SWIMMING IN CIRCLES

JO DIXON

Wrate's Publishing

First published 2021 by Wrate's Publishing

ISBN 978-1-8383400-4-9

Edited and typeset by Wrate's Editing Services
www.wrateseditingservices.co.uk

A CIP catalogue record for this book is available from the British Library.

To clean water everywhere.

CONTENTS

PART I

Stranger in the house

'You jus' get your 'ands off of 'em. I know jus' what you're up to. I saw ya! I saw ya—trying to nick 'em!'

'Shhh, Joe, keep your voice down!' Michael looked nervously around.

'You no good son of a bitch,' Joe carried on, seemingly oblivious.

'Hey! There's no need for that sort of language!' Michael was becoming alarmed. Things were getting out of hand.

Joe mumbled incoherently; he was clearly unhappy with the situation. Michael had never seen his father so agitated and distressed. Last night, when he'd first visited him at the hospital, he'd barely woken up. Now he was puzzled about what had been stolen.

Michael was a gentle soul. An only child, he had always been close to his parents, Joe and Renie. He hated commotion and worried about causing offence.

'Off 'em, ya hear me?' Joe was shouting out again, making random motions with his hands. He would definitely be heard now. Michael thought how he should find someone to help. It upset him to see his father in this state.

Just at that moment, the nurse entered the side room, as Joe started up the tirade again.

'You're nuffink but a filthy . . .'

'Joe!' Michael cut him off but felt sure the nurse had heard.

'Now, mister, you jus' need to calm yerself, all this shoutin' ain't gonna help.' The sister, a heavy-framed lady, spoke in a kind but firm voice.

Michael didn't know what to say. 'He didn't mean it, ma'am, he's not himself,' he eventually explained.

She laughed. 'He's been cursin' anyone and everyone. I ain't takin' it personally.'

She left quickly, before Michael had a chance to talk with her.

'Joe, calm it! You can't go blurting out like that.' Michael tried to both reassure and reprimand Joe at the same time. His father just carried on glowering into space.

★

A week earlier, Michael had been about to set off for work when his mum had phoned to say that she was worried about Joe. He seemed confused. She'd started rambling on about his blood sugars being fairly good and that he wasn't freezing or jerky.

'He was sitting at the kitchen table when he just started talking to himself,' she explained. 'Something 'bout a Jack. I couldn't work out who Jack was, so I just replied, "Yes, dear."'

Michael knew that he was about to get a reconstruction of every conversation Renie had had with Joe.

'OK. What did the doctor say?' he had butted in impatiently.

★

Michael wished now he hadn't been so dismissive. He felt bad for being irritated with his mother. Holding his head sadly in his gloved hands and shaking it slowly side to side, he let out a shoulder-tugging sigh.

He was brought sharply back to the present to find Joe trying to stand up. The tray table was across the armchair, preventing him from moving too far.

Seems like a deliberate ploy. Clever, Michael thought to himself.

'Damn cheating. I won't have it. I won fair and square. Cheats! Liars!'

Joe was off again.

'Joe, it's all right. No one's cheating. Take it easy.'

Michael tried once again to make Joe see reason. It was as if his father was talking to someone across the table, but there was no one there except for Michael, who was perched on the bed to his right. Michael tried to push his gloved hand through his mane of dark, slightly greying hair, but he felt static. Instead, he gave his light brown beard a scratch. The beard hung suspended over his mid-chest, its thick curls touching the top of his thin, plastic hospital apron. His facial hair almost had a life of its own—*a whole ecosystem*, he joked to himself—in contrast to his floppy locks, which were always lifeless. He was thickset, with widely spaced piercing blue eyes and an oddly delicate nose. His broad shoulders slumped forwards, worry clearly evident in his facial features and posture. His wide neck was mostly hidden by his beard.

*

Joe's doctor had diagnosed a water infection. Apparently, he had strong smelling urine and was suffering from incontinence, and this was the most likely cause of his confused state of mind. He'd been prescribed antibiotics.

Michael had kept in regular contact with Renie during the week. The day before he was admitted, when Michael had phoned home again, Joe was no better and Renie had not slept. Joe had been shouting about an intruder in the house. He'd also developed diarrhoea, and it had become clear that Renie was no longer able to care for him. Luckily, Uncle Arnie, Joe's brother, had volunteered to stay with Renie. Michael was able to speak to Arnie later and obtain a fuller picture of what was going on.

'It was as though he were playing a game of cards or something. He kept talking about the ace and the jack. Then he started cursing and swearing. Renie was so shocked. I reckon there was some cheating. That'd make him real cross!'

'It's all complete nonsense. Cheating! Cards!' Michael had muttered to himself, frustrated with the lack of clarity. Michael sensed that Arnie was worried and just trying to make light of the situation. He was grateful for his uncle's help. Even though Arnie was older than Joe, he was still extremely fit and active. Unlike his brother, he hadn't developed diabetes.

The hospital staff had told Arnie that aggressive outbursts were not uncommon with a water infection, and that Joe was having visual hallucinations. He was seeing people in his house. Sometimes, these were friendly folk and Joe talked to them as though they were quite familiar, but at other times he found their presence distressing, particularly at night if he saw them coming into his bedroom. Michael also learned that the medication he had been prescribed for Parkinson's disease could make his hallucinations worse.

The other problem was that the diarrheal illness had caused Joe to become dehydrated, which meant he'd needed an intravenous infusion of fluid. He had been agitated and the doctor had given him a sedative to try to help him relax. This was now wearing off, but the side effects were lingering. Joe was more unstable, and even his sitting balance was off kilter, which wasn't helped by the gesticulations.

Michael was glad that Arnie was present to help calm the situation. Joe always listened to his older brother, and Michael was sure that if anyone could keep Joe settled and persuade him to cooperate, it would be Arnie. Then Michael received a call from Arnie. Joe's stool test was positive for an infection. It was a bad line, so Michael didn't catch the details, but it seemed that the poor chap had yet another infection on top of everything else.

Michael decided that he couldn't leave Arnie and his mum to deal with the situation on their own, so he took some time off work and booked the next available flight from New York to Illinois. At Peoria International Airport, he hired a car and drove straight to the hospital. He was keen to get an update from the medical or nursing staff, as the information he had received from his mother and uncle seemed oversimplified at best, and possibly inaccurate. The visiting time had finished as Michael rang the bell to the ward.

Joe had been admitted to the same hospital just six months ago, after falling and fracturing his hip. It was during this stay that doctors made the diagnosis of Parkinson's disease.

This time, instead of being on the orthopaedic ward, he was on a unit with closed doors. Michael wasn't sure whether this was to protect the other patients from Joe's verbal outbursts or because of the diarrhoea, although he suspected the latter. The nurse's manner was initially brusque, and she instructed Michael to don an apron and gloves; a mask would not be necessary. She told him he couldn't stay long, before quickly disappearing to answer a bell on the other side of the ward.

Joe was calm and sleepy, and although he opened his eyes, he didn't seem to take in Michael's presence, or any of his surroundings. This was probably a blessing, as he would have hated being seen like this. It struck Michael how quickly his father had deteriorated. Joe had been a similar build to Michael, broad and solid, taller than average, with a tendency to carry more weight than was considered healthy. Now he seemed to be wearing his skin as an oversized layer. In the dimly lit room, his greasy skin was almost transparent. He had unkempt, lank, sparse grey hair, and his usually clean-shaven face was sporting stubble, making him appear dishevelled.

He's fitting the gangster image quite well, Joe thought to himself, trying to maintain a modicum of humour in what felt like a desperate situation. There were bruises on Joe's arms and face—*an' he's been in a fight*—and a vacant, hard stare in his eyes—*a gamester mustn't give the game away*—which were sunken into their sockets. The image of his father as a hardened gambler shattered and the realisation that Joe was extremely ill hit Michael hard. It was difficult to believe that the sick, weak, wasted man lying before him was the same person who had taught him to fish and got him interested in the world around him. Joe had inspired him to pursue research, to be curious, imaginative, and to always maintain a sense of humour.

The nurse drifted back into the room. 'You have to leave,' she said curtly. 'He needs to rest. It's time for lights out.'

Michael had left the hospital feeling utterly gloomy. Renie stayed up to welcome him home, but neither of them felt like talking. They were both exhausted. Renie probably would have talked endlessly through the possible outcomes, but she realised that Michael wasn't prepared to do that. It was a hopeless situation and Michael hated speculating, especially when he felt that he didn't have a clue what was going on or where this was all leading.

★

As the afternoon wore on, Joe finally composed himself a little, and he was now sitting back in his armchair. Michael left him to go and find the sister in the corridor. Taking off his apron and gloves and washing his hands as she had done, he felt he ought to say something more, to apologise for Joe's behaviour. He wasn't sure how to broach the subject. It could just make the situation worse.

'I'm real sorry for his language. He was out of order.' Michael shook his head, dropping it slightly, rubbing his damp hands and shuffling his feet. Hating direct eye contact and confrontation, he didn't know where to look.

The sister smiled. 'He's confused. He doesn't know what he's saying. Besides, it wasn't directed at me, was it?'

Relieved, Michael glanced at her and saw that she was smiling. A real smile, which reached her eyes. He wasn't sure if he was supposed to respond.

'It was "them cheats" at the card game!' she continued, chuckling.

Michael warmed to her. She had a sense of humour. He guessed you needed one in her profession.

'We get far worse than that, mister, you wouldn'av' believed it!' she said, before hurrying off along the corridor.

Joe's behaviour was completely out of character and made no sense. Michael really appreciated the nurse's comments, but more than that, he appreciated that she was caring for this curmudgeonly old man, who right now didn't seem deserving of her attention. She was doing her job and acting professionally, turning a blind eye to the lewd comments and abuse, and even finding a way to make light of it. There was a shared sense of understanding. Perhaps it wasn't Joe she'd been amused by, but Michael's reaction. He had turned puce with embarrassment. Michael hated a scene. He liked order, routine and calm, preferring solitude and knowing how things worked.

Michael had hoped to ask the nurse a few questions, but she was obviously busy, so he took the opportunity to slip out for a cappuccino. He had to return a few calls.

'Hi, Carol, just got your message, I'm still in hospital with Joe. Is everything OK?'

Michael made the call from the corner of the café, overlooking an area of landscaped pathways with ornate grasses of various shades and heights.

'Yes, everything is fine. How is he?'

'Oh, you know, he's been really sick this time, but once they get on top of it, I'm sure he'll bounce back.'

Michael chuckled half-heartedly, as he realised how hard he had found the last twenty-four hours. He really appreciated hearing from Carol. She had been a good friend since he had started at Ithaca. One of the lab technicians, she seemed to have been there for years, and knew everyone and everything.

'Just let me know when you're back in town, hon, and we can meet up and maybe try to get that paper done.'

Carol ended the call in her typical effusive manner, leaving Michael blushing. He was sure his ears were red, although thankfully, they were mostly covered by his hair.

Total recall

Left to his own devices again, Michael thought back to when Joe had last been taken into hospital, six months earlier. At this point, Michael had only just moved to New York from Michigan, to work at the prestigious Cornell University. He had joined the Department of Animal Science in the College of Agriculture and Life Science. This meant he had to set up a laboratory, recruit researchers, buy equipment and consumables and, as ever, find funds, which was always the most time-consuming part of his job. He was also asked to teach biochemistry on the undergraduate curriculum, whilst continuing his research; it really wasn't strenuous.

To prepare to lecture the college students, Michael had revised the basic metabolic pathways, the breakdown of carbohydrates and other nutrients and their resynthesis to produce useful chemical products in the body. As a student during lectures, he had copied these reactions with meticulous precision into his hardback book, obsessing about the intricate relationship between each one. He had been intrigued by the inter-reliance of one chemical on another and how a small change had rebound effects on all the other products. These weren't always predictable. Perhaps they should have been anticipated, but they weren't foreseen. At the time, he had been more interested in the length of the carbon chain. He had since realised the essential nature of the vitamin thiamine and had, therefore, become particularly fascinated by its role in the body.

Other students were more interested in doodling or folding pieces of file paper to make into airplanes; the airplanes were sent amidst fits of sniggers whenever the lecturer turned their back. Michael was aware of similar antics in his lectures now. Some things never changed, although his students could send electronic airplanes to each other in the form of tagging or memes. Little did his students realise the relevance of the concept of the meme to the subject at hand. Originating from the Ancient Greek word mimeme, literally meaning something imitated, a meme is an idea that spreads quickly—even becoming viral.[1] Memes can self-replicate, and in doing so went through a kind of natural selection, just like genes in organisms. The meme is the science of dissemination; an airplane just pure fun. He decided he wouldn't spoil it for his students.

A few of the keen students in the group asked more in-depth questions about the biochemical pathways. It was like holding mini tutorials, and he enjoyed the fact that he knew so much more than they did, but also that by trying to explain things clearly to the students, he was testing his own knowledge. If you didn't allow yourself to be stretched, it was all too easy to become stale.

He enjoyed the teaching, but had difficulty fitting in with his fellow scientists. They had all been there a lot longer, and although they were polite enough, they had their own lives and tended to disappear home at the end of the day, except Carol, who had been really friendly towards him. The lead scientist, Diane, must have been about the same age as Renie and had a similar bobbed hairstyle, although that was where the likeness ended. She was tall, lean, with high cheekbones and a prominent nose, although not unattractive. She wore suits and high heels. Michael was secretly afraid of her.

Checking his phone after one lecture, he noticed a missed call from Renie and phoned her straight back.

'Sorry I missed your call,' he said. As he was preparing to tell her that trying to contact him during his working day could be difficult for him, due to his unpredictable timetable, he suddenly heard her sobbing on the line.

'It's Joe, he's fallen'—sniff—'ambulance'—sniff—'pain,' she sobbed.

'Slow down,' he replied, trying to sound calm. He used his most patient voice.

'Joe's in hospital. They think he's fractured his hip . . .'

'I'll get the next flight,' he replied immediately, cutting her off mid-sentence. He knew he wasn't going to get anything more out of the conversation. He would have to go. There was no alternative. His mind was suddenly a whirl of activity.

He considered the worst-case scenario and then imagined the chaos he would find at home without his father at the helm. His work schedule for the next few days flashed through his mind—the lectures, the half-completed projects, the meetings, the deadlines . . . it would all have to wait, or be delegated to a colleague. Renie needed him; there was no debate. He had to go home.

Within two hours, he was at the airport waiting to board a plane to Peoria. He telephoned home from the airport to let Renie know when he would be landing, but there was no answer. He tried his parents' joint mobile number, but realised that doing so would be useless, as they only turned it on "in an emergency".

At 7 o'clock that evening, he had walked onto the ward and found Joe asleep in his hospital bed. He appeared much paler, with a grey hue, unless it was the lighting in the room, and smaller than Michael had remembered. Renie had been at his side, her complexion betraying the fear and exhaustion that she had experienced over the last few hours.

★

That time, Joe had been in hospital for almost two weeks. He had a nail fixed into his hip to stabilise the joint. Because his diabetes was poorly controlled, he had been started on insulin. He had been lectured on his diet and the need to lose weight. He was given information on a strict, low-sugar, low-fat diabetic diet. None of this was a surprise to Michael, but he was shocked to hear that Joe had also developed Parkinson's disease. Apparently, he was only mildly affected, but it still made it more difficult for him to mobilise post-operatively. Joe had been started on medication for the Parkinson's, which was supposed to make his walking easier, but the side effects were troublesome. His blood pressure dropped whenever he stood up, and the nurses worried that he was at an increased risk of falling again.

Renie and Michael visited Joe every day, sometimes twice a day, and in between visits Michael got to work sorting out their kitchen at home. He was determined to make sure Renie understood the diabetic regime. Now Joe was on insulin she would have to be much stricter. He started clearing out the food cupboards, intent on restocking them with healthier staples and preparing a list of safe meals.

This flustered Renie. 'It's perfectly good!' she said, as Michael threw away a ten-year-old tin of spam.

He realised then that he would have to make more regular journeys home, something he had subsequently failed to do.

And now look what had happened.

As he returned to Joe's bedside, he wondered when the parent-child reversal of responsibility had happened. He surmised that there had been a period of anarchy lasting a few years, but that he just hadn't recognised it.

★

After a couple of weeks of hospital visits, Michael had been relieved to get back to the routine of work. In this new position he had diversified his interests and was not spending quite as much time in solitude reading papers and conducting experiments. And, mainly thanks to Carol, at the age of forty, his social life was also beginning to take off. They worked in the same lab and had been collaborating on a research paper. When he first arrived in New York, she had really made him feel welcome, inviting him along to social events. She was outgoing, bubbly, and a little bossy, so it was hard to say no. As they supped lattes in the campus cafe, she brought him up to date on the latest issues, including the fact that Diane was introducing new rules in the lab.

Carol had long, honey-coloured hair, which she would often wind her fingers through. She dressed in low-cut dresses and high heels. Whenever he was with her, Michael wasn't sure where to look, and he shied away from direct eye contact or even glancing at her face.

He was still catching up on emails a week after returning from his parents'. Fortunately, having had more than two weeks away, many of the issues arising within the messages had sorted themselves out. There weren't too many disasters. He found it illuminating that you could simply walk away from an intensely busy role and not be missed. No one was indispensable, he certainly wasn't at work, but at home, well, that was a different matter.

Michael was fascinated by the steps involved in each biochemical pathway, and how incredibly clever the body was to have evolved to enable such sequences of balanced, dynamic chemical reactions all going on at the same time in the interior milieu. Each reaction depended on several others to ensure that at no stage would there be an excess or a deficiency of any products—unless there was an inherited enzyme deficiency, in which case there would be a build-up of a substance, often causing harm. By studying these specific genetic conditions, scientists had worked out the crucial steps.

As a student, Michael had been so engrossed in minute details—the number of carbons in each molecule, the way the chemical groups were switched by each enzyme—that he wasn't able to see what was screamingly obvious. Metabolism in the body was thoroughly disrupted by a lack of this one small molecule—thiamine. *Maybe the body isn't so clever after all*, Michael thought. It seemed to have a monumental design glitch.

'Faulty! Recall all humans!' he chuntered to himself, something he often did, especially if he thought of a catchy phrase for his lectures. He chuckled at his own humour, another habit of his. It was a line he had often used, usually showing a slide with a photo of a car that had been recalled for a problem with EMS—engine management system.

He had surprised himself by how much he enjoyed giving the lectures. It also gave him a platform to spread the message about thiamine. This molecule was essential for all living things, and yet its levels were often precariously low. Absorption was often limited, and adversely affected by the customs of modern-day life, such as consuming regular alcohol or sugar.

Without thiamine, the cells are unable to release energy from food. He would show how several crucial metabolic processes were affected by thiamine deficiency, leading to a domino effect, with far-reaching ramifications. He enjoyed getting this message across, and the buzz from being around young and enthusiastic students.

★

Still sitting in the hospital café, Michael realised he had been daydreaming. Finishing his drink, now unpleasantly tepid, he decided he ought to get back to the ward to see Joe. He felt better for having spoken to Carol. It was easy to feel cooped up in the hospital and forget the existence of life outside this family drama. He walked back along the corridors, moving to the side each time he spotted a porter pushing a patient in a bed. He arrived on the ward just as lunch was being served. It wasn't even midday. At least he could make himself useful by feeding Joe. Unfortunately, his father had been given one of his medicines late that morning, as they had run out of his drug on the ward. The nurse was apologetic. It meant that Joe was very stiff, and each mouthful took an age to process, almost as if Joe's life was now a slow-motion movie. Open mouth, navigate spoon, tip in contents, close mouth, masticate, swallow and repeat. There were occasional variations on this—a failure to line up the spoon with the mouth, a resistance to swallowing, perhaps due to a dry mouth—but you'd think this was hardly a problem given the amount of drool—a slurp of water and a spluttering cough. Michael wasn't sure he was any good at this. Perhaps if they could just sort out the medicines, Joe would be back to his normal self in no time. But at least he was no longer shouting out constantly.

Renie was visiting in the afternoon and Michael needed a break. He drove back to his parents', his mind busy thinking through how this had happened and wondering if he could have prevented it.

★

Before Joe's fall and all these recent problems, it had been over six months since Michael had last been home. That was over a year ago now; it was difficult for him to believe that this was only last spring.

He knew a visit was overdue, but he had been putting it off, partly because he was so busy with his new post in New York, but also after a disagreement with Joe. It had been a difficult weekend. He understood that his father was disappointed in him. Joe had really hoped that Michael would move back to Illinois and be close by to help him and Renie as they grew older. Instead, he had moved further away. As an only child, there was a lot of pressure on him. He could see that his father was ageing and beginning to find it difficult to continue his work in the salmon fisheries, especially since a mystery illness had killed so many of the young salmon—the fry. His mother had always helped where she could, but now she was tiring easily too.

As a boy, Michael had loved helping at the fisheries. He found watching the salmon fry swimming in their large steel vats mesmerising. When the fry started to die, he had listened to all the conversations between Joe and the other workers. It was a complete mystery. There were a few clues, but no one really understood why so many of the young salmon weren't able to survive into adulthood. This mystery continued to bother Michael as he grew up—the more he understood, the more intriguing the problem became to him. Joe was clearly angling for Michael to solve the problem—just like that—and then settle down with a nice local girl.

During this visit, Joe had been sullen—more so than usual—and Michael wondered if he was being given the silent treatment. On reflection, Joe had been uncommunicative for years. Michael had assumed it was the stress of the business. Then there was his recent diagnosis of diabetes, new treatments and a new diet. Michael knew that Joe hated cutting back on his food, so perhaps his general grumpiness had simply been because of his health kick, or maybe the tablets. All drugs have side effects and Joe was taking a right concoction. The diet was certainly fraught with problems, though, as Renie had very little understanding of what was required and assumed that anything homemade was perfectly good and that all they had to do was avoid fast food. She continued to feed Joe just as many meat pies and cakes as before his diagnosis.

'It's just fruit!' Renie had announced, whilst serving Joe a large portion of apple pie with a thick piecrust, all of it swimming in cream. Michael found this frustrating and admitted defeat. He had tried his best to get her to understand. All she knew was that the best way to care for her husband was to feed him with hearty, home-cooked food.

★

Relieved to be away from the hospital at last, Michael sat at his father's desk and reflected on the time before his fall and how he had seemed more withdrawn. Michael hadn't thought anything of the tremor, or the fact that Joe was slouching. He had just assumed that his father was concentrating on something, rather like he did when he was reading something intently.

He began to sort through the letters and papers in Joe's office. There was a large pile of correspondence that needed attention. He noticed Joe's handwriting on a pad, and then he looked at the letters Joe had opened and annotated. Michael was stunned.

Michael checked the symptoms of Parkinson's disease online: tremor, slow movements and stiff muscles also affecting the facial muscles and the muscles in the hand. This causes *micrographia*—small, cramped writing. It was so obvious now, and Michael couldn't believe he hadn't noticed the deterioration earlier. Joe's letters were scrawly and small and some of the words were joined together. Michael rifled through his father's filing cabinet to try and establish when Joe's handwriting had changed. He wondered just how long he had missed the fact that his father was ill—the bent posture, his lack of expression and the tone in his voice, which Michael had mistaken for disapproval of his life choices—it had all become startlingly clear. There were all sorts of other symptoms mentioned online, such as balance problems leading to falls, dizziness, insomnia, excess sweating, swallowing difficulties, drooling, loss of smell and constipation.

Of course, Joe wouldn't have complained about feeling unwell. He never complained. He had carried on as if nothing was wrong. Michael was at a loss. He wondered whether Joe knew he was getting worse. He must have done. How long had he known about the Parkinson's disease? How long had he been this bad? *How come we didn't know? Did Renie know? Why didn't I know?*

He felt dismayed, guilt-ridden. He had lost control of the situation. He just didn't understand how this had all happened and he felt the urge to do something to grasp the state of affairs. That night, he had troubled sleep, as he dreamed about losing all the fish, being chased, searching desperately for something. He often had vivid dreams.

He was worried about Joe and wanted to be more involved. As a scientist, he felt he should be concentrating on finding a cure for Parkinson's so that his father could recover. He had to believe that he was going to get better, even though deep down he knew this was completely unrealistic.

'What even causes Parkinson's disease?' he muttered out loud, despite the fact that there was no one with him.

By the following morning, he had resolved on a course of action. He would talk to Joe about the good times they had spent together. He had found it difficult to communicate with Joe for a while, as he seldom received a positive response. However, he now recognised that this void of expression was a feature of the Parkinson's disease and that it didn't mean that Joe wasn't enjoying the conversation—if you could call it that, it was all a bit one-sided. Michael was determined to persevere. Since his medication had been changed to reduce the hallucinations, Joe had been much slower to respond. At least, he assumed that was causing the change in his personality. After all, he was taking so many drugs now. Michael could also update Joe on his work. He hadn't shared this side of his life for many years.

The following day in the hospital, he started telling Joe about his latest research. He felt as if he was a child again, with Joe in the large metal shed that housed the fisheries, listening to the screeching of birds in the distance and the constant scratching and knocking from tree branches, the wind and the gulls.

He thought back to a conversation they'd had when he was much younger. Joe was his hero.

*

'It's real queer!' Joe was puzzled.

'What is, Pop?' Michael was bobbing up and down behind Joe, holding his hand as they walked on the raised wooden walkways between the tanks containing thousands of small fish, and trying to peer in. Joe was staring into the water. Michael was too short to see over the rim.

'The fry. The young. They're behaving strangely.'

'Can I see them? Please, Pop?'

They had gone to the fishery together, and as Joe held him up, Michael watched the young fish struggling to swim straight. If you put your hand in the water, they jerked away. It was as if they were over-stimulated. Then the fry started swimming in circles. Michael spent hours watching the young fish, and then he persuaded Joe to let him video them.

Swimming in circles

'Do you remember my trip to Sweden, Joe? Did I ever tell you about my talk? They were so interested in those videos I took. Who would have thought?'

Michael tried to keep the conversation going, sitting uncomfortably in one of the stunted, plastic, low-backed chairs that he'd found on the ward, while Joe was propped up in the armchair. Joe no longer needed a tray table to keep him in place, but there was a table in reach, with a glass of water and a straw. Michael glanced at Joe to see if he was still listening. Joe appeared to be interested in what he was saying. There was a subtle change in his expression and his eyes seemed brighter.

Encouraged, Michael continued. 'Did I tell you about the flight? There was this guy . . .' somehow, Michael could relax and talk when it was just him and Joe '. . . he was so big, and he spilled over onto my seat the whole flight.'

Michael chuckled, checking Joe's face for a reaction. He was often accused of making fattist comments, but this time they weren't aimed at Joe, and anyhow, he didn't seem unduly upset.

★

Michael hadn't visited Sweden before, but he had heard the capital referred to as the Venice of the North and knew that it was built on interconnected islands, so the vast watery landscape should not have been a surprise. The maze of islands, shining in the light like hundreds of submerged alligators, was far more extensive than he had expected. It was stunningly beautiful; there was water everywhere. It would have been great to explore the area in a boat or stay in a cabin for a few days. Sadly, he was expected back as soon as the conference had finished.

As the plane descended into Stockholm, the battle Michael had waged silently with his oversized neighbour for the armrest was coming to an end. He had spent much of the flight rehearsing his presentation. He wasn't anxious but looked over his slides and considered likely questions. He owed much of his confidence to Joe. Michael had spent his holidays working with him, learning how to manage the brood stock. Spawning practice in hatcheries had changed very little in thirty years, but this workshop was different. Most of the conferences on fisheries were only interested in making money. This time, the industry was meeting to face a threat to its existence and to answer the question of why so many fry—in both the Great Lakes and the Baltic Sea—were dying.

He pulled his attention back to the images he planned to use in his presentation. His audience would recognise the first slide as an adult male salmon with its bold, hook jaw—the kype. The text under the image stated:

Prior to spawning, adult brood stock are separated into pools by gender, anesthetised and identity tagged.

Michael turned the page. The next slide showed a brood stock female having compressed air injected into it to ease the pale orange eggs into the fresh water.

He could sense his neighbour looking across him. Assuming he wanted to look out of the window, Michael sat back in his seat.

'Mister, if I'd known you were going to spend ten hours looking at pictures of fish jerking off into buckets, I'd have asked for a different seat,' he said in a slow Chicagoan accent.

Michael looked up. He was startled and, he realised, a little embarrassed by the man's comment.

'Oh, yeah! Sorry! I'm giving a lecture tomorrow. I guess I'm a little obsessive about it,' he replied.

'That's OK, man, I'd be happy to land a fish like that. What're you talking about in your lecture?'

'Well, I'm a scientist, a biochemist,' Michael stuttered, scratching his beard. He was unused to someone showing interest in his work. 'But I'm talking at a fisheries conference tomorrow.'

Once he'd started, Michael didn't know how much he should tell him. He was probably a little nervous, and he was exhausted too. His speech sped up and he continued in a higher-pitched voice. 'It's the second workshop on reproductive disturbance in fish. It's in Lidingö, there are big salmon fisheries in Sweden, and it seems they're having the same troubles that we are in the United S—'

'Ling-dingö, huh?' the man's booming drawl interrupted Michael. 'The Swedes are holding the party, but I bet Uncle Sam gets sent the bill!' He guffawed, rocking the seats in the row.

Michael was irritated that the man reckoned the money was bigger than the problem, and he couldn't even pronounce the place correctly.

'It's Lidingö, and they are paying for this one.' Michael started tapping his finger on the side of his face excitedly, talking quickly. 'The meeting was commissioned by the

Swedish Environment Protection Agency, co-sponsored by the Swedish National Board of Fisheries, the Swedish Council for—'[2]

'That's good to hear, I hope your talk goes well,' the man interrupted again.

The conversation stalled. Michael was relieved. He wondered whether he had told the guy too much. He tended to give more detail than was perhaps warranted. But he found the subject interesting and was proud of the work he was doing. He also hated any perceived criticism. He returned his attention to his notes and the next image with the text:

Milt of sperm are stripped from the males and added to the eggs. The eggs and milt are combined in a spawning pan.

★

Michael turned around to check if Joe still seemed vaguely interested.

'Joe, do you remember how you taught me to use a paintbrush to stir the eggs?' He moved his hand in a circle, holding a pretend paintbrush. 'I had to stir the silver stream of eggs as they were squirted into the bucket.'

Joe moved his eyes. There seemed to be some faint recognition.

'The salmon fry had already been dying. All those salmon fry surveys we filled in!'

Michael laughed, remembering the charts. 'I spent hours watching the salmon fry, observing the irregular swimming patterns, the characteristic hyperactivity. The fry would lose coordination. I found out later that was called ataxia.'

Michael paused and looked across at Joe. Strange that Joe now had a movement disorder. He shook his head and carried on. 'They would respond abnormally when stimulated. They would be swimming in circles. That's when you knew they were gonna die.'

Michael paused, suddenly embarrassed, wondering whether Joe had heard him. *Why did he have to blurt that out?*

★

The salmon fry would start spiralling in the water before succumbing to this mysterious death. The cause was unknown, but it was clear the problem was getting worse. Fish stocks had suffered significant losses for twenty years. Fisheries responded by increasing the number of eggs collected during spawning. Then, in 1993, there was a sudden increase in cases, and now massive numbers of fry were dying in multiple fisheries.

The first conference was held in Sweden because it was increasingly difficult to sustain the numbers needed in the Baltic fisheries. It seemed to be the same illness affecting both the Chinook salmon and the coho salmon in the North American Great Lakes, particularly Lake Michigan, but also Lake Ontario and, to a lesser extent, Lake Huron and Lake Erie.

Sitting on the plane, flicking through each slide of his presentation, while checking the flow and mentally noting the salient points, Michael reviewed the processes involved: taking salmon from the wild, harvesting the sperm and the eggs, the fertilisation of the eggs and finally, incubating the eggs until they were hatched. The young salmon were cast out into the wild. This was all done to sustain a multimillion-dollar sport fishing industry. Michael didn't care much for the industry, except that it obviously pumped money into the system; he was more concerned about what it all meant.

Although dying salmon fry had only been observed when fish were farmed, whatever was causing these deaths probably also explained the decline in the natural lake trout numbers in Lake Michigan and Lake Ontario, as well as the related species, rainbow and brown trout.

*

Back in the hospital, his worries about the fish industry seemed an unnecessary distraction from what really mattered. But he was determined not to wallow in sadness. That wouldn't help anyone.

'January 1993, that's when it got real bad. You remember then?'

Joe seemed to shake his head, unless Michael was imagining it, or Joe was due some more medicine.

'Let me tell you, it was a dreadful time. Ninety per cent! The mortality rate was up to ninety per cent in some hatcheries from an early age, especially those in Wisconsin, but also in Illinois, Indiana and even some in Michigan. Terrible!'

Michael leaned his chin on his hand and scratched his beard. Then he tapped the side of his face, shaking his head whilst remembering how bad it had been. 'That's when I moved to Ann Arbor.'

Michael turned around to look at his father. Joe's head had lolled forwards and drool in a silvery, slimy stream fell from the corner of his mouth. His breathing had become heavy and he was sound asleep.

Michael was left to reminisce on his own. *What a year it had been!*

★

In 1992, in his last year at university in Chicago, there was a terrible storm. In fact, there had been extreme weather conditions for several years. Although it was eighteen years ago, Michael remembered reading about this one in the local newspaper; they were still reeling in shock:

Chicago Daily News

Slayer Storm Washes Summer Away

July 03, 1992[3]

I just knew we had to find a way out. It was gonna kill us all!

Chicago's lakefront has avoided much of the brunt of previous storms, but this time it was hit hard.

'It's a tornado, I just knew it!' Doug Forrell, 66, watched it all from his office window.

Then, in April of that year, there was the Great Chicago Flood, when water leaked through a crack in one of the utility tunnels beneath the Chicago Loop, the central business district. These tunnels, forty-five feet below the streets, were built in the early nineteen hundreds to carry freight, mainly coal, on tiny railway lines. They were now abandoned, apart from a few sections used for services and communication lines containing high-voltage cables. There was initially a whirlpool in the Chicago River on Kinzie Street. Then hundreds of millions of gallons of water flooded into the tunnels and into office and shop basements in much of the downtown area. The flood had major consequences for the business sector. Michael recalled the chaos. There was a power cut, and the underground trains were cancelled. If you had to get somewhere, you were best off walking, as the buses were packed. For days, strewn across the streets were the large pipes pumping water out of buildings.

The Chicago River is a system of rivers and canals that run through the city and provide a link between the Great Lakes, the Mississippi Valley and, eventually, the Gulf of Mexico. In an attempt to control the leak, the Chicago River had been lowered by opening the river locks into Lake Michigan.

This river was part natural and part man-made, an engineering feat dating back more than a hundred years. A freak storm in 1885 had threatened the city's water supply and prompted the Illinois General Assembly to make plans to reverse the flow of the Chicago River, so that water from Lake Michigan was discharged into the Mississippi River via a canal. Even today, it would be a huge civil engineering achievement.

In 1889, the Illinois General Assembly had planned to replace the Illinois to Michigan canal, which had become inadequate to carry the city's increasing sewage and commercial navigation needs, with the Chicago Sanitary and Ship Canal, a much larger waterway. This man-made hydrologic connection between the Great Lakes and Mississippi watershed was completed in 1900.

Michael's grandfather—Joe's father—had been born in Chicago to immigrant parents, who lived in a close community not far from the water. He had taught Michael to think of the geography of the land in the way fish would see it, by its rivers. The Mississippi (Misi-ziibi—literally Great River) had the largest drainage system in North America, flowing from Minnesota and meandering two thousand, three hundred and forty miles through Wisconsin, Iowa, Illinois, Missouri, Kentucky, Tennessee, Arkansas, Mississippi and Louisiana. The Illinois River was a major tributary.

Then, in the summer of 1993, the year after the Great Chicago Flood, the Mississippi River had burst its banks, causing vast damage and destruction, so that much of Iowa was underwater. A satellite image showed the flooded area resembling a second Lake Michigan. As the floods receded, the surrounding countryside was covered in brown silt and littered with debris from fallen trees and washed-away parts of roads and property. Landslides added to the destruction, riverbanks tumbled into the river, bridges collapsed and roads cracked and bulged. And then there was the stench . . .

★

The arrival of the lunch trolley brought Michael sharply back to the present. He put a gentle hand on Joe's shoulder, as Joe slowly opened his eyes.

'Welcome back! Jus' wondering when you'd come to.' Michael spoke softly, not wanting to startle Joe, or set off more yelling. 'Feeling hungry?' he enquired, not expecting a reply. 'Meat pie and mash, carrots and peas—yum!'

He tried to sound cheerful, whilst dreading trying to feed Joe again.

'Did I tell you how warm it was compared to Chicago? It was November, we'd had snow weeks earlier.'

★

A friend had advised Michael to bring plenty of layers, as it would feel cool in Stockholm, but landing on the tarmac at midday it was surprisingly mild, considering how far north he was. It was the end of November, so Chicago had already seen its first snowfall. That September, the city had experienced the earliest fall freeze since records began. The North Atlantic Drift certainly made a difference to the climate in Scandinavia.

The fry had been dying prematurely since 1968, even though the hatcheries had been operating the same methods. Granted, there had been no infusion of new genetic material, but it was now agreed that this phenomenon was unlikely to be due to inbreeding. There was no increased mortality in fish caught and maintained under controlled conditions and then bred in captivity, yet any progeny from these farmed fish released into Lake Michigan to mature before being recaptured were affected. It was becoming obvious that only the progeny from salmonids (including salmon and trout) that mature under environmental conditions were afflicted with this mysterious disease. Despite rigorous screening for pathogens, none had been detected. It was most odd.

In his talk, Michael explained how the salmon fry with the disease don't thrive because they fail to feed, compared to healthy fry of the same age. Within the egg, fry develop alongside a yolk containing nutrients, such as vitamins, minerals, fats and proteins. The sick fry had large amounts of residual yolk because they did not completely use it. Slides were shown with the salmon fry swimming in spiral or corkscrew patterns due to having lost their equilibrium. They also displayed a curious dark pigmentation. The fry seemed lethargic, yet they were also hyper-excitable when touched. Michael had taken sequences of photos of his hand in the water, showing the fry overreacting to his touch, as though an electric current had been passed from his hand to the fry; they eventually developed tetany (spasms) and haemorrhages (bleeding), before dying. There were other presentations with slides of autopsies showing hydrocephalus (brain swelling), retrobulbar oedema (swollen, protuberant eyes), subcutaneous oedema (skin swelling) and pericardial oedema (heart sac swelling).

Despite all these images showing the clear signs of disease, tests so far had failed to show a cause for the illness. It seemed there was nothing discernibly wrong with the salmon fry.

★

With Michael's help, Joe was slowly making his way through the mash.

'You know that meeting was a real success, thanks to you, Joe. The talk went down well, and they really liked my home movie of the fry swimming in circles. There were lots of positive comments. I'm not saying I solved the mystery or anything, but it was a good meeting. I felt I'd contributed, done my bit. You'd have been proud.'

Michael praised Joe, whilst stuffing stodgy potato into his mouth, which was easier to manage than either the crumbly pastry or the rolling peas.

★

Following the conference, the general consensus was that the mortality syndrome in the Great Lakes was the same as the Baltic Sea condition known as M74, and also the Cayuga syndrome in the New York Finger Lakes. The panel of experts in the closing session had referred to Michael's work in their concluding remarks and had agreed on a universal term for the condition: Early Mortality Syndrome, or EMS.

Michael learnt that the Cayuga syndrome seemed to be maternally transmitted. Joe had also noticed that progeny from different females had a variable mortality rate in his hatchery. Whatever was causing EMS, there was a female-dependent factor. It was a maternally transmitted disease.

In an attempt to build up numbers of salmon to compensate for the decline in wild salmon, there had been mass breeding of Baltic salmon. Unfortunately, this meant that the majority of females from the Baltic Sea were now physiologically incapable of producing viable offspring outside of the hatcheries.

At an earlier meeting in Uppsala in 1993, there was an agreement that the cooperation would continue to serve a coordinated research programme, developing new networks, with transatlantic communication and participation. The meeting in Stockholm had reinforced these ties. There was a strong sense of optimism that the mystery illness would be solved, and that a treatment strategy was feasible, although at the moment there were few clues. Michael had made contacts throughout Scandinavia and had become friends with a like-minded scientist, Eriksson, who worked at Stockholm University. He had also met colleagues from Cornell University, New York, who were studying the Cayuga syndrome, and also from Finland.

On the plane home, he reviewed his notes from the meeting and sifted through the abstracts. He was searching for similarities.

*

'There was a link,' Michael explained to Joe. 'Whether the EMS was found in fry from the Baltic Sea, the Great Lakes or the Finger Lakes, each time the condition was related to the abundance of forage fish.

'The following year, I went on another trip to a conference held in Dearborn, a suburb of Detroit. It wasn't quite the same deal. I don't know if you've ever been, Joe, but I wouldn't rush back. Flying over Detroit, I could see water and trees and islands, but it was so built up and everything was a dull brown. But hey, at least on this occasion "Uncle Sam" did pick up the tab!'

Michael chuckled, remembering how awkward he'd felt squeezed in next to the Chicagoan on the plane.

'This time, the symposium was sponsored by The American Fisheries Society and the Great Lakes Fishery Commission, as they both had a vested interest in reducing the salmon fry mortality. The title of the meeting was, "Early Mortality Syndrome: Reproductive Disruptions in Fish from the Great Lakes, New York Finger Lakes and the Baltic Region." Catchy, huh?'

The meetings in Sweden weren't the first workshops on EMS. There had also been one in Romulus, Michigan, but the success of the meeting in Lidingö, with interested parties on both sides of the Atlantic prepared to collaborate on research to investigate the underlying cause of EMS, had led to another international meeting the following year.

Michael didn't expect to learn anything new in Dearborn, as the presentations were very similar to those in the meeting in Lidingö. He accepted that it had probably helped to spread the message locally, since a greater American contingency had attended. He didn't want to speak out against these scientists, but, frustratingly, it was as though little progress had been made. He appreciated that the symposium had allowed for a cross-fertilisation of ideas and had certainly made him think more laterally. As is often the case, it wasn't the lectures and workshops that stimulated new ideas, but a chance comment as he supped his coffee; a brief snippet of a conversation over lunch, whilst standing with a plate of buffet food and an orange juice, or overhearing the alcohol-fuelled remarks whilst drinking beer in the bar in the evening—statements thrown in purposefully to challenge current thinking.

'I knew all about Dearborn by reputation. After the war, it became home to lots of Eastern European immigrants, just like Chicago. Then Henry Ford set up the motor trade.'

Michael paused and scratched his beard, becoming cross. 'It reminded me of my conversations with Grandpa. Back then, Polish immigrants were mistrusted. They thought we were all communists. Now there are lots of hardworking Muslims in Dearborn, and they think they're all terrorists.'

Michael shook his head and tapped his cheek. 'It's ridiculous! There are so many more important things to worry about. Real crises! But we ignore them. These are understated—played down. Instead, we make up predicaments and exaggerate dilemmas.'

Ford was apparently anti-Semitic, and for that reason he had employed immigrants from the Middle East. There were now many Muslims in Dearborn. It was interesting how history had a habit of repeating itself. In the past, it was the Eastern Europeans, now it was the Muslims, prior to this the British—there were puritans from East Anglia and Quakers in Pennsylvania, establishing land devoted to their religion. The Germans and the Dutch have also migrated to the States in large numbers.

'I've worked with people of all nationalities and cultural backgrounds. They all bring something unique with them. Populations change—that's evolution. Now, where was I? Oh yes, Dearborn.'

Michael returned to telling Joe about the meeting. 'Well, there was confirmation that a hundred per cent of the salmon fry from a specific female were affected.'

In each of the conditions—the Great Lakes Syndrome (EMS), M74 in the Baltic, and the Cayuga Syndrome from the New York Finger Lakes, it was clear that maternal factors were the cause.

'You see, it couldn't be down to genetics, because this would only affect, at most, fifty per cent of the offspring, but it affected all of them.'

The delegates agreed that further research should be directed away from genetics or pathogens, as these seemed unlikely to explain the disease. By this point, Michael had already diverted his attention from genetics, as he was sure that EMS was due to something in the environment. It was encouraging that there was to be a greater focus on environmental studies, and his biochemical expertise would no doubt be useful.

'It was environmental. Forage fish were the clue! Who'd have thought!' Michael told Joe, as he shook his head, having enjoyed going through the details of the conferences with his pop. He turned round to see that Joe had drifted off again, head tilted to the left, drool mixed with pie spilling out onto his shirt. Michael discreetly placed a tissue on Joe's chest and left silently to head home to Renie.

Thanksgiving

When Renie and Michael visited Joe the following morning, he seemed brighter; perhaps he was better at the start of the day. Michael had told Renie about the way he had tried to connect with Joe, and they'd agreed to talk about happy family times together.

The doctors were doing a ward round as they arrived, and one of the interns spoke with them briefly. Tests had revealed a toxin in Joe's stool, from *Clostridium difficile*. This is a species of bacteria that can occur after taking antibiotics, as the medication alters the balance of bacteria in the gut. Michael had had some experience of *Clostridium*, but thankfully not personally. He had used probes to look for another species of *Clostridium* in salmon.

'Joe?' Renie started talking hesitantly, looking from Joe to Michael for approval. 'Michael and I were talking 'bout your sixtieth birthday up at the club. That was fun, wasn't it?' Renie was desperate to see a response from her husband.

'I'll never forget seeing those ducks skating on the ice, they were comical.' Michael took over, smiling to himself. He believed that Joe could hear and appreciate the conversation without necessarily showing any emotion. Michael would just carry on talking at him, just like he'd done the day before. Asking questions and waiting for a response wasn't likely to achieve much. And if nothing else, the one-way conversation had passed the day pleasantly for the two of them. 'It was a great walk along the river. So beautiful with the frost all over the rushes.'

'That was ten years ago this year, it seems only yesterday,' said Renie, squeezing Joe's hand. She was beginning to get the idea.

★

For Joe's special birthday that year, a huge family reunion had been planned for the weekend after Thanksgiving. The party was held at the Illinois Valley Yacht Club, which had been like a second home to Michael when he was a teenager. He had been looking forward to revisiting it, although there was no sailing at that time of year.

Arnie lived in Wisconsin and Joe's sister had moved to Texas. They were both visiting for the birthday celebration. Although he was an only child, Michael had four cousins. Arnie was a proud granddad.

Michael somewhat dreaded these sorts of gatherings. He felt awkward and was always relieved when he could escape. Although, looking back, he had mostly fond memories. The occasions usually turned out to be more enjoyable than he'd anticipated.

Arriving home on the Wednesday night, his mother Renie was fretting as usual, complaining that she hadn't even started to make the dumplings; it was increasingly difficult to buy good suet for the recipe. Renie was short and round, with permanent smile lines in her kind face. She was bustling by the stove, her tidy, ash-blonde bob complemented her rosy pink cheeks, which were flushed with heat from the salmon steaming in the fish kettle.

Michael hadn't been home for several months and he was looking forward to spending time out of the city. He had recently been appointed as Associate Professor at the University of Michigan. His undergraduate studies had included a major in chemistry and his research mainly focused on the development of assays—processes used to analyse substances. He had moved into a small apartment in Ann Arbor and relished the order and isolation of finally living alone. Even though he had a good relationship with his parents and had coped with shared accommodation for years, he appreciated his own space. He had initially enjoyed the anonymity of living in a larger city, but more recently was missing home, or rather the sense of belonging somewhere. He always enjoyed Thanksgiving and felt the pull to spend time with his family.

Renie had chitchatted about the sleeping arrangements and meal plans. Michael was told about the conversation at the butcher shop and the breakfast sausages that she always bought.

★

'Do you remember those sausages I'd get from the market, Joe? You used to love them. Do you remember? You couldn't beat them.'

Renie talked excitedly, whilst chuckling with a motion that shook her small, plump frame. She was enjoying seeing Joe engaging with her. She had been nervous about coming to the hospital and was worried about what state she would find her husband in. Her relief was clear. As for the sausages she was talking about, they had become something of a family tradition. Michael wasn't sure if Joe liked them quite as much as Renie made out. He preferred his steak. However, talk of them seemed to bring a flicker of recognition, followed by more spittle out of the corner of his mouth. Joe was certainly nodding more today, and he was beginning to make vocal sounds. His cough also sounded stronger.

'You used to tell me all about what my old school friends were up to, Renie,' said Michael, turning affectionately towards his mother. She put her head on his shoulder, but he tensed up at her touch. He immediately regretted his reaction. It was an awkward moment.

★

Whenever he came home, Renie would bring Michael up to date on the news of his former classmates, many of whom he had lost touch with, though his mother still enjoyed tracking their progress through the local paper or events at the church or the yacht club. She sometimes told him about old acquaintances, but more often than not they were complete strangers Renie had misidentified.

Joe's thickset features had changed little over the years, as though cast in clay, and neither had his personality. He was insistent on routine and appeared distracted or withdrawn, seeming not to notice his wife fussing. He looked tired, pallid and worn out. He was breathless just walking from the kitchen. Although he was still working at the hatcheries, for the last decade they had been run by the Illinois Department of Natural Resources. With so many of the fry dying, it had been hard to make a living and there had been considerable state investment to try to understand the cause of the increased mortality. Michael understood Joe's dilemma: he had no choice but to bail out, or rather 'cooperate' with the authorities. Contrary to expectations, he had enjoyed his work far more since he no longer had the hassle of running the business and trying to survive the financial losses.

Michael followed Joe's example and slipped through the open door, escaping the frenetic activity in the kitchen and finding his way to the living room. He sat down heavily on the sofa to relax in solitude. Despite living in the centre of a city, he had become used to calm through living on his own, and he found the constant clatter and commotion at his parents' bothersome. On the coffee table was Joe's familiar collection of fishing magazines and newsletters. Michael flicked through the pages without really paying attention to any of the details. He wasn't expecting to find anything of any real interest. Then he noticed some news headlines on the sizes of some of the alligators in Florida. The article described in detail the complex method used to measure the reptile's size. The longest male alligator in this report was almost four hundred and thirty centimetres, and the largest ever recorded was four hundred and ninety. Unlike salmon, alligators seemed to be thriving. Michael spent the next couple of hours with his head pleasantly immersed in the magazines.

The hatcheries were also on the River Illinois, near Peoria, the main city on the river. Michael passed many evenings as a child being told about the river's history and the importance of the waterway connecting the Great Lakes at Chicago to the Mississippi River. His grandfather had told him that in the early nineteen hundreds, more fish were caught in the Illinois River than any other river in the United States, except perhaps the Columbia River. He'd also taught Michael all about salmon fishing. He remembered learning how to identify the salmon, with their wide middle and well-developed teeth, like many predator fish. He knew about the fins, including the back fin, the caudal fin and the fat fin. The fat fin was now being cut in artificially bred salmon, so that the fisherman could easily tell the difference and return the wild salmon, now an endangered species, back to the water. The wild salmon had a silver-blue sheen, with black spots above the lateral line. Their flesh was white, as their diet comprised mostly of small fish, rather than pink, which is the result of a diet of crustaceans.

Sadly, this had all changed with the pollution of the water, particularly now that the sewage from the city of Chicago flowed down into the Illinois River. Michael was pleased that his grandfather was not around to see what had happened. It seemed common knowledge that there would be regular episodes of untreated sewage overflowing into the river. Obviously, this only happened when there was a flash flood, and thankfully these didn't occur very often.

★

'It was lovely to see so many friends and family, Joe. There was Cousin Jan, with little Lucas and Matius, and Cousin Peter. He's doing so well with his business. It was really good to catch up with everyone and find out what they were all doing. Among Michael's friends, there were a few babies on the way even then. They were all so interested in his studies, and the fish.'

Renie looked proudly towards her son. Or was there a touch of disappointment that he hadn't provided them with grandchildren?

★

Renie had been fussing about the food so much that she had hardly spoken with anyone all evening. Michael circulated among the friends and relatives. By the time he had recounted a dozen times what he was doing now, he was finding the celebration a chore. It was a good reminder of why being away was such a release. The company was well meaning but stifling.

His answers varied between:

'No, I'm not married.'

'No girlfriend, no.'

'In Ann Arbor.'

'An apartment.'

'The university.'

'Setting up an assay to measure . . .'

He stopped himself short as Cousin Peter drifted off to open another can. It seemed that as soon as Michael began to find the conversation interesting himself, he simultaneously became a science bore. He'd have to stick to standard topics: food, drink, fish and the weather.

Uncle Arnie was an exception. He always seemed interested. Despite being the older brother, he was much fitter. Arnie was taller and had energy that his sibling lacked. He looked out for Joe. They would often discuss the river. With the articles he'd been reading still fresh on his mind, Michael talked with Arnie about the alligator farms. Back in the day, the brothers had been enthusiastic fishermen and knew of the fishing in Florida. However, Arnie kept switching the conversation to the subject of his five-year-old granddaughter, Tiffany, and how the family was planning a trip to Disney World. Tiffany apparently loved dressing up and was really looking forward to seeing the fairy -tale castle. She also wanted to see the dolphins in SeaWorld. Michael thought back to when he was a child; his favourite book was the *Big Book of Animals*, which included the names of the animals in Latin. He had loved that book. He would look at the photos of all the animals and read the details about their habitats. Even then he preferred nonfiction and didn't really see the point of storybooks. Tiffany was happier in the land of make believe, but Michael didn't understand fantasy.

While he was talking to Arnie, Michael noticed Joe tucking into the selection of cold meats, quiche and spicy chicken wings. As usual, Renie had over catered; church friends and relatives had arrived with plates piled high for the festivity, and Joe seemed to feel the need to keep eating whilst the food was there, as though he would be letting people down if he didn't try his hardest to at least make a dent in the feast. He hadn't started on the desserts yet, which would no doubt involve a small portion of each one. There was apple pie, cheesecake, devil's food cake and pumpkin pie, as well as Renie's specialty: sweet fruit dumplings topped with melted butter, whipped cream and sugar. Joe would certainly enjoy his birthday celebration.

Over fed, bloated and feeling sluggish, brain dead and exhausted by the small talk, Michael was ready to escape back to the university for the last few weeks prior to the Christmas period, when the scoffing would no doubt start again. He really felt he needed to detox. He made a mental note that when he returned home for Christmas, he would talk to Joe about his diet. It would have been cruel to mention it on his birthday, but Joe was literally popping out of his shirts; they were tight across his belly and the buttons were struggling under the strain. He was carrying far too much extra weight.

*

'Such a nuisance this diabetes. Joe did so love his puddings. You loved my dumplings, didn't you, Joe?'

Michael's eyebrows arched. Renie hadn't meant the double entendre and would be embarrassed if she realised what she was saying.

'And the pies and cakes, but not on a diabetic diet,' Michael said in a mocking tone. Renie was clearly aiming for quality rather than quantity of life, but Michael hadn't given up on Joe, not yet. He could still get better, lead a normal life and appreciate the things he used to enjoy. They had found a cause for Joe's deterioration and hopefully, with treatment, he would be able to return home again and get back to his old self. Meanwhile, Arnie had persuaded Renie to accept help. She would employ a carer to wash him each morning and help him to get dressed. She could then focus on making sure his medication was correctly administered and that he was well fed and watered.

Michael wondered whether his father had always had the *Clostridium* bacteria, and if the antibiotics had simply unmasked the infection, or could he have picked up a bacterial infection while in hospital? He'd heard about so-called 'hospital acquired' infections. If Joe hadn't been infected in the hospital, could he have picked it up by the river? It was worth looking into. What happened to the *Clostridium* once it was flushed away? Was the wastewater treatment effective enough? Michael had heard that periodically there were outbreaks of these kinds of infections, although he wasn't sure whether this particular strain was the sort that broke out.

Griffin gators

Joe was still in hospital. It was now almost four weeks since he'd been admitted, and Michael was visiting for the weekend. Joe had clearly made progress and was more stable walking. He was even talking a little more coherently.

'Morning, Joe. How's it goin'?' Michael breezed into the side room in the hospital ward.

'Oh . . . hi . . . Mich . . . ael,' Joe stuttered, his head shaking and his fingers tremulous, as though he were trying to roll a cigarette in both his hands. There was a suggestion of a smile from his mouth, but a definite brightness in his eyes, or perhaps he was just more alert. Michael felt a wave of reassurance come over him. There may have been little change, but he felt there was definite cause to be optimistic. He resumed his patter. He'd already decided what he was going to talk about with, or rather to, Joe.

'Did I ever tell you about the alligators?' Michael started the tale. 'It's a fascinating discovery; I wonder why more people don't know about it, to be honest. I learned of it in one of your magazines. No, that wasn't it. I read about alligator farming in the magazine, but there was this reference to alligator patrols, which I found interesting. I think it was the following year. Yes, the year after your sixtieth.'

★

Michael was home again briefly for Independence Day and the

local celebrations in the town. He and Joe were sitting quietly together in the lounge reading, whilst Renie was deciding what to wear. Despite repeated attempts to tell Joe that he should refrain from eating too much, he was still putting on weight, though Renie insisted they were both on a low-fat diet. Joe seemed sullen, and he was certainly more sedentary. Michael found another article about alligators, which caught his attention. This time the alligators were dying unexpectedly. He looked up at Joe, but realised there was no point asking him anything at that moment.

Michael reflected on the other articles he had read concerning the ban on hunting alligators in the 1970s, and then how successful gator farming had been in the '80s, and still seemed to be. Once back in Michigan, he searched online for the original paper, finding an abstract from a report produced by the Florida Fish and Wildlife Conservation Commission (FWC). His curiosity was aroused when he read that there had been a dramatic increase in alligator mortality, with no clear indication as to the cause. He was determined to look up the full journal in the university library. It didn't take him long to find it. The study had taken place around Lake Griffin. He knew the area by reputation, as Joe had told him that back in the 1950s, it had the most prestigious fishing.

Michael read the paper, immediately absorbed because the figures were dramatic. The FWC reported that the three-monthly daylight surveys conducted between December 1997 and November 2000 had detected three hundred and six alligators that had died of undetermined causes.[4] It was this particular description that really sparked interest. There would normally be two or three alligator deaths a year, so this was a massive increase in mortality and there was no identifiable explanation. Another report from researchers at the University of Florida confirmed the high mortality rate of two hundred over a two-year period.

★

'Obviously, they blamed blue-green algae, just like with the salmon fry,' Michael explained to Joe, who seemed really interested to hear more about the alligators and what was killing them. 'But I thought it was strange, because these gators didn't have anything wrong with their livers. With blue-green algae, you would definitely expect the liver to be affected.'

★

It seemed that a toxic strain of blue-green algae was initially thought to be involved. The offending algae, *Cylindrospermopsis*, accounted for more than ninety per cent of the microscopic floating algae in the lake and, as it was known to produce toxins that can cause death in animals, it was the obvious culprit. The toxin most often caused damage to the liver, a so-called hepatotoxin, and to the kidneys. A new study had demonstrated that these algae also produced toxins that affected nerves—neurotoxins. However, preliminary examinations of the dead alligators revealed nothing unusual. Curiously, there was little evidence of damage either to the liver, kidneys or brain in the affected animals.

Michael was intrigued—this novel illness had similar features to the Early Mortality Syndrome in salmonids. Like the fry with EMS, the dead alligators had very little wrong with them and the increase in mortality was sudden and inexplicable.

Michael was distracted for the rest of the day, pondering over the alligator syndrome, its lack of an obvious cause and minimal, almost insignificant positive findings. He wondered whether there could be any links with the equally perplexing EMS.

The rates in mortality peaked in the spring, which was also unexplained. It was suggested that this could have been due to the resumption of feeding, or, in the case of a nutritional deficiency, caused by a depletion of tissue reserves during the winter. Michael wondered whether this really was the reason. Why would that suddenly cause such a dramatic increase in mortality?

Searching online, he discovered that there were other papers about alligators; it was clear that research had been carried out on some of the diseased animals, comparing them with alligators from other lakes in the local area. Some of the live alligators had been observed to be lethargic and unresponsive to humans approaching them. These sick alligators had been captured. The researchers wondered whether they would recover when they were removed from the lake environment, rather like the salmon fry in hatcheries surviving in the artificial conditions.

The alligators had been observed and were noted to have weak limb movements; each alligator would drag the dorsal surface of their hind feet, while trying to avoid being handled. In some ways, this abnormal response to stimuli and the disordered movement was not dissimilar to the fish Michael had observed swimming in circles. There had also been alligator attacks, and this type of aggressive behaviour was akin to the hyperexcitable salmon fry.

One alligator was much sicker than the others; it was completely unable to use its rear limbs, and subsequently this poor creature became increasingly sluggish and less responsive. The behaviour of the sicker animal resembled the fry prior to death. Before this alligator died, more in-depth tests were performed. Scientists measured the functions of nerves and muscles with electromyography (EMG), looking at spikes of the nerve impulses, and they also tested brain activity using electroencephalography (EEG), observing the pattern of brain waves.

A more extensive examination was possible on the alligators at post-mortem. Although their internal organs and systems appeared normal, and their blood values similar to the control animals, there were subtle differences. The affected alligators from Lake Griffin had nerve impairment. This was not something Michael had been able to test for in salmon.

The conduction along the sick alligators' nerves was about half that of the normal alligators. Many of the diseased reptiles had microscopic signs of damage to the nerves in their limbs, as well as brain lesions. The alligators were diagnosed with peripheral neuropathy, which was more prominent in the lower parts of their limbs. The more severely affected the alligator, the worse the nerve conduction was found to be. The nerve damage was a sure clue to the mystery illness.

Baffled by the findings, Michael leafed through the technical histological results. Another alligator had damage to the midbrain. There was a loss of nerve fibres, described as chronic degeneration. *Neurodegeneration*—deteriorating nerves. Michael had heard of similar conditions affecting humans.

The histological findings of the nerve tissues seen under a microscope were indisputable. There was clear evidence of a chronic process damaging the alligators' nerves, but also their brains. This wasn't due to an algae toxin. The researchers had had similar thoughts and had measured 'heavy metal' levels. The concentrations of arsenic, cadmium, mercury, lead, selenium and thallium in the liver and kidney were all either at or below detection limits, indicating heavy metal poisoning was not the cause of the nerve damage and, therefore, this insidious disease.

In true fashion, the report finished by raising more questions than it answered. It claimed that due to financial restrictions, it had not been possible to conduct regular daylight mortality surveys of any lakes other than Lake Griffin. However, the report questioned whether the disease had spread. The Lakes in the Harris Chain or Ocklawaha Chain, named after the Ocklawaha River, are all interconnected. Lake Griffin is the historical and original source of the Ocklawaha River.

There were limitations to the study, as the entire brain was not examined histologically. The area examined in detail connected the auditory input with the motor centre. Michael had no idea of the equivalent in fish. This part of the brain enabled the alligator to move away when it heard a human approaching. This made sense, as the diseased creature had not seemed able to do this.

Was there a correlation between alligators dragging their hind legs with peripheral neuropathy and brain damage and salmon fry swimming in circles?

★

'So, these alligators weren't just dying suddenly, they were sick. It was as if they'd been poisoned.'

Michael's explanation was cut short by the supper bell. He'd smelt the food before the bell had sounded, a combination of warm cardboard and oil vapours.

'But no one knew what was doing it,' he finished, as the scent wafted in. It didn't register initially, he was just aware of a sense of nausea creeping up, turning his stomach. He was overly sensitive to smells, always had been.

Talking of poisoning, he thought, but managed not to blurt it out.

'Supper. Great! Hmmm! Wonder what's on the menu today?' He managed to sound enthusiastic. 'I'll head off now and see Renie. I'll be back again tomorrow to tell you more.'

He gave Joe a nod. Michael didn't see the need to be overly affectionate. He escaped before the supper trolley arrived. It didn't do either of them any good seeing Joe struggling to eat. Anyhow, Joe was getting the hang of feeding himself again, he just had to have the proper equipment: scoops, a bowl with suckers and a plastic bib. The dynamic of the parent-child relationship really had reversed.

The Disney Decade

As Michael walked onto the ward first thing the next morning, he was met by the nurse who had seen him on the first night, when Joe had been behaving badly. She clearly recognised Michael, who immediately blushed. She looked worried.

'Didn't you get the message?' she enquired. She was the one who seemed awkward now.

'No! Er, wha . . . what message?' Michael stammered a little, feeling flustered. What was wrong? The door to Joe's room was ajar and the bed had been stripped. The name on the outside of the door had been removed. 'Where is he?' Michael tried to keep the alarm out of his voice.

'Oh, it's just that his stool came back clear and so he's on the general ward now.' She smiled and indicated the bay that Joe had moved to. He was sitting next to the window, the sun shining onto his face, clearly enjoying observing the goings on outside.

'Howdy, partner!' Michael almost shouted out, relieved to see Joe looking so well. 'You've been allowed out for good behaviour, I see!'

Michael was laughing, and Joe practically grinned back. Well, his mouth opened, and his teeth were visible, as he stuttered a guffaw.

'Would you like to make a real bid for freedom? I could find a wheelchair and we can go find the café?'

An hour later, Michael was wheeling Joe along the corridor and briefly out into the fresh air, before heading towards the hospital café for a superior cup of coffee in a china mug, rather than those plastic cups they served on the ward. Once he'd bought them both cappuccinos, he positioned Joe so he could see out to the sky and trees, popped a straw in the cup and then carried on with his fascinating discoveries, which he had to admit were increasingly sounding like conspiracy theories.

'Where were we? Oh, yes, alligators! Well, it got me thinking. Not about alligators exactly, or EMS, but about water. Did you ever taste the water in Chicago, Joe? It's foul.'

Michael screwed up his face and stuck out his tongue to emphasise the point. He wasn't shy as he was doing it, it was just something he was aware of whenever he spoke to Joe. He talked louder and slower, using his hands to tell a story and making faces, as though by exaggerating he could make sure Joe understood. Did Joe understand? Sometimes he thought he did. Maybe he just liked the company. 'I started to get really concerned about the quality of the water. It began after I discussed the state of the River Illinois with Arnie years ago, at Thanksgiving.'

★

Michael had noticed the distinctly off-putting taste of the water when he first moved to Chicago; it was a combination of a fishy flavour with a tincture of chlorine. He asked his colleagues about it and learned they all used water filters. The drinking water was pumped from Lake Michigan, but apparently it tasted better than the drinking water on the outskirts of the city, which was pumped from the wells. Michael became rather obsessed with the quality of the water treatment. He researched the history of the Chicago water supply and discovered that a hundred and fifty years ago, the drinking water had been mingled with sewage. Now it was deemed safe to drink. Nevertheless, he was becoming increasingly wary about the local water.

At first, he was just sceptical, but then his concerns really started to grow. Close to home, there was pollution in the River Illinois and the hatcheries were affected by EMS. More recently, some bad press about it meant there were now proposals to improve its water quality.

*

'If they were actually planning to do something about it, it must have been atrocious,' Michael said bitterly to Joe. 'I was beginning to dwell on the problem. I couldn't understand why other people weren't as concerned.'

Michael shook his head in despair. 'I was biased, I don't mind admitting it. I saw all these cruise ships, read about the pollution and worked it out in my own mind.'

*

Over the last decade, there had been a noticeable increase in the lake traffic in and out of the Chicago harbours. Lake Michigan was the most popular for cruises, but now, to Michael's horror, there were voyages that incorporated all five lakes. He had initially assumed that his reaction was linked to his general prejudice against cruise ships and the increasing gluttony and obscene overindulgence that he knew occurred on them. But there was more to it than that, so he felt his feelings were justified. Their growth in popularity meant there had been a massive increase in the number of cruise ships on Lake

Michigan discharging effluent into the water. He read there had also been a dramatic increase in the number of cruises on the Baltic Sea, and that the Baltic states had acknowledged the problem and campaigned to prevent the dumping of sewage into their waters. Michael wished that a similar policy could be applied to the Great Lakes, but he thought it unlikely that any changes to the current status quo would be applied any time soon.

★

'I was trying to find a link between the Baltic and Lake Michigan. I thought this was it—cruise ships. Well, cruise ships in a relatively contained area of water,' Michael explained, while he and Joe finished their drinks. 'I remembered Eriksson from Sweden complaining bitterly about them. He was really knowledgeable about the sewage, sorry, wastewater treatment in the Baltic countries. I guess I was a bit preoccupied. Eriksson was, too, worse than me even, I'd say.'

★

Eriksson had got Michael to question how effective the wastewater treatment facilities were in the major cities around the Baltic, such as Riga and Tallinn.

Comparing the two geographical areas in his mind, Michael realised that both the Baltic and the Great Lakes had a limited flow of water in and out of a relatively closed basin of water. Did this contribute to EMS? As far as he knew, no one was testing for the levels of human soiling in these water reserves.

Since reading about increased alligator mortality, he had been wondering whether there was an association between pollution from human effluent and the mysterious disease afflicting them. He recalled discussing the demise of the Lake Griffin alligators with Arnie when he'd been home.

★

They finished their cappuccinos and walked the long way back to the ward, dawdling and stopping to let Joe look at life outside the confines of a single hospital room.

'I'd tried to find out what Arnie knew. But he only knew what he'd read about in the press, not the facts. He told me there'd been an increase in attacks. He was more concerned about the odd report of someone being mauled to death by an ill-tempered alligator,' Michael told Joe. 'It made me angry that no one seemed to be trying to work out why these alligators had suddenly started attacking humans.'

Michael sensed he was getting frustrated again. 'Shall we get some fresh air on the way back to the ward?'

Joe nodded. Although it was difficult to detect with all the general head movements, having spent so much time with Joe recently, Michael was getting much better at understanding his father's body language. As they walked back through the glass walkway, on the way to the automatic doors and fresh air, Michael continued. 'I even talked to you, I'm not sure if you remember. You made me realise the problem. You seeded the idea. At the time, I was cross with you for doing your usual trick and switching the subject of conversation. You told me that Lake Apopka near Orlando was now badly polluted, and what a great shame it was. You said it was the finest bass fishing in all the country and that there were almost no bass in the lake anymore, but that there were lots of catfish and other such species that do well in muddy, murky water. You were quite angry about it and made it abundantly clear that catfish were no match for bass. That really got me thinking.'

★

Orlando, home to Disney World, was near Lake Apopka and the other Harris Chain of Lakes. Lake Griffin was also in the vicinity. Michael remembered the conversation with Arnie, who was going to take his granddaughter, Tiffany, to the famous resort. He couldn't remember exactly when it all started, but it didn't take him long searching online to secure a few facts and figures. Disney World opened in 1971, and in the early days had fifty-two million visitors annually. Next there was Epcot, Disney's Hollywood Studios, and the Animal Kingdom, all of which opened throughout the 1980s and 1990s. Then the chairman unveiled the ten-year building plan, an ambitious programme known as the Disney Decade. The growth of the company during this timeframe was phenomenal. It was a hugely successful venture. By the mid-1990s, attendance had passed five-hundred million guests every year.

During the '40s and '50s, bass fishing had been one of Florida's main attractions, and anglers would travel from all over America to fish for trophy-sized catches. In 1964, with his grand scheme in mind, Walt Disney began secretly buying up millions of dollars' worth of central Florida farmland in lots of five thousand up to twenty-thousand acres. The two-year construction employed nine-thousand people, and when Disney World first opened, Orlando was the fastest growing city in the States, with hundreds of firms relocating to the area.

Lake Apopka is fifteen miles northwest of Orlando, in the headwaters of the Ocklawaha River. In 1987, it was targeted for a clean-up under the Surface Water Improvement and Management Act. The surrounding marshland and floodplains were restored, and a marsh flow way system was created to ensure filtration of the lake's waters by circulating it through the restored wetlands. Disney World was actually closer to a town called Kissimmee. Michael felt as though he was on the verge of discovering something, but he was struggling to find a geographical link between Kissimmee, Orlando and Lake Griffin.

★

'I don't mind admitting, I was starting to get fixated on the subject,' said Michael. 'I was getting obsessed really. The increase in alligator deaths occurred between 1998 and 2001, peaking in 2000. By this time, there was a massive increase in the number of people in the area. It would have been similar to a cruise ship docking every two minutes. It must have put a strain on local facilities. There must be a limit to sewage capacity.'

Michael and Joe were now back on the ward. Being the weekend, it was relatively quiet. 'I made very little progress until these scientists from the US Geological Survey agency published a paper on the brain abnormalities in the alligators, which were typical of thiamine deficiency. There were also abnormalities in part of the midbrain. You remember that it was the midbrain that was affected in those alligators last time, when they couldn't find anything wrong? This time they measured the thiamine levels, and they were low, but only in the Griffin gators, not the ones from the other lakes.'[5] Michael checked to see if Joe was still listening. 'Strange, huh? So, I set about trying to find out why. But first I had to find out more about wastewater management.'

★

Michael read up about the various stages of wastewater treatment. Pretreatment removed the bulky material, such as rags, wipes and plastic, to prevent blockages. It also extracted oil, grease and grit and other substances that would interfere with downstream processes. Bar screens were mechanical filters generally consisting of narrow metal grills, although some looked rather like stepladders with very narrow rungs. Moving water carries more sediment, so static tanks were used to de-sludge the water and allow solids to settle. Next came the clarifiers. These were the settlement tanks—circular ponds, each one divided into two semicircles by a rotating arm steadily turning through the water, removing suspended solids. Michael had seen these in action—there were several by the Illinois River, and another near Peoria Lake, not far from the hospital. He learned that this step concentrated the impurities. The sludge sank to the bottom and the scum floated to the top, allowing both to be removed. There were methods of making small particles clump together to encourage them to sink. This was called coagulation-flocculation, and it was generally achieved by adding chemical coagulants, such as iron or aluminium salts, to neutralise charges. This was followed by gentle stirring or agitation with flocculants, such as activated silica and talc, to promote clumping. These substances encouraged the particles to form masses large enough to either settle or be filtered out. Equalisation basins maintained the inflow of water and also ensured the water remained aerated and not stagnant. Michael had had no idea that there were so many stages. The current wastewater treatment processes were designed to substantially degrade the biological content of human and food waste, as well as the soaps and detergents that contaminate water supplies. Bizarrely, the processes utilised certain bacteria and protozoa to help degrade the organic impurities, such as sugars. Water was so vitally important, and

Michael wondered why he hadn't been taught more about the cleansing processes at high school.

★

'It was actually quite fun. No, that's the wrong word. Mesmerising? All that spinning. Addictive? No, well, you know what I mean. I was hooked. It was fascinating.'

★

The final treatment stage improved the effluent quality before discharging it into receiving environments, such as the sea, lakes, rivers, wetland or the ground. There were other more sophisticated methods of treatment, which included the use of activated carbon to draw out toxins, and the biological removal of excess nutrients. Eutrophication was due to excess nutrients. Large amounts of the basic nutrients, namely nitrogen and phosphate, in the water caused an overgrowth of weeds, algae and cyanobacteria.

★

'Putting it simply, eutrophication is a result of modern living, overcrowding and inadequate water purification. We humans are producing fast food for pond life!' Michael laughed at his own joke. 'McPoo! Do you get it?'

Joe was shaking, but Michael couldn't tell if he was happy or repulsed. Perhaps he had been too graphic?

★

In an algal bloom, most of the algae simply die, since the explosion in numbers is unsustainable; bacteria decompose these dead algae and, hence, the toxins are released. This also uses up the oxygen in the water, and consequently the fish die.

Michael wanted to understand more about the biological processes that purified water without using chemicals. In order to make it clean enough for drinking, a significant amount of nitrogen has to be removed from wastewater. Nitrogen mainly exists as part of the compound ammonia, one of the most common pollutants in wastewater. As well as being used in most cleaning products and fertilisers, ammonia is produced in the human body after the breakdown of nitrogen-containing proteins. It is then converted into urea and excreted as urine. Aside from human concerns, ammonia is harmful to aquatic life. The biological processes to remove ammonia from wastewater use bacteria to convert it to nitrogen oxides, which are subsequently converted to nitrogen, an inert and abundant gas forming approximately seventy-eight per cent of the earth's atmosphere.

Michael imagined a picture of a slide he could use to drive these facts home to his students. This was important. He thought he should be able to incorporate it into one of his lectures, starting with the sources of ammonia—food protein, fertilisers and cleaning products—and resulting in a happy ending with nitrogen gas released into the air.

The wastewater management process for the removal of phosphates did not seem quite so straightforward. From his reading, Michael determined that phosphate was the key component feeding algal blooms, which harm aquatic life by depleting the water of nutrients, such as oxygen, as well as producing harmful toxins. Vital for plant growth, phosphate is also used in fertilisers. The removal process similarly used bacteria. Many bacteria have phosphate-grabbing properties, with some able to take on up to a fifth of their weight in phosphates. Reading through the relevant species of bacteria, Michael found one of the Latin terms particularly amusing: *Candidatus Accumulibacter phosphatis*. Standard, non-biological systems for phosphate extraction use aluminium, calcium salts or a soil rich in iron, which all bind to phosphate.

Somehow, it seemed that many of the phosphate-removing processes were insufficient for the current needs of the population, especially when there were so many occurrences of blooming algae.

Very few summers passed by without a warning of excess blue-green algae. Michael felt sure treatments weren't able to keep up with human production, as each adult apparently excretes two hundred to a thousand grams of phosphorus annually, in addition to which there were another thousand grams from detergents. He also wondered whether it was possibly related to the end product—phosphate isn't simply released as a harmless gas into the atmosphere, like nitrogen. Once the water systems have been cleansed, the phosphate-rich sewage sludge is either dumped in landfill or used as fertilisers on the land, so-called biosolids.

⋆

'They're putting human excrement on fields—for growing crops! It contains lots of phosphates, so it makes things grow.'

Michael seemed to have passed most of the day talking about sewage. He could tell that his father was tiring, and that it was time to let him rest.

'Same time tomorrow, Joe? You up for more of the same shit?' Michael laughed as Joe's face lit up.

El Niño

The next morning, Renie decided to go to the Sunday service at her church while Michael was at the hospital. They both thought it wouldn't be long before Joe was back home, and although that would bring new difficulties, especially for Renie, it would be wonderful all the same.

The morning was still and bright. Michael said his farewells to Renie, as he was planning to go straight to the airport from the hospital. When he arrived on the ward, Joe was sitting up and was washed and dressed, and eager to go on another café trip. Michael found a wheelchair and started to talk.

'Going back to the Florida story, I tried to discover information about the local sewage plant, known as the Iron Bridge Water Pollution and Control Facility. Well, I found out that it was designed to serve a population of four-hundred thousand in the area around Orlando. I thought to myself that this seemed rather inadequate given the rapid expansion of the Disney resorts. But what do I know?'

They arrived at the café and Michael bought them both a latte.

'I began to think I'd been on a wild goose chase for nothing. The cause of the mystery alligator illness seemed to be thiamine deficiency. I wasn't convinced that my search for a link to wastewater had revealed anything out of the ordinary. I tried to find another explanation linking the alligator deaths to environmental conditions. I wondered if the deaths were related to certain weather patterns, climate change or even a freak storm. Thinking again about the Chicago floods leaching sewage into the River Illinois and Lake Michigan prior to the increase in salmon fry mortality, I wondered if maybe there was a similar event occurring in Florida, as there was always news of a hurricane or unseasonal weather in that part of the country.'

*

Each year, the peak in alligator mortality occurred in the spring. It was highest in April and May. This variation was also unexplained and, in retrospect, seemed much more likely to be related to climate. Michael thought he had made a breakthrough. The Chicago storms in 1992 had happened just before the increase in salmon fry deaths, and a record-breaking El Nino event in Florida had marked the winter of 1997-98. That winter had been the second warmest on record. Not only that, it was also the seventh wettest since 1895. There were reports of flooding and much wetter conditions across much of the southern part of the state. Furthermore, a series of tornadoes had caused destruction and fatalities. There had been a loss of power to one hundred and thirty-five thousand homes.

*

'Of course, the wastewater treatment facilities must have had independent generators and, therefore, would have been unlikely to be affected by power failures. So, I dug a bit deeper, metaphorically speaking!'

Michael and Joe were sitting in the corner of the café again. Even though there was no one around, Michael dropped his voice and spoke closer to Joe; he didn't want to shout it out. He felt as though he was disclosing a terrible secret.

'And I found out more about the surrounding area. What I discovered was that they were putting human excrement, you know, poo, on the fields that were being regenerated as part of the programme to restore the marshland around Lake Griffin.'

*

The nearest town to Lake Griffin was Leesburg, which had, as expected, undergone growth and economic development as a result of nearby Orlando. The City of Leesburg's wastewater system had been established in 1920, and by then served approximately thirty-seven thousand residents. The city treated its effluent to an advanced level, removing more solids and bacteria than the standard 'concrete pond' stage. It could then be used legally for the irrigation of six hundred and seventy-five acres of city-owned property. The resulting biosolids generated from the wastewater treatment process were disposed of at permitted sites on three hundred and forty acres of city-owned hay fields.

There was also another website with an update on the Iron Bridge treatment plant. In the mid-1980s, it was recognised that it needed more effluent capacity than the Little Econlockhatchee River. In 1986, the city of Orlando purchased one thousand, six hundred and fifty acres, and in July 1987, the wetland treatment system, which was one thousand, two hundred and twenty acres, was completed, and reclaimed water from the Iron Bridge plant began to flow. It was designed to 'polish' up thirty-five million gallons a day of reclaimed wastewater. Water was conveyed through a four-foot diameter pipeline of approximately seventy miles. All this was designed and constructed before the so-called 'Disney Decade'.

★

'Was this sufficient for the massive expansion in the number of visitors?' Michael asked Joe. 'I'd tried to reassure myself, but the more I read, the less sure I became.'

Michael told Joe how, apparently, the best time to visit Orlando was January to April, and the busy season was March to April. Coincidently, alligator mortality peaked between April and May. It was also interesting that the alligator deaths reduced dramatically after 2001. Following the September 11 terrorist attacks, there was a significant drop in the number of international and national tourists to Disney World.

'There has to be a link,' Michael said. 'I wonder whether Uncle Walt noticed a fall in the number of customers?'

Michael had a flight to catch and left Joe back on the ward. He promised to return in a few weeks and hoped that by then his father would be home.

Cruise ships

Although he'd begun to enjoy his visits home again, Michael was pleased to be back at work. Shortly after arriving back in Ithaca, he was having a coffee following a lecture when a few of his tutees walked into the café. They were chatting and laughing, and their high spirits were infectious. Michael offered to buy them a coffee. He'd often wondered where they were from and what their plans were, things not discussed in the lecture theatre. It was fascinating to hear so much optimism and enthusiasm for learning, life and living. The students were chuckling together, and he was standing on the periphery enjoying the scene. Youth, merriment, health; it provided a stark contrast with the sights in the hospital. Among the group was an English student called Luke, whom Michael hadn't seen before.

Michael discovered that Luke was on an elective, which was a period of study away from a scholar's base university, which in Luke's case was Granada, in the Caribbean, where he was reading medicine.

He and Michael talked briefly about his motivation to pursue a medical career and why he had chosen to spend his weeks on the much sought-after placement studying biochemistry. Then the murmuring of students disappeared, almost in an instant, and Michael found himself standing alone. He was smiling, and he felt curiously happy. He didn't know why, but despite all its complications, life suddenly felt good. He felt a glow, and this time not from embarrassment.

He was jolted from his reverie by a phone call. He fumbled in his pocket and saw that it was from Carol.

'Mikey, can we meet up tonight?' she pleaded.

'OK, why don't you come to mine, I'll cook?' Michael said, surprising himself with his boldness. He wasn't known for his culinary skills. Accuracy and efficiency in the lab didn't transfer well to the kitchen, although he couldn't quite work out why. After all, both had the same features: ingredients or chemicals, a recipe or method, basic equipment and some expensive machinery, and then the result, which was sampled or simply recorded for future papers or presentations. The steps were not very different if you thought about it, but somehow producing edible food was more difficult. He decided on a simple beef stroganoff. Unfortunately, he only had a small amount of steak left, having cooked most of it the previous night. He didn't have all the other ingredients either and had to improvise. Perhaps this was the problem. There was always more pre-planning in the lab and supplies were delivered regularly.

He'd finished the mushroom and beef stroganoff with tomatoes, as he didn't have cream, just as the doorbell rang. Carol pushed a bottle of wine into his hand and immediately hugged him. He backed away, taken a bit by surprise. He could smell alcohol on her breath. It was clear she had already been drinking. She stumbled as she put her handbag down and took off her strappy high-heeled sandals and coat. He took her coat from her, turning away to hang it up. She was casually dressed in tight fitting bleached jeans with a lime green t-shirt that looked as though it had shrunk in the wash. She swept her hair off her face, revealing slightly smudged red lipstick, and tried to force her usual breezy smile. Michael wasn't usually good at picking up these cues, but her face was blotchy, her eyes were swollen and her makeup was streaked around them. He wasn't sure how women applied their makeup, but this didn't look right. She had either been crying or was extremely allergic to something. No, she was definitely upset. He should say something, but what? He concluded it was much simpler to pretend he hadn't noticed.

'I'll get us a drink. What can I get you?' Michael asked, even though it was clear that Carol had already imbibed plenty. 'You OK?' he asked nervously. He knew he should ask, but if he were honest, he didn't really want to know.

'Supper's ready!' he announced, quickly changing the subject. Carol winced as she clumsily bent down to pick up her handbag. There was a bruise on her wrist. She saw Michael looking at it.

'I fell,' she stated, inviting no further questions. It seemed a reasonable explanation given the state she was in.

He showed her to the sofa, whilst he finished making supper, but she joined him in the kitchen, asking him too many questions about his culinary skills. She found anything he said hilarious and kept touching his arm, his back or his hair. Throughout the evening, Michael felt uneasy, and he didn't find Carol as relaxing to be around as usual.

The meal was, well, food. It was edible, but hardly the dinner Michael had hoped to prepare. He wasn't trying to impress her; he just appreciated her friendship. She seemed to have other ideas. She sat opposite him at his small, round table. During the meal, he moved his legs several times so as not to kick her, but wherever he placed them, hers seemed to follow. He moved his legs again, only to bump into hers once more. He was alarmed. She was definitely rubbing her legs up his.

He stood abruptly, knocking her wine glass over in the process and splashing wine onto her top. He was horrified.

'Oh, no! Oh, um, I'm sorry!' he stuttered, and before he knew what was happening, she had removed her top in fits of giggles and was mopping up the dripping wine on the table.

'It'sh fine,' she smirked, standing up in her lacy bra. She was definitely slurring her speech now.

'I'll find you a top.' He swallowed his words as he ran towards his bedroom, intending to grab a t-shirt from one of his drawers. He was having difficulty choosing a suitable top when she grabbed him from behind.

'Uh, Carol?' his voice was surprisingly high pitched. He just wanted the evening to end. He wished it had never started. 'Try this one.'

He turned round, knocking her onto the bed in the process, before rapidly leaving the bedroom.

'I'll make coffee,' he called out from the small hallway.

He busied himself clearing up the mess on the table and in the kitchen, relieved to be on his own for a few minutes.

After about twenty minutes, he thought he ought to see where she was and found her asleep on his bed. She hadn't managed to dress herself.

This is no good, no good at all, he berated himself.

He gently woke her up and, after she had dressed herself and drunk some coffee, he called her a cab. Carol seemed disappointed. Michael felt confused. Maybe he had misread the signals.

★

A week after the disastrous dinner with Carol, Michael decided to head to the college bar to unwind after a long day. He had managed to avoid his colleague by spending more time reading in the library. Fortunately, she was nowhere to be seen in the bar, but Luke was there with the other students. He looked up as Michael walked in. Luke was tall and had a tanned complexion, sandy hair and smiling, hazel eyes. He offered to buy Michael a drink and Michael began telling him about home, and the situation with Joe and Renie. It was really good to offload. Luke was well informed about Parkinson's disease and Michael was reassured to find that the kind of presentation Joe had was not unusual. He quizzed him on the causes and discovered that no one really understands why people develop Parkinson's disease. He also learned that there isn't a treatment that alters the course of the disease, but that the pills worked reasonably well for most people.

At thirty, Luke was older than the average medical student. In his twenties, he had worked in the City of London, but he hated the fast-paced life, and whilst his work earned him a lot of money, he came to feel that what he was doing was worthless. Now he was paying his way through medical school, and he loved it. He wanted to understand how best to treat any patient with any condition. Michael really admired this. Although Luke hadn't decided what he would specialise in yet, he suspected it would be a medical specialty rather than surgery. He liked the idea of neurology, hence his curiosity about Joe's problems.

Michael swapped telephone numbers with Luke and the following day called to arrange to meet him at the weekend. 'Do you fancy doing one of the trails? I hear the falls are good, or there's the gorge trail?'

They opted to walk towards downtown Ithaca and then

follow the stone trails and steps back to the campus along Cascadilla Creek. It was a short but pleasant walk. The day was dry, with a refreshing breeze. They passed numerous waterfalls and chatted to the background noise of rushing water.

'These are the Finger Lakes,' Michael explained to Luke. 'There are eleven of these long, narrow lakes, which are obviously glacial in origin.'

'It's stunningly beautiful here.' Luke took a deep breath. 'So, how far from the Great Lakes are we? Aren't they what you're focusing your research on?'

'Yes. We've been trying to find out about this mystery illness in salmon—EMS—early mortality syndrome. It affects the young fish—the salmon fry—in all the Great Lakes. The nearest one to here is Lake Ontario, due north, but it's still a fair way away. Lake Michigan and Lake Ontario are the worst affected. EMS has also affected the Finger Lakes; it's called Cayuga Syndrome here. These falls flow into the nearby Cayuga Lake.'

Michael really enjoyed sharing this information with Luke; he found him incredibly easy to talk to.

'There are beautiful rivers in Suffolk, too,' said Luke. He began telling Michael about his hometown, Ipswich, which was on the River Orwell. Then there was the River Deben and Stour. 'They are all wonderful rivers for sailing,' Luke commented.

They swapped sailing stories and Michael told Luke all about the sailing club in Peoria. This led onto tales about his family, Chicago and Lake Michigan.

'Joe worked in the fisheries,' Michael explained. 'That's when we first noticed the illness. He's always loved fishing. His pa taught him about rivers. He grew up in Chicago. Life was tough back then.'

Michael recounted how his great-grandfather had lived in South Side after emigrating from Austrian Poland before the First World War. He had worked in the steel works. 'His father worked long days, seven days a week,' he said, 'he never really saw his family and turned to alcohol, as so many of the steel workers did.'

★

Michael was born in Chicago, but moved to Peoria as a small child, returning to study at the University of Chicago. His childhood memories of the city of his birth were from visiting his grandfather and listening to his stories whenever he came to stay. As a teenager, Michael joined the yacht club in Peoria. Starting in the junior fleet, he had enjoyed being close to nature and the feeling of harnessing energy from the elements. There was always something requiring attention in a dinghy, whether it was trimming the sails, adjusting the rigger or watching out for other boats. He no longer sailed but still enjoyed watching other people out on the water.

Meanwhile, Luke grew up in Suffolk but went to boarding school like his father. After completing his A levels, he went to work in the City. He was successful, but he hated it. He was out every night in bars and clubs, and he was drinking and eating excessively. His father had suffered a heart attack five years earlier, aged just 51, and it was a wake-up call. He knew he needed to drastically change his lifestyle. He'd been impressed by the doctors who had saved his father's life, but that wasn't why he chose medicine. He disliked the greed and futility of his chosen career path and wanted a vocation where he was giving rather than taking. He wanted to contribute wholesomely to society rather than simply living in it or, worse, contributing to the downfall of others. He'd seen people's lives destroyed by alcohol. He hated the pollution in the city and yearned to live in the countryside again.

'London is just so busy. Everyone is on top of everyone else—commuters, tourists, super-wealthy, super-poor. There are massive inequalities.'

'Chicago has massive inequalities too.' Michael stopped on one of the bridges to admire the view. The trail was relatively quiet compared to midweek, when the students used it to cut across campus. 'What's the population of London?' he asked out of the blue.

'Eight million, I think.' Luke wasn't sure why his friend was asking.

'Lake Michigan is popular with tourists. Chicago is the largest city on Lake Michigan. It has a population of two point seven million, making it the second largest city on the Great Lakes after Toronto, which has over five million inhabitants.'

★

Initially, Michael had wondered if EMS was a result of urbanisation—the two lakes mostly affected were Lake Michigan and Lake Ontario. In recent years, he'd also become concerned about the increasing number of ships departing on lake cruises on Lake Michigan. Following a brief overview of all that the Windy City has to offer, passengers would embark on a week-long trip from the historic Navy Pier. Compared to the lake and surrounding countryside, Chicago was a city of giants. Humans were dwarfed by the colossal buildings. The Wrigley Building by the Chicago River, with its steel frame, was once the tallest building in Chicago. It was clad in white terracotta and lit up at night. The Willis Tower had a similar hollow tube design, like a menacing grey dinosaur. This helped it to withstand the wind. There were concerns about wind tunnels in cities with a large number of skyscrapers. Michael thought it was a shame they didn't harness the energy. Architecturally, the Smurfit-Stone Building looked as if it had been folded like a paper rocket. It was known as the diamond building but was in fact composed of two almost identical triangles. The walls were clad in steel, aluminium and reflective glass, producing gleaming white stripes.

The other contrasting building was the Water Tower, which was one of the only buildings to survive the Great Chicago Fire of 1871. It was built of limestone blocks and looked more like a Bavarian Castle, with its elaborate towers and castellation. A grand spiral staircase encircled the main tower, concealing the water standpipe, which was once the nucleus of the city. The pumping system was built to provide the city with clean water, taken from intake bins situated in Lake Michigan. Until then, the water had been pumped from basins along the shoreline, which had been polluted with water from the contaminated Chicago River. Not surprisingly, the bins also became polluted. It was only when the Chicago River was reversed that the problem was solved, and in its centenary year, the Water Tower became the first American Water Landmark.

★

It hadn't taken Michael long to turn the conversation to water pollution.

'The most historic building along the Deben is the Tide Mill,' Luke said, 'they're still making flour there. It's eight-hundred years old and still working. It's in Woodbridge, a pretty, old market town. The coastline is beautiful, too; it's labelled as a heritage coast. In many ways, it's very different to Chicago, though.' Luke seemed wistful. He hadn't talked about home much. He soon clicked out of it. 'So, what's your favourite building in Chicago?' he asked.

'Now? The Smurfit-Stone Building, it looks like the sails on a boat. It's very different to the other buildings. When I was younger, though, it was definitely Big John.' Michael laughed, remembering a trip to see the skyscrapers as a boy.

*

Big John still contained the world's third highest residence and America's highest indoor swimming pool, on the forty-fourth floor. The Aon Centre had the world's largest public library (the Harold Washington Library Centre) and the world's largest exhibition and convention complex (McCormick Place), as well as the largest collection of Impressionist paintings outside the Louvre, if you were interested in that kind of thing. As a boy, Michael had been impressed by these incredible engineering feats, but now he only saw excess and unnecessary luxury. Even so, there was an incredible view from the three-hundred-and-sixty-degree observation deck. The north view was of skyscrapers, the city and beaches—Chicago boasts fifteen miles of beaches. The south view overlooked factories and smoke. Looking east, there was the flatness of the prairies—grasslands. Known as 'tall-grass' prairie, typical of the eastern Great Plains, the grass grew to six feet, producing lush pastures with rainfall. In the spring, it was awash with wildflowers. Dominant features included the skies and spectacular cloud formations. To the west was the vast, watery seascape of Lake Michigan. Despite urbanisation, Chicago remained the centre of the Midwest, and the inhabitants still had their roots in the land.

★

'It's a big city, but it's more down-to-earth compared to most.' Michael had fond memories of his time in Chicago. 'And while the locals, the Chicagoans, are known for being direct, on the whole they're friendly and pretty humble.'

'There's a divide in Ipswich. It's commutable to London, so the rich people who work in the capital are pushing up house prices. In another world, that could so easily have been me.' Luke shrugged, sounding relieved to have left his old life behind. 'But then there are generations of families who have never left the county. Out of town, most of the land is owned by a few super-wealthy farming families living on large estates. I guess both the Suffolk rivers and Lake Michigan lakefront have the clanging of masts in the harbours, but Suffolk doesn't have the cruise ships. Although we do have Felixstowe container port, which is the busiest in the UK.'

'At least the port has a function.'

'Importing plastic rubbish from China,' Luke retorted.

'Well, I loathe these floating hotels,' Michael complained. 'Talk about unnecessary excess. Each one has several restaurants, music venues, cinemas and swimming pools, not to mention the air-conditioned suites on a choice of decks.'

Michael had seen them departing and knew that the routes were all similar, leaving Chicago in the southwestern corner of the lake and taking in the full splendour of the city skyline, before departing for their cruise of Lake Michigan.

'After dark, each city tower is alight with thousands of

twinkling stars, but these are the only stars you'll see over Chicago, as the city itself lights up the whole sky.'

'Rural Suffolk doesn't have the same problem with light pollution,' Luke admitted. 'Have you been on one of these cruises?' he asked, wondering why Michael knew so much about them.

'Oh, no, absolutely not! I'm just interested. Curious. OK, a little obsessed.'

Michael continued telling Luke about the standard itinerary. 'The cruises take you to Milwaukee, known as Brew City, in Wisconsin. Then onto Manitowoc, to see where the Russian satellite Sputnik 4 crashed onto the street. Next is Sturgeon Bay, which has spectacular limestone cliffs and is one of the largest shipbuilding ports on the Great Lakes. Then you cross the lake to reach Mackinac Island, located at the isthmus in the Straits of Mackinac, between Lake Huron and Lake Michigan. Strictly speaking, it is actually in Lake Huron. Mackinac Island was once important in the fur trade and contained many fur farms. The two most commonly bred animals were fox and mink. It is now a popular tourist destination. All vehicles are banned, so everyone cycles. There are some pretty old buildings there, by American standards, and some were apparently built by the original French settlers. But there's nothing as old as the mill you mentioned.' Michael continued with the virtual cruise. 'The largest island in Lake Michigan is Beaver Island, which has beautiful beaches and numerous lakes. It's part of an archipelago of islands, including South and North Fox Islands, Hog Island, Gull Island and Trout Island. Then there are Whiskey, Hat and Shoe Islands, which were named after local industries. In the sixteenth century, Michigan was the centre of the beaver hunting grounds; mammalian winter pelts were popular for keeping warm. In particular, beaver wool felt hats were a status symbol and were expensive purchases in Europe.'

'Sadly, across the Atlantic, the European beaver has been hunted almost to extinction,' Luke interjected. 'They've just started reintroducing it in some areas in Scotland. When we were last there, the beavers had caused localised flooding with their dams,' he laughed. 'The footpath was completely submerged.'

'Then finally to Holland, which was founded by Dutch Americans,' continued Michael. 'Its main industry is the Heinz Company, which operates America's largest pickle and sauce factory.'

Michael had finished the tour, and for a few minutes they both carried on in comfortable silence. Michael's mind drifted back to his research and the salmon fry. It was great to have a willing ear.

'It's not just Lake Michigan that has its cruise ships. There are also cruises in the Baltic,' Luke volunteered, almost reading Michael's mind.

Michael beamed with enthusiasm. 'There certainly are. An increasing number are visiting Stockholm, St Petersburg, Copenhagen, Tallinn, Oslo, Helsinki and Riga. My Swedish friend Eriksson and I discussed the cruise ships when we were at a workshop in Stockholm. He's keen to protect the natural environment.'

Eriksson and Michael had compared the conurbations along the Baltic Sea with those of the cities on the shore of Lake Michigan. Michael hadn't realised how big some of these Baltic cities were. St Petersburg had a population of four point eight million, virtually the same as Toronto. Eriksson had emailed Michael recently announcing that the states in the Baltic Sea region had decided to adopt something called the HELCOM Baltic Sea Action Plan to reduce pollution. The plan was to restore the ecological status of the Baltic marine environment.

Michael frequently referred to cruise ships as floating gin palaces. He resented their presence and, like his uncle Arnie, felt that they didn't contribute much to the tourism of the area; most of the clientele would rather be entertained on board, being too lardaceous to walk far on shore and only really interested in the next meal and what to drink with it, before it and after it. It was becoming clear that these ships really were a hazard, and not just an obsession and prejudice of Michael's.

'It's not just the cruise ships polluting the lakes; there are also cargo ships—lake freighters or "lakers". The smaller lakers use the Saint Lawrence Seaway to reach the ocean. The ocean vessels, or "salties", come from the Atlantic Ocean,' Michael explained. 'These ships brought the zebra mussel to the Great Lakes in their ballast water—you know, they have to take on water when they unload cargo and discharge the water wherever they load up with more goods. The problem is that the zebra mussel is an invasive species.'

*

Completed in 1959, the Saint Lawrence Seaway was a series of locks and canals along the banks of the Saint Lawrence River; it enabled the lakers and salties to bypass the rapids and dams, but the zebra mussels they introduced affected the fish population. They were freshwater mussels, probably originating in the Ural and Volga rivers in South Russia. As they are adept at adapting to changes in the environment, they gradually encroached on most other freshwater supplies worldwide. They can thrive in inhospitable terrains and are even able to survive out of water for a time.

Zebra mussels were first detected in the Great Lakes in 1988. As filter feeders, they remove huge quantities of plankton from the water. Unfortunately, they lack a natural predator in the lakes, and so their numbers had escalated.

★

Michael and Luke met up for coffee every day between lectures. Joe had been discharged from hospital and Arnie was helping him and Renie. Michael felt bad for delaying his visit. Joe seemed a long way off his former self; even though he was home, he was far from independent. Michael had felt helpless in the hospital. He was frustrated that Joe wasn't improving more quickly, and he was interested in talking with Luke about Parkinson's disease. By way of diversion from Joe's condition, he turned his attention to looking into the putative cause of Parkinson's disease, and the likelihood of Joe's recovery. He was hoping that with his scientific knowledge and Luke's medical background, he would gain a greater insight into the world of human diseases.

He searched for clues online, substituting 'salmon and alligator mystery ailments' for 'Parkinson's disease' and 'increased prevalence' in his browser. In one article, he came across some world statistics: interestingly, one of the highest prevalence of Parkinson's disease in the world was in Egypt, along the River Nile.[6] It was more common in poor, rural areas with open sewers.

Hmmm, Michael thought, suspicious for a few minutes before shaking off his worries. The second highest place was in the Amish community; this was thought to be a genetic form of the disease. The Parkinson's Disease Foundation was one of the most helpful resources. There was a list of factors that increased the risk of developing the disease, including being more than sixty years of age, gender (it is more common in men than women) and a possible complication following a head injury. Curiously, the risk may be reduced in smokers, coffee drinkers and those with high vitamin D levels. He read more than once that there may be an increase in Parkinson's disease in rural areas, and the site specifically mentioned Central Valley, California.

First off, Michael investigated Central Valley, as it was closer to home. This is the most productive agricultural area in California, as well as one of the most prolific in North America. It's known for its large expanse of interconnecting canals, streambeds, sloughs, marshes and peat islands. The Sacramento-San Joaquin River Delta, in the western part of Central Valley, drains into the San Francisco Bay and eventually into the Pacific. These wetlands had recently been targeted for a rescue operation to try to restore them to their former natural state. After many years of cultivation, its natural habitats had been destroyed.

The run-off from the Sierra Nevada flows into the Central Valley and is one of the largest water reserves in California. The Sacramento River is the largest river in California. It flows into the Sacramento-San Joaquin River Delta. Decades ago, it had been recognised that water control was needed to prevent the overflowing of the rivers from snowmelt in the spring, and to avoid them drying up in the summer and autumn. The rivers had been dammed, resulting in the unfortunate loss of Chinook salmon—the largest of the salmon species. Post-war, the predominantly coastal urban development had stretched the water resources even further. The subsequent rapid development of agriculture in the southern Central Valley had then required far more water than was available locally. As part of the California State Water Project, an aqueduct was built. This transported water from northern California, using some impressive pumps. Water had also been pumped from the delta, and this was yet another hazard for the spring-run salmon. He had started by looking up reasons for an increased prevalence of Parkinson's disease in Central Valley and ended up thinking about fish again.

Despite the lack of progress, Michael felt strangely happy, as though he were onto something. He was spurred on to see if he could find out any more information on the underlying causes of his father's disease. It had become important to him. The last thing he read before going to bed was that as well as the association with rural living, Parkinson's may be linked to well water, manganese and pesticides.

Neurotransmitters

Luke had been spending more and more time at Michael's apartment, and before long he had practically moved in. There was no fuss; it just seemed more convenient and they enjoyed each other's company.

Michael quizzed Luke on the *Clostridium difficile* infection that Joe had in hospital. He wanted to find out more about them, wondering if they provided a clue to the cause of Parkinson's disease.

'They are spread by spores, so they are persistent and difficult to get rid of. They stick around in dust,' Luke explained.

'But what happens in the water?' Michael was still puzzled, and Luke shrugged his shoulders. While Luke enjoyed these medical discussions, Michael pushed the boundaries of his knowledge. He didn't always know the answers. He sometimes doubted there *were* answers to Michael's questions.

'So, what causes Parkinson's disease?' Michael gave up on *Clostridia*.

'It's a deficiency of dopamine, which is produced by a specific area in the brain called the substantia nigra—part of the basal ganglia, and—'

'Yeah, I know that—you said that already—but what *causes* it?'

'No one knows. It's just one of those conditions. We know where the problem is in the brain, but we don't know how it gets there.'

'I mean, I know there's no quick fix or anything, but surely we have some idea about why it happens?' Michael sounded frustrated, the exhaustion of the past few weeks was beginning to show. Luke shook his head, empathising with his friend as best he could, before returning to his studies. Meanwhile, Michael clicked away on his computer.

During his undergraduate studies, Michael had learned about neurotransmitters—the chemical messengers acting between nerves primarily in the brain. However, he felt a bit of revision would reassure him that everything possible was being done to help Joe. Studying fish, he'd had little need to read anything about dopamine recently. He wasn't even sure whether they used dopamine in the same way.

In humans there are seven neurotransmitters: acetylcholine, dopamine, GABA (gamma-aminobutyric acid), glutamate, histamine, norepinephrine (noradrenaline) and serotonin. All these interact with each other. Low acetylcholine is implicated in dementia, while GABA plays a major role in the regulation of anxiety. It is an inhibitory neurotransmitter, which means that it inhibits nerves, dampening their response. The antianxiety drugs benzodiazepines increase the GABA effect, leading to a feeling of calm. Glutamate is important for learning and memory. Michael knew of histamine. As well as acting as a neurotransmitter, it also causes itching and inflammation, hence antihistamines are used for hives and insect bites. Noradrenaline acts in the autonomic nervous system, the nerves that humans have no control over. It is the main neurotransmitter in the sympathetic nervous system, which gets the brain and body ready for action—the fight or flight response. It is an excitatory neurotransmitter, meaning it enhances the nerve's potential. It is particularly good at increasing the heart rate and blood pressure. Serotonin is the happy chemical because it improves our sense of wellbeing. It seems to inhibit dopamine, and low levels of serotonin lead to an overproduction of dopamine and impulsive behaviour. In fact, whilst too little dopamine causes Parkinson's disease, an excess brings on hallucinations; an overactive dopamine system has been linked to schizophrenia.

Michael read that dopamine has an effect on several other neurotransmitter receptors; it doesn't just bind to the specific dopamine ones. Dopamine deficiency leads to hypotension. The exact mechanism wasn't entirely clear, but Joe had certainly had problems with low blood pressure. Depressive symptoms were also common in patients with Parkinson's disease. This was presumably due to an interaction of the neurotransmitters, especially serotonin. *Had Joe also experienced depression?* Michael wondered.

Apparently, recent studies were testing a fish diet, which is high in omega-3 fatty acids, in order to promote dopamine levels. It was a slightly strange proposal and Michael wondered how this idea had come about. It seemed to be on the basis that omega-3 fatty acid deficiency in utero leads to a reduction in the number of dopamine receptors. Do fish get dopamine deficiency? Michael thought he was being ridiculous even searching for this, but here was a paper—from Uppsala, Sweden, of all places. Dopamine-deficient zebra fish display an increased number of freezes—where they simply stop moving momentarily—and an increase in erratic movements. Just like Joe! Michael smiled to himself, amused that he was comparing his father to a zebra fish. He was somehow much more at ease reading about dopamine deficiency in familiar creatures.

Dopamine is involved with mood regulation and cognitive function, as well as physiological homeostasis—keeping bodily functions, such as blood pressure, stable—motor coordination and the reward system. Amphetamines increase levels of dopamine by reducing its breakdown.

'Perhaps Joe needs speed!' Michael said out loud.

Luke chuckled at his sense of humour, which was whacky at times, and carried on reading.

'Ah, perhaps not!' The next line revealed that a sudden increase in dopamine triggers the reward system, which is why humans become addicted, seeking ever more reward. Food, particularly sugar and fat, is a potent stimulator, promoting eating as a way to gain more satisfaction. In times of plenty, gorging on such palatable foods was advantageous, as the body would store the energy as fat for when food was scarce.

There is a reason why people are fat and happy! thought Michael, quietly amused.

Rather oddly, doctors were using low dose amphetamine for attention deficit hyperactivity disorder. Even though Michael understood that this was also partly a movement disorder, manifesting itself in too much activity, he couldn't understand how slightly increasing dopamine levels would help. Apparently, low dose dopamine had an effect on glutamate receptors, the inhibitory neurotransmitters, thus improving attention. Conversely, a high dose causes an increase in movement.

'So many connections, so finely balanced, so easy to tip the balance.' Michael hadn't meant to vocalise his thoughts. He'd spent too long living alone.

'Sorry?' Luke said.

'Oh, nothing.' Michael shook his head. 'So, the treatment Joe's on, does that increase dopamine? It says here that it causes increased but abnormal motor activity.'

'It's called dyskinesia; literally bad movement,' Luke replied.

'That's the name the specialist nurse used for Joe's body movements,' replied Michael. 'I've seen drug addicts with jerky movements on the streets in Chicago. I'm guessing they must have been using too much amphetamine to get their reward.'

'That sounds about right. The involuntary repetitive movements are caused by too much dopamine. Joe will be taking L-dopa, a prodrug.'

'Prodrug—sounds like something professional athletes take.'

Luke laughed, 'No, not that kind of pro. Pro as in an inactive drug—that is, metabolised, converted in the body into the active drug. L-dopa—as in a *pre-drug*, levodopa, which is taken up in the brain and then converted where it is needed, to dopamine.'

Reduced dopamine causes a decline in memory and problem solving, as well as motor function. Perhaps this was its effect on acetylcholine receptors, the neurotransmitter affected in Alzheimer's disease. So far, it was all doom and gloom.

What about the cause? he asked himself despairingly. Surely with the facilities and intellect invested in research, it must be possible to elucidate the cause. It was a bit like reading papers about EMS a decade ago; there really seemed to be no clue. Maybe it was environmental; Michael felt fortunate that very few cases seemed to be genetic in origin. Conversely, genetic studies were easier to acquire funding for, the hope being that through research the cause of the neurodegeneration would be identified. This is what Parkinson's disease is; it occurs when there is excessive degeneration in a specific part of the brain, the part that produces dopamine.

'Find out anything?' Luke asked kindly. 'Keep in mind that in many cases, we don't know the cause of cancer. I mean, there are a few cancers that we can say with certainty are caused by things, for example, the human papilloma virus can lead to cervical cancer, but there's a vaccine against that now. There's a lymphoma called Burkitt's lymphoma, a cancer of the lymph glands, that's caused by a virus too—the Epstein-Barr virus.'

Michael wasn't sure where this was going, and there were a lot of big words.

'In fact, there are clear environmental causes, too, asbestos in mesothelioma, a lung cancer affecting the lining of the lung, and there's a chemical called aniline that's linked to bladder cancer.'

Michael was nodding, wondering if there was such a thing for Parkinson's.

'But the current theory is that most cancers are multi-hit diseases, meaning they are a result of multiple accumulating factors over years. Maybe it's the same with neurodegenerative diseases? Who knows?'

It was fish all over again. That night, Michael had vivid dreams of fish struggling to get moving before swimming with stutters and shakes; salmon on speed!

Wild gulls and herrings

Recalling his conversations in the hospital with Joe, when he told him about the alligators and the biosolids distributed around Lake Griffin, Michael mulled over the subsequent revelations. He hoped to be able to update Joe when he returned to see him, but he supposed that with him now back at home, it would be difficult to chat in the same way.

Michael strongly suspected that the alligators, and more specifically thiamine deficiency in the alligators, would provide an important clue to EMS. He had searched for evidence in other creatures and was surprised to discover that another animal had been reported as showing a similar syndrome. This time it was herring gulls in the 1970s and 1980s.[7] The majority of these gulls had an abnormal thyroid, which was not due to iodine deficiency. Interestingly, the gulls' disease was associated with forage fish, just as EMS was shown to be more common where there was an abundance of them.

'So, what are forage fish?' Luke asked.

Michael looked behind him to see Luke peering over his shoulder at the doodles he'd been making on a piece of paper—what had started off as a plan to update Joe on the salient points of his theory.

'They are the smaller fish that the big fish—such as salmon—eat,' Michael replied, slightly stunned. He was used to quizzing Luke on his medical knowledge, so it was amusing to hear Luke ask basic questions about his work. 'It's now mostly alewives, a type of herring—*Alosa pseudoharengus*. They're not native to the Great Lakes.'

'Are the salmon?'

'There were native Atlantic salmon—*Salmo salvar*—in Lake Ontario, but they vanished before the last century. The tributaries were blocked by mill dams,' Michael replied. 'The lake trout—*Salvelinu namaycush*—was also native, but numbers plummeted after the sea lamprey—*Petromyzon marinus*—invaded the lakes through the Saint Lawrence Seaway.'

Michael was bothered that this creature had become a pest as a result of human action. 'Sea lamprey are parasitic— they attach themselves to the trout and suck, like a vampire, or a giant leech.'

He shuddered at the thought. 'They also preyed on other fish, like the lake chub—*Couesius plumbeus*.'

'So, where do salmon—or '*Salmo*'—come from?' Luke asked, trying out the scientific names.

Michael laughed. 'They are mostly in the order of Salmonids. The salmon were introduced largely to boost the sport fishing industry in the late 1960s, after the decline of the lake trout. Coho salmon—*Oncorhynchus kitutch*—was the most successful, but they also introduced Chinook salmon—*Oncorhynchus tshawytscha*—also known as king salmon.'

'EMS. That's the Early Mortality Syndrome, right?' Luke asked, still looking at the scribbles on the page. 'And the Cayuga Syndrome in the New York Finger Lakes.' Luke had remembered Michael telling him.

'Yes, that's right. The immature salmon in the hatcheries were dying young,' Michael replied, surprised by how easy it was to condense decades of work into one sentence. For most people, that's all it took for them to lose interest, but Luke was different.

'What does it have to do with Parkinson's disease?' Luke was confused.

'Oh, nothing. I've got this theory and I'm still trying to make it all fit together,' Michael explained succinctly, expecting the conversation to be dropped.

'Let's hear it, then.' Luke pulled a chair up and sat next to Michael at the table, trying to decipher the other words on the crib sheet.

Michael briefed Luke on the alligators dying of a mysterious illness, which turned out to be thiamine deficiency, and how the timings aligned with the local population explosion and the changes to the nearby water treatment plants. He explained that obviously he couldn't prove anything and moved on to talking about his childhood and the fisheries.

★

Michael didn't enjoy school. It wasn't because of the work, which became easier when he was able to focus on the subjects he excelled at, namely the sciences; it was more that he didn't really have any friends. He didn't say much, and he had a tendency to stutter, which he eventually grew out of. In truth, though, he preferred his own company. One of his more peculiar traits was to break things. Joe and Renie assumed it was a phase he would grow out of, but then it became clear to them that he was actually trying to grasp how things worked by attempting to put them back together again. This was what he was doing now—fixing things. He had found something he was good at and, as it required precision and attention to detail, it suited him. When he started working for his PhD in

Ann Arbor, he finally felt as though he fitted in, or at least that he no longer needed to try and fit in. He would spend hours on one particular paper and then discuss it at length with his colleagues. No one in the lab thought he was strange.

★

Although Luke was pretty much living in Michael's apartment, they were careful not to be seen together at the university. Luke was openly gay and self-confident, so he was relatively relaxed about the relationship, but Michael felt that as he was an Assistant Professor and Luke was a student, it would be frowned upon. This was the only disagreement between them.

'No one cares!' Luke stated, adamant that what was going on between them was no one else's business. Michael admired his self-assurance and wished he could be more like him, but he also knew what his colleagues were like.

'So, what did you learn from the gulls? Herring gulls you say, does that mean they eat herring? Herring are forage fish, correct?' Luke was smart; he picked things up so quickly.

'There were large-scale mortalities, just as with the salmon,' said Michael.

★

Michael went home to visit Joe and Renie for the weekend. It had been a month since he'd last seen Joe, and he was really hoping to see an improvement. He arrived home on Friday afternoon. Joe was sitting in the armchair in the lounge, head bent forward, hands subtly rotating, as though he were trying to turn a doorknob with each hand.

'Hel-lo, Mich-ael,' he stuttered, looking up and shifting forwards on his chair.

Michael walked over to him. 'Don't get up.' He put a hand on his shoulder. 'You're looking so well.'

Joe had put on weight. He'd regained some of the pounds he'd lost in hospital and had more fullness and colour in his cheeks. Michael was pleased to see that he and Renie were coping; however, Joe was no better. He was limited by shakes and stiffness. Consequently, Renie had to do everything around the house. Thankfully, Joe could still read, but he tended to spend most of the day watching television. It wasn't clear how much he was taking in. He seemed to sleep on and off all day, but he had trouble sleeping at night. His mood was generally low, but he had periods when he seemed more lucid. Renie told Michael that there were other times when he seemed confused.

'He's not always with it,' she said quietly. 'One moment he's taking it all in, the next, well, I don't know where he is, but it's not here.'

Michael was beginning to feel cross. *Not here! Where did she think he was?*

'He just loses it, gets angry, for no obvious reason. Starts blaming me for things, like spending his money and losing his stuff. It's not Joe. Not the old Joe.'

As Joe was more anxious, Renie was seemingly less flustered and more resigned to her caring role, as though she had already grieved losing him. There was a certain sadness about her. She also appeared more organised, which was probably out of necessity, but perhaps it was also her coping strategy. Looking after Joe's medicines and needs was a full-time job. There were so many pills. The various concoctions all had multiple side effects, and all interfered with and counteracted each other. There were drugs to stop him shaking, help him move, stimulate his gut, bung him up, prevent him refluxing, sedate him, make him less anxious—the list was extensive, the potential interactions countless.

Michael returned to sit next to Joe. Joe's mouth sluggishly opened, but no words were emitted. Michael was about to interrupt, but after a painfully long intermission, Joe managed two barely decipherable words in a broken voice. 'How's . . . work?'

Michael needed no further invitation. He smiled cheerily, sat opposite Joe and started telling him about his latest discoveries. 'I've been looking at the work on gulls. You know, herring gulls. As both salmon and gulls consume forage fish, I thought it might give me a lead.'

Michael looked across at Joe to see if he was following; he seemed interested, well, less vacant.

'Turns out gulls get a bug similar to the one you got in hospital, Joe, *Clostridium*—not the difficult one though!' He laughed at his own joke. 'No, this one's called *Clostridium botulinum*, and it's caused large-scale mortality in these birds, mostly around Lake Erie.'[8]

This was thought to be linked to the birds' forage fish diet. The toxin produced was a neurotoxin. Michael had talked to Luke about it and discovered that botulinum toxin causes problems in humans, too.

'Botulism caused muscle paralysis, constipation, facial muscle weakness, difficulty swallowing and slurred speech, but the most worrying feature is the breathing difficulties. It could stop you breathing,' Michael informed Joe crassly, before continuing, unaware. 'It turned out that the scientists conducting the study on gulls were from Canada.' Michael thought it incredible that simultaneous research into similar fields could be carried out without any shared knowledge; his group was interested in fish and these scientists were focusing on gulls.

There was a further study into gulls in the Great Lakes area by another member of the group. This study looked at the health of the gulls in relation to breeding locations dating from the early 1990s, which was when EMS suddenly became a problem. It was far easier to look at the breeding locations of gulls than it was salmon. The study surmised that the gulls had been exposed to chemical stressors. However, there was no indication as to what these might have been. Michael had then searched for 'thiamine deficiency' and 'birds' and found a paper from Sweden, which provided details of wild birds dying from thiamine deficiency.

Michael had fond memories of his brief trip to Stockholm, which had spurred him on to do the research. The 'M' in M74, the Baltic equivalent of EMS, stood for 'Miljöbetingad', meaning environmentally related, and 74 was the year it had been discovered. This had been almost two decades before the significant jump in the number of cases of EMS in the Great Lakes. Now a group from Stockholm University had found that a significant number of wild birds of several species were dying of an idiopathic paralytic disease. The location of these birds was the Baltic Sea.

'I had a tremor of excitement,' he told Joe eagerly, before immediately regretting his choice of words. Joe didn't seem to notice and was waiting to find out what was so amazing. Michael always felt a kick when he thought he might be on the brink of a discovery, which in this case was the linking of all these diseases together. The birds were failing to breed, but not only that, the yolk, liver and brain were found to have low thiamine levels. There was evidence of thiamine deficiency in both the chicks and fully grown birds, and treatment of the paralysed birds with thiamine had led to a cure.

'I remember the rush of brain activity, the surge of adrenaline. It was thrilling, exhilarating!' Michael explained, struggling to contain his enthusiasm for the topic. 'Alligators had low thiamine levels and now gulls had low thiamine levels. Gulls from the Baltic Sea had low thiamine levels, gulls feed on forage fish and salmonids feed on forage fish. We knew EMS was related to an abundance of forage fish. There had to be a connection. I was on a roll!' He turned to Joe. 'You see, forage fish increase when there are increased nutrients.' By now he was almost shouting. 'Nutrient increase is eutrophication. It was accepted that algae increased with eutrophication. But the algae were a red herring!'

Michael was clearly delighted with this discovery, and he started chuckling at his own humour 'A red herring!' he repeated, laughing out loud again. Then he suddenly became more serious. 'The algae were the innocent bystanders and something else was leading to the thiamine deficiency in each species. It had to be.'

Chastek paralysis

'Would you like a beer?' Luke called out from the kitchen. 'I picked you some up from the store today.'

Michael had returned to Ithaca after spending the weekend with Joe.

'Yeah, good job!' Michael replied. Not so long ago he would have been sitting alone drinking a beer while reading papers. Before meeting Luke, he met very few people, other than colleagues and trainees. Once he moved to New York and was no longer living close to his family, he led a solitary existence, which for thc most part suited him.

'What happened next?' Luke was sitting back at the table with a beer for Michael, a lime soda for himself and a bowl of olives to share.

'Do you ever drink alcohol?' Michael asked.

'I stopped when I started applying for my medical degree. It wasn't doing me any good. I could definitely have become an alcoholic. I was becoming dependent, really craving the next drink. Anyway, thiamine deficiency from eating forage fish, tell me more.'

'I wondered whether any other animals had been affected by thiamine deficiency. The obvious ones to investigate were the fish-eating sea creatures. Well, a colony of Pacific Harbour Seals—*Phoco vitulina*—had been dying of a strange affliction. It was yet another mystery illness.'

The clinical signs included anorexia, apathy, incoordination and lying on their sides. The affected seals suffered acute neurological problems and had specific pathological defects in their brains. This sort of abnormality and distribution was highly suggestive of thiamine deficiency.[9] After reading early studies, Michael found out that thiamine deficiency had already been recognised in captive seals in the 1970s, along with recommendations for its prevention.[10]

'I assumed it would be treated with thiamine, and I was right,' Michael explained; he was enjoying himself. 'They then induced thiamine deficiency under controlled conditions by feeding the seals forage fish. Only this time it was in captive harp seals—*Phoco groenlandica*—and they were fed Atlantic herring—*Clupea harengus*—and rainbow smelt—*Osmerus mordax*. Not only that, a thiamine-responsive nervous disease had also been described in saltwater crocodiles—*Crocodylus porosus*—in Australia. In addition, it occurred in cats and dogs fed a diet of meat that had been preserved in sulphur dioxide, which meant it had a low thiamine content.'[11,12]

'And the Latin for cats and dogs is?'

'*Felis catus* and *Canis*, as in canine,' Michael replied in all seriousness, not noticing at first that Luke was teasing him. 'Hey!' he laughed, realising that he had been a little pedantic with all the Latin names. 'It's just that's how I think of them,' he tried to explain, before brushing it off and continuing with his tale. 'Then I read a line in a book that made the hairs on the back of my neck stand up.'

'Scary, was it?' Luke joked again.

'It was in a Food and Agricultural Association book. These captive harp seals developed thiamine deficiency because the herring and smelt were both high in thiaminase—'

'An enzyme that breaks down thiamine,' Luke interjected with a nod. He was enjoying the discussion.

'That's right. Thiaminase, an enzyme that destroys thiamine, is present in the seals' diet, through the forage fish they consume. I knew this was it!' he exclaimed. 'The book helpfully explained that if the diet is known to contain thiaminase, thiamine supplementation is recommended. Or the seals could be fed a wide range of fish, meaning thiamine deficiency could be avoided.'

'So . . . EMS?'

'The salmon weren't able to feed on a wide variety of food when there was an abundance of forage fish available.' Michael explained how he now felt positive that he would get to the bottom of the mystery illness, and that a cure was feasible.

'What type of fish is the farmed salmon in Scotland?' Luke asked, suddenly interested to understand more about the different types.

'It's Atlantic salmon—'

'Ah . . . *Salmo salva!*' Luke joined in. 'Is that why you avoid eating fish?' he asked.

'It's partly why. Environmentally, it's really not a good idea now. Tons of wild fish are used to sustain the farmed salmon industry. But mainly it is fear of the unknown—with fish you just don't know what you're eating anymore.'

Michael typed 'thiaminase' or 'thiamine inactivating enzyme' into his computer. He wanted to show Luke the sheer number of papers on the subject, some from decades earlier. One of the reports was not surprising, as he recalled Joe telling him a story about a strange affliction that caused paralysis in foxes. He had a vague recollection that it had something to do with giving raw fish to the animals, and that cooking the fish avoided the problem. The disease in the foxes was first recognised following an outbreak at Chastek Fox Farm in Minnesota, and it was subsequently known as Chastek paralysis.[13] He thought about the fur farm on Mackinac Island. Clicking on the abstracts, he read that there had been a number of cases. He showed Luke the report of a paralytic disease of foxes and mink, which rapidly resulted in death. It was first reported in Canada in 1943, a few years after the Minnesota cases, when a fox started staggering.[14] Prior to its death, the fox was sensitive to handling. This was subsequently shown to be due to thiamine deficiency, and several foxes had been successfully treated with thiamine injections. The foxes feeding on fish mixed with meat were the ones to succumb, and this was thought to be due to inactivation of the thiamine by the fish. The types of fish implicated were both fresh and saltwater, such as carp, suckers, northern pike, Atlantic whiting, quillbacks and freshwater herring. The inactivating factor was found in the 'trimmings' too—the head, skins and viscera. The first symptom was a lack of appetite.

'That's when I realised it all fitted for the disease in salmon. The Great Lakes have massive numbers of clupeids—the term for alewives or herring. The main diet of salmon is the herring, especially alewives, since the sea lamprey had wiped out all the lake chub.'

Michael sat back in his chair and took a swig of beer, letting Luke mull it over. He was keen that Luke understood.

The ecosystem in the lakes was complex, but the clupeid population had been building up for decades. It was now the dominant forage fish, and hence the main diet for salmon. The clupeids were probably introduced in the 1800s, but numbers were kept under control by the predatory lake trout. It was in the 1960s and 1970s that the clupeids proliferated. This was about a decade after lake trout numbers declined; at the time, it was thought that this was due to overfishing, as well as sea lamprey parasitism.

'I wonder whether lake trout reproduction was affected even then,' Michael said to Luke. 'It's possible. EMS also affects lake trout—*Salvelinus namay . . .*' He stopped himself saying the full Latin name.

There seemed to be little reduction in clupeid numbers, even when the lake trout numbers had recovered. The clupeids were able to undergo massive proliferation. At the meeting in Sweden, Michael had learned that Baltic clupeids, in this case sprat (*Sprattus*, he thought to himself, not being able to resist such a cool name) and Baltic herring, had increased with the decline in cod, their main predator. His Scandinavian friends had tried to explain that the loss of cod was due to reduced saltwater washing into the brackish Baltic Sea. More recently, the freshwater conditions had improved, but the cod numbers had remained low.

Returning to the Chastek paper, Michael thought it was strange that the thiaminase was found in the viscera—in the head and on the skin—but not in the fillet—the muscle. *Why was that?*

Thiaminase assay

It was the new year and Michael was back in Ithaca. He and Luke had a few days of peace and quiet, as term was yet to start. Joe and Renie were coping at home so Michael had made only one flying visit to see them at Christmas, partly because he was satisfied that Arnie was taking care of things, but also because he found it increasingly difficult to see his father so changed. It made him sad how much Joe now had to depend on Renie, and to realise how vulnerable he was to infection, however mild. He had suffered a chest infection and had been treated with yet another course of antibiotics, which had then caused more diarrhoea. With a juggling of doses, his medication had been tapered. Thankfully, the visual hallucinations were no longer an issue, but his mood was still a problem and he was definitely having memory lapses. Even so, his parents were managing.

Michael talked to Luke about Joe's infections. It was a comfort to share the burden. Luke was pragmatic and made Michael realise that there was a limit to healthcare. He didn't mean regarding a monetary ceiling, but in terms of how much of the illness was irreversible and untreatable. The drugs Joe was taking were filling in gaps and alleviating symptoms, but they were also causing other problems. Michael now understood that Joe was on a slow downhill descent, and it was the quality rather than the quantity of what life he had left that was important.

Since he'd been back in New York, he and Luke had been to a New Year's Eve party, mainly attended by a few of the post docs and some of the other academics. They also spent a weekend together in the city. Michael was collaborating with the microbiologists there. He had not had a chance to explore the Big Apple before and found that it was much more fun with company. He had thought about taking Luke with him on his next visit home but decided that Joe would not be able to cope with the implications involved. He wasn't sure he ever would be, which saddened Michael, but that was just the way it was.

Michael had been struggling to cater for Luke, as he was a vegetarian, which seemed to require so much more planning. Increasingly, it was Luke who prepared food for them both, while Michael baked a chicken breast, lamb cutlet or pork fillet to eat on the side.

For this evening's meal, Luke had made a sweet potato risotto and Michael was frying some bacon, while quickly catching up with the day's emails. One of them, entitled 'Success!', was from Eriksson, his friend in Sweden. He opened the attached link:

'Ship's sewage banned in Baltic Sea

The International Maritime Organisation (IMO) ban sewage discharge and dumping of wastewater from passenger ships and ferries.'

Michael continued to the end of the article and read that the ban would be imposed from 2013 for all new ships, and from

2018 for all ships, depending on when ports had updated their facilities.[15] Since there were already more than three hundred and fifty cruise ships a year making more than two thousand port calls, this was set to make a huge difference to water quality in the Baltic.

Michael had to smile. Eriksson had been one of the campaigners. It seemed he'd had a victory, although it was sad that it had taken so long and then would not be brought in for another eight years. Michael had positive recollections of his time in Sweden fifteen years ago, although it seemed like another world. A lot had changed since the conference in 1995, and yet so much had remained the same; some interventions were moving at pace and yet other developments, such as preventing pollution, took an interminably long time to prove and become established policy.

★

Michael was finally able to share the alligator story with his colleagues at a departmental meeting. He described the discovery of thiamine deficiency in foxes and explained how thiaminase was destroying thiamine in other creatures, such as alligators, gulls and salmon, rendering them thiamine deficient. The group accepted that thiamine deficiency was due to thiaminase.

Later, he reiterated his theory to Diane, the lead scientist. He explained, 'In the instances when the alligators' diet consisted mostly of gizzard or mud shad—*Dorosoma cepedianum*—a type of herring, the level of thiaminase activity in the shad was sufficient to cause the disease seen in the wild.'[5]

Michael didn't particularly respect Diane, although he had to admit she had achieved a significant amount for her department. She had set up the lab, managing to bring together the right people to make progress in their field. His main issue with her was more to do with her demeanour. She was incredibly stern, and on the rare occasion she did smile, it was more of a grimace. Michael had held back his revelations and it had taken a lot of courage to come forward now. Diane sat at her desk looking nonplussed, her eyebrows disappearing under a heavy fringe and her prominent nose slightly tilted upwards.

As he had recounted his theory, Michael had shifted further and further towards the edge of his chair. He was now conscious of his precarious sitting position, concerned that to reposition himself would hamper the impending judgment or convey disinterest. Diane stuck her large jaw forward, pouting in the process, as though she could read his mind. She wasn't keen on chasing environmental issues and thought them a waste of time. In her view, modern science should revolve around molecular and genetic studies. Anything else was terribly old-fashioned. She gave him a rare smile, but it was one of pity, and Michael knew why. What was still not clear was where the thiaminase was coming from. There was no explanation for the variation in the level of thiaminase in the forage fish. Michael was convinced that the forage fish flourished when there was an excess of nutrients. He wondered whether the thiaminase varied with this surplus.

'Forage fish increased when there were more nutrients or eutrophication,' he told Diane, desperately hoping she would see the connection. He had wanted to add that the gizzard shad were filter feeders, but Diane stood up, indicating that the meeting was over.

★

In the lab one afternoon, Michael looked into thiamine assays—techniques for measuring thiamine levels. He wondered whether he could develop an ELISA—an enzyme-linked immunosorbent assay. This was a common immunological method used in many tests, and it would require a special absorbent surface to bind an antibody to thiamine, and a second antibody attached to an enzyme to produce a detectable chemical reaction. Michael suspected it would be possible to measure thiaminase using this novel technique. He would need to purchase the reagents, but the equipment would be the same. Having recently been successful with a grant application, he had the funds to do it.

'Wanna come for a beer?' Carol asked, opening the door and popping her head through it.

'Maybe later. Where are you going?' Michael asked, without looking up from his screen. Carol replied that she was going to the basement bar; the drinks were cheap and she liked the music. She wiggled her hips provocatively as she left the lab. She and Michael had recently submitted a paper with the rest of the group, and they had been spending quite a lot of time working together, although since the supper he had purposely kept his distance, keeping their discussions limited to experiments and science matters. Although he still enjoyed their intellectual discussions, Carol had started frequently calling him, and it was becoming irritating. He figured he would probably go along to the bar later; there was usually a crowd of post docs there and he had enjoyed himself on the last few occasions.

He carried on investigating the new assay, enlisting the help of a colleague in the lab along the corridor. They found a potential chemical that seemed specific to thiaminase. He worked much later than usual and completely forgot about joining Carol.

When he returned to the apartment that night, Luke was frosty. 'Who's Carol? Were you going to tell me?' he demanded.

'Oh, she's just a colleague in the lab. We've worked together on a few projects. She was very kind when I first moved here,' Michael replied, completely straight, before wondering whether, from the tone of Luke's question, he was missing something. 'When did you meet her?' he asked. He was puzzled, as he couldn't recall a time when Luke and Carol had met. *Why would they?*

'You've just missed her. She said you had a date tonight and that you stood her up.' Luke was pointing his finger at Michael and speaking slowly, whilst almost spitting the words out.

'A d . . . d . . . date? What? I . . . don't understand.' Michael was flabbergasted, and he smiled inappropriately out of embarrassment. He tried to remember what he'd said to Carol earlier. Could she have misinterpreted something?

'She told me all about your cosy dinner a deux!' Luke continued. He was clearly upset by Michael's attitude and the fact he seemed to be treating this as some big joke.

'I invited her here to discuss a paper. It was a disaster, to be honest. I tried to cook. Nearly poisoned her!' Michael tried to laugh it off. 'Nothing happened. She arrived, she ate, she left, and we really didn't make any progress with the journal article.'

Michael remembered how frustrated he'd been. 'What did she tell you?' he asked, now worried.

'Only that you had a night of wild passion, and . . . how could you, Michael?' Luke was exasperated.

'And what?' Michael was interested to hear Carol's version of events. 'What else?'

'Gourmet cuisine!' Luke retorted, really angry now, as Michael almost collapsed with laughter.

When he had recovered his composure, Michael could see that Luke was ashamed to have been gullible enough to believe Carol's story.

Michael explained how she had arrived at the apartment half wasted, carried on drinking, tried to seduce him and switched between being alluring, argumentative and agitated all evening. Her glass tipped over, spilling wine, and he'd ordered a cab to take her home.

'Perhaps she was referring to the origin of the word "gourmet"? A French "gourmand" was a wine taster.' It was Luke's turn to joke. 'Sorry I was such a fool,' he said, tentatively moving his hand towards Michael's forearm and stroking his bare skin. He'd become attached to Michael and hated the rift. He was so far from home and had really appreciated their relationship. Moreover, knowing he would soon have to return to the UK was unsettling him.

Michael grabbed Luke's hand and squeezed it warmly. The two men embraced, kissing each other urgently. Their companionship meant so much to Michael, and he couldn't imagine them parting.

*

In the lab, there was increasing controversy about the origin of the thiaminase. Was this enzyme being produced by the forage fish in response to some—as yet unidentified—trigger, such as the increasing availability of nutrients? Or was there another source? Michael was not convinced that the forage fish were the ultimate source.

The assay seemed to be a success. As with previous processes, it still involved the measurement of consumption of thiamine, but it no longer relied on antiquated reactions involving radioactive chemicals.[16] By using a chromophore—a chemical that emits light waves of different frequencies—Michael was able to produce a simple assay that only used readily available store-cupboard compounds. It would be possible to extend it to a high-throughput testing—a set-up of ninety-six wells that meant they were able to test multiple specimens simultaneously.[17] They would need the right equipment for this, but it was essential if they were planning to assess the large numbers of samples from forage fish, salmon and other organisms. The test required a spectrophotometer (a machine that measures light wavelength), and Michael's bid had included monies to purchase a brand new, state-of-the-art machine. They had not been able to formally investigate it to compare it with established methods, but Michael was eager to see the project through.

It was becoming clear to Michael and others that certain bacteria produce thiaminases. One type of thiaminase-producing bacteria was the *Paenibacillus thiaminolyticus* species. These bacteria were originally thought to be identical to a type of bacteria called Bacillus (the descriptive term for rod-shaped bacteria.) But as they weren't quite a bacillus, they had recently been reclassified as almost rod-shaped—literally, that is what '*Paeni-bacillus*' means. Michael liked this logic. The *Paenibacillus* formed spores, which meant they were able to withstand extreme conditions and survive for a long time. They had been detected in soil, fresh and salt water, compost and sewage. They had even been found in sea lion faeces in Antarctica. It was when he imparted this information to his colleagues that they began to question his mental stability.

'And how do you think it got there?' The question was rhetorical. 'It certainly didn't fly.'

He hadn't meant to sound angry. He wasn't even sure if he had mentioned the cruise ships. Obviously, in Michael's mind, they were the source of the bacteria.

Diane stepped in to change the subject. 'Thank you, Michael. And when will the assay be ready for the ninety-six well plate reader? That's if we can get hold of any sea lion poo.' She winked at him. She hadn't intended to be unkind, but the others in the lab all laughed and Michael's face turned puce. He felt miserable.

He had looked into *Paenibacillus* in more detail, but he decided not to share this. Another type—*P. larvae*—was causing a lethal condition in honeybees. It killed the honeybee larvae, wiping out colonies. *P. apiaries* was found in dead honeybees and produced thiaminase, but apparently didn't harm the bees. It was so confusing. *P. polymyxa* was added during the water management process to fix nitrogen, and *P. alvei* had caused human infections. These bacteria were in the Firmicutes division—a group of bacteria with similar structures, many producing spores, which was interesting, in that he had discovered that patients with type 2 diabetes had an imbalance, with more Firmicutes than Bacteroides. The human gut seemed to be just like Lake Michigan—alter one species and produce knock-on effects. There were even *Clostridium* species that had been known to produce thiaminase and spores, such as *Clostridium sporogenes*, which produces thiaminase in the guts of ruminant mammals that die of thiamine deficiency.

Michael and his colleagues were specifically looking for the *P. thiaminolyticus* in the forage fish. If they could demonstrate that the forage fish ingest the bacteria that produce thiaminase, and that these bacteria are the cause of the thiamine deficiency in prey fish such as salmon, then it would be ground-breaking science. Michael was optimistic that this would be the key. Further research would still need to be done into the original source of the bacteria, but they would be one step further to unravelling the mystery.

There were several major breakthroughs. His colleagues had managed to isolate *P. thiaminolyticus* from the guts and gills of frozen alewives—the forage fish. However, this was difficult to interpret because positive cultures, showing the presence of bacteria, were only possible in a quarter of fish.[18]

In another experiment, they had then given the lake trout a diet with varying amounts of the thiaminase-containing alewives and non-thiaminase containing bloater fish. They showed that it took a minimum of two years to develop full-blown EMS on a diet of highly concentrated alewives, but that even a diet of thirty-five per cent alewives could have a significant impact on lake trout reproductive function.[19] At their peak, the forage fish had consisted of ninety-nine per cent alewives. In addition, another group collaborating with Michael's team had been able to demonstrate that when the *P. thiaminolyticus* was fed to the lake trout in the laboratory, all the trout developed disease.[20] Trout fed either a high proportion of alewives or fed the thiaminase-containing bacteria developed EMS.

Spurred on by these positive results, Michael managed to toe the line. He launched himself into reading a whirl of articles, publications, papers and journals, determined to find out all there was to know about thiaminases. He learned about the different types, as well as the various incidences of odd diseases due to thiamine deficiency. He was going to be the expert on this, and he relayed all the information he'd gleaned in an article summarising the main facts. He was resolute that in the future there would be no further confusion about this enzyme.

The group at Ithaca continued their research into factors that might be responsible for an increase in thiaminase levels. Michael's colleagues put the alewives under stress, subjecting them to harsh conditions, such as reduced salt levels, and restricting their food, but they found no discernible difference in the levels of thiaminase.[21] Michael wasn't surprised, as he thought there would be a higher level of thiaminase when there were surplus nutrients due to higher bacterial load, for example, in sewage. Reduced food availability would not increase thiaminase.

Michael's colleague in Sweden was also investigating the thiaminase theory. Michael corresponded over email with Allan, one of the scientists he met through Eriksson, and with Allan's colleague, Liisa, from Finland, who had been infecting carp with live pathogenic bacteria to see if this affected their thiaminase levels.[22] Liisa had been keen to update Michael on the results of her group's work. There was a competitive edge in research. Everyone played by the same rules so that any potential ideas were kept secret, but once the results were through and the paper had been accepted for publication, there was no holding back. It was fair game to boast. Michael was pleased for Liisa but secretly disappointed for himself.

Even though the bacteria Liisa had injected into the carp did not contain any thiaminase, the thiaminase level was increased in the muscle tissue and the blood in these fish. The control group of carp, with no injected bacteria, had no increase in thiaminase, and similarly, a second treatment group, injected with formalin-killed bacteria, also displayed no increase. It was only the carp that had live bacteria injected into them that produced this response.

'How could that be?' Michael muttered, at a loss to explain this phenomenon. It was as if the thiaminase was being made by the carp, rather than exclusively by the bacteria.

Accused

Michael continued to look for clues in the Great Lakes area. He wasn't convinced that all fish produced thiaminase; after all, the enzyme had mainly been found in the parts of the fish that come into contact with water, the guts and gills, not the muscle. They had found evidence of the bacteria too.

One paper caught his attention; it was about the variation in thiaminase activity in the Great Lakes.[23] This made sense, as the thiamine levels in the eggs had clearly varied. He read on. An analysis had been carried out on thiaminase activity in Dreissenid mussels that had been collected at different depths and during different seasons from various locations in lakes Michigan, Ontario and Huron. Two species of mussels, the zebra and the quagga mussels (*Dreissena polymorpha and D. bugensis*) had increased thiaminase activity. Michael already knew about this, so perhaps the article was not as helpful as he had initially suspected, although it would be useful to know the exact locations where the mussels had been collected.

Michael had not realised just how much thiaminase was in the mussels: somewhere between five and a hundred-fold greater than that observed in the fish of the Great Lakes. He was astonished; five to a hundred is a wide variation. In fact, the activity was greater at shallow depths: *less water, less dilution than those those living at greater depths,* Michael thought to himself. Lake Michigan was a deep lake in the northern part. Bivalves, such as mussels, oysters and scallops, are filter feeders and take up bacteria in the water. Some of these bacteria can persist in the bivalve, and levels can even be concentrated. Could this explain the high level observed? The activity increased in the spring, was reduced in the summer and fell to its lowest rate in the fall. Michael was not able to find an explanation for this.

Is there increased thiaminase activity when the mussels are reproducing or is there increased thiaminase activity when they are feeding more? he mused. He had hoped that forage fish would provide the clue, but he wondered whether they should look further down the food chain. *Salmon eat thiaminase-containing forage fish. Gulls eat thiaminase-containing forage fish. Forage fish eat zooplankton. Gulls feed on sewage!* He mulled over the possible connections in his mind. He was only brought back to the present time when an email flashed across his screen.

Michael

Come to my office tomorrow morning at 9.

Diane

The email wasn't unusually abrupt for Diane, but he couldn't remember receiving one directed only to him before. He was usually included in the group emails. Perhaps he had gone up in her estimation and she wanted to congratulate him on the assay, or better still, discuss his career intentions. He hoped to take on more responsibility.

The following day, he was outside Diane's office at 9 am sharp. He waited for ten minutes, debating whether to knock, and he was about to leave when she opened the door.

'Morning. You're late.' She ushered him into her room.

'I'm sorry, I should have knocked, I wasn't sure if you were . . .'

'Of course I was here,' she interrupted, sounding irritated.

This wasn't what Michael was hoping for.

'Sit down.'

He'd barely taken a seat when she began. 'There's been an allegation, of a serious nature.'

Allegation? He was trying to work out what she meant.

'I'll need a full report from you.'

Michael had always known that he and Luke would be found out. He didn't know whether to stand his ground, as Luke would do, and tell her it was nothing to do with her.

What I do in my own time is my business, he thought about saying, before deciding he wasn't brave enough. Perhaps he should deny it. He could pretend nothing was happening. How did she know anyway?

Carol! Of course.

'Michael?' Diane was talking at him again. 'Were you listening?'

'Er, no, I was a little shocked, ma'am, I'm sorry, you were saying?' He was sure his face and ears must be bright red by now.

'I need to know if there were any witnesses?' She seemed a little less hostile.

'Witnesses?' He was totally confused.

'Yes, Carol has accused you of sexually assaulting her, in your apartment a few months ago.'

'W. . . w . . . witnesses? Me? What? That's not true,' he stuttered, horrified by what he'd heard.

'Was she in your apartment, then?'

'Yes, b . . . but, it was . . . it wasn't like that.'

Diane took a deep breath in. 'I think you'd better tell me what happened.'

She stood up and offered him a coffee, which he accepted.

Michael closed his eyes and thought back to that night. Luke had just arrived at Ithaca. 'Carol was very kind to me when I started here,' he explained. 'She and I have been collaborating on a few projects and we tend to bounce ideas off each other.' He realised this had been happening a lot less since Luke arrived. 'We had a paper to finish and I offered to cook her supper. It was months ago. I don't really understand why she's come forward now.' He hesitated. 'Not that I did anything . . . anything at all wrong.' He was shaking his head as he spoke.

He explained how Carol had arrived at his place already drunk. 'She must have fallen over before getting to mine, as I saw a clear bruise on her wrist.'

He didn't feel the need to tell Diane how bad his cooking was, but he did relay that they hadn't discussed the paper at all. He admitted that he had brushed against Carol's legs under the table. When he thought about this, he remembered that she had deliberately touched him. 'I jumped up hastily and spilt wine over her. I found her a spare t-shirt, but she'd already taken off her wine-stained top.'

He covered his face with his hands, slowly shaking his head as he realised how this must sound.

I'm not a rapist! I'm not a rapist!

He told Diane how they had both drunk too much, but Carol certainly didn't seem much worse than when she had arrived. Eventually, he had ordered her a taxi, despite her protests, and guided her out of the door.

'There was one thing, though,' he added, sipping coffee and feeling relieved to be able to finally talk about that night, 'she looked like she'd been crying.'

'Thank you, Michael. I'll talk to Carol. This has happened before.'

Diane stopped short, lowering her voice, as if hoping that Michael hadn't heard that last remark. 'I'll see if I can find an alternative space for her.'

The matter was resolved more quickly than Michael had expected. They parted company on reasonable terms and, as Michael opened the door to leave, Diane asked, 'How much longer is Luke here for?'

*

Luke finished his elective in New York and returned to Granada. It was impossible to see any future between them, living as they were in different countries, but they were determined to keep in touch. With Luke gone, Michael resorted to his old ways and became a hermit once more. He was working long hours in the lab, writing papers and submitting grant applications. He managed to avoid Carol.

He wanted to brush up on his knowledge of the lower realms of the food web. A bit of planktology was in order. *No kidding!* he sniggered to himself, and as he did so he realised how lonely he was. At times like this, he would have shared the joke with Luke. *The study of plankton actually has a name.*

He was amused to find out that the word plankton derived from the Greek word for wanderer. *Luke would have known that.* These were the nomads of the water world, as their movement is largely determined by the current. This differentiates them from fish, which tend to move against the current; fish are called nekton.

I must be a nektologist, Michael smirked. Phytoplankton are algae that have to live near the surface of the water to undergo photosynthesis. Zooplankton include the small protozoa, as well as small crustaceans and jellyfish. There was a term Michael had not heard of before—bacterioplankton, bacteria that play an important role by absorbing nutrients dissolved in the water. In order, and from the bottom up, the food chain consists of phytoplankton, zooplankton, predatory zooplankton, filter feeders, and predatory fish. Michael guessed that bacterioplankton must be at the bottom of the chain with phytoplankton. Apparently, plankton outnumber all the fish in the lakes and oceans, but bacteria outnumber plankton.

Variation in thiaminase

It was now two years since Joe had first been hospitalised, and he was finding things difficult. Michael knew that, so he tried to go home to see his father every other month or so. On his last visit, Joe had been struggling to sleep at night and dozed throughout most of the day. He had become depressed and morose. He was back in a wheelchair, and if he wanted to get out of the house, only Michael and Arnie could take him, as it was too heavy for Renie to push.

Michael decided to try and cheer Joe up with a trip to the yacht club to look at the boats. The clanging masks and lapping water had a soothing, mood-enhancing effect. There was a bit of fuss getting Joe in and out of the car, and it was even more bother getting the wheelchair in the boot, however, it was a lovely spring day, with a fresh breeze, so the effort was worth it. There were goslings on the river, with a noisy gander calling out to its mate from the bank; the mother goose was tending to her brood in the water.

Sitting on a bench along the path from the club, Joe tried to grab Michael's arm.

'What is it, Joe?' Michael asked gently.

'I . . . need you to . . . to do something,' Joe replied, his words stalling intermittently.

'What's that, Joe?' Michael was worried.

'I . . . can't . . . go on . . . like . . . this.' Joe seemed desperate.

'What d'ya mean?' Michael didn't like the sound of this. He wasn't sure what Joe was trying to tell him. *Had he succumbed to a terminal illness? No, that wasn't it. Joe was miserable. That was it.* He had recently become incontinent and was wearing nappies at night. He had developed sores as a consequence. *Nappy rash.* Michael thought of how Joe was regressing back to being a baby. At times, he was also struggling to swallow. There had been the usual rejigging of medicines; add in a bit of this, take away something else, up one dose, down with another, try an antidepressant, suffer the side effects, give up on it. Michael had the lowdown whenever he spoke to Renie.

'I can come home more often,' Michael offered, not knowing what else to say.

There was silence, as he and Joe listened to the chinking of the masts.

'Time to go home, Joe, Renie will have those breakfast sausages cooked by now,' Michael said, without thinking how pureed sausage wasn't quite the same.

*

Back in Ithaca, Michael struggled to focus on anything. He needed a project. He hadn't previously paid much attention to geographical location, but then he received a copy of a special publication issued by the Great Lakes Fishery Commission.[24] It summarised the last five years of research in the Great Lakes area, even providing a line graph showing the variation in thiamine in the eggs at different locations in Lake Michigan.

This was just what Michael needed as a distraction, although the section on salmon and trout numbers made for depressing reading. Despite all the expensive research, the lake trout yield had continued to decline. There was a chart showing the potential for recovery, with a minor peak in lake trout yield in 1997, and a swell in numbers of Chinook salmon between 2002 and 2006, but then the yield had dramatically fallen for all species. The reasons given were inadequate numbers of stocked fish, suboptimal stocking practices, excessive mortality from sea lamprey and overfishing, as well as the negative impact of the non-indigenous species such as clupeids and zebra mussels.

The line graph was the closest to fish epidemiology Michael had seen. The colour-coded lines showed the amount of thiamine in the eggs at nine locations around Lake Michigan between 2001 and 2009. The graph gave the impression that egg thiamine levels were generally improving, but this contradicted the previous chart on salmon and lake trout yields. Whilst studying the lines again, Michael noted that the main improvement hadn't been until 2009, which meant that the effect on lake trout would not have been published in the 2011 report.

The worst affected areas were Grand Traverse Bay, Little Traverse Bay and Clay Banks. The area with the fewest problems was the Port of Indiana, whereas Michigan City, Portage Point, Waukegan and Milwaukee were in the middle. Some of these were well known tourist spots. He wasn't sure he could make a reliable link to the pollution caused by floating gin palaces.

He returned to the graph and highlighted each location on a hand-drawn map of Lake Michigan. He then searched for data on wastewater management for each of the areas affected. Grand Traverse Bay was an inlet of water, where, as a consequence, there may have been less circulation of water. He discovered the existence of a wastewater management facility that was discharging processed effluent into the bay, and Little Traverse Bay was in the same geographical area. There didn't seem to be any wastewater management facility at Clay Banks. He wondered whether his theory was incorrect, but he was determined not to give up.

Next, he searched for Milwaukee and wastewater and found a facility there. In the history section, he read about a proposal for a multibillion-dollar programme starting in 1979 to upgrade the facility, with the construction of a deep tunnel system. The aim was to reduce the sewer overflows and basement back-up. The Water Pollution Abatement Programme became operational in 1993. However, further investment to expand these deep tunnels had not been completed until 2010. Michael suspected that the original capacity of the deep tunnels had been insufficient to prevent the storm water overflowing the system. Interestingly, there had been a gradual improvement in the egg thiamine levels from 2004 onwards.

Waukegan had a large wastewater management system covering a wide area on the north shore, so he went on to discover more about the area around Michigan City. He came across news articles on 'reporting violations' and one entitled: 'A sanitary district employee fired.' The system was described as poorly run. There were regular overflows of raw sewage into the lake from an inundated system, and these had often gone unreported. Repairs and upgrades had apparently only started in 2011.

Michael tried to find out the dates of any significant floods. He remembered the Great Flood of 1993 along the Mississippi River; the soils had become saturated during the previous fall. Was this enough to cause an overflow? This was when the EMS had first become noticeably worse. Then there had been storms causing localised flooding in parts of Michigan and Illinois in 2007 and 2008, but he found it difficult to get specific information on which drains had then overflowed with raw sewage. It was a highly sensitive issue, causing chiefs to lose their jobs, as had happened in Michigan City.

Michael felt frustrated. There was simply insufficient evidence to prove anything. He looked up the Port of Indiana and wondered why the egg thiamine levels there had been consistently good. It was home to large steelworks and wasn't a place of particular interest to tourists. There had been a fall in the population in recent years and there seemed to be no wastewater management system in place. In addition, there had been no reported cases of algal blooms.

He returned his attention to Clay Banks, the one outlier, and tried to find out more about this area. Farming was an important industry and, as the land was flat, it was prone to flooding. The only other finding was that the population seemed to rely on water from wells. Now, obviously, this wouldn't affect the fish! There was that nagging, twitching feeling that Michael experienced when he thought he was onto something. Persisting with this topic, he read a report acknowledging that due to the farming activity there was often increased nitrogen in the water. Not only that, the high nitrogen levels were attributed to the contamination of the ground water by human or animal waste or fertilisers.

Suddenly, he had a flash of inspiration. Lake Michigan was not the only lake affected. Lake Erie was also a problem. He searched 'Lake Erie' and 'wastewater management' and read with horror but quiet satisfaction a revelatory journal article:

Eco Watch - December 1st 2011

'The largest single sewage plant in the USA, the Detroit wastewater plant, dumped nearly 30 billion gallons

> of raw and partially treated sewage into Lake Erie between January and July this year. It is the single largest contributor of phosphorus to Lake Erie.'[25]

Lake Erie was also the shallowest lake. Double whammy! It was effectively being poisoned by human effluent. The fish didn't stand a chance.

★

A few weeks later, Michael returned home. Joe's condition had deteriorated, and he had been in bed for days, with Renie nursing him. She was exhausted, emotionally and physically, but had accepted that her husband probably wouldn't recover this time.

'He's not the same Joe,' she said to Michael during a brief moment away from his bedside, when they were snatching a bite to eat. 'He's given up.'

'He's not fighting it anymore,' Michael acknowledged, knowing full well Joe's wish. He wanted his suffering to end.

★

Michael sat with Joe as he drifted in and out of consciousness. He had been coughing, but his cough was too weak. The doctor said he could have more antibiotics, but the likelihood was that they wouldn't work, or would only delay the inevitable. Michael wondered whether he should have persuaded Joe to take them, but it was clearly too late now. Should he have done more, rather than watching him fade away? He quickly put the notion out of his mind. This was what Joe wanted.

Joe's breathing had been fast for hours, and then it became

raspy. He was still shaking—his hands rolling on the bed sheets in a continuous, rhythmic motion, like the waves on the shore of Lake Michigan, like the ripples on the River Illinois. Then he was stuttering. Finally, there were gasps, like a fish caught in a net. The tremors were no more. Joe stopped struggling. No longer swimming in circles, he was peaceful.

★

The funeral took place at the graveside two days later. Michael stood by Renie. After prayers, they both placed a handful of soil on the plain wooden coffin. Luke travelled to be near Michael but stayed in a hotel and kept his distance at the funeral, remaining at the back of the crowd made up of relatives, a few work colleagues and many of Renie's friends. Later, he was introduced as a friend from England.

Purple sea urchin

The following year, Luke was in England for the final few months of his degree. He had exams in Granada and then he would be qualified. He and Michael remained in touch, but mainly through WhatsApp messages and emails, as the time difference made verbal communication tricky.

Renie had become more involved with the local church. She had a network of close friends, and they all looked after one another. She had started cooking meals for others and doing their shopping, basically continuing her role as a carer. Michael had been home for the first couple of weeks after Joe's death, but since then he had barely seen Renie, however, he dutifully spoke with her on the phone every weekend. She eemed content. She had never had high expectations of life nd was pleased that Michael had settled down.

★

ichael continued to suspect that there might be a link tween thiamine deficiency and sewage outflow. He told ke about his suspicion that water was a problem, and that herever he turned he found himself delving into the same ues. Luke teased Michael gently for obsessing, sending ghing emojis whilst at the same time admiring his tenacity.

Michael was curious to know more about water resources the arid Southern California region. Reading about tewater management in Los Angeles, he discovered

that the city had one of the largest wastewater recycling programmes and laboratory facilities in the world, which apparently enabled thorough microbiological analysis of even low-grade pathogens. Michael reckoned this claim was a little overconfident; low-grade pathogens were extremely difficult to culture on account of their slow growth. In fact, several human pathogens are impossible to culture in laboratory conditions. It was also entirely possible that there were still some pathogens undiscovered by man, which meant they could not be analysed. It was likely that new microorganisms were still evolving.

Whilst reading about Southern California, he started to drift off course. One minute he was getting to grips with water supply and wastewater treatment in California, and the next he was perusing an article about purple sea urchins that were dying unexpectedly, without an obvious cause.[26] Perhaps what he was actually obsessing over was death. It was alligators and salmon all over again!

This particular paper described mass mortalities of purple sea urchins, or *Strongylocentrotus purpuratus!* It was such a great Latin name that Michael couldn't resist saying it out loud. The deaths had occurred at Malibu Lagoon State Beach, Southern California, in 2010, and again in 2011. Both events followed the first heavy rain of the season and coincided with the coastal lagoon breaching. The sea urchin deaths could not be explained. *Yet another mystery!*

Incidentally, the day the deaths occurred in 2010 coincided with the first World Surfing Reserve, which had been set up to protect areas used for surfing and was run by Save the Waves, a non-governmental organisation. As the surfers and officials arrived, they were greeted with literally thousands of dead purple sea urchins washed up on the beach. There was no obvious cause. The author of the paper made the pertinent observation that the time of the breach seemed significant. Sea urchins are remarkably tolerant and able to withstand huge variations in environmental conditions. Initially, it was thought that they had died from a disease or after being poisoned by toxins, however, none of the dead animals carried signs of being killed by either of these things. They obviously had not been killed by predators, as they hadn't been injured. In the past, sea urchins have died after exposure to variations in salinity, extremes of temperature or severe storms, but this hadn't been the case here.

One of the lifeguards had helpfully recorded that the lagoon had been breached on October 7th, at 9.30 am. The dead sea urchins began to wash ashore the following morning. In addition, nearly every year, varying numbers of sea urchin carcasses were washed up on the shore after the flooding of the lagoon, but these recent episodes affected far more of the creatures. Michael became fixated on these incidents of mass extinction.

The remainder of the paper described how the deaths seemed to be due to environmental toxins or hypoxia, but essentially the cause was unknown. Keen to pursue this further, Michael looked up 'Malibu Lagoon' and 'sewage'. He found a reference in a publication from an international conference on environmental pollutants, explaining that oxygen and hydrogen isotopes were used to determine the percentage of wastewater from leaking sewers in groundwater supplies. This isotopic analysis of wastewater and groundwater samples showed that there was up to seventy per cent imported water in the groundwater samples. The possible sources of bacterial contamination to Malibu Lagoon and the near-shore ocean were the onsite wastewater treatment systems—modern day cesspits—for off-grid sewerage. These were frequently used to store and treat residential and commercial sewage in the area. Clearly, there were concerns about sewage contamination of the lagoon and the beach. Michael wondered why there were so many of these onsite wastewater treatment systems in a built-up area. In a different report, however, another indicator of human faecal contamination—human-associated *Bacteroidales*—was not detected in water from wells, Malibu Lagoon or the near-shore ocean. So, it seemed that human effluent was not actually the cause of the problem. It was baffling.

Michael then found a newspaper article on septic tanks in Malibu.[27] It featured a photograph of a surfer standing in the shallow waves, with filthy, brown sand along the shore. It went on to describe how Malibu has a high water table; septic tanks rather than mains sewers provide the wastewater drainage. The surfer described swimming as 'dirty business', and he was in no doubt that Malibu Lagoon was polluted, as it had been for decades. The surfers all suffered multiple infections. Finally, there had been an order that Malibu must phase out septic tanks and that mains sewage must be installed.

This was fishy!

Michael pardoned himself for the pun. Malibu was just north of Los Angeles, and it was where all the rich and famous people lived. Michael wondered to what extent this initiative would succeed. It seemed that all it took to fill the lagoon with sewage again was heavy rainfall. Was it only sewage? Does cannabis affect sea urchins? Or for that matter, cocaine?

Michael returned abstractedly to his prior investigations into Parkinson's disease. Recently, he had not thought much about it, as Luke had dismissed trying to fathom a cause for the disease as futile. Looking at the world figures for the disease,[6] he saw that the country with the highest prevalence in the world was Albania, one of Europe's poorest countries. It had no municipal wastewater treatment plants, and water privatisation catered for only a fifth of its population. Moreover, it wasn't just Parkinson's disease—there was a higher incidence of neurological diseases generally. The reason for this had not been established.

Michael was beginning to see a strong pattern developing between neurodegenerative disease and water pollution. Waterborne infectious diseases spread by the faecal-oral route had been known about for years. One hundred and sixty-five years ago, the British physician John Snow had discovered that drinking well water caused outbreaks of cholera; the story involved the infamous Broad Street Pump in Soho, London. Snow drew a map of cases of cholera, showing the geographical relationship to the pump. He hypothesised, correctly, that cholera was spread through infected water. It wasn't just the well water that was polluted; the River Thames was also contaminated. Until that time, the major concern had been air pollution. Had we come full circle? Again, there was a great deal of focus on air quality and perhaps not enough on sanitation.

The more Michael thought about it, the more he realised that there was very little difference between the Broad Street Pump, Lake Michigan, Lake Griffin, Malibu Lagoon, probably Central Valley, the River Nile and even Albania. In London, the well had been dug close to a previously used cesspit, resulting in raw sewage effectively contaminating the drinking water. In Lake Michigan, there was a greater volume of water in the 'well', but an increasing amount of raw sewage was contaminating this water.

Maps

Michael read the headline from July 2014:

'Storm forces officials to open Lake Michigan Locks'[28]

It wasn't a great surprise after the sheer volume of rain. The sluice gates had been opened and the result was plain to see. It made for stark reading. The report didn't hold back on the details, describing the mix of sewage and water as 'noxious'. They might as well have called it poisonous. Once again, there had been a surge of the foul water, which overloaded the city's underground sewers and storm water tunnels. Once again, the raw and partially treated wastewater entered the lake, the same lake that supplies water to millions of people in Chicago.

Michael was horrified that Lake Michigan was still being polluted at regular intervals, and it seemed that no one had made the link between raw sewage and sick fish. He was becoming increasingly concerned that it wasn't only the fish that were affected.

He searched for data on the prevalence of Parkinson's disease in North America. After several attempts he found what he was looking for: a colour-coded map showing the numbers of patients affected by Parkinson's disease in each region; red indicated high prevalence and green low.[29] It was red around the Great Lakes and then there were patchy areas of red in other places, including a few scatterings in Florida and an area of red in Southern California.

He searched for another map, which displayed an almost identical pattern of red, except that there was no shading in Florida. He knew that he had to show Luke. He took a screenshot so he could easily flick between the two images.

Luke was visiting for a couple of weeks over the summer. By now, he had been working as a junior doctor in England for almost six months. He had a further eighteen months of posts organised in the UK, and he also needed to apply for his specialist training in neurology. Michael had been looking forward to his trip for weeks. He had so much to tell him. He really wanted to work through some of his ideas and discuss a few of the papers with him.

When he arrived, Michael covered up the titles to the maps. 'What do you think of these two?' he asked.

Luke was intrigued and queried what he was supposed to be looking at.

'The red shading is almost identical on both maps,' Michael said, almost bursting with enthusiasm.

Luke agreed that the shading was similar. Michael explained that the first map showed the prevalence of Parkinson's disease. This came as no surprise to Luke, as Michael had been bent on finding the cause of Joe's illness. The second map showed areas of flood risk in North America.

Initially, Luke remained unconvinced. 'It'll be related to population density,' he argued.

They searched for a map showing population density and found that the match was nowhere near as compelling. They also looked for prevalence maps showing other factors, such as obesity.

What was really striking was that the areas around the Great Lakes matched; the valley of the Mississippi was highlighted in both maps. There was a slight difference in Florida, which had a hint of red on the Parkinson's disease map, despite not being in a high flood risk zone. On both maps, the same areas in Southern California were highlighted. The similarity between the two maps was uncanny.

Michael showed Luke the result of his searches of Parkinson's and water. 'Do you remember me saying that the Amish community had a high prevalence of Parkinson's disease?' he said. 'I originally believed the assumption that this was mainly due to genetics, but now I'm not so sure.'

It was well known that farmers were prone to developing Parkinson's disease, and the Amish people were predominantly farmers. The tendency for farmers to be at an increased risk had been explained by their exposure to pesticides; however, not all farmers exposed to pesticides developed Parkinson's disease. That argument lacked some credibility. In fact, in his search for direct evidence of pesticide use and Parkinson's disease, Michael found several articles that took into account other factors, such as rural living and well water.

The Amish used wind power to pump water to their homes, and in recent times there had been several issues with water supply. State and local government had implemented new standards for the treatment of wastewater, and the Amish believed that these modern conveniences did not comply with their religious beliefs. It seemed that in many of the wells, the water contained nutrient levels above the safe drinking water standard. In Michael's mind, 'excess nutrient levels', or eutrophication, was becoming a euphemism for contamination. The reason for this increase in nutrient levels was blamed on run off from animal yards. Manure was spread on the fields as a way of disposing of animal excrement rather than as a means of boosting nutrients in the soil. There were large populations of Amish people in Indiana, Ohio and Pennsylvania, and there were increased nutrient levels in these states, which all bordered the Great Lakes. They were also in the flood zone.

Michael continued telling Luke what he had discovered about risk factors. Luke enjoyed seeing his friend so motivated by such an important cause. Plus, he hadn't mentioned fish once!

'There's no doubt that the use of pesticides increases the risk of Parkinson's disease, particularly the organochlorines and the organophosphorus compounds,' Michael said. 'I wondered if Joe had used any of these chemicals in salmon farming?'

Luke smiled at the reference to salmon and listened attentively to Michael's commentary.

'He wouldn't need to, I thought, if the local farmers had used them and he had been exposed to them through the water. Don't you think that would probably be significant?'

Luke replied that paraquat was the pesticide he had heard of as causing Parkinson's disease. 'It's not an organochlorine or organophosphate, though, it's in its own class,' he explained. 'I'm sure it's banned in Europe. Every so often we have a case of poisoning, either accidental or attempted suicide. It's a dreadful chemical; it causes ARDS.'

Luke saw the confusion on Michael's face and realised he had switched unwittingly into medical speak. 'That's Acute Respiratory Distress Syndrome,' he said. 'It causes severe, acute lung injury, and then scarring—pulmonary fibrosis. Low dose, chronic poisoning has been linked to Parkinson's disease, though.'

Michael continued with his ideas about organochlorine pesticides. These chemicals, consisting of only chlorine, hydrogen and carbon, were also banned due to their toxicity, but because they were so stable, they persisted in the environment. 'Well, I wondered whether this linked in any way to thiamine deficiency,' he said.

The best-known organochlorine pesticide was DDT—dichloro-diphenyl-trichlorethane. It wasn't a new study, but DDT had induced thiamine deficiency in rats. Another organochlorine pesticide, PCB—polychlorinated biphenyl—a manmade chemical primarily used in the electrical industry in the 1970s, was problematic because it was easily absorbed and carcinogenic. Tests found it to be associated with thiamine deficiency. Michael knew about the PCB pollution in Lake Michigan, which had come from local factory effluent decades before. Lake Michigan was the worst affected of the Great Lakes, and although levels in the lake were finally improving, because of its persistent nature there were still high levels in fish. Michael felt sure that the thiaminase levels were not reducing either.

There was another poison, a piscicide that Joe had mentioned. It was one that had been used in the fisheries to specifically poison the spawning grounds of the sea lamprey. Michael found the name of the chemical without too much difficulty—TFM, or trifluoromethyl-4-nitrophenol—and read a few articles. It was strange. It seemed to work specifically on sea lamprey. *Really?* The way it killed the parasitic fish was unclear, as was its effect on other fish or humans.

★

Luke's visit was so short that Michael hadn't planned anything for them to do in particular, although they did manage to walk the trail again. They just enjoyed being in each other's company.

'Have you seen much of Carol?' Luke asked, concerned for his friend and still conscious over how he had overreacted to her visit.

'No, she's working in another area now,' Michael said. He wasn't particularly interested in discussing Carol.

'I found out more about her from the other students, that's all,' Luke added. 'She's done this before.'

'That's exactly what Diane said,' Michael replied. 'But why? I thought we were friends.'

'Apparently, she's in an abusive relationship with an alcoholic. She also has a history of alcohol abuse herself.'

'There were bruises,' Michael added. 'Yes, she definitely had bruises on her wrists and arms. I believed her when she said she'd fallen. I should have questioned her about them, done something.'

'She latched onto you as someone who would rescue her from her life. I guess she was bitter and resentful that this wasn't the case,' Luke replied. 'It wasn't your fault.'

There was a pause. Michael felt relieved. He knew he wasn't in the wrong, but it was still good to hear it said out loud.

The conversation moved on, and Michael told Luke about an article he'd read concerning another toxin that was clearly linked to neurodegenerative disease. 'It's another story with maps!' he joked. 'It's a report on a condition called amyotrophic lateral sclerosis, or ALS, also known as Lou Gehrig's disease. Do you know about it?'

'Yes. It's a type of motor neurone disease. There's degeneration of the motor nerves, the ones that carry impulses from the brain to the muscles,' Luke explained.

Michael nodded and continued telling him about the findings of the study. The researcher had entered the addresses of the patients suffering from ALS onto a computer-generated map; an epidemiological technique used by John Snow but this time incorporating modern technology. Michael looked up the scientific article and discovered that the cases of ALS were clustered around lakes or water, particularly around the Mascoma Lake in New Hampshire. The toxin—BMAA, or beta-methylamino-L-alanine—was produced by cyanobacteria, a type of algae prevalent in the lake. It was thought to be responsible for ALS, but it wasn't clear exactly how these people were exposed to the toxin. 'I couldn't find out whether they were drinking the water, swimming in the lake, eating contaminated fish or just breathing the toxin in. Curious, don't you think?'[30]

Luke thought that exposure to the toxin seemed eminently plausible as a cause of ALS, except for the fact that surely massive doses of the toxin would be required to produce the condition. It wasn't clear if the algae were causing the disease or were simply associated by chance. Michael thought that maybe the dose of toxin required would be less if patients were already susceptible to neuronal damage, for example, if they were also thiamine deficient.

Apparently, the clue leading to the suspected toxin had come from a disease prevalent on the Pacific island of Guam, a tiny United States territory in Micronesia, midway between Japan and Australia. The disease was called lytico-bodig—*lytico* meaning paralysis and *bodig* dementia. The presentation of the condition was inconsistent; sometimes patients had an ALS-type paralysis, whilst symptoms were more in keeping with

Parkinson's disease in others, which Michael found interesting. In fact, some patients also had the cognitive impairment seen in Alzheimer's disease. The disease profile was highly variable. Lytico-bodig was only found in people who had lived on the island for at least a decade. It was found in certain areas and was particularly prevalent amongst the indigenous people, the Chamorros. All these features were thought to suggest either a toxin or an infective cause. British biochemists found that the Chamorros used flour made by grinding seeds from the cycad plant to make tortilla, and that this plant contained the toxin BMAA. In fact, all cycads have a symbiotic relationship with the nitrogen-fixing cyanobacteria—the source of BMAA.

More alarming still was the suggestion that fruit bats had also eaten the seeds from the cycad plant. Since the local people ate fruit bats, it was proposed that the toxin might have become concentrated in the bats in sufficient quantities to cause neurological damage in the indigenous population.[31] However, this was never proved and was only surmised when the petering out of the disease coincided with a fall in bat numbers; the bats had been hunted to near extinction. The other explanation was that when the outbreak occurred after the Second World War, the Chamorros had resorted to eating cycad nuts as an emergency food source. Apparently, they had soaked the nuts first to minimise their toxicity, but they were already malnourished and were also, therefore, thiamine deficient.

From 1952, starting in the Philippines, it was mandated that rice should be fortified with thiamine. This timed with no more reported cases of lytico-bodig. Michael was sure this was more than just a coincidence—increased thiamine intake must have led to a reduction in cases. This was only Michael's theory, but he was rather pleased with it.

There wasn't a coherent theory on why BMAA was toxic and caused variable neurodegenerative diseases. BMAA is structurally similar to the amino acid alanine. Michael suspected that thiamine deficiency would make someone more susceptible to the toxin, interrupting the normal metabolism of alanine in the body. Perhaps starvation meant more toxin was taken up in lieu of alanine.

The concern was that it was not just the people in Guam that were at risk of BMAA poisoning. There were multiple reports of outbreaks of cyanobacteria causing algal blooms in lakes throughout the United States and the rest of the world. Cyanobacterial crusts and dust were widespread in the deserts of Qatar. There was double the usual rate of ALS in Gulf War veterans, occurring at an unusually young age. Although they were dormant for much of the year, cyanobacteria would bloom after rainfall or if disturbed by military activity.[32] If potentially harmful cyanobacteria were present in these geographically diverse locations, then it could be a worldwide phenomenon. Flooded rice fields must be at risk, especially as they are treated with fertilisers and then cyanobacteria are utilised to encourage nitrogen fixing.

Vancouver

It was Luke who pointed it out. 'Take a look at the headline,' he said.

Michael read the article, unsure why Luke was so excited. Then he realised that he was reading about sewage.

> **'Metro Vancouver guilty of dumping sewage in Burrard Inlet. Greater Vancouver Sewerage and Drainage District agrees to fines and environmental contribution.'** [33]

Michael still couldn't quite see why Luke had been so eager to show him the article; this sort of incident was becoming commonplace.

'Did you ever hear about the TV show *Leo and Me?*' Luke asked. Michael looked at him blankly. 'The one starring Michael J. Fox, before he became really famous with *Back to the Future.*' Another blank look. 'You have heard of *Back to the Future?*'

Luke felt he had to explain everything to his friend. It was as though Michael had been brought up on another continent!

Michael wasn't aware of the Canadian TV show. Joe hadn't really liked that kind of humour and anyway, Michael preferred the outdoors and books to television. He had seen *Back to the Future* and knew that its lead actor had sadly developed Parkinson's disease at a young age. Over recent years, Fox's work supporting research into the disease had been admirable.

'The show was filmed on a yacht.' Luke was speaking clearly, so that Michael would understand the significance of his words, but Michael could already predict what was coming next. 'The yacht was moored at the Westin Bayshore, in Vancouver, right by Burrage Inlet.'

Luke looked up Burrage Inlet online to give Michael an idea of what he was talking about. The inlet was a shallow-sided fjord, which ran almost directly east from the Strait of Georgia.

Michael read the article with a newfound interest. Environmental groups had claimed there were ongoing problems concerning the drainage pipes, which were getting backed up, resulting in raw sewage bypassing the filtration plants and flowing into the natural water sources.

'The thing is, Michael J. Fox wasn't the only one to develop Parkinson's disease.'

Luke had lowered his voice, as though gossiping and aware that this was not something they should talk about freely. 'It was in the news a few years ago. Out of a film crew of a hundred and twenty or so, I think four developed Parkinson's disease, all within a few years of each other, just over a decade after filming *Leo and Me*.'

Luke showed Michael a newspaper article to confirm his revelation.[34] It seemed Michael had at least persuaded one person that his theory was correct.

★

Back in the lab, a week after Luke had left, Michael's studies looking for the offending thiaminase-producing bacteria were proving fruitless. His colleagues had used genetic techniques to search for the *P. thiaminolyticus* genes. Unfortunately, despite eloquently conducted experiments using PCR (polymerase chain reaction) to identify these genes, there was no evidence of the specific thiaminase-producing bacteria in the wild lake trout.[35] Quantitative PCR assays can detect the gene from as few as a thousand cells per gram, and by using the specific RNA probe (16S rRNA) it can identify the gene from as few as one hundred cells per gram. Their conclusion was that *P. thiaminolyticus* was not the primary source of the thiaminase. Michael didn't understand how this had happened. He didn't want to believe it, and he was extremely concerned that it would direct further research away from bacterial thiaminase.

Meanwhile, Michael's group had decided to use his rapid assay to test how much thiaminase was present in alewife guts and innards. Unexpectedly, as with the lake trout, no relationship could be found to link the thiaminase activity and *P. thiaminolyticus* protein or cells. Michael and his group were disappointed, but even negative studies have their role.

Michael's interpretation of the results, however, differed from that of his colleagues. He was still convinced that thiaminase-producing bacteria had been present at some stage, even if they had been unable to demonstrate it. Nevertheless, based on the findings of the group, the paper was written up and published.

Michael was annoyed. His reading had led him to be sure that once the bacteria had produced the thiaminase in the forage fish, the thiaminase would be active; that is, unless the lake trout started cooking the alewives! 'Ridiculous!' he muttered, frustrated with his colleagues' inability to see the obvious.

'Thiaminase is the problem!' he chuntered. His understanding was that thiaminase was a stable enzyme that was inactivated by heat, hence feeding raw fish to the foxes had caused disease. The absence of bacteria simply meant that the trout still had the thiaminase enzyme, even though the bacteria had disappeared. It didn't necessarily rule out bacteria as the source.

Michael was now also concerned that neurodegenerative conditions were related to thiaminase activity and, therefore, to the salmon fry deaths too. All those years that his father had worked for the fisheries in the contaminated water of the River Illinois, Joe had been anxious about the salmon fry, but he ought to have been worried for his own health, too.

Red cornetfish, blue jeans

2015

Michael's colleague, Craig, was asked to speak at the thirty-third Annual Salmonid Restoration Conference in Santa Rosa, California. Michael agreed to go along and was looking forward to the meeting. Luke would usually join him on such occasions, but he had just started a new training scheme and couldn't get the time off to travel to the West Coast. There were some interesting presentations in the programme, including, 'California's climate in perspective—paleoclimate records of past droughts and floods' and another entitled, 'The West without water.' His colleague was talking on 'The case for de novo production of thiaminase by alewife.'

At the conference, it was generally agreed that thiamine deficiency is an impediment to the restoration of native lake trout stocks, and that non-native alewife is the preferred prey for lake trout. However, the source of the thiaminase was still controversial. Craig was set to argue that the evidence was consistent with the hypothesis that alewives have a gene encoding thiaminase.

Michael listened to Craig preparing for his talk. 'A gene for thiaminase was first identified in zebrafish,' he said, showing Michael the first slide of a striking zebrafish.

'Zebrafish—*Danio rerio,*' Michael added.

Michael's problem was that he switched off as soon as a

genetic study was mentioned. At least at the conference he would be exposed to the whole shebang, genes 'n all. He tried to focus on Craig's slides. He discovered that the zebrafish weren't the only fish that produced thiaminase; the red cornetfish—*Fistularia petimba*—also has the gene for thiaminase. This creature was a strange, worm-like fish found off the coast of Japan, where they were more appropriately called rifle fish. The zebrafish and red cornetfish thiaminases were similar.

The strongest evidence for the fact there was a gene coding for thiaminase in alewives, and therefore that these fish produced the enzyme, was that the size of the protein and the chemical characteristics predicted by the putative thiaminase gene were the same as the size and chemical characteristics of the thiaminase protein found in these other fish. What was a bit odd was that the fish thiaminase type I was similar to the bacterial thiaminase type II (TenA). The TenA pathway was called the thiamine salvage pathway and was thought to be useful if there was a shortage of thiamine.

Michael wondered whether this was why thiaminase activity was increased by the presence of other bacteria, as shown by Liisa from Finland. Otherwise, what benefit did it confer to these bacteria? It had to be thiamine salvage. Organisms were competing for the basic ingredients for thiamine synthesis. Breaking thiamine into constituent parts would possibly give the thiaminase-containing bacteria a survival advantage over the non-thiaminase-containing bacteria and other organisms, as they would be able to use the ingredients to make more of this life-sustaining commodity, to secure a supply of thiamine. Perhaps the thiaminase-producing fish were similarly competing for products for thiamine synthesis, and thiaminase production was increased when they were threatened.

Thiamine was the rate-limiting step, Michael thought smugly, as his colleague's talk drifted past him, like fish swimming into the current.

In his search for other factors that increased the activity of thiaminase, Michael had been up the night before looking for evidence. He had expected to find up-to-date papers on other potential factors and was surprised when his search directed him to an interesting paper written in the 1950s.[36] He read that thiaminase activity was increased by certain aromatic amines, including dyes, such as aniline and quinoline. The chemical that activated thiaminase the most was aniline. Pyridine activated thiaminases in bacteria, but less so in shellfish, and it was the same for quinoline.

Michael went over in his mind what he had gleaned from reading information and papers online. Aniline was the dye used for making denim jeans. Denim fabric originated in Nimes, France, to make hardwearing workwear, but now there were factories all over the world making denim products. India had recently overtaken China as the denim giants. There was significant bad press about the effluent from the factories, but seldom any direct evidence of toxicity. There would be no evidence if all that happened was the activation of thiaminase and then thiamine deficiency. Yet again, thiamine deficiency seemed to go under the wire, and because it affected the function rather than the structure of tissues, many of the tests for toxicity were unremarkable.

After aniline, *o*-aminobenzoic acid and *m*-aminobenzoic acid have the most potential to activate thiaminase. *P*-aminobenzoic acid is associated with less ability to activate thiaminase, but still activates thiaminase by approximately a third as much as *o*-aminobenzoic acid. Because it blocks ultraviolet light, *p*-aminobenzoic acid is used in sunscreen; it is also a constituent of dyes. Michael couldn't find much use for *m*-aminobenzoic acid, but *o*-aminobenzoic acid is also used in dyes, as well as in perfumes, drugs such as furosemide, and as a mould inhibitor in soy sauce. A derivative is used in some of the stronger, non-steroidal, anti-inflammatory drugs, such as mefenamic acid. Like many of these chemicals, back in 1951, it wasn't something that the researcher would have had available to test on his thiaminase assay. The most recent potential use is for insect repellents. Other chemicals mentioned were *o*-aminophenol, which has been used to develop black-and-white photographs, and in dyes, and toluidine, a chemical similar to aniline.

Pyridine is interesting, as it activates bacterial thiaminase more than the thiaminase found in shellfish. It is one of the components of the 'volatile organic compounds' that are produced in roasting and canning processes, for example, fried chicken and potato chips, as well as fried bacon.

The standard American diet—fast food, Michael thought.

Aromatic amines were also present in crude oil. Another paper had caught his attention:

'Very low embryonic crude oil exposures cause lasting cardiac defects in salmon and herring.'[37]

Michael was seventeen at the time of the disaster the paper referenced, and he remembered it well. The Exxon Valdez, an oil tanker, ran aground in the Prince William Sound, Alaska, and caused one of the largest oil spillages ever. He read on. The paper focused on the cardiac anomalies, but Michael was more interested in the collapse of the herring industry four years later.

Crude oil leading to herring death. He repeated the words in his head. Could the mechanism really be aromatic hydrocarbons in crude oil, activation of bacterial thiaminases, thiamine deficiency and death? He really wished he had Luke with him.

Through reading the paper on crude oil, he learned that scientists had reported higher mortality rates in the pink salmon embryos and significant reductions in juvenile-to-adult survival. He scanned the rest of the paper to see if there was any mention of swimming patterns; these fish were swimming slowly, and had other features similar to thiamine deficiency, such as oedema and intracranial haemorrhages, but they weren't reported to be swimming in circles.

Michael was aware that thiamine deficiency in humans had a varied presentation. He and Luke had discussed it regularly. Neurological symptoms were only part of it; wet beriberi was the term used when humans had heart failure. It seemed plausible that thiamine deficiency could cause cardiac abnormalities in fish. Did this activation of thiaminase by certain chemicals explain the variability in the enzyme activity in some clupeid?

Factory effluent, having an indirect toxic effect. 'A magic, invisible bullet!' Michael muttered.

*

'What do you think?' Craig asked. He had finished his talk, and with a start Michael returned from his private thoughts. Luckily, Craig didn't seem to have heard Michael's totally irrelevant comment.

'Great! Yeah, really great, all those genes. Wow!' he said, trying to look impressed. Craig was deeply committed to genetics research and Michael's vague response bounced off him, allowing him to return to his own ideas.

There would be no evidence of increased thiaminase activity, because no one would think to look for it. It would certainly explain why thiamine deficiency was still rife in these parts, Michael pondered; he had been musing and was still grappling with the real world.

'Can I get you a coffee?' his colleague interrupted him.

'Er, yes, please. White Americano. Thanks,' he replied, finding himself suddenly back in the present and in California.

★

Michael would have liked to have shared these ideas with someone. He often thought about Joe; he would have been interested to hear Michael's theory on crude oil and aromatic hydrocarbon activation of thiaminase leading to thiamine deficiency.

Parkinson's disease was supposed to be more common in rural areas. There were obviously toxins and pesticides that could increase the risk, but Michael wondered whether there were other factors. He remembered that biosolids—the solid residues left after sewage treatment—were being used on agricultural land as fertilisers. Luke had told him that the *Clostridium* bacterium produced spores and was persistent. Michael had wanted to investigate whether it escaped wastewater treatment processes.

He found some relevant publications. Interestingly, *C. difficile* wasn't completely cleared by wastewater treatment. Following local outbreaks, investigators had found *C. difficile* in ninety-two per cent of raw sludge and in ninety-six per cent of anaerobic digested sludge. This was in Ontario, Canada. More concerning was the fact that it was detected in seventy-three per cent of dewatered biosolids and effluent discharge, as well as in thirty-nine per cent of river sediments.[38] Biosolids contain bacteria, some of which are known to be harmful to humans. It was clear that pathogens could be disseminated into the environment through the land application of biosolids, as well as via effluent. The papers on *C. difficile* were proof.

Michael recalled the Prairie Lake Parks by the Illinois River; beautiful, natural environments providing nesting habitats for many bird species. He'd spent much of his childhood outdoors, away from urbanisation, spotting the white-tailed deer, herons, kingfishers and ducks. He realised now, not for the first time, that living by the river certainly hadn't been as healthy a lifestyle choice as his family had imagined it was going to be.

Sea lions and stars

The conference had just ended, and Michael was spending a few days in the Santa Rosa Valley. He'd decided not to read too much about the region's water quality or the local laguna but had taken to drinking bottled water or coffee in the hotel. As he was sitting in the lounge, a news article drew his attention. Reading more about it online, he found comments on blog sites.[39]

'Crisis on one of California's islands. | Thousands of baby sea lions dead. | Locals burying the rotting mammals along the shore.'

The sea lion pups were being washed up on the California shore, anywhere from San Diego to north of San Francisco. There were vast numbers; so far, the rescuers had picked up more than one thousand six hundred carcasses. It appeared that only the pups had been affected; the adults were not dying. It was estimated that tens of thousands of babies born in the previous summer were dying on the islands. At that stage, there were over a thousand pups famished and stranded on the California Channel Islands, due west of Los Angeles. Scientists blamed the phenomenon on unseasonably cold waters, but to Michael this seemed an unlikely cause—after all, hadn't these creatures evolved to live in cold water? There had to be another cause.

The next explanation given was that the ocean temperature was actually warming, resulting in mass death. The experts felt it had to be linked to climate change. Michael was cynical again—not about climate change, but about the fact that it was becoming the excuse for everything. It was lazy thinking, just as a virus is said to be the cause of all modern ailments, and genetic research was predicted to solve every medical mystery.

The final remarks were that the locals were distressed and didn't know when the back-to-back events would end.

Back-to-back? He re-read the report.

`'The sea lion emergency is back . . .'`

There had been other occasions? Michael thought it was suspicious. This was a repeated incident, not a one-off tragedy. At the bottom of the article, a linked report flashed up.

`'Scientists report on exceptional rates of mortality . . .'`

Michael clicked on the link and read on. There were other events involving sea lion pups, starting in 2013. In addition, other creatures had been affected prior to this. There were images of dead and dying sea stars—starfish—washed up on the Californian beach; in pieces, inverted, folded over, their bodies riddled with sores. Several had limbs that were curled at the edges, or else they were piled up in untidy heaps, like cars on a scrap heap. These creatures had rapidly degraded to mush, as though they had simply melted. The larger sea stars had detached limbs, as if the arms had walked off by themselves in a scene from a creepy horror movie. It looked as if whatever was causing the deaths was getting worse rather than better.[40]

To Michael, this smacked of salmonids and alligators all over again. He wondered how the events might be linked and noted the years: 2011, 2013 and 2015. There had been floods in Southern California in December 2010 after a week of stormy weather—Disneyworld, Los Angeles and San Diego had all been affected. The 2010 and 2011 storms had been associated with the purple sea urchin deaths at Malibu Lagoon, north of Los Angeles. Could the deaths of the sea stars be linked to the sea urchin mortalities?

The disease that was causing deaths in sea stars had been termed Sea Star Wasting Syndrome, and it had wiped out literally millions of the creatures. It had occurred over a few days across a large region, and the mortality rate had been estimated at ninety-nine per cent. In addition, marine invertebrates kept in laboratories in the area, at the UC Davis-Bodega Marine Laboratory, just north of San Francisco, had been found dead in their tanks. Seawater was used in the laboratories.

There were carcasses of red abalone, large sea stars and other snail-like chitons. Most significant, though, were the sheer numbers of purple sea urchins that had washed ashore along the sixty-two-mile stretch of coast. There had been no obvious physical stresses, for example, storms or heavy rainfall, and so biologists were initially at a loss to explain the 'die-off'. Subsequently, it had been attributed to a red tide and, predictably, an algal bloom was blamed. The underlying problem was eventually identified as a toxin, the 'yessotoxin', which is produced by these algae. Strangely, there was no previous evidence of yessotoxin being the cause of a lethal disease.

Funny that, Michael thought, as he put his tablet down and scanned the view from the hotel lounge window.

The report went on to state that the possibility of unidentified species or toxins being responsible had not been ruled out. It sounded as though the scientists were not convinced about their own theories. Michael decided to return to the original research for clues.

Online, he found more information when he went over the data on the purple sea urchins, feeling sure this would lead to the root cause of the trouble. Purple sea urchins are known as 'ecosystem engineers'. Michael thought this was an interesting term, and he guessed it must mean that they are important for the local ecosystem. The sea stars are voracious predators, feeding on sea urchins, mussels and other shellfish that have no other natural predators. Many, such as the six-armed sea star (*Leptasterias aequalis*) and the large, three-foot in diameter, twenty-six-armed sunflower sea star (*Pycnopodia helianthoides*) had completely disappeared from a hundred kilometres of coastline. The deaths extended along a vast distance, from Baja California in Mexico, to southern Alaska.

He tried to find out more about the wasting disease affecting the sea star and found an article claiming a viral infection was responsible.[41] The full scientific lowdown was that there had been at least twenty asteroid species affected. The disease led to behavioural changes, lesions, loss of turgor and limb autonomy, and, finally, death.

Experiments had been conducted; small amounts of material from symptomatic animals were injected into healthy animals, causing the wasting disease, but when the animals were injected with heat-treated material instead, there had been no effect. Researchers identified that the disease appeared more severe when the animals had more virus particles—the viral load. Worryingly, though, the virus was detected in plankton, sediments and other echinoderms.

Two thousand and fourteen seemed to be the year of the virus. At that time, the Ebola virus had ravaged humans in West Africa, and again it had been the result of an animal harbouring the virus that had made eradication almost impossible. Strangely, in the case of Ebola, a marked difference in mortality was evident in developed countries compared to West Africa. From the few cases that had been brought to the States, almost all the victims had survived.

Michael wondered whether this virus would cause the extinction of the sea star. Bizarrely, the virus had also been detected in museum specimens of sea star dating from 1942, and it had been found more recently in some healthy sea star. These were asymptomatic carriers. This was a sea star epidemic. Had there been others?

He read on and found that the disease seemed to have started in Southern California, thereafter spreading north and south. Aquariums that sterilised inflowing seawater with ultraviolet (UV) light did not have the disease, but sand-filtered aquariums had been affected. It seemed likely that they were dealing with a microscopic, waterborne infectious disease; one that was heat sensitive and destroyed by UV light.

The explanation given for the detection of the virus in asymptomatic starfish was that the disease takes two weeks to become established, and so these starfish had simply been in the preclinical stage. Michael wondered whether the disease had a predilection for the younger species and found that there did seem to be a higher viral load in the smaller creatures; there was an inverse relationship between viral load and size. He presumed that the size of a particular creature correlated with age. This seemed to be the case, meaning that the younger animals were more vulnerable to the disease. Smaller creatures also had a larger surface area to volume ratio.

But why does the virus disproportionately affect the young? he asked himself. He was perturbed that this virus seemed unselective when it came to species, which was highly unusual. He discovered that the scientists had faced the same conundrum. The rationale given was that this 'densovirus' was a member of the parvovirus family of viruses. These are renowned for gaining entry via a specific receptor, and this type of receptor was common to most of the starfish suffering with the wasting disease.

However, the virus was not unique to the Northwest Pacific coast; it was also detected in similar species along the Northwest Atlantic coast. Like Michael, several scientists seemed to think it was strange that the virus had not elicited wide disease outbreaks in the past. Was the epidemic due to overpopulation or virus mutations? Or was there an unidentified environmental factor?

It was interesting because the virus was detectable on particles suspended in seawater, as well as in the sediment. It was also found in purple sea urchins, where it was thought to form a reservoir—the sea urchin possibly acting as an intermediate host.

He returned to the demise of the sea lions. The theory was that these young creatures had literally starved to death. Sea lions usually feed on a wide variety of fish, including salmon, sardines and anchovy, but for some reason there were fewer fish. Hence, they were largely dependent on a more restricted diet of hake, squid and rockfish. It was the term 'variety', or rather the lack of variety, that alerted Michael to a familiar feeling. He searched for 'squid' and 'thiaminase'. Squid contain a moderate amount of thiaminase, but so do sardines and anchovy. He wondered whether the sea lions had in fact become thiamine deficient as a result of eating a limited type of fish prior to dying of starvation. This was similar to the salmon fry eating a diet mainly consisting of forage fish and the alligators eating gizzard shad. The sea lion and sea star deaths had to be linked, and he felt sure that water pollution was the underlying problem. He just couldn't prove it.

Red fish, dead fish

'One Fish, Two Fish, Red Fish, Dead Fish.' The keynote talk had a catchy title. Michael didn't usually travel to Europe for conferences, but it was an opportunity to see Luke again. It was July and Luke had planned to take a few days of annual leave to join Michael in Vienna for the thirty-ninth Annual Larval Fish Conference. There was also an Early Life History section, which was actually a subunit of the American Fisheries Society. It was the only meeting devoted to the early stages in the fish life cycle. Michael was also hoping to meet up with some of his Scandinavian acquaintances.

There were some other interesting lectures, such as, 'Natural mortality in the egg and larvae stages of fish.' He read through the programme online.

'The session aims to bring together empirical and conceptual insights into these key processes and address issues relevant to ichthyoplankton surveys, general population dynamics and, ultimately, management.'

Ichthyoplankton was a term for the eggs and larval stages of fish. The next session dealt with the 'importance of plankton seasonality on larval herring'. There was also a talk on how larval fish were less tolerant of the effects of low oxygen than low pH, but that the impact of both were synergistic—more than just additive, the effects were amplified, and they were much more toxic to young fish.[42]

Michael's research interests were diverging from those of

the rest of the group. He hoped to be able to persuade the other members that they should study the animals and plants lower in the web. He wanted to start by taking samples of water from locations known to be near wastewater facilities and tourist areas. He was tempted to sample effluent from tourist ships, too; he was sure they would find thiaminase. Perhaps the thiaminase was actually coming from human faeces, doing the full cycle through phytoplankton, plankton, forage fish, predatory fish and back into humans through water or fish. Smoked trout or salmon wasn't so appealing anymore.

Michael had spoken with Diane before leaving for Europe, trying to get her approval, but she was annoyed with him. She wanted his support for her theory that forage fish produce thiaminase from the thiaminase gene in their genome. She also wanted his assistance in getting the new genetic studies underway; there were new techniques to master and the equipment required to perform the relevant tests would be extremely expensive. She thought that they might be able to collaborate on the genetic work and, as Michael had a good track record for gaining funds, she was desperate to make him see sense and work with her. Collaboration would certainly reduce their individual costs but doing so would take time and he had other lines of enquiry he wished to pursue.

Diane was adamant that cooperation was the best thing for the department. She told Michael that everyone was doing genetic research and that they would be left behind if they didn't follow suit. There simply would not be the time or resources for him to branch out on a whim. He was cross and felt betrayed.

Michael was even prepared to pursue his beliefs in his own time, but because of his title, assistant professor, this was frowned upon. The atmosphere between him and Diane became hostile. He realised he would be unable to follow his own interests whilst working in this laboratory. He felt miserable and missed having someone to talk to. He knew he had become a loner again. Although he kept in touch with Luke, the time difference, compounded by Luke's fixed and busy schedule, meant that an occasional email was often all they managed.

They were in the hotel room and Michael was in the bathroom.

'What do you think?' he asked, as he appeared through the door.

'Wow. You look . . . different. So much . . . younger.'

Michael had shaved off his beard.

'I'm not sure you should have done that, though,' Luke continued.

Michael looked worried; Luke appeared serious.

'You've just destroyed the natural habitat for a number of . . .'

He wasn't allowed to finish before Michael threw a cushion at him. Unused to change, it had taken a lot of courage for him to shave off his facial hair, but he felt it was time.

They had a great time together in Vienna. Michael enjoyed being in the centre of Europe. There were signposts to Czechia, Slovakia and Hungary, and he knew that his great-grandfather's homeland, Poland, was close too, on the other side of the Czech Republic, beyond Brno.

The Vistula, which flows through Krakow, is the largest river in Poland. It begins in the mountains on the border of Czechia and what is now Poland but was formerly the Austrian part of Ukraine. Michael remembered his father talking about how his great-grandfather had sought refuge in the States during the First World War. They set quotas shortly after, restricting the number of visas available each year for each country. The number of Jewish refugees applying for entry to the US was much higher than the number ultimately accepted into the country. Michael's great-grandfather was one of the lucky ones.

Luke was enjoying his work in England. He enthused about his subject and the research. He had attended a few of the basic science lectures at the university, as well as spending time on the wards. The university scientists were interested in gut bacteria, the role of nutrition and neurodegenerative diseases. He mentioned that there was also an interest in omega-3 fish oils and that environmental and microbiological departments were strong. Half joking, Luke suggested that Michael should apply for a post there. At first, Michael thought this a ludicrous idea. He hadn't ever imagined leaving New York. He had designs on a professorial position in Ithaca, but the likelihood of achieving this was becoming increasingly remote, unless he retrained as a genetic specialist. He thought he would look up what the university had to offer, and whether it might even be worth organising a visit. At the very least it would be a good way to see Luke again. The research interests, gut microbes and neurodegenerative disease, seemed much more akin to his hypothesis, even if the research didn't involve fish.

PART II

Pulp and paper

Michael had moved to the UK as a Professor in Ecology and Environmental Science at the University of East Anglia in Norwich. It had been a hectic twelve months, applying for and being appointed to the post, organising the visa, packing and redirecting mail. He now had three months off to finalise contracts and paperwork, prior to starting in the department at the beginning of the new academic year. He had been torn, but it was Renie who encouraged him. She had a new life in the church and had plenty of friends and a large support network. It was definitely time for him to start living his own life, and if that meant living in a different country, on a completely different continent, then so be it.

He parted company with Diane amicably. Increasingly he had been engrossed in papers on thiamine deficiency and the wider implications of water pollution. He had found a number suggesting that thiamine deficiency was also important in Parkinson's disease, and it was clear his focus had drifted away from the rest of the group. Now Diane would be able to recruit a genetic specialist who would be able to work with her and carry out her tasks.

In preparation for his interview, Michael had looked into whether there could be a link between water pollution and dementia. The department he would be working for had close links with neuroscientists, gastroenterologists and academic microbiologists, who were all exploring the link between the gut and neurodegenerative diseases. He started with a review of the prevalence of dementia. However, there were very few studies showing any geographical preponderance. He discovered that the prevalence of dementia was higher than expected in Latin America and that Japan seemed to have the lowest risk.

Meanwhile, Luke was writing up his PhD thesis. He had specialised in neurology and was hoping to start as a consultant in the next year. There had been a certain time pressure over the last year, as he tried to conduct research while writing up and submitting papers, as well as applying for substantive positions. At the time, it had seemed impossible.

Luke was renting an apartment in the old part of the city. Michael thought it was quaint. None of the walls, windows or floors were straight, and the plumbing was atrocious. If the building had to deal with the traffic in Chicago it would have fallen down years ago. It had originally been in a yard for one of the many industries that had started up during the city's textile-manufacturing boom in the seventeenth and eighteenth centuries. It was in the centre of a commercial hub, yet hidden away behind a gate, opening onto cobbled streets. Cafés, restaurants, galleries and antique shops were all within a short walking distance. The street across the road was regularly used as a film set whenever there was a need for a traditional, old-world English backdrop. Michael laughed at them trying to film a snow scene during one of the hottest Julys on record. There was fake snow everywhere for days.

Michael hadn't intended to lodge permanently, but they enjoyed each other's company and besides, he didn't really know where to look for a property of his own.

Luke had almost finished his dissertation; he still had to check references and set a date for the final viva. They were sitting together in the lounge on a couple of wingback chairs, drinking tea—an English habit Michael had adjusted to well—whilst reading papers.

'Here's one you might be interested in.' Luke handed Michael a neurology journal opened at a specific page. He knew how much Michael liked maps; this time it was a world map. The article was about the prevalence of Parkinson's disease throughout the world, with numbers for most but not all countries, allowing for a comparison.[43] Luke had spent some time reading through the data. It was an impressive piece of work, and worrying, because it showed that Parkinson's disease had increased between two and four-fold in almost three decades. In fact, it claimed that Parkinson's was now the fastest growing of the disabling neurological disorders.

'The country with the highest incidence is now Canada. Then the USA and Alaska, followed by Argentina. There was a higher incidence than most other European countries in the Baltic: Poland, Lithuania and Estonia, but also a couple of South American countries adjacent to Argentina, namely Chile and Uruguay and, curiously, Iran.' Luke showed Michael the map, with Canada shaded dark red and Alaska, the US and Argentina in orange.

'What do these countries have in common?' Michael asked, suddenly fascinated. In his new position working alongside clinicians with an interest in neurodegenerative diseases, he had a strong sense of optimism that the mystery of Parkinson's disease would be solved, and that a treatment strategy would be found. Speaking his thoughts out loud, he pondered, 'Hmmm, it can't be sewage. Sewage doesn't explain these differences.'

'Could it be mercury?' Luke asked. The way he phrased the words, it didn't sound like a question. He obviously knew something.

Michael quickly latched on. 'What are the industrial uses of mercury?' He was looking it up, trying to catch up with Luke. 'Electrical equipment—batteries and semiconductors, medical appliances—sphygmomanometers and thermometers, dentistry—mercury amalgam, barometers, paper manufacturing and paints.' Michael read the list out loud.

'Look, I found a newspaper article reporting on the Ontario government trying to get two former pulp mill owners to pay for ongoing monitoring, after tons of mercury was dumped into the English-Wabigoon River system in the 1960s and 1970s.' Luke put the article in front of Michael. 'I think it might be mercury.'[44]

Luke let Michael ponder it for a few minutes. He knew how determined Michael had been with his theories on thiamine deficiency, and he didn't want him to feel his hard work was being dismissed so soon. At the same time, Luke was really keen to show Michael what he had been working on, and he hoped it would interest him.

Michael read the excerpts; he could understand why Luke wanted to share this with him '*. . . dead fish floating . . . the mink and otter disappeared . . . eagles and turkey vultures flying as though drunk . . . a kitten walking in circles.*'

'The mink, otter, eagles, turkey vultures and even the kitten, all poisoned by eating mercury-contaminated fish,' Luke explained. 'Canada's pulp and paper industry was one of its most important and profitable. It's the same in Alaska. It's not just the Dryden mill in Ontario, though, there are also lakes in British Columbia with high levels of mercury.' Luke showed Michael another paper he'd found.[45] 'It's especially common downstream of mercury mines. The mercury is taken up by fish.'

'And the humans eat the fish.' Michael was nodding pensively. 'What else did you find out? Why paper mills? You mentioned the United States; are there any recent studies on Parkinson's prevalence?'

'There is one, and it confirms regional variations, which does suggest an environmental cause. For some unexplained reason, it's almost always higher in men.'[46]

Luke was relieved that Michael was happy to discuss this. He'd been concerned that he would be cross with him for mentioning it. He was worried that he would be dismissive now that Joe had died. After all, it couldn't help him now.

'Where did you say there was a high prevalence before? Was it Northern California?' Luke asked.

'Yes, Sacramento, and the Nile Delta in Egypt, and Albania,' Michael replied. 'That's why I was pursuing water pollution as the underlying cause.'

'Well, this study also shows a high prevalence in Northern California.' Luke showed Michael the online paper.[46]

'So, how did you come up with mercury?' Michael had to admit he was intrigued.

'Well, there was this other study, but I already knew a bit about heavy metals and Parkinson-like symptoms, or parkinsonism. You must have heard about mad hatters?'

In the past, Mercury toxicity was well known in hat makers. Chronic mercury poisoning caused tremors as well as visual, sensory and cerebellar disturbance. It was also called mad hatter's disease, or erethism.[47] Luke told Michael about the eccentric Hatter in Lewis Carroll's 1865 novel *Alice's Adventures in Wonderland*, and how he was probably inspired by the term 'as mad as a hatter', which was linked to the hat-making industry and mercury poisoning in the eighteenth and nineteenth centuries.

'Mercury nitrate was used to turn animal fur into felt,' Luke explained. 'Hat makers were known to get tremors, known as hatter's shakes, and suffer with speech problems, mood swings, excessive drooling and hallucinations. Prolonged exposure to mercury vapours caused severe, uncontrollable muscle twitching in the limbs. It also led to hair loss, a lurching gait, difficulty talking and thinking, clumsiness and insomnia.

'The USA had its own "hat capital" in the city of Danbury, Connecticut. There the tremors were called the Danbury shakes,' Luke continued, while Michael thought about the hat-making industry on Mackinac Island in Lake Huron.

'Do you think Joe . . .' Michael started quietly, and his voice faded. 'No matter.'

He stopped and let Luke talk some more. It was easier to listen and keep his thoughts to himself. Luke hadn't seemed to notice and carried on, chuckling as he relayed more tales of intrigue.

'I read a funny story. Apparently, in Turkey, felt producers used camel urine, whereas in France, they used their own urine. It helped to remove the fur from the animal skin, but also softened it. This one French guy produced superior quality felt, and it turned out that he was taking mercury treatment for syphilis. I'm not sure how reliable this is, it's just amusing. Funny how discoveries are made, eh?' Luke took a slurp of tea. 'It wasn't until the 1940s that the use of mercury in felt production was finally banned.'

'And then there was another study linking Parkinson's disease to air pollution.'

By this stage, Michael was thoroughly mystified, and Luke spent the rest of the evening talking him through the various ideas he'd hatched. He had found a study in Ontario that showed a definite association between Parkinson's disease and exposure to fine particulate matter.[48] These tiny particles were also called PM2.5, because they were less than 2.5um in diameter, and made the air appear hazy. 'Mercury is mainly produced by burning fossil fuels. Because of the direction of the winds, the north tends to be more polluted with mercury.'

'Hence Canada,' Michael said with a nod.

'In fact, an international declaration on mercury pollution took place in Madison, Wisconsin. It stated that three times more mercury falls from the sky compared with the time before the industrial revolution. Not only that, but in the last thirty years they reckon emissions have increased from developing countries, offsetting any decreased emissions from elsewhere.'[49]

'These countries are having their own industrial revolutions,' Michael said. He thought that Luke might be right about air pollution and Parkinson's disease. He shook his head in despair.

Luke explained that there were three different kinds of mercury; elemental mercury—pure mercury; inorganic mercury—like mercury chloride and other such compounds; and organic mercury—mercury bound to carbon, which was mostly methylmercury. These different types varied in toxicity and absorption. Methylmercury had the highest absorption through the gut and passage into the brain, but inorganic mercury vapours from fossil fuels were also absorbed through the nasal mucosa and crossed the blood-brain barrier to enter the brain, albeit in smaller amounts.

'You'll find this interesting,' Luke said, speaking more slowly. 'Inorganic mercury, released by coal-power plants into the atmosphere, falls to the ground. Methylmercury is formed from inorganic mercury—' he paused, enjoying teasing Michael, waiting for him to be on the same wavelength, then he started speaking faster '—in warm, shallow waters, which have low oxygen levels and lots of dissolved organic matter, acidic pH, and large numbers of bacteria—'[49]

'Sewage! Water pollution!' Michael interrupted, almost shouting and jumping up from his seat, delighted that Luke was back on side. 'So, it is important after all. OK, Sherlock—or perhaps I should call you Quicksilver? Can you explain the gender differences?'

'I'm not entirely sure about that, but first I want to tell you about China.'

Luke showed Michael another paper, with yet another map showing regional differences, this time in China. He explained how he had initially looked into it after a conversation with his mother. He mentioned that he was interested in the effects of mercury on the brain, and she had asked if he'd heard about the 'rivers of mercury' flowing under the Terracotta Army.

'I'd heard about the Terracotta Warriors, obviously, but I didn't really know much else about them. Emperor Qin—pronounced Chin, hence China. Anyway, Qin Shi Huangdi wanted to live forever, and when he realised he wouldn't, he built an enormous burial chamber, complete with its own army of at least eight-thousand characters, including clay horses and wooden chariots. He also used mercury to create the rivers, lakes and seas of China and make them flow. It was a miniature creation of China, for him to rule over for eternity.'[50] Luke paused again; Michael wasn't sure whether it was for effect. 'Where was I? Oh yes, Parkinson's prevalence in China.'

Luke showed Michael the map, this time the colours were faded. 'I ran out of colour ink, but I think you can see the regions with the highest prevalence: Xinjiang in the far northwest, Shaanxi, Hubei and Hebei in central China, and Guanxi, Fujian and Taiwan in the southeast.'[51]

Michael waited for the explanation, smiling at his friend, who he knew must have put a lot of hours into this research.

'The Terracotta Army are located in the Shaanxi region. The soil mercury levels there are very high. Then there's the Xinjiang region, which, in 2008, had one of the most polluted cities in China, with severe air pollution as well as water pollution. In fact, it's known to be one of the unhealthiest regions in China. It's the number one coal consumer in the country, so the air pollution is mainly from coal-fired power plants. They even have underground coal fires, which have lasted for decades. Surrounded by mountains, its only water supply, via underground channels, is melted glaciers, which are retreating. The combination of massive immigration, excessive water demand for coal production and the drying up of well-water has led to years of water shortages. Locals had described drinking water from puddles. Water pollution was inevitable.

'It's the same in the other areas. Hebei burns a lot of coal. Hubei, not to be confused with Hebei, is China's centre of pollution—' Luke took a sharp intake of breath, making sure Michael was following every word. '—Hubei has twice the amount of atmospheric mercury deposited on the land as the rest of China, but it's also a major rice producing area. Rice paddies, as you know, are kept flooded—'[52, 53]

'So, what you're saying,' Michael interjected, 'is that the

rice paddies convert inorganic mercury from the coal power stations into the more dangerous methylmercury, is that right?'

'Absolutely, the paddies form the ideal environment: warm water, organic matter, bacteria—'

'But what about these areas in the south? Is there coal there?'

'There is in Taiwan. The Taichung Power Plant is the third largest coal-fired power plant in the world, and it's the main source of mercury in Taiwan. In fact, the lowest levels of PM2.5 are found in February, when the factories close for Chinese Lunar New Year. That's the same for much of China, too; February is usually less polluted. One of the biggest problems with methylmercury is that the levels build up. Once it's in the environment, mercury doesn't break down. The levels actually build up towards the top of the food chain, so-called bioaccumulation. Mercury is, therefore, found in fish like tuna. This is a major issue in Taiwan, where they consume a lot of seafood.'[54, 55, 56]

'They do like their tuna.' Michael nodded in appreciation. Now that Luke was talking about fish, he was on solid ground. He stretched back in his chair, took in a long, satisfying breath and listened carefully as Luke explained further.

'Fuqing is in the Fujian Province and it has a high density of fish farms. There is a large chloralkali plant there.'[57] Luke was on a roll but could see Michael's brow furrow.

'Chloralkali? Have I missed something?' Michael asked, suddenly confused.

'Chloralkali factories produce chlorine and caustic soda,' Luke explained. 'The Dryden mill in Ontario used chlorine for bleaching paper. Do you remember I said about the mercury being dumped in the English-Wabigoon River? In the past, mercury cells were used in chloralkali plants.'

'Oh, you mean for electrolysis?' Michael was nodding, having suddenly caught up. Electrolysis uses electricity passed through solutions, in this case a salt solution, to split it into constituent parts: chlorine and sodium hydroxide. He could see how these chemicals would have all sorts of uses. 'And the mercury was then disposed of into the water supply,' he mused, rubbing his stubble and shaking his head slowly, as he recognised the gravity of the situation. 'The kitten walking in circles.' He remembered the effects on the wildlife in Ontario.

It had been a long session, but Luke wanted to finish. 'There's one more region with a high incidence of Parkinson's—Guangxi, and this has mercury toxicity from mining, smelting and the electronics industries.'[58]

Michael's mind was reeling. He felt both excited and confused. There were so many questions. Luke had an early clinic the next morning and retired to bed, leaving Michael with a pile of his papers and notes to go through. He started by finding out more about mercury. The original outbreaks of mercury poisoning were discovered in Minamata, Japan, in 1956. Much of the work had been reported since then by Herada, a Japanese scientist, who had made it his life's work.[59] Approximately six hundred tons of methylmercury had been discharged from the Chisso chemical plant into Minamata Bay. Fish and shellfish had absorbed methylmercury, and then the local fish-eating people had succumbed to strange neurological diseases. Those poisoned suffered severe paralysis, coma and death. It was twelve years from the first reported case to the first action. Luke was right—the industrial inorganic mercury, which had been used as a catalyst in the chemical factory, had been converted to the more toxic organic mercury and had accumulated in fish. Through the food chain, the industrial pollutants had been transferred to humans. This was serious, as it didn't just involve poisoning of those involved in the industry. A whole community had been poisoned, including unborn babies, who were subsequently born with horrendous defects, as methylmercury crossed the placenta. Michael was fascinated in the symptoms described: disturbance of coordination, trouble speaking and tremors were among the commonest symptoms.

It sounds just like Joe, he thought.

Another paper showed that there was a higher prevalence of Parkinson's disease in Hong Kong, Sydney in Australia, and Bambui in Brazil.[60] This confirmed that the male predominance was more common in the studies of Western countries.

Michael knew what he would find even before he searched for it.

Hong Kong was still reliant on coal, as it had been since 1890. Three quarters of Australia's electricity generation was from coal. He wasn't sure about Brazil. He wondered whether there was a lower incidence in countries that weren't as reliant on coal. First, he looked for a pattern in Sub-Saharan Africa. The rates of Parkinson's disease were low in Ethiopia and moderate in Nigeria.[61] Until 1960, coal had been the main energy source in Nigeria, whereas ninety per cent of Ethiopia's power supply came from hydroelectricity. Next, he scanned the incidence rates in Europe. Interestingly, Finland was one of the countries with the highest prevalence of Parkinson's disease. Sweden had one of the lowest and was closing coal-fired power stations ahead of many of its European counterparts.[62] Meanwhile, Finland was importing millions of tons of coal from Russia, where it was used in household heating. Finally, Michael looked up Albania. There had been a chloralkali plant in Vlora, which closed in 1992, but not before dumping mercury into the bay, causing heavy contamination. Subsequently, high levels of mercury were found in the fish.

All that glitters

Whilst Luke was in clinic, Michael spent the morning walking around the city, visiting the market. He thought how Renie would love the traditional sausage store, which sold every feasible flavour of sausage. Luke was a vegan now, and unfortunately there were no meat-free options. Michael thought it strange that the market seller seemed to bristle when he said the word vegan. Surely it was better to cater for all-comers. And wasn't the customer *always* right?

He phoned Renie religiously every week. She was always pleased to hear from him and told him about the meals she had cooked and delivered to neighbours, who, for various reasons, some more plausible than others, were in need of hearty, home-cooked food. She had promised to visit her son, but no firm plans had been made.

Wandering through the cobbled lanes, there were numerous second-hand shops—the locals didn't seem to throw anything away. Some were cluttered with stuff no longer wanted, waiting for a second home, other items had been upcycled, lovingly repaired, repainted or rebranded to produce something saleable. There were charity shops too, with seasonal, colour-coordinated window displays.

Michael waited for Luke in one of the many cafés. He'd found an independent one heading towards the old monastery, which was now part of the university. They served a daily dish, which Luke enjoyed; he thought it rather continental. Sitting in the window, Michael could watch the students passing by, whilst drinking coffee and reading the papers.

'Hi! How was clinic?' Michael stood up as his friend entered the café.

'Fine, the usual clientele, although there was one really interesting case.'

'Can I get you a coffee?' Michael asked, as Luke put his things down on the bench by the table.

'Yes, please, black Americano. And you, what have you been up to?'

Michael ordered Luke's drink and ordered a white Americano for himself; they exchanged stories whilst drinking their coffees and then Luke ordered the dish of the day—a garlic, butter bean and vegan chorizo casserole, served with a sourdough roll. Michael had a New York deli pastrami ciabatta.

'I read the papers from China last night. How can you be so sure it's mercury?'

Luke laughed. 'I'm not, but it's quite convincing—a globally-polluting, toxic heavy metal causes Parkinsonian symptoms, while the levels of mercury are increasing, as are the number of cases of Parkinson's, and the countries with the highest prevalence also have the worst pollution?'

Michael had to admit it was suspicious. He didn't want to offend his friend, but he also wondered why no one else had made the link. He wanted to know about other countries, and whether this information meant Parkinson's was treatable. There were so many questions.

Luke read his thoughts. 'There's a lot to take in, but let me start by showing you the data from other countries.'

Pulling out a laptop, he opened a file and said, 'This paper looks at the cases in the UK over a ten-year period.' He scanned through the abstract and added, 'Yes, here it is,' before moving the screen so Michael could read it. The study showed that the incidence of Parkinson's disease in the UK seemed to be steadily falling.[63] It still followed the same pattern, though, being more common in men and, curiously, in urban areas. 'Here it's definitely related to pollution rather than pesticides. The laws on the use of pesticides are strict and have been for decades, unlike in the States.'[64]

Luke opened another file. 'Here, read this,' he said. He showed Michael a further report, which confirmed that epidemiological studies suggested a decline in the incidence of Parkinson's in the UK. However, it also showed that there was actually a steady rate of new cases in Wales.[65]

'I started thinking about this. Why is Parkinson's disease increasing in China and Canada whilst declining in the UK?' Luke asked. 'Simple. Coal.'

Once they had finished eating, they packed up their things to leave the café, whilst Luke continued asking Michael questions. 'And why was Parkinson's disease first recognised in the UK?' He chuckled, as he was really putting the question to himself. 'Originally, I thought it was because of the millinery business—the world's largest hat makers was in Gracechurch Street, just round the corner from where James Parkinson worked in the East End of London. He practised in Hoxton, between Spitalfields and Hackney. Gracechurch Street is near Monument. I thought it was that. Then I tried to find out about coal-fired power stations in the vicinity, but this was the early nineteenth century, before the power stations were built.'

They were walking down the cobbled streets back to Luke's apartment.

'So, the UK was one of the earliest countries to use coal, and it used to be ahead of the world in coal production, which peaked in 1913. These days, it's back to the levels it was three hundred years ago. The decline in imports in recent years had been dramatic. Anyway, enough on that for now. What about elsewhere?'[66]

They reached the riverside and strolled along the bank. Like much of the UK, the river, once an industrial zone, had been transformed. There was a beautiful river walk and the old warehouses and Victorian buildings had been refashioned as apartments or repurposed as offices to suit modern service employment rather than manufacturing.

'In Rotterdam, they've noticed a fall in the number of cases of Parkinson's. But if you look at Europe overall, the city has an above average number of cases compared with the rest of Europe. France and Aragon in Spain have a lower prevalence,which is interesting because France has developed nuclear and hydropower, and in Aragon, hydroelectricity is the dominant technology, and they also have a lot of wind power.'[67,68]

They arrived home and Luke walked over to his desk. 'Let me show you this paper. It's interesting.' He shuffled through a neat pile of printed papers on his desk and handed a few pages to Michael. The cases were from different parts of the world. Taiwan was one of the places with a high incidence of Parkinson's. Interestingly, Copiah County in Mississippi, a relatively poor, rural area, also had a low prevalence. Overall, it was the same in China, too.

'China includes regions with low numbers of cases,' Luke explained. 'It just shows how much regional variation there is, and it emphasises the importance of environmental causes.

It was Copiah County I wanted you to see. In this area, there are no coal-fired power stations, no mercury, no mining even. Whereas if you look at central Spain, there are coal power plants, and Almadén town in Ciudad Real province is one of the world's richest mercury-producing regions. There's a large mercury mine there.'

He was about to finish when he remembered something else interesting from the paper. 'Oh, and there isn't a coal-fired power plant in Sicily, I checked, it's gas, but there is an active volcano—Mount Etna. They measured high levels of mercury in the air following the last eruptive phase. Not only that, but they eat a lot of fish and Sicilian fisherman have been shown to have high mercury levels.'[69]

Michael was presented with more and more information supporting Luke's claim. He was told that of all the energy sources, coal was known to have the largest negative health and environmental impacts, both in the short and long term.[66] The coal-fired power stations in England were widely dispersed, whereas in South Wales, several coal-fired power stations, at Aberthaw and Uskmouth, were situated in the most densely populated area of the country. Both were major emitters of mercury, but thankfully had now closed—Aberthaw only recently. Several power stations had already been converted to gas or biomass, and this reduction in coal burning, Luke hypothesised, was why there was a falling number of cases in England, but still the same caseload of Parkinson's disease in Wales.

Most studies showed that there was a gender difference; Parkinson's disease was more common in men than in women, but there were some countries with a female preponderance. Luke had highlighted this and scribbled question marks in the border. It was clearly something he wanted to try and explain. Moreover, unlike many modern diseases, there was no difference in socioeconomic groups. *Why was this?*

'I have a meeting to go to this afternoon,' Luke said, as he stood up. Then, recalling his morning at work, he added. 'I didn't tell you about the interesting case I saw. This lady had a peripheral neuropathy. In the past, she'd also had symptoms that sounded like dementia, and she had a tremor. She was convinced it was thiamine deficiency and had been treated with intravenous thiamine. It was incredible. She was taking a supplement to boost thiamine levels—it's one that the diabetics take. I can't remember the name—sounded like thiamine, though. Oh, and she also claimed that she had bacterial overgrowth in her small intestines and had been taking an antibiotic—rifaximin.'[70]

Luke was deep in thought, trying to remember more details. 'Nice lady. Fascinating case, don't you think?' He didn't wait for a response. 'Is that the time? I better go.' He shot out of the door, leaving Michael absorbed with the material he had collected so far.

A study from Scotland showed a definite geographical difference in cases in West Scotland. There were significantly fewer cases in the urban area around South Glasgow compared to the more rural South Lanarkshire. Researchers suggested that the lower rate of cigarette smoking in South Lanarkshire was a contributory factor, accounting for a higher prevalence. Curiously, smoking seems to reduce the risk of Parkinson's disease. Luke had made a note that this was apparent in many studies. Michael discovered that a higher-than-average number of people smoked in the Copiah County. The rates for lung cancer there were particularly high for men.

Luke had also highlighted that the Scottish report seemed to show a higher incidence of Parkinson's in rural areas.

He'd noted that an inner-city Yoker coal-fired power station closed in 1976, but that there were many sites of previous coal mines in South Lanarkshire, and there were concerns that new developments may have disturbed the workings of the old mines. Michael wasn't sure if this would increase mercury pollution in the environment.[71]

Luke had also done his research on the USA. He'd obviously remembered Michael telling him about the Amish community and people around the Great Lakes having a higher incidence. There was also Sacramento, and Egypt along the River Nile. Michael could see Luke had filed papers for each location.

Luke had clearly used different sources for the research into pollution in the area around the Great Lakes. He'd written various notes from a few websites. New England was called the 'tailpipe' of the nation, because of the pollution that blows over it from the Midwest. Ohio was in the centre of one of the worst areas.[72] Apparently, more than a third of all the mercury pollution from power plants in the States derives from the plants in Texas, Pennsylvania, Ohio and West Virginia. There had been concerns about mercury pollution in Pennsylvania for years—with good reason; Keystone and Conemaugh coal-fired power plants in Pennsylvania were the second and fourth worst mercury emitters in the States. In addition, the other mercury polluters in the neighbouring states of Ohio and West Virginia contributed to the toxicity.[73] In fact, three power stations in southwestern Pennsylvania were among the top ten emitters in the nation; the fact that they were all so close in one region was clearly a cause for concern.[72] Luke had made a note of the fact that journalists were reporting that coal was making the residents sick, and that they faced continuing risk from mercury pollution. The American Medical Association stated that mercury was causing global pollution—it was contaminating fish and it was neurotoxic for humans, particularly in developing foetuses, and they suggested that it might even provoke cardiovascular disease.

There seemed to be some progress in the States, although there was some backwards thinking taking place too. In 2011, it was recognised that coal was the largest domestic energy resource, but that it was also needed for energy security. The reason there was such a lot written about it at that time was due to the change in emission rules by the Environmental Protection Agency (EPA). The Madison Declaration on Mercury, which convened in Madison, Wisconsin in 2006, recognised the impact of mercury pollution. In fact, it stated that the majority of deposited mercury was anthropogenic—chiefly environmental, due to human activity—and that there were minimal effects from natural emissions from the earth's crust. According to the EPA, fifty per cent of mercury air pollution in the States is from power stations. The newer power stations were able to control emissions to some extent, and some of the older ones had been converted, but forty per cent of power plants did not have the advanced pollution control equipment required to do this. They were continuing to produce toxic emissions twenty years after the USA produced its Clean Air Act Amendment in 1990.[74] In this year, three industries made up two thirds of the mercury emissions, namely medical waste incinerators, municipal waste combustors and power plants. Since then, there has been over a ninety-five per cent reduction in mercury emissions from medical and municipal waste, but only a ten per cent reduction in emissions from power plants.

Michael read an explanation on how power plants can reduce mercury emissions, but it was highly technical, with abbreviations that probably only made sense to engineers. It reminded Michael how he had tried to understand water treatment plants. Basically, the bottom line was that it was possible to reduce mercury and still burn coal. Although the best solution by far was to find alternative sources of energy, and this seemed to be something that most of Western Europe was leading on.

Luke had printed off a map of power plants. At the top of the page, he'd scribbled, 'For you, Michael!' which made him chuckle, especially as it wasn't that useful. It was supposed to be colour-coded, but Luke still hadn't replaced his colour ink cartridge. Perhaps that was a job Michael could do now he was here with time to spare. The map was supposed to show the location, type and size of the power plants. It seemed to correlate with the map of Parkinson's disease rates that Michael had shown Luke all those years earlier.

Finally, the EPA website had shown, using two maps, how depressingly reliant the US is on energy, with consumption increasing year on year and still a firm reliance on coal, although natural gas and petroleum were increasingly being used. Luke had made notes that this energy consumption was primarily driven by weather-related factors: heating or air conditioning, depending on the season. Michael thought that demand was likely to increase further in the future, thanks to the extremes of weather due to climate change.

Luke had been busy. He had made the association between Sacramento, and its history at the centre of the California Gold Rush, and increased rates of Parkinson's in Central Valley. It looked like he had resorted to tourist websites. Michael wondered how he had missed it. He had been so focused on his thiamine studies that he hadn't recognised something so obvious. It had taken an outsider to see it clearly. Reading through Luke's notes, he was reminded that gold had been discovered by James Marshall in 1848, in what is now

State Historic Park. The Empire Gold Mine was a working mine for over a hundred years between 1850 and 1959. It is the site of the oldest and largest—as well as the richest—mine in California. Then there was the Kennedy Gold Mine near Jackson, which was famous for being one of the deepest gold mines in the world. Luke had printed out another map showing the location of gold mines in California. There were hundreds throughout the state, with a glaringly obvious concentration around Sacramento.

The next article contained photos of a large, spherical silver mass of mercury, perhaps the size of a table tennis ball, being held in a grubby palm. There were several photos illustrating the process of mining gold. Michael had images in his mind of miners wading through shallow rivers, using a large sieve to filter through rocks for gold. The captions told a different story. This globular mass was actually an amalgam of gold and mercury. Mercury bonds with the gold so that it becomes easier to separate the gold from the ore. The pictures showed men squeezing mercury amalgam in a net using their bare hands, and then rubbing mercury into the ore with their bare fingers. There was another photo of a man burning off the mercury from the gold mix. He was covering his face with his T-shirt, but this would provide no protection from the vapor. Mercury use in gold mining was largely unregulated. The miners inhale mercury and also return to their families with it infused in their clothes, contaminating their homes. In many developing countries, this small-scale mining was deemed to be the largest source of mercury pollution. The example from the photographs was in Ecuador,[75] but there were similar cases in Brazil—*of course!* This is why it had higher numbers of patients with Parkinson's disease. Other places where this happened included French Guiana, Peru, Burkina

Faso, Tanzania, the Seychelles, the Philippines, Indonesia, and even Slovenia and the Faroe Isles.[76] There seemed an endless list. In the Philippines, it was clear that mercury wasn't only affecting gold mine workers; it also polluted the water downstream and caused mercury poisoning in a significant amount of the population there.[77] In populous areas, with the bacterial contamination of water supplies, the conversion to methylmercury would be significant and the potential for damage even greater.

In the section on gold mining, Luke had printed a paper on the prevalence of Parkinson's disease in the Coquimbo region of Chile. This study looked at different communities, Paihuano in the mountains, and La Serena by the coast. Paihuano had a rate of two hundred cases per one hundred thousand people, which was the highest Michael had seen.[78] Paihuano is in the Andes Mountains. There are still active mines in the region, including the Andacollo mine, although they now use the cyanide leaching process to separate gold from the ore.

And this is safer? Michael wondered.

The Andacollo mine is located in the urban area of the city of Andacollo, which is in the Elqui province of this region. Michael was cynical. Even though a different extraction method was being used, there was still a significant amount of mercury in the soil and atmosphere within the vicinity. There were reports of a lack of monitoring by the companies—it was coal-fired power plants in the USA and chemical companies in Ontario and Minamata all over again. Mercury occurs naturally in ore, and high temperatures are required to evaporate it during extraction. Miners in the Andacollo region displayed more symptoms of mercury-related toxicity, including tremors, Parkinsonism associated with cognitive deterioration and difficulty speaking.

Michael was becoming obsessed with this line of research. He was desperate to know more. How did mercury cause the neurological damage, and were other factors important?

He referred back to the first six cases of Parkinson's Disease, as described by James Parkinson in his 1817 essay 'The Shaking Palsy'. Luke had tried to link them to the conditions in London. Michael remembered Luke chuckling at himself that he had been blaming the milliners' factory. It was funny how they had both obsessed about something, Luke the mercury from hat-making and Michael the water pollution in the Thames, arising from the massive population increase at the beginning of the nineteenth century. It was staggering to think that, even then, Parkinson's disease could be linked to burning coal.

One particular article compared air pollution levels in London with those of other world cities over the last few centuries. From 1700 onwards, the capital's air had become increasingly polluted. There was data on the suspended particulate matter—the fine solid or liquid particles suspended in the earth's atmosphere—namely soot, smoke, dust and pollen. Looking at the graphs, Michael could see that the suspended particulate matter peaked in the late 1800s, at a level of six hundred and twenty-three. Delhi currently had a level of four-hundred and eighty. The Indian city was now in the early stages of industrial development and was heavily polluted, with a high death toll as a consequence. The current relatively low level of air pollution in London reflected its economic development.[79]

To think that London then was worse than Delhi is now, Michael thought to himself.

There were more notes on the subject. Luke had written that fogs were quite common in the 1700s, but by the early 1800s, the time when James Parkinson recognised the patients with shaking palsies, these fogs had become deadly. It was due to smoke and fumes from industrialisation and population expansion in the city. One of the main contributors was domestic coal burning—crowding within the city confines had its consequences. There were no coal-fired power stations then, but even in 1817 there was still coal burning on a massive scale, albeit for domestic purposes—heating homes and cooking.[80] Michael looked forward to showing this to Luke—particularly to demonstrate that he liked graphs as well as maps!

Synthetic heroin

Luke was working in the morning and had given Michael a list of groceries to buy. While Luke did all the cooking, Michael tended to do the shopping. As much as possible, he used the market for buying his vegetables. He could understand Luke wanting to avoid fish. Michael hadn't read anything bad about North Sea fishing, but neither of them wanted to chance it. Luke had continued his vegan diet, while Michael adopted a flexitarian approach, enjoying tasty vegan dishes with additions such as eggs. He had definitely reduced his meat consumption, particularly red meat.

He picked up a pack of six eggs and whilst waiting for the cashier checked to make sure none were broken. He was surprised to find that there were only five eggs. He asked the cashier if he could get a replacement carton.

'It's Pride,' she told him by way of explanation. He must have looked nonplussed. 'The eggs,' she said, nodding at the pack. 'They take an egg to chuck at the marchers.'

Michael was shocked. He and Luke hadn't experienced any trouble. He was surprised to hear there were locals with such strong feelings.

Back in the apartment, he waited for Luke to finish his morning ward round and glanced through some of the other papers that Luke kept in his file. He happened across one highlighted 'a medical detective story'. Michael liked the sound of it and read on. Essentially, the Director of Neurology in San Francisco had been asked to see a patient who was catatonic—virtually completely unresponsive. The strange thing was that the patient appeared fully alert. It was as though he were awake, yet he made no spontaneous movements. The neurologist described how, when he lifted the patient's arm, it stayed up in the air, something he called 'waxy flexibility', which, in Michael's opinion, seemed an odd and totally useless expression. On bending the patient's arm, the neurologist could demonstrate the rigidity similar to that seen in Parkinson's disease. He subsequently discovered six more identical cases, eventually identifying the common factor in each as the use of a synthetic heroin—a designer drug used recreationally. It was chemically similar to pethidine, but far more potent. These cases had almost all the motor features of Parkinson's disease. After treatment with Parkinson's medicines there was a dramatic improvement.

Real detectives assisted by carrying out police raids. A few friendly dealers were on side to supply a batch of this synthetic heroin—also known as MPPP or 1-methy-4-phenyl-4-propionoxypiperidine—for research. It seemed that MPPP was converted to another, slightly different chemical called MPTP, and this derivative was able to enter the brain by crossing the blood-brain barrier. Once in place, it is converted to an active, charged compound—known as MPP+—which is harmful. This chemical then destroys the substantia nigra, the specific area in the brain affected in Parkinson's disease, leading to permanent damage. It works in a similar fashion to the herbicide paraquat, which has been banned in the EU since 2007. However, it was still being produced in the UK and then sold abroad, including in the States.

Double standards, Michael thought, irritated by the hypocrisy.[81]

Later, sitting outside in the small courtyard drinking coffee, Michael asked if he could help with Luke's line of investigation. 'I think we need to find out more about heavy metal poisoning in general, specifically mercury,' he said. 'I found a few articles, and if this hypothesis is to have any grounding, I really need to link low-grade mercury exposure to the pathology found in Parkinson's disease.'

Heads down, the two of them scouted through papers. Much of what they read was established fact or just not too surprising. Some of it, Luke remembered from basic science at school. Metals are good conductors of electricity; they are malleable and have a lustre—they are shiny. Michael felt comfortable with the knowledge that there were varying degrees of naturally occurring metals in the earth's crust, depending on the site. The heavy metals are just that—heavy—weighing in at more than five grams per cubic centimetre. Neither of them realised that the body utilised twelve of these trace metals in normal bodily functions, although it shouldn't have been a surprise.[82]

'OK, pub quiz! Which metals are essential in the human body?' Luke teased Michael. He knew he would be obsessive about getting them all right.

'Sodium, potassium, calcium, magnesium, iron, copper, zinc, um, that's . . .' Michael faltered, clearly unhappy that he was struggling.

'Seven down, missing five.' Luke was enjoying himself, but quickly filled in the gaps: 'Vanadium, chromium, cobalt, molybdenum and, of course, manganese. Who would have thought it! Vanadium, chromium! Not so different from your car engine after all,' Luke smirked, recalling Michael's lectures and reading his mind.

'Xenobiotic metals—that's a good term—are foreign, alien, imposter metals. They include mercury, cadmium, lead and aluminium.'

Michael joined in, having grabbed the article before Luke could test his general knowledge again. 'These ones have no physiological function, and look, they enter the body by mimicking the other useful metals, using the transporter systems in place for the essential metals. That's definitely a design glitch!' Michael chuckled.

The other papers filled in gruesome facts about how heavy metals disrupted biochemical pathways, bound to crucial chemicals in the body and disturbed bodily functions. Even the essential metals were toxic in excess, including copper and iron, something Luke knew about from medical school, as there were genetic conditions; Wilson's disease for copper and haemochromatosis for iron, where an excess caused organ damage.

'Aluminium is probably a risk factor for Alzheimer's disease,' Michael announced. 'Excess aluminium results in loss of memory, and problems with balance and coordination, and the toxicity worsens with more acidic conditions, such as with acid rain.' Michael was quiet for a few minutes. 'There's a theme here. Everything is made worse by human activity. Everything!'

It was true. Aluminium silicates are abundant in the soil. Acid rain, mainly caused by the burning of fossil fuels, causes the silicon to leach out of these stable aluminium compounds, producing unstable aluminium compounds, which are then able to interact with cells in the body. Interestingly, ionic magnesium and iron can be replaced by aluminium. Magnesium is vital for respiration and the thiamine- dependent pathways. Michael wondered whether this was one of the ways that aluminium caused Alzheimer's, by replacing magnesium with aluminium. Going back to basic biochemistry, it seemed to make sense. Perhaps it reduced the effectiveness of respiration, specifically the conversion of pyruvate to acetyl-CoA—the thiamine-dependent part of the reaction. The changes in neurons with aluminium toxicity were similar to the changes seen in Alzheimer's disease. It seemed that urinary excretion was particularly important for this metal, and that patients with kidney disease were known to accumulate aluminum.[82]

Meanwhile, Luke was reading up on mercury, so Michael moved onto manganese poisoning. 'Did you know manganese oxidises dopamine, the neurotransmitter that is destroyed in Parkinson's?' he asked.

'Yes, it's known to cause manganism—a condition that resembles Parkinson's.'

Luke seemed to know already. Michael was confused. 'So, it's already known that heavy metals can cause Parkinson's disease?'

'It's a different disease.' Luke confidently dismissed Michael's concerns, before reiterating his point. 'Mercury produces a colourless, odourless gas when heated, which is very toxic and bioaccumulative. Anthropogenic actions, such as agriculture, municipal wastewater discharges, mining, incineration and discharge of industrial wastewater are all sources. It's neurotoxic but can impair any organ.' He put the paper down. 'That much we knew already. Tea?' he asked, while getting up, stretching and walking towards the kitchen. Michael gave him the thumbs up and carried on reading about other metals.

Iron is one of the most abundant metals in the earth's crust. It exists predominantly in either the pale green ferrous (2+) form or the rust-coloured ferric (3+) form, depending on the charge on the iron ion. *Iron ion.* This appealed to Michael. Ions were formed when an atom lost an electron—a negatively charged particle. Ferrous iron ions have lost two electrons and ferric iron ions have lost three. Ions are able to cause a charge in other compounds or are more likely to bind onto other chemicals by grabbing their electrons—so-called ionic bonding. In the body, iron is bound to proteins called metalloproteins—literally, a protein bound to a metal.

Nothing too clever there, Michael thought. *Chemists say it as it is. Waxy flexibility! Honestly, neurologists!*

Michael continued reading about these proteins. Minor changes in the way the proteins folded, caused by a change in the charge, influenced the bodily functions and, therefore, caused illness. There was no evidence that an excess of iron caused neurodegenerative disease directly, however, there was an increase in brain iron in these conditions, particularly in Parkinson's disease.

The change in iron status by oxidising or reducing agents is crucial for energy production in the cells in many living organisms. Michael was suddenly on the alert. In his mind, he could picture lecture slides:

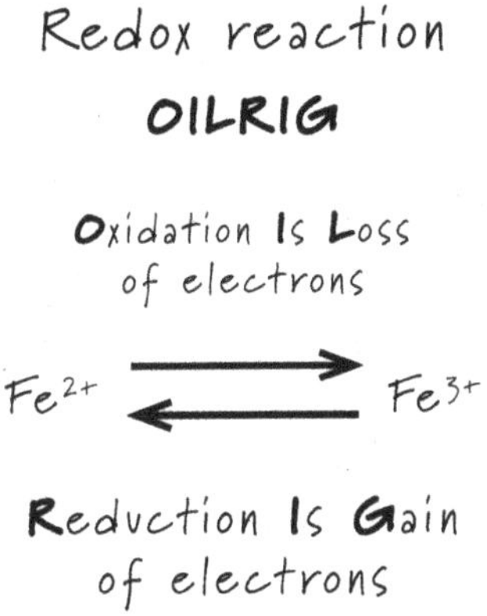

He shouted out to Luke in the kitchen, 'Of course, it's the mitochondria!'

This reversible redox reaction of iron formed an essential part of the electron transfer chain—the transport of electrons from the oxidation of food. This electron transfer chain was responsible for releasing most of the energy from food in the respiration process. This electron transfer chain was actually a series of reactions that took place in the mitochondria. Paradoxically, the 'redox' properties, the ability to alter charge from 2+ to 3+ meant that iron was potentially toxic to cells. The ability to switch iron state was essential for energy production but also extremely hazardous. The main reason it was so damaging was that it increased the production of hydroxyl radicals—highly reactive oxygen-containing molecules. The Fenton reaction—the formation of hydroxyl radicals ($OH^{\cdot}$) from hydrogen peroxide H_2O_2—used ferrous ions as a catalyst.

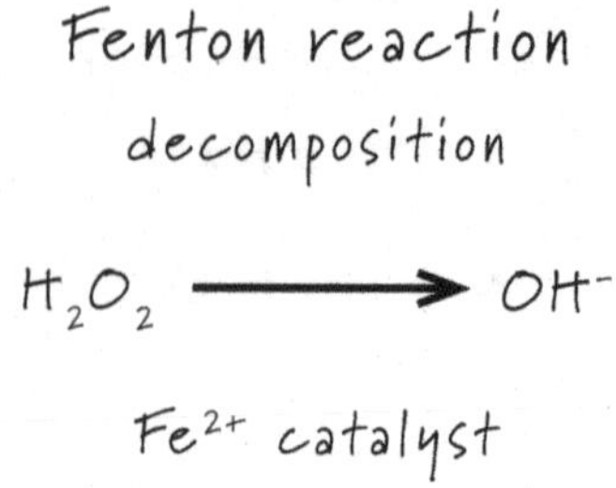

Not only that, but the ferric iron was reduced to the ferrous iron states by reacting with another reactive oxygen compound, the superoxide anion ($O2^-$). Hence, even small amounts of loose iron were exceedingly harmful to the cell. Iron absorption was finely tuned, and there were several mechanisms to control the amount absorbed, but there were no mechanisms for iron excretion.[83] Iron had to be kept safe once inside the oxidative environment of the cell, and one way this happened was by binding it to chaperones—molecular housekeepers, such as citric acid, also known as vitamin C. Michael ran through the facts in his mind, summing up as he would do in a lecture.

So, excess iron is bad. Oxygen in many compounds could be charged, becoming extremely reactive and destructive. Even so, both oxygen and iron are essential. And vitamin C is good at protecting the body from any iron that escapes, keeping it away from the reactive oxygen.

Gender differences

Luke wasn't sure how iron toxicity was related to mercury poisoning, but he was grateful for Michael's input and customary enthusiasm. Luke then explained that manganese toxicity caused an 'extrapyramidal syndrome'. Michael looked baffled and Luke realised he had ventured into medical jargon, which was easily done as Michael understood so much science terminology, particularly if it was the same in fish.

'It refers to our motor—muscle—control, and coordination. It also stops us making movements we don't want to. Many drugs will have extrapyramidal side effects,' Luke explained.

Michael nodded and asked, 'So, how does 'manganism'—is that what you called it—affect you?'

'It causes the same symptoms and signs: hypertonia—increased muscle tone, and cogwheel rigidity—the jerky movements you get when someone actively tries to straighten or bend your arms—'

'I saw the doctors check Joe's arms like that,' Michael interrupted, finding the fact that he recognised the problems Joe had experienced strangely fascinating.

'I'm sorry about Joe,' Luke responded softly.

Even though a couple of years had passed since Joe's death, he and Michael never talked about it. Luke thought Michael would want to open up about his feelings, and on a few occasions, he had tried to prompt him. As usual, Michael just changed the subject. Luke was particularly concerned because Michael often talked in his sleep. It was as though he was having nightmares. Luke found it all quite strange, but Michael seemed to have put Joe's death firmly in the past and had moved on.

'What are the other symptoms of manganism?' Michael prompted.

Luke continued, 'There's the bradykinesia—literally slow movements, tremor and a tendency to fall backwards due to postural instability. Apparently, you can also get a cock-walk gait, where you walk on your toes, but I've not seen any cases, just read up about them. So, there are differences, you see.'

Luke carried on talking about how manganism classically didn't respond to Parkinson's treatment, featured more problems with dystonia—the abnormal movements—and caused less of a tremor. Manganese toxicity also produced sensory disturbances, as well as the neuropsychiatric and cognitive issues. The patients with manganism had typically been intoxicated at work and were either manganese miners or farmers and food producers who had come into contact with the fungicides maneb or mancozeb, both of which contained manganese. Also affected were welders, steel manufacturers and manufacturers of glass, ceramics, matches, fireworks and textiles—the list, which Luke was now reading from one of his many articles on the subject, seemed endless. It was obviously a well-researched area of interest.

'So, can you always tell the difference?'

'Yes, sure you can,' Luke replied confidently, before adding, 'I mean, in the cases where there is obvious exposure you can. Chelation therapy can be used to bind the manganese. It works.'[84]

'Chelation?'

'Yes, substances that bind well to heavy metals to draw them out of the body.'

'So, they can detoxify?'

'Yes, to an extent.'

For a while, they both sat there deep in their own thoughts. Michael found a review and started reading up on manganese toxicity. He had an idea, but he didn't want to challenge Luke's medical knowledge without some idea on the background. He read that drinking water had been contaminated by manganese in Bangladesh, but also in Canada. Soymilk infant formulas had a minimum manganese concentration, as it is an essential element, but no maximum. There had been outbreaks of manganese poisoning in intravenous drug users in many countries in Eastern Europe and Canada, as the oxidising agent potassium permanganate had been inadvertently added to the drug ephedrine, used in an uncontaminated form during surgery, but abused as a stimulant similar to amphetamines. The report suggested there might be lower levels of exposure below the guidance set for occupational standards that still caused neurological damage and, therefore, could be significant in neurodegenerative disease.[85]

He read on, getting more interested with the next paper. Manganese disrupted energy production, by inhibiting a specific mitochondrial enzyme.[86] The cells most susceptible were the ones requiring the most energy, such as the nerves and brain. In fact, chronic exposure to manganese led to high levels of the metal inside the mitochondria.[87]

No point measuring the blood levels! Michael decided.

It was even more worrying than he had first thought. The fuel additive 'MMT', an organomanganese compound, was added to unleaded petrol, or 'gasoline', as Michael knew it. This happened in several countries: the USA, Canada and Australia, for example, and combustion in the motor engine released the manganese salts into the air. Hence, in places of high traffic density, there was increased exposure. By filtering down through the soil and into the ground water, it ended up in the water supply.

How predictable! Michael thought.

It seemed that the differentiation between manganism and Parkinson's disease wasn't as simple as Luke had made out. There were exceptions, in addition to an overlap of symptoms and variable presentations. In fact, there was a case of manganism in a welder who had responded to Parkinson's drugs.[85]

Perhaps it wasn't quite so straightforward, Michael thought.

Furthermore, manganese, like iron, existed in two different oxidised states in the body: manganese II (Mn^{2+}), which was bound to albumin, and manganese III (Mn^{3+}), which was bound to the iron transporter transferrin and formed a very stable complex. This transferrin complex was able to enter the brain. The interesting thing was that the absorption of manganese III from contaminated water through the gut lining was increased both in those with iron deficiency and pregnant women. Additionally, manganese levels were found to be significantly higher in women of all ethnicities.

Women were much more susceptible to manganese poisoning, because they were more likely to be iron deficient.

Michael wanted to share this revelation with Luke. 'I've done some digging around,' he started, 'after you piqued my interest in manganism.'

'Oh, yes,' Luke laughed, waiting for what Michael was about to tell him.

'Manganese levels are much higher in women, and they are often over the limit in water supplies throughout the world. Did you say that Parkinson's is more common in men in most countries, but not all of them?'

'Yes, that's right.' Luke was always impressed by Michael's ability to pick up on the minutia. 'Here are the papers.' He handed him a cardboard file. It was obviously something he'd wanted to look into in more detail.

The male-to-female ratio was usually about 2:1, but in several countries, the ratio was closer to 1:1.5. Parkinson's disease in these countries was more common in women. The first country in the file was Japan, in the Yamagata Prefecture.[88] The next country was South Korea.[89] Additionally, Luke had found a review on Parkinson's disease in Central Asia and Transcaucasia. In Kazakhstan and Uzbekistan, the disease was also more common in women.[90] Finally, Egypt was also in the file, but because here there was no significant difference in the male-to-female ratio.[91]

They started looking for specific data on manganese mining and toxicity, as well as water pollution in these countries. It didn't take long for them to uncover some interesting information. The first paper Michael found was on manganese being used in cosmetics. There were other reports of much higher levels in ground water, particularly in urban areas, which would fit with the industrial and vehicle sources of manganese.[92]

'There's a Yamagata mine,' Luke read out, 'it has manganese deposits.' He stopped, adding, 'It won't let me open the page.'

'How about this paper?' Michael pointed to a report of a

sabo dam in the Yamagata Prefecture that had led to an almost three hundred per cent increase in manganese concentration in the river downstream. Sabo dams were built in mountainous areas to prevent flooding and were commonplace due to the heavy rainfall typical of this region. Damming the river caused some of the elements, such as manganese, to accumulate.[93]

'The Yamagata plant was used for mining manganese in the 1940s, so there are deposits, but it's likely that the dam is the main problem,' Michael went on. 'The bottom line is that there is increased manganese in the water supply there.'

In agreement, they started looking for evidence in South Korea, but they found no significant manganese deposits or mining.

'It's steel!' Luke suddenly announced. 'They are the world's fourth largest steelmaker. It's their main industry.' Michael looked doubtful and Luke continued to explain that manganese is added as an alloying or a deoxidising agent to steel, and that over half of this is lost in the steelmaking slag.[94]

'There is still mercury pollution from iron and steel manufacturing, partly from burning coal, and also via blast furnace gas and limestone production,'[95] Michael said. He liked to put the other side to an argument.

'I agree, though manganese is possibly a greater issue. It's interesting that UK steel production has also decreased as Parkinson's disease prevalence has fallen, although there are still two steel works in South Wales, one of which is the largest in Europe.'

Michael was quiet for a while, busy looking up something. 'We never really explained the increased rates of Parkinson's in South Lanarkshire.' Michael looked smug. 'There was also a large steelworks in Motherwell, North Lanarkshire, and there's a cement factory in South Lanarkshire. Both processes increase mercury pollution.'

'Anyway, Egypt next,' Luke teased, feigning impatience to move onto the next country on their list. 'It's not strictly meeting the criteria for female preponderance, but it would be nice to explain why it's not more common in men like in the rest of the world.'

It was quiet for a while as they both tapped away. It felt strangely like they were in a race to explain the mystery of gender differences in the world. Luke banged his hand on the table, pressing the imaginary bell to end this exciting round of questions, as Michael imagined them both in a TV show, just without the witticism.

'I've got it!' Luke announced, perhaps slightly louder than was necessary, as Michael was sitting right next to him. 'The Nile Delta aquifers are contaminated with manganese as well as iron.'

It was true. There were several reports.[96, 97] The main sources seemed to be fertiliser use, as well as industries and petrochemical activities.

'So, they have manganese pollution in their water supply, but didn't you say that iron deficiency increases manganese absorption?'

'That's right,' Michael replied, failing to understand why this was so relevant in Egypt.

'Iron deficiency anaemia is a major problem in Egypt, due to hookworm infestation—it affects some forty per cent of the population. Both men and women are iron deficient. That's despite having iron in the water supply!'

Luke looked pleased with himself; he had definitely won that round. They celebrated with a drink.

Later that evening, Michael quietly investigated Kazakhstan and Uzbekistan. He didn't like to leave a job half done. Apparently, in the past, manganese deposits were widespread and extensively used for industry.[98] Manganese certainly seemed to be important in Kazakhstan, even more so now.[99] This probably meant it was in the water supply.

Michael also completed an investigative spiral and discovered a couple more interesting facts about manganese. Similar to iron, there was no obvious transporter to rid manganese from the brain after it had been taken up. It was fairly clear that repeated excess exposure would lead to toxic brain levels.[100] Dried leaves, eaten by the Chamorro people in Guam when they had their outbreak of Parkinsonian-like ALS, contained extremely high levels of manganese. He remembered reading about the cases of ALS, or Lou Gehrig's disease, that resembled manganism. Michael wondered whether manganism had actually been a contributory factor.[101] It was interesting that there had been no significant gender difference in the Parkinsonian-like disease on Guam.[102]

Mitochondrial poisons

Michael had noticed that suddenly there were a lot of people with tattoos locally, or maybe it was just that as the weather warmed up, the body art was revealed. It was springtime and the river walk was alive with daffodils, which wasn't something Michael had seen much of in the Midwest. After a Saturday morning stroll for provisions, they returned home for a midmorning coffee. Michael had a pastry while Luke had bought himself a vegan nutty flapjack.

'Did you read about this guy who developed Parkinson's from a tattoo?' Michael said.

'It wouldn't be Parkinson's disease; if the cause is known, it's Parkinsonism,' Luke retorted, trying to sound clever, but it didn't work.

'Ah, well, this is *The Sun* newspaper. Readers understand Parkinson's disease, so that's what it's called in the article. Anyway, the important thing is that he was twenty years old when he started twitching. After covering more than three quarters of his body with tattoos, he was diagnosed with Parkinson's disease. He thought he had a hangover twitch, so presumably he drank heavily too.' Michael showed Luke the article.[103]

Luke was able to explain that the toxic tattoo ink contained small amounts of the organic mercury, ethylmercury, which is closely related to methylmercury. The culprit was the chemical thimerosal—a preservative used in tattoo ink. In the past, thimerosal had also been used in multi-vial vaccines and some medicines.[104] It was scary that these products had been used on patients, particularly as the levels build up over time and are toxic to developing foetuses.

Michael felt he was overdue a little revision of the electron transfer chain—the high-energy-producing series of proteins in the mitochondrial membrane. With his competitive edge, he thought he would possibly have an advantage over Luke. After the end of medical school, the British system tested little in the way of basic physiology, while in the States, medics are routinely examined on basic physiology and pharmacology, as part of the licensing exam USMLE. Michael wasn't sure about the system in Granada, but Luke had also completed an elective in biochemistry, so his knowledge of these pathways was probably better than the average British-trained doctor.

Michael went over how the brain uses twenty per cent of the oxygen in the body, although it only makes up two per cent of the mass.

It's like a 6L engine requiring a high-performance fuel, he thought.

He recalled the car analogy he'd used to get the message across to university students back home. He tried to imagine how he would get the next part of the process across. There is a series of electron carriers in the inner mitochondrial membrane. *Like reusable bags*. It's the job of these electron carriers to transfer electrons from high-energy molecules, produced by earlier parts of respiration—the tricyclic acid cycle—onto oxygen.

It's like a relay race. The baton is the electron. Oxygen is waiting at the finish line to be turned into water, with the help of a little hydrogen.

The electrons flow through these electron carriers or protein complexes. As the negatively charged electrons flow out, positively charged protons—hydrogen ions—accumulate inside the inner part of the mitochondria, leading to a concentration gradient. As the hydrogen ions move through the mitochondrial membrane from a high concentration to a low concentration, they activate the enzyme ATP synthase, which converts ADP to ATP (adenosine di to tri phosphate). The extra phosphate group is added by phosphorylation. This is a high-energy reaction, and the final P-P bond is a high-energy bond. This energy can then be used anywhere in the body.

The P-P bond resembles a purse full of gold coins. Michael changed his mind. *No, more like a contactless debit card, tap and go, or tap-p, tap p and go.* These reactions were happening so fast, all the time—ATP produced in the mitochondria—broken down to ADP in the nerve and muscle cells—releasing energy. *And every day is Black Friday!*

There was an intricate relationship between each of these reactions, but the overriding equation was quite simple really.

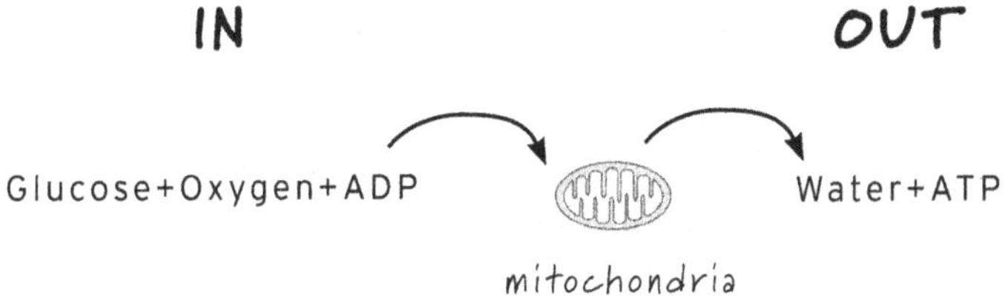

The most relevant part of this pretty complex energy transformer—*that's exactly what the mitochondria are, highly-efficient, miniscule transformers—the powerhouse of the cell*—is that methylmercury binds avidly to sulphur, and hence, it reacts with the iron-sulphur groups in the transmembrane complexes and interferes with enzyme function. Consequently, it disrupts electron transfer. *The fuse wire breaks. A mitochondrial power cut—a black out!* The most susceptible seemed to be complex I, because they contain eight of these iron-sulphur complexes. Damage to complex I causes premature electron leakage. *A hole in one of the carrier bags.* This leads to the production of superoxide anions—$O2^-$ and oxidation.

Even worse, methylmercury binding to sulphur leads to the release of free iron from the iron-sulphur compounds. Free iron generates free radicals. *Those Jacobins on the loose!* The most dangerous is the hydroxyl radical.

Likewise, other chemicals known to cause Parkinson's disease, the pesticides paraquat and rotenone, and the derivative of synthetic heroin, MPP+, also inhibit complex I.[105] Interestingly, cocaine inhibits complex I too, potentially lowering the threshold for the development of Parkinson's disease.[106] Did all these toxins—mercury, synthetic heroin, cocaine and paraquat work synergistically to destroy the mitochondria in the basal ganglia?

Post-mortem studies on the brains of patients with Parkinson's disease have shown three things: reduced activity of complex I, increased iron, and an increase in free radicals.

This was it. The evidence Luke had been searching for.

This was how mercury could cause Parkinson's disease, but it wasn't the only toxin capable of doing damage. Once the cascade of events had been unleashed, it continued to cause widespread chaos and disruption.

The highly oxidising hydroxyl radical precipitated a series

of harmful reactions, damaging mitochondrial DNA, the genetic material in the mitochondria that maintains the proteins required for energy release. Mitochondrial DNA was more vulnerable to oxidative damage, as it wasn't protected by histone—housekeeping proteins, unlike DNA in the cells' nuclei. Abnormally produced proteins disrupted the electron transfer chain, releasing yet more of the free radicals. *Prison outbreak!* The end result was a cycle of free radical production and, ultimately, senescence—ageing, due to an increased number of errors in the mitochondrial DNA.[105]

Michael had to admit that the evidence was definitely stacking up against mercury as the culprit. *Circumstantial evidence, but nonetheless compelling*. It clearly wasn't the only environmental agent, but in the current climate, as toxins go, it was probably in the lead. *Still, innocent until proven guilty. No!* He disagreed with himself. *No amount of mercury is safe, advisable or, therefore, acceptable.*

The next part made him very excited. After giving rats methylmercury, they were treated with a specific iron chelator (deferoxamine) and the rats' brains were protected. Free iron was definitely implicated in the damage in Parkinson's disease.[107] Other studies have looked to see if the deferoxamine binds to mercury, and it doesn't.

Michael wondered if this would contribute to the gender difference, which was particularly prominent in Western countries; the lower iron level in women provides some protection against mercury toxicity but makes them more vulnerable to manganese pollution. He'd read that there was also an increased risk of Parkinson's in those who consumed a lot of red meat.

Joe!

It seemed too simple, and yet iron appeared to be central to the damage, and reducing iron levels seemed to confer some protection from the effects of mercury. Importantly, the mercury was concentrated in the nerve cells and then super-concentrated in the mitochondria.

Can't beat the real thing

Michael and Luke had explored the riverside, and the nearby broads, which were classed as an 'area of outstanding beauty'. The overarching skies and marshland fields with whispering reeds reminded Michael of the prairies back home. Luke also took Michael to see the seals on the north Norfolk coast. The city of Norwich was pleasant, with some charming old buildings and lots of history, but the surrounding countryside was stunning, particularly south of the city, which had remained largely unspoiled by urbanisation.

Michael told Luke about the way mercury destroyed mitochondria—the cells' batteries. It was good to understand the mechanism. Meanwhile, Luke was still tracking cases all over the world. 'Do you remember the other countries with a higher prevalence of Parkinson's disease? I think we should check them out too. I looked up Alaska but drifted over to Greenland.'

There was no data from the global study in Greenland, but they clearly had a problem with Parkinson's disease. 'The crude prevalence is eighty-one per hundred thousand,' said Luke, 'but this is because there are fewer people over fifty, and Parkinson's disease basically presents in older people—'

'When the toxins of your misspent middle-age catch up with you!' Michael interjected.

'Yes, that! Well, the age-adjusted prevalence is a whopping one hundred and eighty-eight.'[108] And the answer you've been waiting for,' he was back in TV-host mode, 'mercury concentrations in Greenlanders were elevated due to exposure in their diet.'[109]

'Fish!' Michael shook his head sadly. 'We've poisoned the fish and now they're poisoning us right back.'

'It's not always about fish!' Luke said in a mock retort. 'Hey, this is interesting,' he was off again, 'mercury concentrations are even higher in Faroe Islanders, and they have a high prevalence of Parkinson's disease.'[110] He was on another spiral.

'That's to do with artisan gold mining,' Michael said. He remembered reading about the countries with significant gold reserves and unregulated mining. Meanwhile, he had tried to find out more about the Inuit people and had ended up back in Canada. 'Apparently, the Inuit hunt for seals all year. No wonder they have high levels of mercury. They are eating from the top of the food chain. That's where the methylmercury levels will be highest. Oh, now this is hugely controversial. The local government is damming a waterfall in Labrador to produce hydroelectricity, but they know it will pollute the river that the Inuit people depend upon for their livelihood.' He showed the paper to Luke. 'It's well known that hydroelectric development leads to increased methylmercury levels.'

Studies on other dams had shown that there was more methylmercury downstream, as it is produced in the organic matter at the bottom of the lake, and it is these lower waters that tend to flow through the dam.[111]

'First we poison the water with coal and then we make it worse by damming it.' Luke sounded angry, then bothered. 'So, you're saying damming rivers can actually make mercury contamination worse?'

'Yes.' Michael thought Luke already knew this.

'So, the dam across the Yangtze River, what's it called?' He clicked his fingers trying to recall the name. 'Yes, the Three Gorges Dam, that will increase the mercury levels downstream.'

Michael was looking it up. 'It flows through Hubei province, into a city called Wuhan. Yes, it will. Hang on! There are dams on the Sacramento River too. Do you think that'll increase the methylmercury levels downstream?'

He remembered the impact that these dams had had on the Chinook salmon. 'Dammed if we do, dammed if we don't,' he laughed, rather too loudly. 'Do you get it?'

It was one of his dreadful jokes that really made no sense, but that he found funny, and Luke couldn't help chuckling too. Michael now had total body shakes, with tears rolling down his face. The two of them were hysterical at the direness of their discoveries.

When they had finally recovered, Michael pointed out that Canada's guidelines on the amount of methylmercury that can be consumed were laxer than in the United States.[111] He was shaking his head in despair.

'If it's in the soil and the water, and it contaminates fish, then surely it could affect crops?' he said, checking out how mercury infiltrated crops. 'Here, look.' He showed Luke an abstract from a mining area that confirmed his suspicion that mercury enters the food chain and accumulates in crops, animal feed and even cow's milk.[112] Interestingly, there seemed to be quite a lot of evidence that dairy consumption increased the risk of Parkinson's. Michael also read that there was a greater prevalence of Parkinson's disease among Hispanics in California.[113] He wondered why this was, and whether mercury accumulated in corn, but he could find no evidence of this.

'In fact,' he said, 'it's a good way of ridding mercury in the atmosphere. Corn is a biospheric sink!'[114] As a biospheric sink for mercury, corn took up atmospheric mercury into the leafy parts of the plant. Plants were biospheric sinks for carbon, too—they took in carbon dioxide from the atmosphere for photosynthesis. Some of this carbon was transferred to the soil as plants died and decomposed. Michael loved new words. *Biospheric sink*. Luke could see how he was trying to turn this into a memorable ditty for his students. 'That's a corny story!' he added, pleased with himself.

'But there is mercury in other crops,' Luke added, 'vegetables are worse than grains, but both exceed standards. It's especially bad near coal-fired power stations. Leaves are worse than roots. Rice is bad too. Apparently, by washing the vegetables or grain the levels can be reduced. In heavily contaminated areas, it's best to grow maize instead of rice, as it contains less mercury.'[114, 115]

'Obesity is more of a problem in Mexican-American children,' Michael chirped up. He was still chasing an explanation for the increased prevalence in Hispanics. If it wasn't cornmeal, what was it? The major sources of mercury seemed to be air pollution from coal-fired power stations. There were no such power-generating plants in California, as the state imported energy from neighbouring Utah, New Mexico and Arizona. Yet it still had mercury pollution from historic gold mining in the middle of the nineteenth century. Fish consumption was a major cause worldwide of mercury poisoning. Chemical industries had also caused outbreaks, such examples were Minamata in the 1950s and Grassy Narrows in the 1960s. In Grassy Narrows, it was caused by a chloralkali plant. There was a chloralkali plant in Santa Fe Springs, California. It now seemed likely that low-grade, chronic exposure might be an issue.

'Mercury can be found in high-fructose corn syrup, not corn, but cola!' Michael sounded very pleased with himself. 'Chloralkali plants are also used to produce food stuffs, such as citric acid, sodium benzoate and high-fructose corn syrup. They tested samples and found that there was mercury in the syrup. This is not only added to soda, but also some food, such as sweet yoghurts and frozen junk food, to increase the shelf life.'[116]

'Yuk!' Luke was horrified.

'Yes, they use caustic soda and hydrochloric acid to produce high-fructose corn syrup,' Michael added. 'Seriously, you drink lots of this stuff with mercury in it, then it rots your teeth and the dentist fills them with yet more mercury to top up the levels!'

★

Luke had finished early for the day and was preparing roasted pepper and squash risotto for supper, served with cavolo nero and yeast flakes. Michael would have parmesan, but this wasn't vegetarian, as it contained rennet, an enzyme from goats or calves' stomachs. The yeast flakes contained vitamin B12, which was a good supplement essential for vegans.

Michael was on his way home, after attending one of the regular departmental meetings at the university. He was hoping to collaborate on some of the ongoing projects. It had taken ages to sort out the administration. Thankfully, most of the paperwork had now been completed and he was allowed to stay and work in the UK, although it hadn't been easy. There were so many forms—so much bureaucracy. He had found it daunting, even with good English skills, a friend to call on and years of practice filling in forms.

'I don't understand,' Luke called out as Michael walked in. 'I've been looking for any evidence of mercury in the brain, but if you search "post-mortem", "Parkinson's" and "mercury", nothing comes up. Surely someone would have tested for it, even if it was a negative study?'

Luke continued to tap away on his phone, while waiting for supper to cook. 'Here's one. No kidding! This paper summarises it beautifully. "Methylmercury toxicity is poorly understood." I'll send you the link. Hey, Michael, what do you know about selenium?'

'Is this one of your trick questions? Pub quiz? *University Challenge?*'

'No. Seriously. There's a study on patients poisoned with mercury and they had increased selenium in their brains. I've left it on the desk.'

Michael proceeded to read through the study of five cases, four with varying degrees of mercury exposure and one control. The first case had suffered acute mercury poisoning from eating contaminated pork aged eight. She had lived with brain damage until she died in her late twenties. There was no methylmercury in her brain, although there was an increase in selenium and a mercuric selenide. There were other cases of more chronic exposure, with significant amounts of methylmercury and lower levels of this mercuric selenide, which is non-toxic.[117] Methylmercury, the organic mercury, is more readily taken up into the brain. Inorganic mercury is more likely to get into the brain from the breakdown of organic mercury, and it doesn't cross the blood-brain barrier very well. Once in the brain, inorganic mercury binds with selenium. This is effectively a detoxification process, as mercuric selenide is chemically and physically unreactive. One theory was that mercury scavenged selenium, causing a deficiency of selenium in the brain and other tissues. There was little transport of selenium into the brain and, consequently, only limited potential for detoxification.

'Selenium is an essential trace element and micronutrient—' Michael tried to answer Luke's last question.

'Yes, I know all that,' Luke replied, rather rudely. 'Anything about selenium-containing enzymes?' he asked, looking up from the stove.

Michael sighed, but started searching for information, although he thought supper was more important right now, as Luke was probably hungry, which is why he'd been short with him. 'There are quite a few enzymes that contain selenium. They look important too. They're involved in the cellular response to oxidative stress, protein folding and redox reactions. There are quite a few of these oxidoreductases.'[118] Michael showed Luke the list. He nodded and carried on stirring the risotto.

Michael discovered that glutathione peroxidase is one of these selenium-containing enzymes, and that its main role was to provide protection from oxidative damage, such as from hydroxyl radicals. There were areas in the United States, including one rural location that was predominantly Amish, where the soil selenium was naturally low. Here, people had a significantly lower level of selenium in their blood, and they were found to have a lower concentration of glutathione peroxidase.[119] Michael also found out that there was a variable amount of selenium in the soil due to the type of rock present in China, with a selenium-poor belt across Central China that included parts of Shaanxi, around Xi'an and Hebei, and around Beijing.[120]

Michael told Luke what he had found out and updated him on a few geological facts. 'It seems that it is just unfortunate to have low selenium, as it is generally found in minute amounts virtually everywhere, although rarely unbound and usually as a constituent of a compound. It is found in igneous rocks, sedimentary rocks, hydrothermal deposits, and as a compound, such as with silver, gold and mercury. So, nature put mercury and the natural antidote, selenium, together—it's just that man messed it up!'

★

After they'd eaten, Luke joined Michael and caught up with the latest line of investigation. 'In the Western states, but not in California,' he said, 'selenium content in the soil tends to be high and produces vegetation toxic to animals. In eastern parts of Canada, selenium levels are low.'

'Yep! Double whammy!' Michael added. 'High mercury, low selenium. That can't be good.'[121]

'It's worse,' Luke continued. 'Selenium intake is inversely related to methylmercury toxicity. It's been known for decades.' He was shaking his head. 'It causes far worse disease if there is a dietary deficiency of selenium. In fact, selenium can prevent methylmercury toxicity and even reverse some of the more severe symptoms. They've studied populations that eat fish such as shark, where the methylmercury is higher than the selenium content, and the children do badly. Other populations eat selenium-rich fish, such as yellow-fin tuna and salmon, and there is an improvement in the child's IQ.'[122]

'It's the same with fish and thiamine,' Michael added. Luke stopped talking for a moment, not quite sure if his fellow detective had been following his line of thought. Michael continued, oblivious. 'Some fish naturally have a higher thiamine content, which protects the predator fish from thiamine deficiency,' he said, and by way of an explanation, added, 'taking the poison with the antidote.'

PART III

Blue circles

Michael had been working at the university for a year. Luke had finished his PhD and was now applying for a substantive consultant post. Meanwhile, he was working as a locum consultant pending the advertisement of a permanent position locally. There was no certainty that this would be forthcoming, or that he would be appointed. He'd learnt that it was better not to dwell too much on the future.

Michael had his own work on water pollution to pursue. He was enjoying the company of his new colleagues, many of whom had a background in medicine and shared his interest in the gut-brain link. He had started by setting up assays, then filling in the endless forms for grant money and the ethical approval required before he could start collecting samples. He reflected on the set up he had left behind. At this rate it would be years before he would see any results. The system in the UK seemed particularly cumbersome.

Michael understood that as a possible underlying mechanism for Parkinson's disease, Luke was now investigating infectious proteins. *Proteins causing infections, whatever they were.* This was way outside Michael's field of knowledge. He was aware that most of Luke's time was now taken up with clinical work.

It was the weekend and Michael and Luke were engrossed in their own reading. Michael had recently come across an article about so-called Blue Zones—the five locations in the world where people have been found to live the longest.

Mitochondrial mutations were reported to be associated with ageing. Presumably living longer meant less mitochondrial damage. As mitochondria were allegedly involved, Michael was looking for an explanation at each site. The researcher clearly enjoyed maps, too, and had circled these areas. The blue circles provided the name, Blue Zones.

The places were extremely diverse, not just the locations, but the types of countries: Sardinia in Italy, Okinawa in Japan, Nicoya in Costa Rica, Loma Linda in California and Ikaria in Greece. The obvious explanation was sunshine. These sites were all closer to the equator than the poles. The article also informed the reader that the inhabitants in each case consumed a largely plant-based diet.[123] Michael thought rather smugly about the healthy diet he and Luke had adopted, mostly thanks to Luke. He spent a pleasant couple of hours looking through tourist guides, which were far more descriptive than medical articles. There were very few scientific articles written about these places.

Another factor all of these places had in common was that they were isolated, and much less populated. The descriptions included terms such as 'rugged', 'wild', 'off the beaten track', 'untouched', 'remote' and 'unspoiled'. The description Michael liked the most was 'gorgeously unruly', and he just wanted to add 'darling!' They were generally hilly, or even mountainous; several were volcanic. Ikaria was known as 'red rock', as the island resembles a mountain emerging from the sea. Nicoya was called a steaming volcano. Rising sharply out of the ocean was a definite theme, which wasn't surprising as they were clearly volcanic in origin, but there were also volcanic interiors and emerald mountains.

Michael started looking up each place in turn, focusing particularly on the water provisions. Beginning with Sardinia, he discovered that there was one natural lake—Lake Baratz, and also a number of reservoirs, which had been constructed in 1870 to meet the island's water requirements. As a result, eighty per cent of the water was provided by surface water, with a small contribution from wells. Most importantly, there hadn't been a water shortage, although there were concerns for the future, largely due to reduced rainfall in recent times.[124] The Fukuji Dam on the island complex of Okinawa in Japan was completed in 1972 to provide water and prevent floods. It apparently keeps water supplies flowing.[125]

In Costa Rica, a quarter of the country is protected by national parks, and it has one of the highest levels of biodiversity on the planet. Okinawa also had a huge range of wildlife, much of it underwater, such as unspoiled coral reefs, which showed that the water was not polluted. In fact, each place had ample clean water for most of the year, either due to a rainy season or snow melt. There were lush rainforests, mangrove swamps, jungles, tumbling waterfalls and mineral thermal hot springs.

People generally inhabited villages or lived in the mountains. They had a self-sufficient model of living, eating sustainable foods, locally caught fish or farmed fruit, vegetables, grains and pulses. Okinawa had only two thousand inhabitants.

Michael was particularly interested in the people of Loma Linda, who were the longest living Americans, enjoying a lifespan that was seven years longer than their North American counterparts. They were also religious—Seventh Day Adventists. Michael didn't think God was the reason for their longevity, but the fact that, as part of their religion, they had no caffeine, caffeinated sodas or alcohol may have helped. They also had a 'Garden of Eden' diet, as told in the Book of Genesis, replacing meat protein with seed and grain protein.

Genesis 129

'And God said behold I have given you every herb bearing seed . . . and every tree in which is a tree-yielding seed, to you it shall be for meat.'

They are mostly lacto-ovo vegetarians, consuming some animal products, but no pork or shellfish. According to the Bible, the clean animals are the ones that eat leaves and grass. This is basically advising eating at the lower trophic levels, towards the bottom of the food chain.

Interestingly, there were some scientific studies on the Nicoyan people from Costa Rica, where a man has a seven times greater probability of becoming a centenarian compared to a man living in Japan, where males already enjoy longevity compared to the rest of the world.

Nicoya is a peninsular, where most of the people live in hilly terrain. The mortality rate is lowest for those who are born and live their life in this area. Those who are born outside the peninsular and move to Nicoya have a slightly higher mortality rate, and then for those who are born in Nicoya and move out it is slightly higher still. Clearly, the advantage in Nicoya is the environment.[126]

'What are you reading?' Luke asked, looking up from his computer screen.

'I've just been on a fabulous round-the-world adventure, all without leaving the comfort of my own home, well, actually, your home. It's perfectly marvellous—Dan Buettner's "The Blue Zones". I've been visiting the places where people live the longest. Fascinating stuff.'

Michael started to explain about the five areas he'd read

about in the National Geographic article, written by an explorer, journalist and now author. Another interesting fact was that there was almost no dementia in these places. There were also fewer functional disabilities.[127]

'There was one strange thing. In Nicoya, the longevity advantage only occurs in men, not women. I wondered if maybe there was an external force. Out of curiosity, I searched manganese.' Michael had recalled how manganese levels were higher in women. Costa Rica has manganese, which has been mined. The deposits were all in the Nicoya region.[128]

When he reread the article written about the global prevalence of Parkinson's, he realised there were very few cases on the volcanic African islands of Cape Verde and almost none on São Tomé and Principe. The subtropical island of Cape Verde had recently been discovered by tourists and the natural springs no longer provided a sufficient water supply, so the country was dependent on desalination programmes. Electricity was produced using generators, with an increasing amount from renewable sources. São Tomé and Principe were close to the equator. They were known as the African Gálapagos and they had encouraged eco-friendly tourism. Consequently, there had been far fewer tourists, partly as a result of it being less accessible. The area was described as consisting of steep mountains covered in thick jungle, with subsistence agriculture, which sounded just like a Blue Zone.

'Which countries have the highest prevalence of dementia? Do we know that?' Michael asked Luke.

'The same group who mapped out global Parkinson's disease prevalence collected data for dementia. There's another map.' Luke nudged Michael. 'I'll find it.'

The map and the paper were easily accessible online. There

was no data for Oceania, Central Asia, Eastern Europe or southern Sub-Saharan Africa. There was a clear, deep-orange shade for Turkey, as the worst country for the age-standardised prevalence of Alzheimer's dementia. This was closely followed by Brazil, and then the North African countries: Morocco, Algeria, Tunisia, Libya, missing out Egypt, and then the Middle Eastern countries: Yemen, Saudi Arabia and Syria, through to Iran and Afghanistan.[129]

'Do you think that Alzheimer's dementia could have anything to do with the water pollution in these countries?' Michael asked.

They searched for any information to support this idea. For each of these countries in turn they found incriminating evidence online—'Rivers turned into open sewers,' 'Dirty water mixed with potable water' and 'Contamination of water with faecal material.' In Brazil, there were reports of faecal bacteria befouling waters in the Guanabara Bay, and tons of dead fish had been found floating in the water. In the run up to the Olympics in 2016, the government had denied a problem, but the scientists had blamed water pollution.

'What about the United States? Any stats for the individual states? You know how I like a good map,' Michael chuckled.

'You'll have to draw this one yourself. I have a table with all the states. They've used the Medicare and Medicaid data. Guess which is the state with the highest death rate, and presumably the most severe disease burden?' Luke asked.

'Pub quiz time,' Michael replied, raising his eyebrows, but actually enjoying the banter. He shrugged, 'I really don't know. Florida?' he guessed.

'Mississippi,' Luke replied, studious for a few minutes. 'The prevalence doesn't change that much between states.'

He explained that although the prevalence was between ten and fourteen per cent, the age-adjusted death rate, which gave an easier comparison between states with different age populations, was significantly different. Luke was reordering the states according to the age-adjusted death rate. 'Mississippi, then Tennessee, Georgia, Alabama, South Carolina, Louisiana, Arkansas . . .'[130]

'Tennessee, Arkansas, Mississippi and Louisiana – these states are all downstream of Chicago along the Mississippi River. And the lowest death rate? Which states have the fewest people dying with Alzheimer's?'

'New York State, then Maryland, the District of Columbia and Hawaii. But New York and Columbia both have a high prevalence of cases, whereas Hawaii and Maryland have a low prevalence and a low mortality rate.'

'And Hawaii is a volcanic island,' Michael said to himself. He'd started to look up the island's water supply. 'They have extensive aquifer systems, but demand is predicted to be an issue in the future.'

'The rate of dementia in Hawaii may be one of the lowest in the States, however, the rates of Parkinson's aren't low,' Luke added. There were concerns about methylmercury levels in fish and fish consumption.[131] However, the rate of male to female Parkinson's disease cases was similar to Egypt and interestingly, Hawaii was known to have manganese toxicity in the soil.[132, 133] 'There is definitely a pattern.' Luke shook his head seriously.

Michael was already looking up Maryland water quality. Apparently, no state was blameless, but Maryland was a decade ahead in terms of the standard of the water. The main problems with sewage seemed to occur around the Northeast and the

Great Lakes region, although some of the older cities, such as Atlanta, San Francisco and Memphis, also had problems. These places still had combined sewer systems, where human and industrial waste and storm water are all collected into the same pipe. The problem is that with escalating population growth and industrialisation, in addition to heavier rains, the pipes can't cope with the volume of storm and sewage produced, so there is often overspill. The overspill is a design feature to prevent back up coming into houses, but instead it flows into rivers, the sea or even onto the street, polluting the drinking water. Waste spilled in Ohio or Chicago affects everyone downstream.[134]

Michael thought back to the storm in 1992 and the massive floods across large swathes of the States along the Mississippi and Missouri Rivers. Then there was the Chicago Loop flood in 1993. This was before the massive increase in the deaths of salmon fry and before Joe developed Parkinson's disease.

'Did you know Canada has the highest life expectancy in the Americas?' Michael had been genning up on these facts. 'As Parkinson's disease affects older people, I thought this might be relevant. I mean, clearly, it's not the only reason for the high prevalence. Oh, and I read somewhere that Libya has a low prevalence of Parkinson's disease, but again, that might be to do with a shorter than average life expectancy.'

*

Michael had been enlightening his new colleagues at the university on the putative role of thiaminase, and how it caused diseases associated with thiamine deficiency in the animal world. He suspected it may link to human diseases spread by water pollution. Reading about longevity, clean water and the lack of cognitive impairment in the Blue Zones had only reinforced his belief. He was now aware that eating foods higher up the food chain was potentially harmful due to the toxins that bioaccumulate, and yet eating foods lower down the chain may still contain unfiltered bacterial contaminants.

He had extended his reading to some of the areas mentioned in the Alzheimer's dementia prevalence study; he tried to find evidence of thiamine deficiency in these areas and instead discovered there had been a large outbreak of beriberi, due to thiamine deficiency, among illegal gold miners in French Guiana. These people seemed to have a reasonably thiamine-rich diet, made up of pulses, chicken and fish. Interestingly, there were no figures for this country in the Alzheimer's prevalence study.[135] A quarter of the miners in this article admitted to handling mercury. It was clear that there were multiple mines like these polluting the Amazon River and fish downstream, and that hygiene conditions were poor. These riverbank communities lacked basic sanitation. There were reports of untreated sewage being discharged directly into the Amazon.

Sewage and thiamine deficiency—another recurring theme.

Colour change

Michael had been into the university for a meeting. Since the weekend he had been dwelling on the Blue Zones. He wondered whether this survival advantage would be ongoing if these places struggled with sanitation and water supplies in a changing climate. Or perhaps longevity in other areas would catch up if we all adopted a plant-based diet. He'd read that the most important factor was beans. *Beans!* A balanced vegetarian diet had to contain beans to provide sufficient protein. Beans were also an excellent source of thiamine.

Mulling over this thought, he tried to find out if there was any association between thiamine deficiency and mercury. He ended up on blog sites, as these were the first searches that popped up. It was good to know he wasn't the only one who had made a connection. Thiamine was used in a mercury assay—to measure mercury levels, and mercury was used in a thiamine assay—to measure thiamine levels; so clearly there was a chemical reaction that took place between the two. Mercury seemed to oxidise thiamine, producing a thiochrome—chrome meaning colour. The colour change was presumably what was used in the assay, similar to the thiaminase assay he had used, which involved colour change but not mercury. One site also noted that the symptoms of thiamine deficiency and mercury toxicity were similar. The reason mercury binds to thiamine is because thiamine has a sulphur group. *Of course*. Mercury binds well to sulphur, selenium and gold. Michael wondered whether mercury interfered with thiamine in some way, and if inactivating thiamine caused deficiency.

He remembered the lady from clinic that Luke had mentioned—the one with bacterial overgrowth and thiamine deficiency. He hadn't realised that humans, like fish, could suffer the consequences of thiaminase disease, with the identical bacteria.[136] He looked to see if Parkinson's disease had been linked to thiaminase, but unsurprisingly there were no results. He postulated that mercury would make an individual more susceptible to thiamine deficiency, particularly where there were borderline levels.

Thiamine had been used to treat a small number of patients with Parkinson's disease.[137,138] He wondered whether there was any reason to suspect bacterial overgrowth in the development of Parkinson's. He was astounded to find that there was even evidence that Parkinson's doesn't start in the brain.

'It starts in the gut,' he suddenly announced to Luke, who had returned late from an evening ward round. 'Parkinson's disease. Patients often get constipation and gut disturbance, many years before they notice the tremor.'[139] It wasn't at all clear why, and Luke didn't seem that interested. After all, he was a specialist in brains and nerves.

Researchers had tried to see if there were different bacteria involved. 'The lady from clinic had complained of cognitive impairment, the one with a dementia-like illness.' Michael tried to involve Luke again. 'It had been cured with intravenous thiamine and long-term antibiotics.'

'And intravenous vitamin C,' Luke added, removing his coat.

Michael realised he hadn't actually asked a question. 'So, did she have bacterial overgrowth?' he asked this time.

'I think she may have done,' Luke replied vaguely, sounding tired.

There was a pause, as Luke wandered into the kitchen to find something to eat and Michael returned to his reading. There was an article suggesting that dementia occurs in Parkinson's in up to half of the patients, usually within ten years of diagnosis. Mild cognitive impairment was actually common on diagnosis but didn't necessarily progress to dementia.[140]

A group in Italy had found that more than half of the patients with Parkinson's disease had evidence of small intestinal bacterial overgrowth using a glucose, lactulose breath test. The Parkinsonian motor symptoms were more difficult to control in the presence of gut bacteria, and treatment with antibiotics to eradicate the small intestinal bacterial overgrowth resulted in improvements in motor function, which were repeatable. The patients with bacteria in their gut had slower gut movements. Unfortunately, there was a high relapse rate.[141,142]

Parkinson's often occurred in clusters and one of the explanations was that it was contagious and could be spread by the faecal-oral route, like many gut infections. This report also mentioned Michael J Fox and the fact that he was in his early thirties when he started developing symptoms. Young onset Parkinson's disease is usually genetic and is thought to affect three to four per cent of sufferers, however, the actor was part of a cluster of cases, which hinted at an environmental origin. The reporter suggested that it pointed to an infective cause.[143] Clusters seemed to be more common in certain groups: teachers, medical workers, loggers, miners and farmers. Some of these obviously had occupational exposure to heavy metals or pesticides, known environmental causes—loggers, miners and farmers—but teachers and medical workers? Were they exposed to infections through their occupations?[144]

A Finnish study had looked back at the number of antibiotic prescriptions and found an association between Parkinson's disease and the prior use of certain antibiotics. Antibiotics were known to alter the microbial balance in the gut.[145]

Michael quizzed Luke on the case from clinic and the other interesting fact was that the lady had been severely deficient in vitamin D, which was thought to be due to small intestinal bacterial overgrowth. Interestingly, Parkinson's disease patients were found to have a significantly low vitamin D level, and the lower the level the worse the motor symptoms.[146] Perhaps bacterial overgrowth was important in Parkinson's disease too. He was determined to carry on looking into the significance of thiamine in this disorder.

Lobster

Meanwhile, Luke had been looking to see if there was any support for the use of chelators to treat Parkinson's disease, by detoxing the body of heavy metals. 'Chelation is an interesting word,' he pointed out to Michael. 'It's literally from "Chele"—the claws of a lobster.'

'Reminds me of a mechanical grabber at a pile of scrapped cars, picking up metal.'

Michael had a vivid imagination and Luke could tell he was thinking in lecture mode again.

Instituting chelation therapy for Parkinson's disease was tricky, because by definition the diagnosis of it in the UK was made after excluding known toxins, such as the synthetic heroin, MPTP.[147,148] Surely this also included heavy metal poisoning? Luke found this frustrating, as clearly it is not possible to rule out chronic, low-grade exposure, which is so ubiquitous and had proved to be impossible to measure in any samples, even after death. Taking blood levels in patients to see if they have been exposed to mercury was useless. A blood mercury level might be increased after acute toxicity, but after chronic exposure mercury was practically undetectable. The levels might be increased in the mitochondria, but a mitochondrial biopsy was not feasible. He looked for any evidence of chelator use in cases where heavy metal exposure wasn't known.

Wilson's disease is a rare autosomal recessive genetic condition. Patients with the condition have low levels of the copper-transporter protein—caeruloplasmin—in their blood. This means that they tend to accumulate copper in the liver and the brain rather than excrete excess amounts through the gut. Diagnosis is tricky due to variable presentation, but they could present with Parkinson-like symptoms.

There was a case where Parkinsonism improved with the use of a metal chelator.[149] It wasn't clear whether copper had contributed to the Parkinsonian features or whether the patient had other heavy-metal poisoning in addition to the copper-related damage. Another case was a forty-two-year-old man who had presented with Parkinson's disease five years previously, so at quite a young age. His symptoms were difficult to control, and as his caeruloplasmin—the protein that transports copper—was reduced. He was given the heavy metal chelator penicillamine, which resulted in an improvement in his symptoms.[150]

The first case was from Hong Kong and the second from Kyoto, Japan. Consumption of fish in both countries was common and had long been known to be a significant cause of mercury poisoning.[151]

Michael tried to find out if there were any other reasons why caeruloplasmin might be important. It seemed to be involved in controlling the oxidative status of iron. Michael remembered that this was important in the stability of the mitochondria. Caeruloplasmin oxidises the conversion of iron II (Fe^{2+}) to iron III (Fe^{3+}). Hence, low caeruloplasmin levels might have caused higher levels of iron II, which in turn increases free radical production.

Caeruloplasmin also helps by binding iron to the iron transporters—the transferrins. These are the body's inhouse iron chelators. Low caeruloplasmin was actually recognised in Parkinson's disease, where it was associated with a greater iron deposition in the substantia nigra.[152] It seemed that caeruloplasmin was potentially important in neurodegenerative diseases, not just in Wilson's disease.

The most well-known medical chelator, simply known as EDTA (calcium disodium ethylene-diamine-tetra-acetic acid), is able to remove many different heavy metals. An interesting study from Italy had used intravenous EDTA and collected urine samples after the infusions. Scientists measured the amount of heavy metal excreted in the urine as an indicator of the toxic metal burden. They were able to demonstrate that weekly chelation therapy to eliminate heavy metal poisoning was safe and effective in many cases. Disappointingly, however, although several different metals were mentioned, there were no specific cases relating to mercury and Parkinson's disease.[153]

Another search for chelation in Parkinson's disease led Luke to a review from India, which was interesting, though not quite what he was expecting. He scanned through, looking for the chelation therapy, and read about a reduced prevalence rate of Parkinson's in the slums. In most other countries, there had been no socio-economic impact, and yet here you fared better while living in poverty. The only significant environmental risk factor was well water. Tobacco smoking was protective, by a factor of five. Smoking really did seem to prevent Parkinson's disease. *Curious!* The smoking of bidis, which are thin, hand-rolled cigarettes in leaves, seemed to provide even higher protection. This was thought to be due to their higher levels of nicotine, amongst other things.

Luke finally found the part in the review on Parkinson's treatment that talked about eliminating toxins. Panchakarma was a traditional, alternative medicine known as Ayurvedic therapy. There was a focus on wellbeing through the use of massage and steam baths, as well as certain herbs that induced vomiting and laxatives that caused diarrhoea. It also recommended *Mucuna pruriens*—velvet bean, and *Withania Somnifera*—Indian ginseng, a member of the nightshade family.[154] Ayurvida literally means the 'Science of Life', but to Luke this didn't seem very scientific at all.

Natively unfolded

'Found anything interesting?' Michael asked. He was aware that Luke had been obsessed with something for a couple of days; whenever he was home, he always seemed deep in thought. Michael had also been busy, as he had been lecturing the undergraduates and had their curriculum to incorporate into his research interests.

'I've been investigating the prion theory for Parkinson's disease,' Luke replied.

'Prion?' Michael sensed Luke was onto something. 'You mean the infectious proteins?'

'Yes, there are prions that can move along nerves. It's really quite fascinating. Parkinson's disease occurs less often in patients who have had the main nerve from their gut cut,' Luke explained in non-medical terminology, while Michael winced. 'It's OK, it's called a truncal vagotomy, and in the past, it was used as a treatment for stomach ulcers. The vagus nerve controls acid secretion in the stomach, and so, without an intact vagus nerve, there's no acid and no ulcer. Nowadays, we have pills for this.'

Michael realised that Luke was oversimplifying things, but so far, he had followed. 'These patients were found to have a reduced risk of future Parkinson's disease. But it had to be the full vagotomy. A partial or selective snip didn't protect against the disease.'

Michael mimed snipping with his fingers, whilst pulling a face. He hadn't been totally reassured by the explanation.[155,156] 'Are they sure it wasn't to do with the reduction in acid?' he asked. 'What about the pills?' He was thinking about his findings that linked bacterial overgrowth to Parkinson's. 'Basically, it all starts in the gut.'

'No, I checked. It doesn't happen with the pills. So, I—'

Michael interrupted him. 'But did you see the papers reporting how medication that reduces acid, proton pump inhibitors—is that what they're called?—increase the risk of dementia? Interesting, eh?'[157]

Michael had found out something else that potentially backed up his theory, and he wanted to see whether this was the mechanism in Parkinson's disease. He found what he was looking for in an online biomedical archive. 'You're right! There's no association with Parkinson's disease. And what about dumping? These patients have malabsorption from sudden bouts of diarrhoea after eating. Perhaps that reduces the absorption of mercury, and hence there are fewer cases?'

Michael was challenging Luke, who seemed to have completely changed tack from the pollution and poisoning theory. He felt the betrayal, like in the lab.

'OK, it could be,' Luke replied, 'but I couldn't find any evidence to support that. Let me fill you in on prions.'

'Prions. You mean the infectious proteins that cause mad cow disease,' Michael said sulkily. He had heard about the cull of thousands of cows in the late eighties, but he was unsure how Luke had transferred allegiance from Parkinson's disease to cattle ailments. He huffed, as he drew his chair up closer.

Luke explained a little more about Bovine Spongiform Encephalopathy, which was also known as BSE or mad cow disease. Affected animals would walk abnormally, develop tremors and hyper-responsiveness, and eventually die. BSE was due to feeding cattle the remains of infected cows. Prion proteins were passed on between animals, and they accumulated in the brain.

He showed Michael a review article detailing all the studies that supported the theory that Parkinson's disease was a prion-like illness. It all revolved around the protein alpha-synuclein, which didn't fold correctly, or rather was 'misfolded' in Parkinson's disease. Prions in BSE were also misfolded.

Alpha-synuclein was a small protein, and its actual function in healthy individuals was unknown, although it was suspected to have a role in protecting the nerve cells. It was found in the end of nerves, before the synapse—the gap between nerves. It also occurred in an identical form in many animals. Because it was highly conserved, it was probably quite important. In Parkinson's disease, it was found in both the sporadic kind (with an unknown cause) and the genetic familial illness—where a mutation in a gene leads to a build-up in the protein. Lewy bodies, the proteinaceous deposits, which are the hallmark of Parkinson's disease, are mostly made of alpha-synuclein. Lewy bodies are an aggregation of the misfolded protein.

Proteins are known to fold in certain ways, and the folding enables them to do their job as enzymes. Misfolded or denatured proteins fail to operate. Alpha-synuclein is no exception—it folds. However, when it folds it aggregates with other alpha-synuclein proteins and they stick together in relatively large clumps—this process is called fibrillation and the clumps are called fibrils. The main problem seemed to be the partially folded alpha-synuclein, or oligomers.

'More on these oligomers, or small clumps, later,' Luke said, not wanting to lose his friend in medical and scientific terminology before he had told him about the interesting part.

'Studies showed that a mutation in the alpha-synuclein gene led to early onset genetic Parkinson's disease. A specific type of worm, bred to overexpress alpha-synuclein, developed degeneration of the dopamine-producing nerves, like in Parkinson's.'[158]

Michael had to admit that the evidence against this protein was convincing, although he found the image of shaking worms rather amusing and couldn't help but smirk.

Luke carried on, ignoring Michael's sniggers. 'Alpha-synuclein belongs to a family of proteins that are called "disordered proteins."' Luke knew Michael would like this, because of his intolerance of anything disordered, including a theory that kept changing. 'In fact, alpha-synuclein is one of the most disordered. It's also known as a "natively unfolded protein."'

'Well, why didn't you say? That's just asking for trouble,' Michael joked, beginning to feel more confident and paying attention.

'The alpha-synuclein proteins form well-defined, highly ordered structures. Once the initial binding has occurred, the fibril surface locks the protein in place. The binding acts like a seed for the propagation of folding, making the other adjacent proteins fold in such a way as to bind on. In this way, it behaves like a prion protein, as it is capable of spreading.'

'Holy cow! It's like uncontrollable, contagious origami!' Michael feigned being shocked.

'These fibrils seem to disrupt the nerve cells, but the oligomers are definitely bad news, as they harm the nerve cells —they are cytotoxic.'

'I got it. These proteins and their sidekicks—'

'Groups. Their side groups,' Luke corrected. He could tell Michael was having a bit of fun, entering lecture mode, and he played along.

'They're little devils,' added Michael.

'Well, no, they are useful. We don't quite know what they do, but they are important.' Luke put Michael right again.

'They go around—'

'In nerves,' Luke added.

'Yeah, and they persuade other likely proteins, more of a kind—'

'More of the same kind—other alpha-synuclein.'

'To radicalise—'

'Er, not quite. They alter the naive synuclein, so they—'

'Yeah, I got it, clump together.' Michael was on a roll now. 'But you needn't worry so much about the bigger groups, as they're more stable and less dangerous. It's the little guys you gotta watch out for. They're dangerous!'

'Are you quite finished? Can I go on?'

'There's more? Hit me!' Michael sat forward ready to listen, as Luke explained more about alpha-synuclein, and how it was thought to spread from one part of the body to another along nerves like the vagus that have no myelin sheath.[159] It had even been found in the gut, with a higher concentration in the upper gut.[160]

'How do they know it creeps along these nerves?' Michael asked suspiciously. 'Why aren't these nerves prone to whatever precipitated the alpha-synuclein clumping in the first place?'

'Because it happens at a much faster rate if the vagus

nerve is intact,' Luke replied. 'It's difficult to comprehend, as it challenges our understanding of infections, but there are now plenty of examples of prion diseases, not just Creutzfeldt-Jakob disease, or mad cow disease—'

'You mean BSE? You just called it something else. Some fancy medical term.'

'Yes, CJD is BSE in humans.'

'So many acronyms!' Michael complained mockingly. Luke carried on, regardless. 'There's also scrapie in sheep and goats, and then there was kuru in New Guinea, where it was the custom to eat dead people's brains during a funeral.'

Looking at Michael's horrified face, Luke realised he had definitely gone too far and quickly changed the topic. 'But let's face it, viruses aren't living—they are more than just proteins, granted, but they can't survive independent of a host.'

'And mercury isn't living, but it still induces changes.'

'Yes, agreed,' said Luke tentatively. He wasn't sure it was quite the same thing.

He moved swiftly on to explain something else he knew would interest Michael—genetically modified mice that overproduce alpha-synuclein developed Parkinson's disease.

'Like worms,' Michael interjected.

'Yes, like the worms,' Luke agreed, as he explained that if they were then given antibiotics, their symptoms improved. The same mice with lots of alpha-synuclein, kept in germ-free cages, had fewer motor problems and also less alpha-synuclein aggregation in the brain. When they were given bacteria from patients with Parkinson's disease they deteriorated rapidly, but there was no effect when administering gut bacteria from healthy people.[161]

'I knew it. There's something in the gut bacteria that makes Parkinson's disease worse. That's what I was reading about,' Michael blurted out, suddenly back in the loop. 'How, though?'

They both pondered the question. How can having bacteria in the gut, particularly a certain type of bacteria, make these mice develop Parkinsonian symptoms?

'Even though alpha-synuclein is found in much higher levels nearest the mouth, constipation is the only gut symptom that precedes the motor symptoms,' Michael pondered out loud.[139] 'Did you know that patients with dementia and Parkinson's had low thiamine in their brain at autopsy?'[162] As always, Michael was keen to get the conversation back to thiamine.

'Parkinson's dementia? We know very little about it.' Luke shook his head and then changed the subject, because he wanted Michael to understand about dopamine, too. 'Almost all the dopamine in the brain is found in the substantia nigra, and a few linked areas close by, which also have motor functions. These are the areas of the brain affected in Parkinson's disease, so scientists rationalised that dopamine might be an issue.'

Luke continued with the fact that dopamine is produced from tyrosine, and that the enzyme for this conversion is tyrosine hydrolase, with iron being a cofactor—without iron the enzyme doesn't work.

'I know what a cofactor is,' Michael snapped, pretending to be insulted, while Luke leaned over to grab a pen and a piece of paper.

He started writing equations. 'It helps me to think out loud,' he explained.

'And in colour?' Michael offered him a different-coloured pen.

'If you insist.'

'Ooh, I do!' Michael opened the fridge to get a beer and some olives, and a tonic water for Luke, while Luke finished the first equation and carried on explaining.

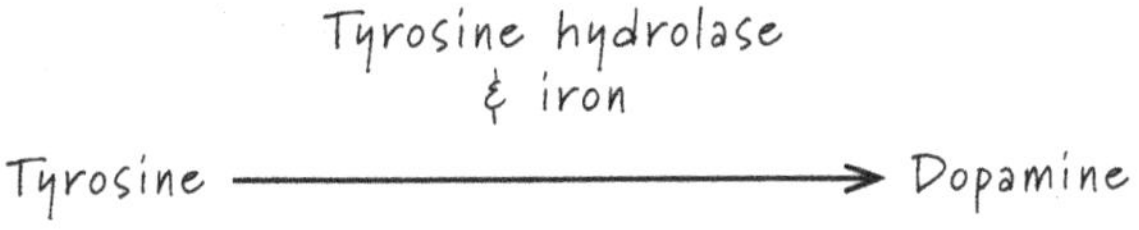

'Dopamine isn't stable. It is broken down by enzymes to produce DOPAC. DOPAC is toxic and makes the alpha-synuclein form oligomers. This rate of DOPAC production is increased by divalent metals, such as manganese, copper and iron II, and reduced by antioxidants such as vitamin C. Metabolism of dopamine also produces hydrogen peroxide and free radicals.'[163]

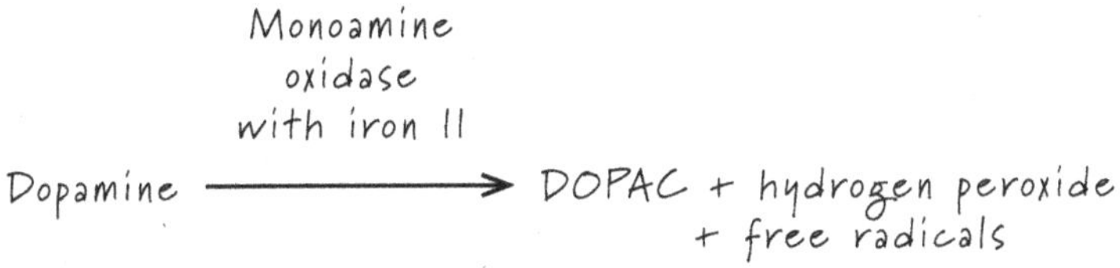

'Dopamine can also be spontaneously oxidised to a quinone, producing hydrogen peroxide and a superoxide in the process.'

'Dopamine isn't safe to be allowed out alone,' Luke said. 'It's kept secure in compartments of the cell, called vesicles. One of the putative roles of alpha-synuclein is making these vesicles and transporting dopamine to the synapses, where it acts as a neurotransmitter.' Luke went onto explain that the by-products of these reactions led to oxidative stress and mitochondrial dysfunction, as well as oligomeric alpha-synuclein. 'Dopamine is fundamental to the underlying pathology in Parkinson's disease. It's not a coincidence that the dopamine-containing neurons are the ones affected.' He took a sip of tonic water. 'Iron is taken up by transferrin receptors, but also by divalent metal transporters.'

Michael popped a black olive in his mouth and continued to listen.

'In the substantia nigra, iron is stored in neuro-melanin—the melanin makes the substantia nigra black. It's easy to spot when you dissect the brain.'

'Oh, no,' Michael choked. 'Please, not while I'm eating!'

Luke was used to Michael's sense of humour and went onto explain that on scanning the brain, the iron content is visible and strongly correlates with disease severity. Iron II is the main form in the cell, but iron III sticks more avidly to alpha-synuclein. Iron II is oxidised to iron III, with all these free radicals swilling around, and this produces yet more hydrogen peroxide and hydroxyl radicals.[164]

'So, the main culprits are alpha-synuclein, dopamine and iron,' Luke summarised.

'The perfect storm brewing inside the substantia nigra,' Michael added. 'Ooh, it sounds just like an Agatha Christie plot. They're all there, no alibis!'

Metallic lustre

'All this is fascinating, but how does it all start?' Michael asked Luke pointedly. 'I mean, what are the actual triggers for Parkinson's disease? How is mercury involved in all this?'

'Well, we already know that certain environmental toxins cause Parkinson's, for example, rotenone and paraquat. Rotenone inhibits the electron transfer chain in the mitochondria, and as a result the mitochondria churns out free radicals. Similarly, paraquat produces a lot of these reactive oxygen species, generally known as ROS.

'In mice, this increase in ROS leads to an increase in alpha-synuclein, and whenever alpha-synuclein is overproduced, like in the mice models, it clumps.'

He drew a simple diagram, doodling as he explained things.

'So, it might start with a mitochondrial poison,' Michael said.

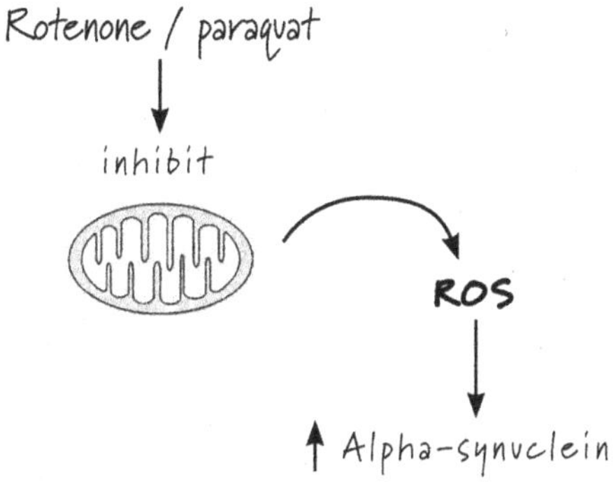

Luke finished his drawing.

'What are you doodling?' said Michael.

'Rude!' Luke retorted. 'It's a mitochondria, obviously. We also know,' he continued, 'that metals are important.'

'Did you know that cannabis also increases oxidative stress and causes mitochondrial dysfunction?' Michael added. 'It might not be such a great idea as a treatment for Parkinson's.'[165]

Luke hadn't known that and wondered where his friend had found this little gem. It was true that there were reports of cannabis improving motor symptoms in Parkinson's disease. However, the main benefit seemed to be mood enhancement. If Michael was right, cannabis might actually do more harm than good.

'There's cannabis in wastewater, that's all,' Michael said. He had somehow managed to return the conversation to sewage again.

Luke explained that other metals were potentially important: aluminium induces oligomers, copper binds to alpha-synuclein, and this complex generates ROS, which leads to the formation of oligomers, and lead promotes aggregation. Nickel also damages mitochondria. Manganese causes alpha-synuclein to misfold, as well as inhibiting a mitochondrial enzyme. It somehow leads to toxicity in a different part of the brain—the striatum and the globus pallidus.

'In fact, one of the causes of familial Parkinson's is a mutation in the gene that codes for a manganese transporter—PARK9,' Luke said. 'Magnesium deficiency is associated with Parkinson's, so magnesium and zinc may protect against the disease, like selenium.'

'So, you have good metals, which are magnesium, zinc

and selenium, and bad metals, which are aluminium, copper, nickel and manganese,'[158] Michael summarised. 'But what about mercury?'

'That's just it. I can't find any specific enzyme that it inhibits or how it causes toxicity. It's just that it's known to be extremely toxic, especially methylmercury. I mean, the negatively charged side chains of alpha-synuclein seem to react with many metals, and this stimulates partial folding.'

'Only that it binds to the iron-groups in complex I of the electron transfer chain in the inner membrane of the mitochondria. The same complex that rotenone and paraquat inhibit. Coincidence?' Michael added smugly.

Luke was thrilled that Michael had found an explanation. They swapped notes.

'What's this ginseng and vanilla bean panchakarma? Is it a new vegan food?' Michael asked, with just a hint of sarcasm in his voice.

'I know. I was led down the garden path on that one. It's Indian complementary medicine,' Luke sighed, raising his eyes to show that he clearly thought it was no use. 'Hocus pocus!'

'Did you look them up?' Michael looked serious and got busy tapping away. 'Well, the vanilla bean is a natural source of L-Dopa, so that's why that works, and—' he hesitated, as he clicked on a few articles, '—the other one, ginseng, has a number of different properties. It's an antioxidant—it contains a very high amount of vitamin C, it's antibacterial, and it also chelates iron.' He paused, 'although not quite as well as EDTA. Not bad for a Parkinson's treatment. *Withania somnifera* is called "poison gooseberries" and also goes by the name of "ashwagandha!"' He started to chuckle to himself.

'The liquorice-tasting root of the plant is used, which has an aphrodisiac action. Should be popular!'

They both continued reading the notes. There were other small molecules that had an effect on the aggregation of alpha-synuclein—how it clumps into fibrils. These mostly inhibited its formation, such as the antibiotic used to treat tuberculosis—rifampicin, and the compound curcumin, which is found in the spice turmeric.

'Another chemical that reduces the cytotoxic effects of alpha-synuclein—' Luke paused, and Michael knew it was for effect.

'OK, what have you found out? Out with it.'

'—is nicotine. Alpha-synuclein seems to produce the larger, non-toxic aggregates with nicotine,' Luke explained.

'Hence why Parkinson's disease is less common in smokers? They are protected?'

'They get plenty of other diseases from smoking—cancer, heart disease, strokes, aortic aneurysms, bronchitis, increased mortality from all other diseases.' Luke was preaching—it was a well-rehearsed line. 'But not Parkinson's.'

'Has anyone used nicotine patches to treat Parkinson's?'

'Yes, but disappointingly they didn't work in the trials. It seems that the treatment comes too late once you've developed symptoms of Parkinson's disease. They may work better as a preventative treatment, if we could predict those at risk, maybe? All the Parkinson mutations of the alpha-synuclein gene alter the secondary structure and promote aggregation.'

Luke was now drawing a spider diagram to illustrate the promotors and protectors for toxic alpha-synuclein aggregation.

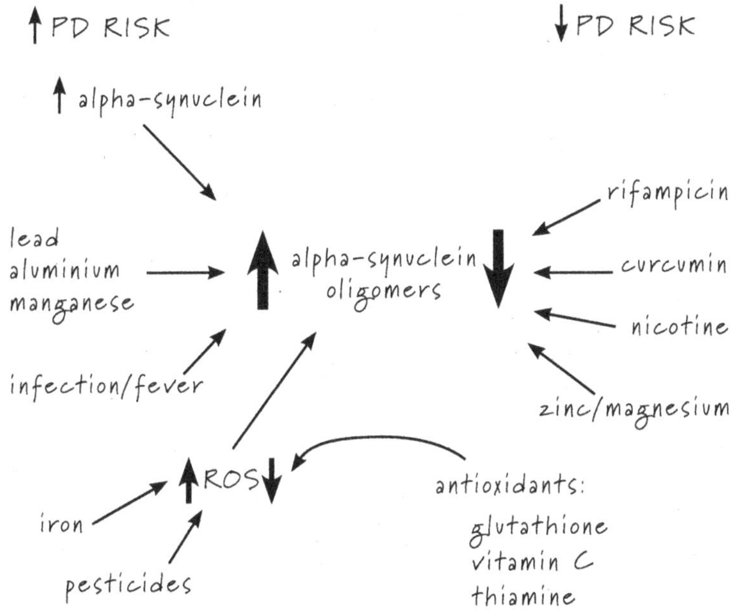

It was beginning to make sense. Alpha-synuclein oligomers are toxic and self-perpetuate once they've started, possibly long after the initiating toxin has disappeared. There were a few things that reduced the toxic collections of proteins: smoking, or specifically nicotine, turmeric, namely curcumin, and the antibiotic used in the treatment of tuberculosis—rifampicin. Then there were multiple factors that aggravate the cytotoxic effects of alpha-synuclein: genetic mutations that increase the concentration of alpha-synuclein, excess alpha-synuclein, acidity and fever, such as with an infection, metals and pesticides. Chronic exposure, rather than acute, seemed to be more important for insidious neurodegeneration. Acute toxicity was more likely to lead to early brain damage and death.

'Alpha-synuclein is found in the gut—' Luke started to explain.

'Hence symptoms starting there,' Michael added, 'the alpha-synuclein must affect the nerve function in the gut.'

'But it's also found in the submandibular glands.' Luke continued to explain that several metals are taken up in the olfactory bulb—the part of the brain that senses smell. Mercury and manganese are both taken up and move along the olfactory nerves.[166]

Michael was horrified to learn that these toxic proteins—a build-up of alpha-synuclein—had been found in the olfactory bulbs of children and adolescents in highly polluted areas. A paper reported that children exposed to the particulate matter PM2.5 in the centre of Mexico City had the first stages of Parkinson's brain abnormalities.[167] PM2.5 contains manganese[168] and mercury.[169] In Mexico City, the pollution is worst in the northeast, especially during cold, dry spells, when there is no heat to make the particles in the air rise or rain to make them fall. The capital city is in the crater of an extinct volcano, and at altitude, so there is lower atmospheric oxygen and, hence, incomplete combustion of carbon, resulting in the production of the poisonous gas carbon monoxide. There are no coal-fired power stations, but there is an iron and steel industry, and lots of traffic, which all account for the mercury pollution.

'This explains how symptoms start in the gut with constipation, which fits if the predominant mercury uptake is ingestion, for example, in water, fish or rice.'[139] Luke was thinking out loud. 'It's also been shown to start in the nose, with loss of smell, which occurs in the majority of patients. The nerves in the nose are sensitive to total body mercury exposure, but this could also be explained by the inhalation of mercury vapour. There is often a stage in the onset of early symptoms that is not recognised as the disease. This is called a prodromal period, and it's characterised by autonomic disturbance: depression, sleep disorder and then this olfactory dysfunction. We know the problem metals that promote aggregation of alpha-synuclein are aluminium, copper and lead, which are found in coal, iron, which is already in the brain, and manganese, which is found in the soil. Zinc and magnesium are protective and reduce aggregation.'[170] Luke took a deep breath. It had been quite a speech.

They seemed to be making progress, although there were still so many questions.

Bright yellow

Luke was preparing lunch.

'It's rather yellow. What is it?' Michael asked.

'Red lentil dhal. Plenty of turmeric,' he smirked.

'I see you're getting your fill of curcumin then,' Michael replied. 'Your alpha-synuclein won't be fibrillating tonight.' He then started to repeat Luke's hypothesis to him, as though summing up at the end of a lecture he'd just given. 'So, let me see if I've got this right. You think that Parkinson's disease is caused by chronic exposure to heavy metals—mostly, but probably not only, mercury, mainly from coal-fired power stations—but also particulate matter from vehicle exhausts, gold mines and chemical industries, such as chloralkali plants polluting waters.'

'That's the theory, yes,' Luke confirmed.

'But other metals are also potentially important. Do we know whether these effects are additive or cumulative, or synergistic and accelerated when more than one metal is implicated?'

'No, we don't know, but presumably it's at least additive?'

'There's so much geographical variation that can't be explained by genetics or by infection.'

'True,' Luke agreed.

'There are some clues. Higher prevalence in areas with

more mercury pollution and falling or stable prevalence in areas with less.'

'Wherever I looked there was a link with mercury pollution,' Luke emphasised.

Michael started talking more excitedly, coming up with ideas. 'You say the unmyelinated autonomic nerves are more vulnerable. The gut and the nose are also the first to be exposed to methylmercury and mercury vapour, respectively. So, damage to autonomic nerves causes constipation through a reduction in motor activity in the gut. This, along with a loss of the sense of smell, is often the first symptom of Parkinson's.'

'That's right.'

'It is less common in smokers, which can be explained by an effect on the prion-like misfolded protein clumps of alpha-synuclein.'

'Yes. Alpha-synuclein is the hallmark of disease. It appears first in the olfactory area and loss of smell, hyposmia, is one of the first symptoms.'

'Mercury binds to sulphur groups located on complex I in the mitochondria and disrupts the electron transfer machinery, which starts a chain reaction, leading to changes in the charge on iron, which leads to an oxidative state in the cell, further changes to the charge on iron and a disordered, unfolded protein to fold. Dopamine is tricky stuff, because it should be kept locked away in compartments—funnily enough, it's made of this disordered protein, which has the ability to spread like an infection when triggered. The infectious protein is toxic to the cell; the charged iron and free dopamine promote free radicals, stress and, ultimately, the death of the nerve cells ensues, resulting in the whole shebang—the shaking, stuttering and dribbling, et cetera, that is Parkinson's disease.'

Luke had to agree it was a fine soliloquy, and Michael had remembered the salient points. There was just a little fine-tuning to be done. Methylmercury induces reactive oxygen species by direct interaction with mitochondria, but also via independent mechanisms that included damaging DNA—the genetic material of the cell—and interrupting calcium and glutamate pathways, which are both vitally important for cellular function.

Michael hadn't finished. 'Let me tell you how thiamine fits into all this.'

'Be my guest, Obi-Wan Kenobi!' Luke joked, pleased with his reference to the *Star Wars* hero. 'Do you get it – O-B1?' Luke laughed. He always enjoyed teasing Michael for his thiamine obsession. 'B1? Thiamine?' Michael looked nonplussed. '*Star Wars?* Jedi Knight? Oh, forget it.' He could tell his sparring partner had just been biding his time, waiting for an opportunity to explain his theory, and he didn't appreciate Luke's humorous interlude.

Michael explained how thiamine has been shown to improve motor features in Parkinson's disease, and how antibiotics have worked too. He also said that there is no doubt that small intestinal bacterial overgrowth or the microbes living in the gut are important. He wondered whether this was secondary to constipation and bowel movements slowing down, due to nerve damage and the resultant reduced motility in the gut.

'In the places we looked at for heavy metal poisoning, there was also water pollution, water shortages or floods. For example, downstream of Chicago along the Mississippi, the Nile in Egypt, the Atacama Desert in Chile, Sacramento in California, Brazil, Mexico, and so on.'

Luke had to agree with all this.

'We've already said that oxidative stress, the release of products that can oxidise body components and cause major damage at a cellular level, is one of the causes of the aggregation of this protein, alpha-synuclein. Well, antioxidants can prevent this. Thiamine, along with vitamin C and glutathione are antioxidants. Glutathione is interesting.'

Michael carried on explaining how glutathione was the most potent antioxidant in the body. It was made from cysteine. In fact, the amount of cysteine available controlled the amount of glutathione synthesised—the so-called rate-limiting step.

He then made a tangential move and returned to living longer. 'Human females tend to outlive males.'

'Except in Nicoya, you said,' Luke added.

'True, but they do almost everywhere else on the planet. This longevity advantage is seen during famines and epidemics. It's all to do with the stress response. There are some factors clearly helped by the female hormone oestrogen.' Michael was on a roll. 'Glutathione seems to be increased in females. There is a decline in levels with age, and this reduction is more pronounced in ageing male mice. This seems to be due to a down-regulation of the rate-limiting step, the one binding cysteine, and the enzyme involved—glutamate cysteine ligase.'[171,172]

'So, is this reduction in glutathione treatable?' Michael continued. He was definitely in lecture mode. 'Glutathione doesn't work. But cysteine can be given, usually in the form of a pro-drug, that's what you called it—N-acetylcysteine.'

Michael explained that a trial administering N-acetylcysteine to patients with Parkinson's disease improved their symptoms.[173] This helped to confirm the mechanisms of action for the disease. Other antioxidants were quercetin, a plant pigment with a bitter taste that is found in capers and red onion, and a related compound quercitrin, which is found in buckwheat. Both protect mitochondria from methylmercury and other neurotoxins: rotenone and MPTP. Admittedly, the quercetin needed piperine to improve its effect. This was found in black pepper.[174,175,176] Not only that, methylmercury forms a complex with cysteine. By mimicking another amino acid—methionine—it uses the methionine transport system and enters the cell.[177]

Luke had read up on chelators and added that the sulfhydryl groups in these compounds, methionine, cysteine and N-acetylcysteine, bound to metals, particularly mercury, and were, therefore, good at chelation and helping with the excretion of metals.[178]

'They might be a way in for the metals, but they're also a way out—a way to detoxify,' Luke added. 'There's a chelator called DMPS. It's approved in Germany. I think it's available over the counter there. Another similar one, DMSA, might be better at disposing of organic mercury. DMPS, sodium 2, 3-dimercaptopropane sulfonate and DMSA, dimercaptosuccinic acid, both chelate mercury—binding mercury to help to clear it from the body.'[179]

'It's surprising they aren't more widely known about or used?' Michael questioned. 'Has it been used? You know, in Parkinson's disease?'

'What is Parkinson's disease?' Luke replied rhetorically, less certain of the notion that it was idiopathic. He went on to tell Michael about a study of gold miners in the Philippines, who were treated with DMPS. They were known to have chronic mercury poisoning and features consistent with this. The chelation treatment improved their tremor, balance and hypomimia—the paucity of facial features often seen in mercury poisoning—and Parkinson's disease. There were other possible benefits on memory, insomnia, anxiety and palpitations.[180]

★

After lunch, Luke sent Michael to a health food store with a list of new products. The following morning, he was busy in the kitchen mixing something gloopy in a jug.

'What's for breakfast?' Michael enquired nervously.

'Buckwheat pancakes, made with soy milk, served with fresh fruit and maple syrup,' Luke announced proudly.

'But what about the eggs, you don't eat eggs?'

'No eggs required. They're more like—' he paused, thinking, '—like, um, I want to say flatbread, but they're flat pancakes.' Luke gave up with explanations. 'Do you think they'd taste nice with black pepper?'

'No way!' Michael immediately responded, screwing up his face in disgust. Luke was beginning to take this health food diet too far. *Next, he'll be asking for supplements.*

'While you're in town today, could you get me some thiamine, vitamin C, vitamin B12 and selenium, please?'

It was as if Luke had read his mind. 'We could also do with some vegan cheese. I'm making caper and red onion pizza tonight.'

Dancing cats

Michael had finally managed to persuade Renie to visit him in England. She had been extremely reluctant to travel, but Arnie had helped to convince her that she would enjoy the trip. The date was set. He just had to find an Airbnb locally, and there were lots available.

Britain had voted some time ago to leave the European Union, and politicians were now in the throes of debating a deal. Michael wasn't sure what the implications would be for a foreigner from outside the EU; even one with European ancestry. Would it now be easier to get residency? He had no idea. Luke had joked that he should try to get Polish nationality. Michael knew it wouldn't be that simple. Many of Luke's friends had applied for Irish passports. Luke was irritated by the political inertia caused by Brexit. The NHS was being completely neglected. No decisions were being made on environmental issues, either. He felt as though the country was in limbo. Increasingly, Michael was becoming aware that the guidelines and standards set by the European Commission were there for good reason, to improve the quality of life of everyone and all living things in Europe—countries working together with a common goal. But it didn't matter what he thought. The majority of British people had voted to leave the EU, and they lived in a democracy.

Luke showed him a European Commission report on tackling mercury pollution, not just in Europe, but worldwide. It was a well-written, thorough report, with an action plan to reduce the pollution, starting by ceasing industrial production and safely decontaminating industrial sites. One of the outcomes from the Minamata Convention, an international treaty to protect human health and the environment from anthropogenic mercury emissions, was that there would need to be a global effort to reduce mercury levels; the agreement had been signed in 2013 by one hundred and twenty-seven countries and the European Union.

'Gold mining is now the largest source of mercury. Illegal gold mining, you know, artisanal and small-scale—ASGM, it's known as. Then burning coal is the second largest source. Obviously, these affect very different countries.'[181] Luke was waving the paper in front of Michael. When the paper finally stopped moving, he could see a section on fish, which caught his attention.

'Tunnus tinnus!' Michael laughed. Luke was rather taken aback. He was used to tangential moves, but this was quite extreme.

'Tin what?' Luke asked, trying to understand what Michael found so funny.

'It's the name for tuna, *Thunnus thynnus*. It's the large, Atlantic bluefin tuna, the one that has high levels of mercury. It's the name—*Thunnus thynnus*—it's such a great name for a fish that ends up in a tin—tinned tuna, but that's just a coincidence. There's also *Xiphius gladius*—swordfish. Gladius? Get it? Sword?' He continued reading the other names of the fish that were high in mercury. The report mentioned weever fish, with their venomous spikes on their fins and gills, and Atlantic bonito, a large, mackerel-like fish. There was no connection, except that these were large, predatory fish that ate smaller, mercury-containing fish. In Europe, apparently, the main dietary sources of mercury were tuna, swordfish, cod *(fish and chips!)*, whiting and pike, as well as non-alcoholic beverages *(presumably fizzy drinks)* and rice.

Michael had seen fish advisories recommending a limited intake of specific kinds of fish in the States. He was surprised he hadn't seen more information about this in England. He couldn't recall seeing any warnings on fish sold at the market, or in the local fish and chip shop. There were no notifications on sodas that they might contain mercury and, therefore, an excess number was potentially dangerous. In England, there were helpful comments on the salt and fat content of food, or whether it contained any fruit or vegetables, but it didn't even have to be fresh, so it seemed. There were age limits for cigarettes and alcohol, but these were less strict than in most of the States. There were the beginnings of attempts to reduce sugar intake.

'Somehow fish have slipped through the net!' Michael joked.

The amount of mercury in an adult's brain was linked to their number of amalgam fillings. This level was increased by chewing gum. In a baby, the amount of mercury was linked to the number of fillings the mother had, as well as to the mother's fish consumption. Michael wondered whether this information was common knowledge. He thought the public ought to be made aware, as they should be about the organic mercury content of tattoo ink and the multi-vial vaccinations in the past. After all, mercury was toxic, potentially building up all the time, and there was no accurate way of assessing one's mercury burden. However, there were supplements that could capture mercury and help detoxify and eliminate it.

The report talked about how mercury moves around the world, cycling between the atmosphere, land and water. It stated that Asia is currently the largest source of atmospheric mercury emissions, with China contributing a third of the global total. However, it also pointed out that as mercury lingers, half of the mercury pollution in the surface layers of the ocean today come from emissions made prior to the 1950s, when the US and Europe were the predominant producers.

The Minamata Convention, named after the city on the west coast of southern Japan that suffered the worst mercury poisoning disaster ever recorded, only came into legal force in August 2017. The aim was simple—to control, reduce and, in the long-term, eliminate mercury emissions. There was then a case-by-case review on how to reduce mercury pollution from different sources. There were helpful suggestions, such as washing coal and avoiding burning certain types. It was possible to filter out particles, and there were directives on monitoring air emissions and water effluent, and how often these should occur. In most cases in Europe, the methods used to reduce other pollutants, such as desulphurisation for sulphur dioxide, and activated carbon, will coincidently reduce mercury emissions. However, the effect on carbon dioxide was not economically viable, and Michael wondered whether there would ever be legislation.

There were a hundred different mercury-producing chloralkali plants worldwide, and these were all built before 1970. The current technology was supposed to be phased out by the end of 2017, and either closed or converted by 2020. This seemed rather ambiguous. Would they continue to pour mercury-laden effluent into the water until then? The main issue wasn't so much closing the plants, which was still essential, it was how to decommission industries, safely store large amounts of mercury and clear contaminated sites. The paper had recommendations for this, which involved temporary above-ground storage and conversion to mercury sulphides, or storing it deep underground in adapted salt mines or hard rock formations.

What was clear over and over again was that toxic levels of mercury were first apparent in animals. In the city of Minamata, locals noticed that fish floated to the surface of the sea, birds fell to the ground and cats went mad.[182] Cats in Minamata were particularly valued because they guarded the fisherman's nets from rodent damage, so there were many of them. In the 1940s, the fishermen noticed that barnacles did not attach themselves to the boats moored near the factory outflow. There were no fish near the outflow either. Then in the early 1950s, a huge number of fish were seen rising to the sea's surface and swimming as though they were crazy. Sea birds crouched on the shores, incapable of flying, and open-shelled oysters and cockles washed up on the beach, where they rotted. In 1953, the local cats started behaving strangely, too. They were drooling, staggering, running in circles, leaping up into the air and charging forwards. Throughout town, the cats dropped dead shortly after exhibiting these bizarre dancing fits.[182]

It was found that the local factory, owned by the Chisso Corporation, a Japanese chemical company, was responsible for a widespread poisoning outbreak after starting to produce acetaldehyde, using mercury as a catalyst, back in 1932. Acetaldehyde is used in plastics and perfume manufacturing. Changes to the process meant that the amount of methylmercury produced and lost in effluent increased in the 1950s. As the factory grew, Minamata city developed and the chemical plant became the main local employer. It provided well-regarded public facilities, including a factory hospital.

Sickeningly, a hospital doctor had discovered early on that by feeding a feline with factory effluent water, he could provoke the dancing cat syndrome, however, he was hushed by the management. The factory manager went on to become the local mayor and served four terms in this prestigious position. Later, a second outbreak occurred in Niigata, close to another acetaldehyde plant. It became more difficult to deny causal association, but it still took years for the government to release an official report that methylmercury originating in the Chisso factory had caused the disease. It was decades before any of the victims received compensation.

Initially, it was thought that the mystery neurological disease afflicting the residents of Niigata might be contagious, and the sick in the area were shunned by society. Then a doctor called Herada brought the disease to international attention. Someone else who was concerned about the impact on her fellow residents was Michiko Ishimure, who wrote several novels and biographies exposing the tragedy of Minamata disease. One novel, *Sea of Suffering*, is particularly famous in Japan, and it motivated activists to keep pressurising the industry and the Japanese government to reduce pollution. It was curious that she should die of Parkinson's, admittedly in her 90s, but perhaps low-grade mercury exposure was a factor?

There was some debate over the safe level of mercury. But this was utter nonsense. Humans are not meant to eat or breathe in mercury—that much was clear. However, there did seem to be certain people who were more susceptible to the effects of mercury toxicity. This was causing controversy. A study in the Seychelles had shown that despite a high intake of methylmercury-containing seafood, there were no long-term impacts on the developing brains of children. The study had started in the 1980s and followed-up children for two decades. Referring back to the Lancet article, the Global Burden of Disease, concerning the number of cases of

Parkinson's worldwide for each country, Michael found that the prevalence of Parkinson's disease in the Seychelles was low. While it was steadily increasing, there weren't large numbers of people affected. He felt sure that the mercury levels now were significantly higher than they were in the 1980s, but it was reassuring to know that these people seemed less susceptible to the effects, unlike the citizens of the Faroe Islands, Grassy Narrows and Minamata.

He tried to find a link between thiamine deficiency and mercury toxicity in these susceptible groups. There was an article from 1979, which seemed to suggest that thiamine deficiency was associated with adverse effects from mercury poisoning, and that the neurotoxic effects may be additive, with alcohol being a contributing factor.[183] Alcohol is known to drastically reduce the body's ability to absorb thiamine, as well as being a direct toxin to nerve cells. There was another article in French, and it seemed to strongly suggest that thiamine deficiency was an issue in the Japanese populations of Minamata and Niigata.

There had to be a link. *Susceptibility to mercury. Thiamine deficiency.* He thought back to the first case of Chastek paralysis. These foxes had been fed raw fish that contained thiaminase. The Japanese ate sashimi—thinly sliced raw food, which included fish such as tuna and mackerel. The Inuit have eaten raw fish for thousands of years. The Faroese cuisine consists of air-dried fermented fish and meats, which are hung outside in slatted sheds to ferment and dry. Hawaiian 'poke' was the equivalent of Japanese sashimi. It consisted of raw fish cut into cubes. The main fish used for this was tuna. Many types of raw fish, including tuna and Pacific mackerel, contain thiaminase. Not only that, but they were also served with soy sauce, which contained o-amino benzoic acid, one of the aromatic amines that increased the activity of thiaminase. Thiamine deficiency would make these people more prone to neurotoxicity from mercury poisoning.

In Minamata, methylmercury had passed through pregnant women's placentas and into their developing foetuses, despite the conviction at the time that there would be no risk to unborn babies. This resulted in significant neurological disabilities, including cerebral palsy. There were now international non-profit organisations, such as IPEN (International Pollutants Elimination Network) and BRI (Biodiversity Research Institute), monitoring childbearing age women in fish-eating communities for mercury levels using hair samples.[184] They sampled cases on small islands in the Pacific, West Indies, Hawaii and the Indian Ocean. Fifty-eight per cent of women had a mercury level greater than 1ppm, the limit recommended by the US EPA (Environmental Protection Agency). However, new data recommends lowering the safe level to 0.58ppm, and seventy-five per cent of women had a level greater than this. Generally, the average level and the highest recorded level were consistent for each geographical location. There was clearly a problem with mercury toxicity in these fish-eating, island communities. The highest level recorded was on the island of Comoros (28 ppm), part of an archipelago just off the coast of Mozambique. Here there were frequent volcanic eruptions. The next highest recorded was in Trinidad and Tobago (24 ppm), by the Ortoire River. Oil was first reported here in the sixteenth century, at the La Brea Pitch Lake, by Sir Walter Raleigh. They had been drilling oil for over a hundred years. Refining oil was a significant source of mercury pollution, particularly given the number of years of cumulative toxicity. Other places with high levels were Sri Lanka (16 ppm), which used coal as its main energy source, and Tonga (15 ppm), which was in an active volcanic area. Not only that, but Tonga also had a reputation for game fishing, particularly for blue marlin, which contained a significant amount of mercury. Michael returned to Comoros, thinking perhaps there was another reason for the high mercury levels there. He discovered there was gold mining in nearby Madagascar, and in Tanzania.

The lowest mercury toxicity was found in the Dominican Republic and St Kitts and Nevis. Both islands had mountains, largely rural communities and crops, which meant they weren't totally reliant on fish and seafood.

The inhabitants of the Seychelles undoubtedly had a high seafood diet, however, by eating the smaller fish and by cooking them, they might have been protected. The other protective factor was selenium. Michael found what he was looking for—a paper on the selenium-to-mercury ratio for fish. Selenium was found in excess to mercury for almost all the fish tested. Marlin, yellow fin tuna and skipjack tuna all had significantly more selenium. Mako shark had less selenium than mercury. Was this relevant in the Seychelles? He had no idea.

The only pattern emerging was that eating a predominantly fish diet, consisting of larger fish, was associated with higher mercury levels. However, that did not lead to a significantly increased incidence of Parkinson's disease. This seemed to require a diet of raw fish, particularly in areas with improper water management processes. The Seychelles seemed to manage water resources well, and most of the water came from streams in the mountainside, with four desalination plants for the drier spells.

The common factor was thiamine deficiency due to thiaminase—Michael was sure of it. Thiaminases were found in raw fish. Bacteria produced thiaminases. Bacteria were found in water contaminated by sewage. He didn't know whether thiaminase was in the water—he still hadn't been able to find out. There was also the higher conversion to methylmercury in the sewage-contaminated waters, which was definitely a factor.

Back in Minamata in the fifties, it was the people living and working by the sea who recognised the strange disease—the fish floating, the cats convulsing and the crows dropping from the sky. The Chisso Corporation chose not to collaborate and actively hindered research. The government concurred. Industrial growth and preserving the economy had been prioritised over public health. Rimiko Yoshinaga, a fisherman's granddaughter, whose family all died from mercury poisoning, now spoke about her experiences at conventions. 'Always listen to the voices of the nameless persons,' she said.[185]

Silver water

'Michael J Fox lived in Burnaby as a child—it's a suburb of Vancouver,' Michael said, whilst Luke prepared the pizza dough.[186]

'And?'

'I was just reading up about the Department of Fisheries and Oceans lab in West Vancouver.'

'So? Spill the beans.'

'It was an article about eating mussels on the shore and swimming in the harbour.'

'OK, out with it.' Luke could tell Michael was now teasing him on purpose.

'It's only that the mussels in Burrard Inlet had the highest mercury levels in the region. Just thought you'd be interested, that's all.'[187]

Luke was very serious for a moment and appeared deep in thought. This told Michael that he had discovered something potentially important, but of course, it didn't prove anything.

★

After supper, Michael sat down to do some studying. Something he'd read had prompted him—that human harm followed on from that seen in wildlife.

'Did you know that algal bloom species are thiamine auxotrophs?'

'What?' Luke put his neurology journal down, sighed quietly and waited for an explanation.

'They're not simply innocent bystanders, or red herrings.' Michael laughed to himself, remembering how he had thought they were just a marker of eutrophication. 'Most of the species of algae that erupt into massive blooms require exogenous vitamin B1.'

Michael was speaking slowly, wondering exactly what had confused Luke the first time. 'Auxograph? They are mutants, like—' he was thinking of a Luke-friendly analogy '—like Ninja Turtles.' He laughed at his own joke. 'The mutants require certain nutrients that the normal strains don't, in this case thiamine. An algal bloom can strip the water of thiamine in maybe a few hours.'[188]

'So, thiamine is important?' Luke asked.

'Do you remember me telling you about the sea lions in 2011? How the pups died in mass numbers all along the Californian coast? Well, there were multiple algal bloom events along the Californian coast, including in Bodega Bay. The deaths could have been chronic mercury poisoning exacerbated by acute thiamine deficiency. Also, the Inuit. They ate seals, which contain high levels of methylmercury. Many seals are thiamine deficient, too, if they have a diet mostly consisting of thiaminase-containing fish.'

⋆

Michael reviewed all the cases of mass mortalities in animals, just in case he had overlooked something. Just as thiamine deficiency wasn't immediately obvious, he wondered whether mercury poisoning didn't become clear until bacteria were involved, and that this was also exacerbated by thiamine deficiency. Anyhow, he wanted to reassure himself that there had been no mercury in the vicinity of these cases.

He searched 'alligators', 'Florida' and 'mercury'. He was horrified to discover that a large part of the Everglades, coloured red on the map in the report, has high levels of mercury.[189] The area was near Lake Okeechobee, which is the largest freshwater lake in Florida and the second largest natural lake entirely within the States, after Lake Michigan. It was a very shallow lake that frequently flooded into the surrounding Everglades. Its source was the Kissimmee River. Michael traced the river back. There was a chloralkali plant in Tampa on the west coast, but that wasn't in the watershed, and it didn't seem to use mercury in its production of chlorine.

So, where did the mercury come from?

There was definitely a problem with mercury contamination, and there were restrictions on eating certain types of fish, again stricter for children and women of childbearing age. Little did they realise that men are just as much at risk. The policies advised against eating large shark and king mackerel, but since you often don't know how big the fish was when you order a shark steak, surely this meant it was difficult to eat shark?[190]

There was a reference to a large fertiliser company in the region. It was one of the largest phosphate mining industries in the world. Apparently, there have been incidents of mercury contamination of soil as a result of long-term fertiliser production due to the use of sulphuric acid.[191] Sulphuric acid is a by-product of zinc and copper plants, and as zinc and copper ores often have an elevated mercury content, mercury evaporates from the ore and can contaminate the sulphuric acid.[192]

In the alligators in Lake Griffin, Florida, the levels of mercury were reported as at or below the detection limit. Michael checked the amount in the original paper—0.5-2mg/kg. This seemed rather high.

The combined effects of thiamine deficiency and mercury toxicity. *Surely enough to cause neurodegeneration*, he thought.

Methylation of mercury would be enhanced in the typical habitat of wetlands, rich with humus—the degraded plant material from bacterial activity, and probable sewage.

Michael looked back at other cases—Bodega Bay, on the coast, near Santa Rosa, was where the baby sea lions had died of a mystery illness, as though they had starved to death. The area around Bodega Bay had mercury mines in the late 1960s. It was well known for the bright red mercury ore cinnabar, which was mined in New Almaden, named after the mercury mining area in Spain; New Almaden was the oldest and most productive in the States.

It wasn't just the mercury on the land, though. The oceans contained significant amounts of the mercury-laden compound dimethylmercury, as well as the toxic methylmercury produced by bacterial action. There was none under the Antarctic ice, so these mercury pollutants originated from atmospheric mercury. At a depth of two hundred metres, dimethylmercury decomposes into methylmercury and some of it escapes into the atmosphere and is transported overland by fog. The coastal fogs in California were known to contain mercury. Unless disturbed, dimethylmercury is stable in the depths of the ocean; it is thought to decompose into methylmercury in acidic conditions. The surface of the ocean absorbs carbon dioxide from burning fossil fuels and becomes more acidic as a consequence.

The timings were curious. California had a drought from 2012 until 2016. In December 2012, construction of a much-needed, massive desalination plant began in San Diego, with ten miles of pipe and six pumps assembled along the sea floor. Mass deaths of the pups were first observed in January 2013, near San Diego.

Michael revisited the cases of ALS on the island of Guam, the ones that sometimes resembled Parkinson's and at other times were more in keeping with Alzheimer's disease. The toxin BMAA had been found in the brains of people who had died of the disease. Interestingly, BMAA had been found in the Baltic Sea, where it bioaccumulated in plankton and fish. He found another article that showed that patients with higher mercury levels had a significantly increased risk of developing ALS. Not only that, but small amounts of BMAA, which caused no toxicity, were found to be poisonous in the presence of methylmercury. The combined effect was worryingly damaging to brain cells. Mercury potentiated the effect of BMAA.[193]

Was there increased mercury in Guam? There were no gold or mercury mines and no coal power station. Michael researched the island's US military base. Historically, Guam was a coaling base to fuel US ships; it was ideally situated for the Philippines and had a large, natural harbour. After World War II, there was a massive installation of military building, supplies and ammunition. The island had one of the military's largest fuel storage facilities. There were also multiple submarine volcanoes in one of the world's most active volcanic regions and near the deepest trench—the Mariana Trench. The Chamorros had a diet that included a lot of fish, as well as the fruit bats that had bioaccumulated the neurotoxin BMAA. There were now advisories on eating fish due to mercury levels. There were also multiple recent reports on polluted waters surrounding the island.

Michael returned to the latest updates in the sea star wasting disease. This had affected sea stars from Alaska to Mexico, and it was being described as the biggest die off ever, predicting that some species, such as the sunflower star, were now close to extinction. It seemed the syndrome had persisted and there was now some doubt as to whether it was caused by a virus. It occurred when there was an increase in water temperature and was reduced by ultraviolet light. It was worse in sheltered water with low oxygen levels.

Perfect conditions for bacteria. Ideal for mercury conversion to methylmercury, Michael thought self-assuredly.

He looked up the dates of the worst outbreaks. It was seen in the Gulf of California in 1977-1978. Mercury had been mined in Mexico since pre-colonial times. From the 1970s and 1980s, hundreds of tons of mercury were produced annually. This officially stopped in 1994 but carried on informally. Michael was dismayed to read that between 2011 and 2015, Mexico reopened many of the previously closed mines.[194]

Another area was specifically mentioned as having dying sea stars—Guemes Island, by Bellingham Bay, between Seattle and Vancouver. Nearby, there were very high levels of mercury found in the mussels at the entrance to Howe Sound. Sea stars fed on mussels. Mussels contain mercury and thiaminase. It was the next part that left Michael stunned. The mussels were from the waters where Burrard Inlet meets Howe Sound.

Hmmm, fish floating or just dissolving! It affects the animals first, Michael thought.

Finally, he read that scientists were perplexed about a sudden increase in the level of mercury in the Great Lake's fish.[195]

Apparently, there had been high mercury levels, but since the 1970s these had been steadily falling. Recently, mercury levels were increasing in some species, such as in walleye and lake trout, and in some locations. One of them was Grand Traverse Bay. *Grand Traverse Bay!* This was the location that had higher levels of thiaminase. He remembered there was an inlet that received processed effluent from the wastewater management facility.

Sewage. Methylmercury conversion.

★

It seemed that whichever industry Michael researched, there was a possibility of mercury being released into the atmosphere, water and soil. It wasn't just the pollution caused by industry, it was now being made worse by trying to reduce fossil fuel use and build an infrastructure for the production of renewable energy. The Three Gorges Dam was a monster of a hydroelectric dam, and even though the idea was commendable, as it would prevent downstream flooding and provide hydroelectricity, it might have made pollution worse. There were mines and industrial waste on the site of the flooded area, and a vast amount of raw sewage was being dumped in the Yangtze each year. The potential for mercury conversion to methylmercury was huge.

In Europe, Poland produced the most coal, although, increasingly, coal was imported from Russia.[196] More worryingly, it was lignite or brown coal—higher mercury-containing coal—that was burnt in the power plants there. Eighty per cent of Poland's energy was from coal. Consequently, Poland had the highest mercury emissions in Europe.[197] Germany burnt more coal than Poland, and historically had been the largest lignite producer. This brown coal was softer, moister and could only be mined in opencast mines. It released less energy, but more carbon dioxide and more mercury.[198] The worst coal plant, Belchatow, was in Poland. The Vistula is the most polluted river in Poland, and the Przemsza is the most polluted tributary to the Vistula, flowing from the Upper Silesian Coal Basin. A lawsuit by in international NGO 'ClientEarth' was underway to sue the state-owned plant.

Michael tried to find a connection with the year 1974, when EMS was first spotted in the Baltic. He found a graph of lignite mining in central Germany. There was a massive increase in the 1960s, peaking in the 1990s. There was a significant flood in Poland and Germany in 2010, with a reported 1.2m tons of mercury fouling the Baltic. The burning of fossil fuels was thought to be causing the current problem there. Poland has almost half of the population and agricultural lands in the Baltic Sea catchment area. M74—the Swedish name for Early Mortality Syndrome—was partly due to the decline in the cod population, as a result of pollution in their spawning areas and overfishing. It was also probably due to the effect of fertilisation, which started in the 1970s. Fertilisation, with probable mercury contamination, caused eutrophication, increasing bacteria, algae and photoplankton, which increases the occurrence of methylmercury.

The Baltic was unique. It was the largest body of brackish water in the world after the Black Sea, but it had an extremely low diversity of species, which meant they were more susceptible to changes in the environment. It was also one of the most polluted seas. Michael wasn't surprised to find out that all the recent reports of M74 salmon were dismal. He read that in the River Simojoki in Finland, the mortality rate was approaching one hundred per cent.[199]

Coal was only part of it. Sweden had found thousands of barrels of mercury offshore that had been dumped by a local papermill.[200] Sweden also has a mining history, but much of the mercury now was thought to originate from outside the country, the majority from beyond Europe.[201] The rivers in Sweden all exceed the recommended maximum mercury level.

In Europe, at six different sites, mercury levels were found to exceed safety standards for fish—the rivers Scheldt (Netherlands), Rhône (France), Göta älv (Sweden), Tees and the Mersey (both in the UK), and Lake Belau (Germany). During the testing period (2007-2013), mercury increased in the Mersey, Scheldt and Göta älv.[202] The Mersey was the area most heavily polluted with mercury in the UK. There was a chloralkali plant nearby at Runcorn, which used mercury until 2017—the heavy metal had spilled into the river. In the past five years, levels have decreased in the Mersey. The Thames Estuary, in London, was also highly contaminated with mercury. There was no specific recent industrial cause, but high levels of mercury in the sediment indicated centuries of pollution.

Blue skies

What a year. Twenty-twenty was certainly one to remember. If you had to get anywhere, you didn't dare risk taking public transport, you walked. The car parks were shut, but there was nowhere to drive to anyway. Shops, offices, schools, gyms and hair salons were all closed, and travel was restricted to essential journeys only. Many parts of the world had banned international travel. England hadn't stopped visitors, but Michael didn't want Renie to risk travelling and asked her to cancel her visit. He was sad that he wouldn't see her, but he thought it sensible and far less stressful. Strangely, he felt closer to her and made more of an effort to speak to her after the country went into lockdown.

Luke was conducting his clinic from home and Michael had to leave the lab and focus on other aspects of his work. They both kept a regular eye on the news, with an almost morbid fascination.

'It's curious,' Michael said.

'What is?' Luke was finishing writing up some clinic letters on his computer.

'It takes so long to implement climate-protecting policies, yet Covid-19 comes along and does it overnight.'

The pandemic had spread from Wuhan in the Hubei province, to Northern Italy and then to London. The footage of pollution clearing over China and Northern Italy was striking.

They both returned to their screens and all was quiet for a few minutes. It was true. People were at home, still living, cooking, washing and heating their homes, yet since the factories had closed, day after day, the skies had become blue and cloudless.

'There are many similarities with Parkinson's disease,' Michael started off again.

'I guess there are,' Luke replied, not looking up from his screen or really taking in what Michael was saying.

'I mean, both Covid-19 and Parkinson's cause loss of smell, both are more common in men, and there is an increased risk of both with type 2 diabetes.' As there was no response from Luke, Michael looked out of the window at nothing in particular.

'Is coronavirus worse with air pollution, do we know?' Luke eventually asked out loud.

'I don't think we know yet,' Michael responded, pleased that Luke was willing to talk, 'but so far the worst places have been Wuhan in Hubei, Northern Italy and London, all of which have a problem with air pollution. Hubei is just downstream of the Three Gorges Dam on the Yangtze River, which means the river is heavily polluted too.'

'Yes, with mercury,' Luke added, returning to his work.

'What about glutathione? Do we know if deficiency makes you more susceptible to Covid? Like it seems to in Parkinson's?' Michael continued.

'I don't know. Maybe.'

'OK, here's another similarity. Both Parkinson's and coronavirus are less common in smokers. Smoking is somehow protective.' Michael was keen to chat. Finally, he had struck a topic that Luke found interesting.

'Yes. Nicotine causes alpha-synuclein to form fibrils, which are less toxic—'

Luke knew that Michael was aware of this, but the open discussions had helped them to gather their thoughts in the past. Michael now had Luke's full attention. He'd finished his letters. Michael was right, there were a number of similarities between Covid-19 and Parkinson's disease. Was this a coincidence or was it a clue to an underlying problem—an accumulation of toxicities making humans more susceptible to this viral illness that was now causing mass death and destruction to certain members of the human race? Why were some regions, some age groups and some races affected more than others? Luke continued with the explanation, '—and nicotine down-regulates the ACE2 receptor, the one in the lungs that coronavirus attaches to. It's why it's so infectious. The virus binds to this ACE2 receptor, making human-to-human transmission easy.'[203,204]

'So, is this why taking ACE inhibitors is bad during a coronavirus pandemic?'

'Yes, it's thought these commonly used blood pressure pills actually increase the receptor ACE2 that coronavirus uses to gain entry into cells,' Luke explained.

'It's not just that though, is it? I mean, hypertension is a risk factor for heart disease and mercury causes cardiotoxicity too. Coronavirus causes significant hypoxia and shunting of blood, which puts the heart under considerable stress. Did you know that patients who have had mercury amalgam fillings *and* hypertension have a greater risk of developing Parkinson's disease?'

'Interesting. I read somewhere that non-dietary predictors of higher levels of mercury include being male, having greater alcohol consumption, being overweight and increased age. Do these have common factors with coronavirus? They do seem to.'[205]

★

'This is startling.' Michael started, leaving Luke wondering briefly what was so shocking. 'In this study in Louisiana, African Americans represent seventy per cent of coronavirus deaths, whilst only accounting for thirty per cent of the population. Why is this? Is it the same in Parkinson's? Here's a study.' He sent the link of a *Lancet* paper to Luke. 'Basically, the blood vessels and capillaries in the lungs were full of clots.'[206] These types of papers were freely accessible during the pandemic and many hypotheses were published without peer review to speed up the transmission of ideas.

'Lupus is more common in African Americans,' Luke stated, and Michael waited for an explanation. 'It's an autoimmune condition. It causes inflammation of the blood vessels—vasculitis—and sometimes more clots.'

'Interesting.' Michael wasn't sure he completely understood it when Luke used medical terms. He also thought there may be other more pressing issues in this group, such as socio-economic status and other cultural factors.

'Covid does seem to increase the stickiness of the blood,' Luke added, looking concerned. The clots were one of the factors increasing the death rate as well as causing chronic health issues. 'Perhaps it will throw some light on other diseases with unknown causes,' he added hopefully.

Michael returned to gazing out of the window, delighted to see so many different varieties of birds.

'What's the small bird called, the one with the black, white and red head?'

'That's a goldfinch. There's a pair. Can you hear them chattering? They're quite common now, unlike the poor sparrow.'

Luke shook his head and quickly changed the subject. 'I saw a kingfisher by the river. I've never seen the river water so clear. You can see through to the bottom, and there are so many small fish. It's incredible.' Luke was enthused by nature returning, as humans remained locked indoors and vehicle use was drastically cut.

'Our goldfinch is much yellower,' said Michael, recalling the American namesake. 'I read that there have been mass deaths of songbirds in the Southwest of America. Suspicious, huh?'

'Where did you read about that?' Luke enquired.

'I'm not sure. It was in the news, though. There were floods in New Mexico just before the birds fell out of the sky. Could it be mercury?' Michael was thinking out loud. 'They were previously worried about the larger, fish-eating birds, now it's the songbirds.' Michael shook his head sadly, adding, 'it's in the beetles. Mercury. I checked. The songbirds are sentinels. As they said in Minamata, it happened to the animals first.'

⋆

'Fantastic news!' In his excitement as he read his emails, Michael was almost shouting. 'The Baltic are the first area in the world to completely ban sewage discharge. The law applies to newbuild passenger ships this year and existing ones in 2021. It's funny that coronavirus has probably had a greater impact than all those years of campaigning.[207]

Cruise ships had been in the press recently. There had been a number of cases aboard them early on in the pandemic, and it was clear that asymptomatic carriage of the virus was a risk for transmission.

'They were basically giant labs—gigantic, floating laboratories of infection,' remarked Michael. 'I dread to think what happened to all that sewage whilst they were floating offshore unable to dock. They found coronavirus in faeces, you know, along with who knows what else!'

Michael was getting angry and flustered. It had also become clear how many of the cruise ships were owned by multinational companies, registered in tax havens and crewed by migrant workers who were paid a pittance. It shouldn't have been a surprise—it was globalisation on full display. Michael read about it in the paper, lapping it up.[208] There was another pause.

'Even coronavirus has failed in some areas, though. Did you read that Trump has given states more time and authority to decide how to implement new technology in coal-fired power stations?' Luke was reading the news online. 'He brought it in right in the middle of a pandemic. He's not invested in lowering mercury pollution.'

'No, he's only invested in his investments,' Michael added cynically.

'There's definitely a link to pollution. The highest extra deaths are in London—one hundred and thirty per cent extra deaths compared to the seasonal average. Ouch! The capital is followed by the Northwest and West Midlands. In France, there were two hotspots: Paris and the other around Mulhouse. In Italy, the epicentre was in the northern region of Lombardy.'

'There were political differences when lockdown was

instituted.' Michael proffered an alternative argument, even though he wasn't familiar with European geography.

'Even with these differences, within countries the most polluted cities have the worst infectivity rate and mortality. It's obvious. It's been linked to air pollution; this report specifically mentions that the amount of particulate matter is associated with increased infectivity.'[209] Luke waved his smart phone in front of Michael.

He sensed that Michael wasn't that well informed and reeled off the cities and associated industries. Paris and London needed no explanation. Mulhouse had a significant textile industry, a chloralkali plant that tipped mercury into the river basin, and a large car manufacturer. Lombardy had metal mining, fertiliser and fungicide chemicals industries, along with steel works and coal-burning, which caused smog. It had been described as having a similar level of air pollution to southern Poland.

As the pandemic continued to rage, other countries that had figured in the Parkinson's disease project as places with pollution and a high prevalence of disease also had worse outcomes from Covid, such as Brazil, India and the States. The numbers were changing on a daily basis, but the worst states for the number of Covid cases per head and mortality were New York, New Jersey, Massachusetts and Connecticut. Wuhan was known to be heavily polluted, and compared with other Chinese provinces, the death rate was significantly higher and the cure rate significantly lower in the Hubei province. Air pollution definitely seemed to be an issue.

As with Parkinson's disease, selenium improved outcomes. This had been shown in China. Enshi City, which was seven hours by car due west of Wuhan, had a much higher cure rate and was known for having elevated selenium in the soil and, consequently, a high oral intake. It was well known that host selenium deficiency led to increasing virulence of other RNA viruses, such as types of Coxsackie and Influenza. Covid-19 had caused cardiomyopathy in some cases. There was even a condition called Keshan disease, which arose due to a combination of Coxsackie infection and selenium deficiency, which amazingly could be treated with selenium.

Michael looked at the other coronavirus outbreak—SARS—which occurred in 2002. In this case, mortality rates increased alongside pollution levels. It was more than a trend; there was a definite association.[210] In fact, other scientists had also worked out that Covid was a mitochondrial disease. The virus apparently hijacked the host's mitochondria.

Michael was fascinated. Mitochondria were making a comeback! They really were the powerhouses of the cells. They had even been found flowing freely through the blood.[211] They were thought to have descended from bacteria and were closely linked to them, both genetically and evolutionarily. Michael looked at an analysis of the antibiotics used to treat Covid patients in different countries. Interestingly, the countries with the highest use had a significantly poorer outcome. It was known that some antibiotics actually inhibited mitochondrial DNA, weakening the immune system.[212] He thought back to the Finnish paper, which showed a higher prevalence of Parkinson's disease after antibiotic use. Perhaps this was because antibiotics were mitochondrial poisons.

He found a clever analogy on a blog, comparing mitochondria to reinforced nuclear power plants like the one at CERN, the largest particle accelerator in the world, boosting the energy of particles with superconducting magnets. It was true, the mitochondria were like mini CERNs, the particles were the high-energy compounds and the magnets were the transmembrane complexes. Mitochondria can safely manage the explosive reactions required to break the oxygen-oxygen bonds between the O_2 in the air. *Of course!* Michael hadn't thought of it like that before. Many diseases were associated with mitochondrial dysfunction, including neurodegenerative diseases. Mitochondria deteriorated with age, losing their respiratory function by accumulating mutations and errors in their DNA. Ageing mitochondria produced excess reactive oxygen species and increased susceptibility to infections. All the major risk factors for Covid-19 involved mitochondrial dysfunction and accelerated ageing, which shortened life. The young were able to generate sufficient ATP from oxidative phosphorylation.[213]

Going back to basics, it was easy to explain why Covid was so lethal, yet still no connection with the fact that ageing mitochondria are poisoned by contaminants of modern-day living was being made. There was definitely a link between Covid and neurodegenerative diseases such as Parkinson's. A few other scientists had recognised that too. It all pointed to sick mitochondria. Covid-19 survivors experienced accelerated ageing, which wasn't just seen in the lungs but also occurred in the brain.[214]

Michael thought he might have found a plausible connection between the virus, pollution and Parkinson's disease. The Covid spike protein binds to the ACE2 receptor. This was well documented by now. It was a critical step in viral replication and, therefore, infectivity, viral load and outcome. In both the spike protein and the ACE2 receptor, there were several cysteine residues, containing sulphur, which binds avidly to mercury. There was a stronger bond between the ACE2 receptor and the viral spike protein when the disulphide (S-S) bonds were present. This occurred in sick mitochondria with an oxidative state in cells. Glutathione was an antioxidant and a measure of cellular oxidative stress. High glutathione levels reduced the sulphur to thiol (SH) groups and weakened the attraction to the Covid spike protein. Mercury increased oxidative stress, thereby potentially enhancing the ability of the virus to attach to the cells and gain entry. Well, this is what Michael thought anyway. It just seemed self-evident.

Obviously, there were other factors affecting the spread, such as early containment, something at which the UK and the US had been appalling. Both countries had put the economy ahead of health. *Minamata*. Some lessons were never learned.

★

Luke opened the paper on global Parkinson's disease prevalence on his laptop, and then clicked on another chart. He started writing down the countries in two columns: China, the US, India, Russia, Japan, Germany, South Africa, South Korea, Indonesia and Poland. Then a second list: China, the US, India, Japan, Russia, Germany, Indonesia, Italy, Brazil and France.

'What are these?' Michael asked, noting the similarities in the two lists.

'The first list is the top-ten coal consumers in order of size.'

'The second list?' Michael suspected he knew already, and there were remarkable similarities that couldn't just be coincidence.

'That's Parkinson's disease prevalence in order, starting with China. It uses one million megawatts of coal. Over forty-nine per cent of the global consumption of coal is in China alone, and one point four million people in the country are living with Parkinson's disease. That was in 2016, and the numbers are still going up. I read in one article that by 2030, China will have fifty per cent of the cases of Parkinson's disease in the world.'[215]

★

The national lockdown was dragging on, and the initial novelty had worn off. Doomscrolling was becoming monotonous.

'Do you have any jigsaws?' Michael asked Luke.

'No.' Luke didn't stop reading.

'Board games?'

'No, afraid not,' Luke replied and continued reading.

'How about some live theatre on the TV tonight?' Michael suggested. Luke agreed. There were some definite advantages to the restrictions.

Michael returned to the *Lancet* paper on the age-adjusted prevalence of Parkinson's disease. He had to admit it had become a fun thing to do, rather like playing *Risk*, the warfare board game. The idea was to identify the higher risk countries in a certain region and work out why this was the case. So, for example, in Africa, the three countries with the highest prevalence were, in order: Egypt, Algeria and Nigeria, with large gaps between them. He knew about Egypt. Algeria? There was a chloralkali plant discharging mercury into the bay. It seemed that mercury pollution was known to be an issue.[216] Nigeria burnt coal.

He looked at Europe and was surprised at the high prevalence in Norway. Not coal, surely? After a little more research, he had it worked out.

'It's fish. Oh, and an ex-Nazi submarine leaking mercury off the coast,' he said out loud, unable to contain his excitement. Norway had tried to address the problem with a comprehensive plan aimed at trying to reduce the mercury pollution. Michael wasn't sure how feasible this was.

*

Luke and Michael's standards hadn't just slipped, they had plummeted. Neither of them missed grooming themselves for work. Luke had regressed from wearing suits to putting on a shirt and jeans, adding a tie occasionally for online clinics. Both men were shaving far less.

'I might get you to cut my hair, is that OK?' Luke asked Michael. 'It's getting quite long and difficult to manage.'

'Oh, I don't know, you're turning into a blue zone,' Michael laughed, and Luke looked confused. 'Gorgeously unruly!'

*

The days were all the same.

'Tea?' Michael asked, clearly not sure what to do for the rest of the day. He'd read the papers, answered emails, checked on Facebook and taken his Government-sanctioned daily exercise. They weren't short of any essential items.

'No, I'm OK.'

'Coffee?'

Without waiting for a response, Michael started telling Luke about the benefits of the drink. 'It's an antioxidant. The roasting process produces melanoidins, apparently, which are strong antioxidants.'

Luke looked up, suddenly interested. 'Perhaps I will have one,' he smiled, and Michael switched on the coffee machine.

'Tea, cocoa, honey and wine have the same benefits,' Michael continued, 'but coffee is the richest source of antioxidants. Coffee and cocoa are better than tea, which is better than red wine. The benefits of coffee are also to do with the chlorogenic acid it contains. Interestingly, the Arabica coffee contains the most; it's the one you typically get from India and Mexico.'

He brought two black coffees over to the table between the wingback chairs. 'I've been looking up foods that contain antioxidants, too, to add to your list of healthy foods.' Michael wasn't overly keen on the buckwheat pancakes, although he didn't mind the maple syrup. 'Fruits and vegetables have antioxidants, but also there are some foods that are naturally high in glutathione, namely spinach, avocados, asparagus and okra. Whey protein is high in cysteine, which increases the rate of glutathione production. Fascinating, huh? You've got your mercury tattoo and your whey protein antidote!' Michael had noticed a number of shops in the city selling whey protein for building muscles, and a number of men with bulging biceps covered completely in tattoos. He laughed at his own joke. 'Glutathione production requires either cysteine in the diet, or it can be synthesised from methionine. Both of these are sulphur-containing amino acids. Sulphur-rich foods include broccoli, sprouts, cauliflower, kale and watercress, as well as garlic, onions and shallots. Cured by kale. That's shallot!'

★

For some light entertainment, Michael had been inventing a new board game. 'Perhaps it should be called *The Game of Death*. You know, like *The Game of Life*, but with higher stakes? You can be posted around the globe as a journalist, musician or engineer, gaining toxicity points and maybe green points. It's a winner.'

'Hmmm,' Luke pondered. 'You might want to rethink the name?'

'It's like *Cluedo* as well.'

'What is?' Luke was still trying to work out how a board game crossing *Monopoly, Risk* and *The Game of Life* would work, and now *Cluedo*?

'Yes, alpha-synuclein in the substantia nigra, with dopamine and the iron. Ha! They all have a motive, well, the putative mechanisms.'

Michael realised he was beginning to get cabin fever. '*How to save the planet and yourself, too?*' he suggested.

Luke didn't look up, but spoke in a droll manner, 'Or *Mikey and the Mercury Factory*.'

Michael laughed, thinking of ideas for cards for the new game. *Songbirds' mass death in New Mexico. Move back three spaces.*

*

Out of the blue one day, Michael asked Luke about Joe. 'Do you think he had Lewy Body Dementia, like Robin Williams?'

He'd read an article about how the actor had committed suicide having suffered terrible symptoms for a number of years. There was a piece by his wife, who described the symptoms that Michael recognised from Joe: constipation, urinary difficulties, heartburn, sleeplessness, insomnia, poor sense of smell, but also paranoia, anxiety and delusions. It was thought he probably also had hallucinations.

'For most of his life he lived in San Francisco,' Michael commented. 'The article was fascinating, as it covered the fluctuating nature of the illness and also the way someone can cover up the worst symptoms.' He shook his head. He'd said enough on the matter.

Luke decided not to push him and changed the subject. 'Robbie Williams has been found to have toxic levels of mercury in his system.'

'Yeah, I read about that. He was eating fish twice a day, and lived in London, Malibu and LA. Victoria Beckham also has high mercury levels—from eating swordfish and tuna. It sounded as though she was having chelation therapy at a spa in Germany.'

'That's interesting,' Luke replied. He remembered reading about the drug DMPS, which had been approved in Germany to detox mercury.

★

A few days later, Michael suddenly announced, 'I looked it up! You know how Parkinson's is associated with oxidative stress, as is Covid-19? Well, mercury poisoning increases oxidative stress. Glutathione is a powerful antioxidant, but you need cysteine to replenish stocks. N-acetylcysteine provides the body with cysteine. Do you follow?' Michael checked that Luke was still listening. 'This is the good part. You see, there's this hypothesis that the patients who develop severe Covid have less glutathione. N-acetylcysteine—NAC for short—helped in other viral infections, so it might help in Covid.'

Like many people, Michael was hoping for an effective treatment and would jump at anything shown to have a benefit.

Luke wondered where Michael was going with this. He replied, 'Yes, useful drug. We've used it in paracetamol overdose and in alcoholic liver failure for years. It was first used as a mucolytic—to break down mucus in chest infections. Funny how it's gone full circle and made its way back to chest medicine again.'

'Well, it's actually been used in a case of acute mercury poisoning, and with selenium it worked better than the chelator DMSA. Interesting, huh?'[217] He had been sitting next to Luke in the chair but stood up in his enthusiasm. 'The thing is, African Americans have lower glutathione levels than whites. This is the case even after adjustments for cardiovascular disease and type-2 diabetes, which are known to reduce levels. So, there are proven racial differences to oxidative stress. That's what we see in Covid.'[218, 219]

★

'It's happened,' Luke announced after reading the news on his tablet.

'What has?'

'They've finally shown that diesel exhausts cause neurodegenerative disease.'

'Really? So, you were right,' Michael acknowledged proudly.

'It's in zebra fish. What is it with zebra fish? They are the monkeys of the fish world.'

Michael started singing, '*Hey, hey, we're the Monkees.*'

'Apparently, freshwater fish neurons interact in a similar way to humans.'

'So, it is all about fish, after all,' Michael teased.

'And unlike humans, zebra fish are transparent, hence you can see what's going on in their brain without killing them. If you could see through to your brain, there'd be fish there.' Luke ruffled Michael's long lockdown hair, causing Michael to squirm.

'Whereas we just kill humans, slowly destroy them,' Michael muttered scathingly under his breath. He then resumed humming the Monkees theme. It was one of those catchy tunes that once started was difficult to shake.

'Anyway, diesel was neurotoxic and increased alpha-synuclein. And we know what happens when alpha-synuclein increases—'.[220]

'It aggregates.' Michael knew the story. *'Here we come, walkin' down the street—'* He was off again.

*

'You've been overwatering again, Michael.' Luke sounded displeased. He was wandering around the apartment with a small watering can.

'Oh, sorry.' Michael didn't look up, but spontaneously announced, 'Amyloid proteins!' He looked round to see if Luke had finished complaining. 'Like your prions? Well, these are also produced by bacteria and promote alpha-synuclein aggregation in the brain and the gut.' It was Michael's turn to boast now. 'Exposure to these microbial amyloids can act as triggers for Parkinson's disease. The bacteria responsible are *E. coli*. The proteins are called curli proteins,' he chuckled, amused by the name. '*E. coli* are found in the gut. I knew gut bacteria were important!'[221]

The presence of *E. coli* in drinking water was recommended

as a test of water cleanliness; *E. coli* indicates faecal pollution. Michael had also found a paper confirming faecal pollution in Iran, one of the countries with a higher prevalence of Parkinson's disease.[222] He was also now getting a very different image of the Baltic Sea. It was apparently one of the most polluted seas in the world, and it wasn't just from industrial waste. Much of the arsenal of Nazi Germany was dumped there after the Second World War. The connection with the ocean was shallow, meaning that any pollution from the surrounding industrialised countries remained in the Baltic.[200]

'Poland is the tailpipe of Europe,' Michael declared. 'Look at this.' He showed Luke a table illustrating that three of Europe's worst coal plants were in Poland. 'Meanwhile, Sweden closed its last coal plant in 2002, and France, Portugal, the UK, Ireland and Slovakia are all moving to cleaner energies by 2025 at the latest.'

Michael was quiet for a while, whilst taking in the statistics on a comprehensive report written by the European Environment Agency. It recognised that there was a big problem. He then blurted out, 'Check this out. Young women in Spain and Portugal have the highest mercury levels in Europe. They're almost ten times higher than here.'[223]

'I wonder why that is?' Luke said, looking at the chart, which confirmed what Michael had told him. He knew an answer would be forthcoming.

'It just has to be fish!'

★

The news was monothematic as coronavirus spread around the globe. The daily death toll in the UK had been replaced by global deaths. Famous people with the virus in the media were usurped by obituaries of stars from the past, many of whom Michael hadn't realised were still alive. Michael's interests had diverted from Covid back to pollution. Since the lockdown, it was clear that industry produced most of it.

He started ranting at Luke. 'The iron and steel industry is required to produce new, eco-friendly cars. However, the iron and steel production process is one of the predominant anthropogenic sources of atmospheric mercury emissions worldwide. The countries with the most electric cars are China and the United States. These are also the countries with the most mercury pollution, and the countries burning the most fossil fuels to produce electricity to run the cars. This is without considering the other toxic metals in the batteries: cadmium and lithium. It's all wrong!' he huffed. 'Comparing the mercury emissions from automobiles using gasoline, diesel and liquid petroleum gas—a low carbon fuel known as LPG for short—LPG produces three times as much mercury as diesel and significantly more than gasoline or petrol.'[224] He shook his head, becoming exasperated. 'Now scientists are encouraging a fish diet high in omega-3 fatty acids to promote dopamine, which means people are taking on yet more mercury poisoning.'

*

During the lockdown, there were occasional upsides and good news. Luke read aloud from his tablet. 'Britain goes coal free as renewables edge out fossil fuels. Only a decade ago, forty per cent of our energy was derived from coal. When Britain went into lockdown, our electricity demand plummeted.'

Michael had to admit this was a benefit. The UK had gone two months without burning any coal. Then there had been a cold spell at the beginning of June—what a crazy world.

'Did you know that the UK now has the biggest offshore wind industry in the world, and the largest single wind farm is off the Yorkshire coast? Way to go!' Michael smiled, but not for long, as a disturbing headline caught his eye.

Hundreds of elephants dead in Botswana's Okavango Delta

He studied the photos. Lying on its side next to a few sparsely scattered trees was the remains of an emaciated elephant, with baggy skin folds, its front limbs curled up. Curiously, its tusks were intact. Nearby, an elephant carcass was lying halfway between the green pool of water and the brown dust. It also hadn't had its tusks removed. He then read through various reports. Many of the dead elephants had been seen close to natural waterholes, some had been found on trails while others had collapsed on their chests, indicating death had most likely occurred suddenly. *Like birds falling out of the sky.* There were stories of dying elephants walking around in circles or dragging their hind legs, as though their rear quarters were paralysed, suggesting that something potentially neurotoxic was causing this bizarre ailment. Locals observed that there were fewer vultures than usual.

By flying over the vast waterscape, it was difficult to estimate the numbers of elephants that had died. Initially, one or two were spotted here and there, then the discoveries accelerated. It was now thought to be around four hundred, making it one of the largest elephant mortality events ever recorded, certainly this century. Conservationists were urging governments to speed up investigations, but still the mortality was unexplained.

Algal blooms were initially blamed for the mass die off. Anthrax, which is caused by bacteria that occurs naturally in soil, has been known to kill wildlife in large numbers, but laboratory testing had ruled it out. Due to travel restrictions during the pandemic, the hunting season in Southern Africa had failed to take off in 2020, but these deaths weren't caused by hunting or poaching—for once the elephants weren't being killed, they were dying of a mystery illness, tusks intact.

Following years of droughts, there had been a huge amount of rain in neighbouring Angola earlier in the year, resulting in the highest flood levels in the Okavango Delta for five years.

Michael showed Luke the article and they both read it quietly, before turning to each other. 'Mercury!' they said in unison.

'It has to be,' Michael insisted.

'But where is it coming from?' Luke asked, searching online for any clues.

'It'll be gold mining in the neighbouring countries.' Michael felt gloomy as he read that there were indeed reports of illegal gold mining. Africa was experiencing a great gold rush.

'So, if we're right about Parkinson's disease and mercury . . .' Luke started saying.

'And thiamine deficiency,' Michael added with a nod.

'And Covid and possibly mercury, or pollution at the very least—'

'Yep, and thiamine deficiency,' Michael added determinedly.

'Aha!' nodded Luke in agreement. 'Then why hasn't anyone else worked it out? It just seems so clear. It's the only thing that links it all together.'

'And fish,' Michael added, concurring.

'Of course, and fish.'

'And bacteria.' Michael was quite emphatic. 'They convert mercury into the dangerous type and make your proteins stick together, which then creep along your nerves and destroy thiamine. In fact, when there are more bacteria around, the response is to increase thiaminase production—whether that's the bacteria producing it or the fish.' Michael was pleased he was able to bring the conversation back to fish and bacteria.

'I hadn't thought about it before, but the mercury cycle is intricately linked to the carbon cycle. We burn fossil fuels, which release carbon *and* mercury. This either warms up the planet, hence more mercury vapour is released, or it cools it down, so we use more fossil fuels to counteract the effects. Flooding means more organic mercury is produced, along with sewage leakage, leading to more organic mercury in the water. Water, water everywhere—'

'—Nor any drop to drink.' Michael continued reciting the famous Coleridge poem. 'Or fish to eat.' He changed it slightly.

Luke smiled. 'It's not all about fish, you know.'

A note from the author

The idea for this novel hatched from my personal experience, after I developed a constellation of odd and debilitating neurological symptoms while working as a hospital consultant in Norwich. In writing this book, my hope was to share with the reader not only the findings of my research, but also the exciting journey behind them. As such, I have created the fictional character, Michael, whose own foray into researching the causes of neurological disease was motivated by his father's Parkinson's diagnosis.

After years of researching the cause of my symptoms, I first wrote about my experiences and my findings in a memoir published in 2020.[70] Through my research, I became increasingly aware of the impact of thiamine deficiency on the nervous system. Thiamine is essential for all of us, and thiamine deficiency is more common than is currently appreciated. In my case, thiamine deficiency was caused by an overgrowth of bacteria in the gut. Bacteria produce thiaminase enzymes, which destroy thiamine. My symptoms improved following the administration of antibiotic treatment and a fat-soluble thiamine supplement.

Having established the link between neurological disease and thiamine deficiency, and the role played by bacteria, I turned my attention to the source of the bacteria. Like Michael, I was convinced that water pollution was the culprit, and that waterborne bacteria were the transmitters of modern disease, causing low-grade infections in the gut and adverse effects elsewhere in the body, over years or even decades.

I searched for evidence to back up my hypothesis. The association of flood areas in the USA with high rates of Parkinson's supported my theory of waterborne bacteria causing disease. However, reviewing a global study of prevalence made me question whether it was quite so straightforward. Canada has a particularly high prevalence of Parkinson's disease, but unlike with other areas, I couldn't find any major reports of pollution from sewage or flooding. There is a problem with water pollution in Canada, but the problem is mercury. Although I remained certain of the link between thiamine deficiency and neurological disease, the cause turned out to be more complex than I had previously thought.

It is well established that mercury poisoning causes neurological injury and death; the impact has been seen in animals and in humans across the globe. In 1995, a medical science journalist, Geir Bjørklund, summarised data from a number of different states and countries, demonstrating that Parkinson's mortality was related to mercury contamination from chemical, paper, iron or copper industries.[225] High levels of mercury in the blood are associated with an increased incidence of Parkinson's disease.[226] Patients with dental amalgam fillings are more susceptible to Parkinson's, and there is a direct correlation between the number and the extent of the surfaces of mercury-containing dental amalgam fillings and the amount of mercury in the brain.[227]

As I delved into the literature, certain patterns emerged, and the same factors became apparent each time: water pollution, mercury, low thiamine and bacteria. Everywhere I looked—every mass death in the animal kingdom, every society with a high incidence of neurological diseases—I found a correlation between these four conditions, disease and death.

Neurological diseases are the main cause of disability throughout the world, and Parkinson's disease is the fastest growing of the neurodegenerative conditions. Treating neurodegenerative disease is really difficult. Parkinson's causes symptoms throughout the body, and the treatment for it is costly and never curative. More often than not, this also causes further illness through adverse side effects—I hoped to illustrate the devastating impact of this disease and the poor treatment options through the character of Joe, Michael's father.

My research for this novel has taken me—virtually—to London, Hubei, the United States, Brazil and Mexico City. I discovered that the places and countries with the worst mercury pollution were in the news with high Covid-19 infection and death rates. I also noticed parallels between the symptoms of Covid-19 and neurological disease: loss of smell, gut symptoms, male predominance, a link with diabetes and mitochondrial involvement. The places with a high incidence of neurological disease and the places worst affected by the coronavirus pandemic were both associated with high exposure to pollution from anthropogenic activity, such as coal and gold mining, diesel fumes, steel and chemical factories.

In writing this novel, I hope to highlight the ongoing issues with mercury toxicity, the likely consequences and the risk factors for mercury excess to individuals and the planet as a whole, so that each of us can review our risk and our impact. The characters in this novel are fictional, but the evidence behind the narrative is based on real news reports and scientific papers. I have kept as close as possible to the original dates of these reports and papers within the timeline of the story.

The underlying problem is straightforward: anthropogenic activity is poisoning the human race and all the creatures on the planet. Our industries continue to produce high levels of mercury, which will persist and continue to accumulate in our environment. We need to change.

References

1 Dawkins R. The selfish gene. Oxford; New York: Oxford University Press. 1989.

2 Bengtsson B-E, Hill C and Nellbring S (Eds). Report from the second workshop on reproduction disturbances in fish, 20-23 November 1995. 1996. Swedish Environmental Protection Agency, Report 4534. 114 pp

3 Swanson S and Kiernan L. Killer storm drowns summer peace. Chicago Tribune. 3 July 1992. www.chicagotribune.com>ct-xpm-1992-07-03-9202290463-story

4 Schoeb TR, Heaton-Jones TG, Clemmons RM, Carbonneau DA, Woodward AR, Shelton D and Poppenga RH. Clinical and necropsy findings associated with increased mortality among American alligators of Lake Griffin, Florida. J Wildl Dis. 2002; 38(2): 320-37.

5 Honeyfield DC, Ross JP, Carbonneau DA, Terrell SP, Woodward AR, Schoeb TR, Perceval HF and Hinterkopf JP. Pathology, physiologic parameters, tissue contaminants, and tissue thiamine in morbid and healthy central Florida adult American alligators (Alligator mississippiensis). J Wildl Dis. 2008; 44(2): 280-94.

6 Viartis. Prevalence of Parkinson's Disease. http://www.viartis.net/parkinsons.disease/

7 Moccia RD, Fox GA and Britton A. A quantitative assessment of thyroid histopathology of herring gulls (Larus argentatus) from the Great Lakes and a hypothesis on the causal role of environmental contaminants. J Wildl Dis. 1986; 22(1): 60-70.

8 Yule AM, Barker IK, Austin JW and Moccia RD. Toxicity of Clostridium botulinum type E neurotoxin to Great Lakes fish: implications for avian botulism. J Wildl Dis. 2006; 42(3): 479-93.

9 Wohlsein P, Peters M, Geburek F, Seeliger F and Böer M. Polioencephalomalacia in captive harbour seals (Phoco vitulina). J Vet Med. 2003; 50(3):145-50.

10 Geraci JR. Experimental thiamine deficiency in captive harp seals, Phoco groenlandica, induced by eating herring, Clupea harengus, and smelts, Osmerus mordax. Can J Zool. 1972; 50(2): 179-95.

11 Jubb TF. A thiamine responsive nervous disease in saltwater crocodiles (Crocodylus porosus). Vet Rec. 1992; 131(15): 347-8.

12 Studdert VP and Labuc RH. Thiamin deficiency in cats and dogs associated with feeding meat preserved with sulphur dioxide. Aust Vet J. 1991; 68(2): 54-7.

13 Green RG. Chastek paralysis — a new disease in foxes. Minn Wildl Dis Invest. 1936; 2: 106-7.

14 Jones TL. Chastek paralysis on Alberta fox ranch. Can J Comp Med Vet Sci. 1943; 7(4): 112-3.

15 Siponen A. IMO bans ships' sewage in the Baltic Sea! 2010. www.panda.org/wwf_news/?195333/imo-sewage-ban

16 Honeyfield DC, Hanes JW, Brown L, Kraft CE and Begley TP. Comparison of thiaminase activity in fish using the radiometric and 4-nitrothiophenol calorimetric methods. J. Great Lakes Res. 2010; 36(4): 641-5.

17 Hanes JW, Kraft CE and Begley TP. An assay for thiaminase I in complex biological samples. Anal Biochem. 2007; 368(1): 33-8.

18 Honeyfield DC, Hinterkopf JP and Brown SB. Isolation of thiaminase-positive bacteria from alewife. Trans Am Fish Soc. 2002; 131(1): 171-5.

19 Honeyfield DC, Hinterkopf JP, Fitzsimons JD, Tillitt DE, Zajicek JL and Brown SB. Development of thiamine deficiencies and early mortality syndrome in lake trout by feeding experimental and feral fish diets containing thiaminase. J Aquat Anim Health. 2005; 17(1): 4-12.

20 Richter CA, Wright-Osment MK, Zajicek JL, Honeyfield DC and Tillitt DE. Quantitative polymerase chain reaction (PCR) assays for a bacterial thiaminase I gene and the thiaminase-producing bacterium Paenibacillus thiaminolyticus. J Aquat Anim Health. 2009; 21(4): 229-38.

21 Lepak JM, Kraft CE, Honeyfield DC and Brown SB. Evaluating the effect of stressors on thiaminase activity in alewife. J Aquat Anim Health. 2008; 20(1): 63-71.

22 Wistbacka S, Lönnström L-G, Bonsdorff E and Bylund G. Thiaminase activity of crucian carp Carassius carassius injected with a bacterial fish pathogen Aeromonas salmonicida subsp. salmonicida. J Aquat Anim Health. 2009; 21(4): 217-28.

23 Tillitt DE, Riley SC, Evans AN, Nichols SJ, Zajicek JL, Rinchard J, Richter CA and Krueger CC. Dreissenid mussels from the Great Lakes contain elevated thiaminase activity. J Great Lakes Res. 2009; 35: 309-12.

24 Claramunt RM, Warner DM, Madenjian CP, Treska TJ and Hanson D. Offshore salmonine food web. The state of Lake Michigan in 2011. Great Lakes Fishery Commission. 2012; Spec pub 12-01: 13-23.

25 Spear S. Lake Erie toxic algae bloom seen as worst in decades. 1 December 2011. www.ecowatch.com/lake-erie-toxic-algae-bloom-seen-as-worst-in-decades-1881558624.html

26 Hendler G. Recent mass mortality of Strongylocentrotus purpuratus (Echinodermata: Echioindea) at Malibu and a review of purple sea urchin kills elsewhere in California. Bull S Cal Ac Sci. 2013; 112(1): 19-37.

27 Glaister D. Why septic tanks are a washout in Malibu. The Guardian. 26 September 2010. www.theguardian.com/theguardian/2010/sep/26/septic-tanks-washout-malibu

28 Hawthorne M. Storm forces officials to open Lake Michigan locks. Chicago Tribune. 1 Jul 2014. www.chicagotribune.com/news/breaking/chi-lake-michigan-sewage-stormwater-mwrd-20140701-story.html

29 Wright Willis A, Evanoff BA, Lian M, Criswell S R and Racette BA. Geographic and ethnic variation in Parkinson disease: a population-based study of US Medicare beneficiaries. Neuroepidemiology. 2010; 34(3): 143-51.

30 Caller TA, Doolin JW, Haney JF, Murby AJ, West KG, Farrar HE, Ball A, Harris BT and Stommel EW. A cluster of amyotrophic lateral sclerosis in New Hampshire: a possible role for toxic cyanobacteria blooms. Amyotroph Lateral Scler. 2009; 10(S2): 101-8.

31 Cox PA and Sacks OW. Cycad neurotoxins, consumption of flying foxes, and ALS-PDC disease in Guam. Neurology. 2002; 58(6): 956-9.

32 Cox PA, Richer R, Metcalf JS, Banack SA, Codd GA and Bradley WG. Cyanobacteria and BMAA exposure from desert dust: a possible link to sporadic ALS among Gulf War veterans. Amyotroph Lateral Scler. 2009; 10 (S2):109-17.

33 Proctor J. British Columbia. Metro Vancouver guilty of dumping sewage in Burrard Inlet. CBC News. 12 March 2014. www.cbc.ca/news/canada/british-columbia/metro-vancouver-guilty-of-dumping-sewage-in-burrard-inlet-1.2570322

34 Davies H. Michael J Fox one of four on TV show hit by Parkinson's. The Telegraph. 29 March 2002. https://www.telegraph.co.uk/news/worldnews/northamerica/canada/1389234/Michael-J-Fox-one-of-four-on-TV-show-hit-by-Parkinsons.html

35 Richter CA, Evans AN, Wright-Osment MK, Zajicek JL, Heppell SA, Riley SC, Krueger CC and Tillitt D. Paenibacillus thiaminolyticus is not the cause of thiamine deficiency impeding lake trout (Salvelinus namaycush) recruitment in the Great Lakes. Can J Fish Aquat Sci. 2012; 69: 1056-64.

36 Fujita A, Nose Y, Kozuka S, Tashiro T, Veda K and Sakamoto S. Studies on thiaminase I: activation of thiamine breakdown by organic bases. J Biol Chem. 1952; 196(1): 289-95.

37 Incardona JP, Carls MG, Holland L, Linbo TL, Baldwin DH, Myers MS, Peck KA, Tagal M, Rice SD and Scholz NL. Very low embryonic crude oil exposures cause lasting cardiac defects in salmon and herring. Sci Rep. Nature. 2015; 5: 13499.

38 Xu C, Weese JS, Flemming C, Odumeru J and Warriner K. Fate of Clostridium diffice during wastewater treatment and incidence in Southern Ontario watersheds. J Appl Microbiol. 2014; 117(3): 891-904.

39 Chossudovsky M. Ten thousand dead sea lions wash up in California. 'This is a crisis'. What is the cause? ENE News Global Research California. https://www.mondialisation.ca/ten-thousand-dead-sea-lions-wash-up-in-california-officials-announce-crisis/5517547

40 Diep F. The sea star and urchin die-off you've never heard of. Pacific Standard. 5 June 2015, updated 14 June 2017. www.psmag.com/.amp/environment/every-single-one-along-sixty-miles-of-coast

41 Hewson I, Button J, Gudenkauf BM, Minor B, Newton AL Gaydos JK, Wynne J, Groves CL, Hendler G, Murray M, Fradkin S, Breitbart M, Fahsbender E, Lafferty KD, Kilpatrick AM, Miner CM, Raimondi P, Zahner L, Friedman CS, Daniels S, Haulena M, Marliave J, Burge CA, Eisenlord ME and Harvell CD. Densovirus associated with sea-star wasting disease and mass mortality. PNAS. 2014; 111(48): 17278-83.

42 De Pasquale E, Baumann H and Gobler CJ. Vulnerability of early life stage among Northwest Atlantic forage fish to ocean acidification and low oxygen. Marine Ecology Progress Series. 2015; 523: 145-56.

43 GBD 2016 Parkinson's Disease Collaborators. Global, regional, and national burden of Parkinson's disease, 1990-2016: a systemic analysis for the Global Burden of Disease Study 2016. Lancet Neurol. 2018; 17(11): 939-53.

44 Mosa A and Duffin J. The interwoven history of mercury poisoning in Ontario and Japan. CMAJ. 2017; 189(5): E213-5.

45 Weech SA, Scheuhammer AM, Elliott JE and Cheng KM. Mercury in fish from the Pinchi Lake Region, British Columbia, Canada. Environ Pollut. 2004; 131(2): 275-86.

46 Marras C, Beck JC, Bower JH, Roberts E, Ritz B, Ross GW, Abbott RD, Savica R, Van den Eeden SK, Willis AW and Tanner CM on behalf of the Parkinson's Foundation P4 Group. Prevalence of Parkinson's disease across North America. Nature NPJ. Parkinson's disease. 2018; 4: 21.

47 Satoh H. Occupational and environmental toxicology of mercury and its compounds. Ind Health. 2000; 38(2): 153-64.

48 Shin S, Burnett RT, Kwong JC, Hystad P, van Donkelaar A, Brook JR, Copes R, Tu K, Goldberg MS, Villeneuve PJ, Martin RV, Murray BJ, Wilton AS, Kopp A and Chen H. Effects of ambient air pollution on incident Parkinson's disease in Ontario, 2001 to 2013: a population-based cohort study. Int J Epidemiol. 2018; 47(6): 2038-48.

49 The Madison Declaration on Mercury Pollution. MBIO: A Journal of the Human Environment, Royal Swedish Academy of Sciences. 2007; 36(1): 62-6.

50 Ball P. Flowing rivers of mercury. Royal Society of Chemistry. 7 January 2015. www.chemistryworld.com/features/flowing-rivers-of-mercury/8122.article

51 Li G, Ma J, Cui S, He Y, Xiao Q, Liu J and Chen S. Parkinson's disease in China: a forty-year growing track of bedside work. Translational Neurodegeneration. 2019; 8: 22.

52 Scull E. Environmental health challenges in Xinjiang. Wilson Center, China Environment Forum. 2018. www.wilsoncenter.org/publication/environmental-health-challenges-xinjiang

53 Zhang P, Zhang YY, Ren SC, Chen B, Luo D, Shao JA, Zhang SH and Li JS. Trade reshapes the regional energy related mercury emissions: A case study on Hubei Province based on a multi-scale input-output analysis. Journal of Cleaner Production. 2018; 185: 75-85.

54 Fang G-C, Lo C-T, Huang C-Y, Zhuang Y-J, Cho M-H, Tsai K-H and Xiao Y-F. PM2.5 particulates and particulate-bound mercury Hg(p) concentrations in a mixed urban, residential, traffic-heavy, and industrial site. Environmental Forensics. 2017; 18(3): 178-87.

55 Hsu C-S, Liu P-L, Chien L-C, Chou S-Y and Han B-C. Mercury concentration and fish consumption in Taiwanese pregnant women. BJOG. 2007; 114(1): 81-5.

56 Chen YC and Chen MH. Mercury levels of seafood commonly consumed in Taiwan. J of Food and Drug Analysis. 2006; 14(4): 373-8.

57 Barboza D. In China, farming fish in toxic waters. The New York Times. 15 December 2007. www.nytimes.com/2007/12/15/world/asia/15fish.html

58 Deng C, Zhang C, Li L, Li Z and Li N. Mercury contamination and its potential health effects in a lead-zinc mining area in the karst region of Guangxi, China. Applied Geochemistry. 2011; 26(2): 154-9.

59 Herada M. Minamata disease and the mercury pollution of the globe. www.einap.org/envdis/Minamata.html

60 Abbas MM, Zheyu X and Tan LCS. Epidemiology of Parkinson's disease – East versus West. Mov Disord Clin Pract. 2018; 5(1): 14-28.

61 Williams U, Bandmann O and Walker R. Parkinson's disease in Sub-Saharan Africa: A review of epidemiology, genetics and access to care. J Mov Disord. 2018; 11(2): 53-64.

62 Von Campenhausen S, Bornschein B, Wick R, Bötzel K, Sampaio C, Poewe W, Oertel W, Siebert U, Berger K and Dodel R. Prevalence and incidence of Parkinson's disease in Europe. Eur Neuropsychopharmacol. 2005; 15(4): 473-90.

63 Horsfall L, Petersen I, Walters K and Schrag A. Time trends in incidence of Parkinson's disease diagnosis in UK primary care. J Neurol. 2013; 260(5): 1351-7.

64 Donley N. The USA lags behind other agricultural nations in banning harmful pesticides. Environmental Health. 2019; 18(1): 44.

65 Orayj K, Akbari A, Lacey A, Smith M, Pickrell WO and Lane E. Incidence and prevalence of Parkinson's disease (PD) in Wales. European J Neurol. 2019; 26: 331.

66 Ritchie H. The death of coal in five charts. Our World in Data. 28 January 2019. https://ourworldindata.org/death-uk-coal

67 Darweesh SKL, Koudstaal PJ, Stricker BH, Hofman A and Ikram MA. Trends in the incidence of Parkinson's disease in the general population: The Rotterdam Study. Am J Epidemiol. 2016; 183(11): 1018-26.

68 De Lau LML and Breteler MMB. Epidemiology of Parkinson's disease. Lancet Neurol. 2006; 5: 525-35.

69 Giangrosso G, Cammilleri G, Macaluso A, Vella A, D'Orazio N, Graci S, Lo Dico GM, Galvano F, Giangrosso M and Ferrantelli V. Hair mercury levels detection in fishermen from Sicily (Italy) by ICP-MS method after microwave-assisted digestion. Bioinorg Chem and Appl. 2016; 5408014.

70 Dixon J. The missing link in dementia. A memoir. London: Wrate's Publishing. 2020.

71 Newman EJ, Grosset KA and Grosset DG. Geographical difference in Parkinson's disease prevalence within West Scotland. Mov Disord. 2009; 24(3): 401-6.

72 Hopey D. Mercury termed a big threat to health in region. Pittsburgh Post-Gazette. 26 January 2011. www.post-gazette.com/health/2011/01/26/mercury-termed-a-big-threat-to-health-in-region/stories/201101260170

73 Biddle TD. Mercury pollution concern grows in Pennsylvania. PennLive. 2011, updated 2019. https://www.pennlive.com/editorials/2011/03/mercury_pollution_concern_grow.html

74 EPA. Power plants likely covered by the mercury and air toxics standards (MATS). 19 January 2017. www.epa.gov/mats/power-plants-likely-covered-mercury-and-air-toxics-standards-mats_.html. Accessed 2020.

75 Rasmussen G. Millions of people being contaminated with toxic mercury used in mines. CBC News. 30 December 2015. www.cbc.ca/amp/1-3375754. Accessed 2020.

76 Rafati-Rahimzadeh M, Rafati-Rahimzadeh M, Kazemi S and Moghadamnia AA. Current approaches of the management of mercury poisoning: need of the hour. Daru. 2014; 22(1): 46.

77 Drasch G, Böse-O'Reilly S, Beinhoff C, Roider G and Maydl S. The Mt Diwata study on the Philippines 1999 — assessing mercury intoxication of the population by small scale gold mining. Sci Total Environ. 2001; 267(1-3): 151-68.

78 Contreras M, Pizarro P, Hernandez U, Gomez C and Gajardo J. Prevalence of Parkinson's disease in the region of Coquimbo, Chile [abstract]. Mov Disord. 2016; 31(Sl2).

79 Ritchie H. What the history of London's air pollution can tell us about the future of today's growing megacities. Our World in Data. 20 June 2017. https://ourworldindata.org/london-air-pollution

80 Heggie V. (The H-word) Over 200 years of deadly London air: smogs, fogs and pea soupers. The Guardian. 9 December 2016. www.theguardian.com/science/the-h-word/2016/dec/09/pollution-air-london-smogs-fogs-pea-soupers

81 Langston JW. The MPTP story. J Parkinsons Dis. 2017; 7(S1): S11-9.

82 Jaishankar M, Tseten T, Anbalagan N, Mathew B and Beeregowda KN. Toxicity, mechanism and health effects of some heavy metals. Interdiscip Toxicol. 2014; 7(2): 60-72.

83 Farina M, Avila DS, da Rocha JBT and Aschner M. Metals, oxidative stress and neurodegeneration: a focus on iron, manganese and mercury. Neurochem Int. 2013; 62(5): 575-94.

84 Kwakye GF, Paoliello MMB, Mukhopadhyay S, Bowman AB and Aschner M. Manganese-induced parkinsonism and Parkinson's disease: Shared and distinguishable features. Int J Environ Res Public Health. 2015; 12(7): 7519-40.

85 O'Neal SL and Zheng W. Manganese toxicity upon overexposure: A decade in review. Curr Environ Health Rep. 2015; 2(3): 315-28.

86 Zheng W, Ren S and Graziano JH. Manganese inhibits mitochondrial aconitase: a mechanism of manganese neurotoxicity. Brain Res. 1998; 799(2): 334-42.

87 Morello M, Canini A, Mattioli P, Sorge RP, Alimonti A, Bocca B, Forte G, Martorana A, Bernardi G and Sancesario G. Sub-cellular localization of manganese in the basal ganglia of normal and manganese-treated rats. An electron spectroscopy imaging and electron energy-loss spectroscopy study. Neurotoxicology. 2008; 29(1): 60-72.

88 Kimura H, Kurimura M, Wada M, Kawanami T, Kurita K, Suzuki Y, Katagiri T, Daimon M, Kayama T and Kato T. Female preponderance of Parkinson's disease in Japan. Neuroepidemiology. 2002; 21(6): 292-6.

89 Park J-H, Kim DH, Kwon D-Y, Choi M, Kim S, Jung J-H, Han K, and Park Y-G. Trends in the incidence and prevalence of Parkinson's disease in Korea: a nationwide, population-based study. BMC Geriatrics. 2019; 19: 320.

90 Kaiyrzhanov R, Rizig M, Aitkulova A, Zharkinbekova N, Shashkin C, Kaishibayeva G, Karimova A, Khaibullin T, Sadykova D, Ganieva M, Rasulova K and Houlden H. Parkinson's disease in Central Asian and Transcaucasian countries: a review of epidemiology, genetics, clinical characteristics, and access to care. Parkinson's Dis. 2019; 2905739.

91 El-Tallawy HN, Farghaly WM, Shehata G, Rageh T, Hakeem NM, Elhamed NM and Badry R. Prevalence of Parkinson's disease and other types of Parkinsonism in Al Kharga district, Egypt. Neuropsychiatr Dis Treat. 2013; 9: 1821-6.

92 Williams M, Todd GD, Roney N, Crawford J, Coles C, McClure PR, Garey JD, Zaccaria K and Citra M. Toxicological profile for manganese. Agency for Toxic Substances and Disease Registry (US). September 2012. www.atsdr.cdc.gov/toxprofiles/tp151.pdf

93 Praise S, Watanabe T, Watanabe K, Ito H and Okubo H. Impact of closed sabo dams on manganese concentration change in mountainous streams. Int J River Basin Management. 2017; 15(1): 61-8.

94 Jeong Y-S, Matsubae-Yokoyama K, Kubo H, Pak J-J and Nagasaka T. Substance flow analysis of phosphorus and manganese correlated with South Korean steel industry. Resources, Conservation and Recycling. 2009; 53(9): 479-89.

95 Wang F, Wang S, Zhang L, Yang H, Gao W, Wu Q and Hao J. Mercury mass flow in iron and steel production process and its implications for mercury emission control. J Environ Sci (China). 2016; 43: 293-301.

96 Salem MG, El-Awady MH and Amin E. Enhanced removal of dissolved iron and manganese from nonconventional water resources in Delta District, Egypt. Energy Procedia, 2012; 18: 983-93.

97 Bennett PC, El-Shishtawy AM, Sharp Jr JM and Atwira MG. Source and migration of dissolved manganese in the Central Nile Delta Aquifer, Egypt. J African Earth Sciences. 2014; 96: 8-20.

98 Maksimov AA. Types of manganese and iron-manganese deposits in Central Kazakhstan. International Geology Review. 1960; 2(6): 508-21.

99 Kazakhstan's mining industry: Steppe by Steppe. Engineering and Mining Journal. September 2015. www.gbreports.com/wp-content/uploads/2015/09/Kazakhstan_Mining2015.pdf

100 Yokel RA and Crossgrove JS. Manganese toxicokinetics at the blood-brain barrier. Res Rep Health Eff Inst. 2004; 119: 7-58.

101 Denton GRW, Siegrist HG and Jano-Edwards JP. Trace elements in Pandanus (Pandanus Testorius) from a manganese-enriched wetland in Southern Guam: a possible Lytigo-Botig connection? J Toxicol Environ Health A. 2009; 72(9): 574-6.

102 Galasko D, Salmon D, Gamst A, Olichney J, Thal LJ, Silbert L, Kaye J, Brooks P, Adonay R, Craig U-K, Schellenberg G and Borenstein AR. Prevalence of dementia in Chamorros on Guam: relationship to age, gender, education, and APOE. Neurology. 2007; 68(21): 1772-81.

103 Larbi M. My hangover twitch turned out to be an early sign of Parkinson's disease – I was only 23. The Sun. 11 April 2019. www.thesun.co.uk/fabulous/8829910/parkinsons-disease-hangover-twitch-early-sign/amp/

104 Sharpe MA, Livingston AD and Baskin DS. Thimerosal-derived ethylmercury is a mitochondrial toxin in human astrocytes: possible role of Fenton chemistry in the oxidation and breakage of mtDNA. J Toxicol. 2012; 373678.

105 Puspita L, Chung SY and Shim J-W. Oxidative stress and cellular pathologies in Parkinson's disease. Mol Brain. 2017; 10: 53.

106 Cunha-Oliveira T, Silva L, Silva AM, Moreno AJ, Oliveira CR and Santos MS. Mitochondrial complex I dysfunction induced by cocaine and cocaine plus morphine in brain and liver mitochondria. Toxicol Lett. 2013; 219(3): 298-306.

107 Le Bel CP, Ali SF and Bondy SC. Deferoxamine inhibits methylmercury-induced increases in reactive oxidative species formation in rat brain. Toxicol Appl Pharmacol. 1992; 112(1): 161-5.

108 Wermuth L, Pakkenberg H and Jeune B. High age-adjusted prevalence of Parkinson's disease among Inuits in Greenland. Neurology. 2002; 58(9): 1422-5.

109 Johansen P, Mulvad G, Pederson HS, Hansen JC and Riget F. Human accumulation of mercury in Greenland. Sci Total Environ. 2007; 377(2-3): 173-8.

110 Wermuth L, Joensen P, Bünger N and Jeune B. High prevalence of Parkinson's Disease in the Faroe Islands. Neurology. 1997; 49(2): 426-32.

111 Cox S. Mercury rising: how the Muskrat Falls dam threatens Inuit way of life. The Narwhal. 22 May 2019. www.thenarwhal.ca/mercury-rising-muskrat-falls-dam-threatens-inuit-way-of-life/

112 Sahakyan L, Belyaeva O and Saghatelyan A. Mercury pollution issues in Armenia's mining regions. International Multidisciplinary Scientific Geoconference. 2015; Book 5(1): 513-20.

113 van den Eeden SK, Tanner CM, Bernstein AL, Fross RD, Leimpeter A, Bloch DA and Nelson LM. Incidence of Parkinson's disease: variations by age, gender and race / ethnicity. Am J Epidemiol. 2003; 157(11): 1015-22.

114 Sun G, Feng X, Yin R, Zhao H, Zhang L, Sommar J, Li Z and Zhang H. Corn (Zea Mays L.): A low methylmercury staple cereal source and an important biospheric sink of atmospheric mercury, and health risk assessment. Environment International. 2019; 131: 104971.

115 Li R, Wu H, Ding J, Fu W, Gan L and Li Y. Mercury pollution in vegetables, grains and soils from areas surrounding coal-fired power plants. Sci Rep. Nature. 2017; 7: 46545.

116 Dufault R, LeBlanc B, Schnoll R, Cornett C, Schweitzer L, Wallinga D, Hightower J, Patrick L and Lukiw WJ. Mercury from chlor-alkali plants: measured concentrations in food product sugar. Environ Health. 2009; 8: 2.

117 Korbas M, O'Donoghue JL, Watson GE, Pickering IJ, Singh SP, Myers GJ, Clarkson TW and George GN. The chemical nature of mercury in human brain following poisoning or environmental exposure. ACS Chem Neurosci. 2010; 1(12): 810-8.

118 Steinbrenner H, Speckmann B and Klotz L-O. Selenoproteins: antioxidant selenoenzymes and beyond. Arch Biochem Biophys. 2016; 595: 113-9.

119 Snook JT, Palmquist DL, Moxon AL, Cantor AH and Vivian VM. Selenium status of a rural (predominantly Amish) community living in a low-selenium area. Am J Clin Nut. 1983; 38(4): 620-30.

120 Sun GX, Meharg AA, Li G, Chen Z, Yang L, Chen S-C and Zhu Y-G. Distribution of soil selenium in China is potentially controlled by deposition and volatilization? Sci Rep. Nature. 2016; 6: 20953.

121 Selenium in Nutrition: Revised Edition. National Research Council (US) Subcommittee on Selenium. Washington (DC). National Academies Press (US); 1983.

122 Ralston NVC and Raymond LJ. Dietary selenium's protective effects against methylmercury toxicity. Toxicology. 2010; 278(1): 112-23.

123 Ducharme J. 5 places where people live the longest and healthiest lives. Time. 15 February 2018. https://time.com/5160475/blue-zones-healthy-long-lives/

124 Sannitu S. Water and land in Sardinia. The integrated water cycle in the context of water management systems: the Sardinian experience. Watershed management: Water resources for the future. www.fao.org/3/a0438e/a0438e04.pdf

125 OkinawaWanderer. Fukuji Dam keeps Okinawa water supplies flowing. 17 March 2014. www.okinawanderer.com/2014/03/fukuji-dam-keeps-okinawa-water-supplies-flowing/

126 Rosero-Bixby L, Dow WH and Rehkopf DH. The Nicoya region of Costa Rica: a high longevity island for elderly males. Vienna Yearb Popul Res. 2013; 11: 109-36.

127 Newman C. How to live to a ripe old age. National Geographic. 29 December 2012. https://api.nationalgeographic.com/distribution/public/amp/news/2012/12/121227-dan-buettner-health-longevity-100-centenarians-science-blue-zones

128 Kuypers EP and Denyer PC. Volcanic exhalative manganese deposits of the Nicoya ophiolite complex, Costa Rica. Economic Geology. 1979; 74(3): 672-8.

129 GBD 2016 Dementia Collaborators. Global, regional and national burden of Alzheimer's disease and other dementias, 1990-2016: a systemic analysis for the Global Burden of Disease Study 2016. 2019; 18(1): 88-106.

130 Wirth J. States with the highest rates of Alzheimer's disease. 25 November 2019. www.aplaceformom.com/caregiver-resources/articles/states-with-highest-rates-of-alzheimers. Accessed 2020.

131 Ramos A, Quintana PJE and Ji M. Hair mercury and fish consumption in residents of O'ahu, Hawai'i. Hawai'i. J Med and Public Health. 2014; 73(1): 19-25.

132 Weiss L. Parkinson's disease in Hawai'i: a study of prevalence and ethnicity. (Thesis M.S.) University of Hawai'i at Manoa. 2007. http://hdl.handle.net/10125/20423

133 Hue NV, Vega S and Silva JA. Manganese toxicity in a Hawaiian oxisol affected by soil pH and organic amendments. Soil Sci Soc Am J. 2001; 65(1): 153-60.

134 Evans MA. Flushing the toilet has never been riskier. The Atlantic. 17 September 2015. www.theatlantic.com/technology/archive/2015/09/americas-sewage-crisis-public-health/405541

135 Mosnier E, Niemetzky F, Stroot J, Pommier de Santi V, Brousse P, Guarmit B, Blanchet D, Ville M, Abboud P, Djossou F and Nacher M. A large outbreak of thiamine deficiency among illegal gold miners in French Guiana. Am J Trop Med Hyg. 2017; 96(5): 1248-52.

136 Matsukawa D, Chang S, Fujimiya M, Takato K and Horikawa Y. Studies on thiamine deficiency due to bacterial thiaminase. III Further investigations on thiaminase disease. J Vitaminol (Kyoto). 1956; 2(1): 1-11.

137 Luong KVQ and Nguyên LTH. The beneficial role of thiamine in Parkinson disease. CNS Neurosci Ther. 2013; 19(7): 461-8.

138 Costantini A and Fancellu R. An open-label pilot study with high-dose thiamine in Parkinson's disease. Neural Regen Res. 2016; 11(3): 406-7.

139 Cersosimo MG, Raina GB, Pecci C, Pellene A, Calandra CR, Gutiérrez C, Micheli FE, Benarroch EE. Gastrointestinal manifestations in Parkinson's disease: prevalence and occurrence before motor symptoms. J Neurol. 2013; 260(5): 1332-8.

140 Lanskey JH, McColgan P, Schrag AE, Acosta-Cabronero J, Rees G, Morris HR and Weil RS. Can neuroimaging predict dementia in Parkinson's disease? Brain. 2018; 141(9): 2545-60.

141 Fasano A, Bove F, Gabrielli M, Petracca M, Zocco MA, Ragazzoni E, Barbaro F, Piano C, Fortuna S, Tortora A, Di Giacopo R, Campanale M, Gigante G, Lauritano EC, Navarra P, Marconi S, Gasbarrini A and Bentivoglio AR. The role of small intestinal bacterial overgrowth in Parkinson's disease. Mov Disord. 2013; 28(9): 1241-9.

142 Vizcarra JA, Wilson-Perez HE, Fasano A and Espay AJ. Small intestinal bacterial overgrowth in Parkinson's disease: Tribulations of a trial. Parkinsonism Relat Disord. 2018; 54: 110-2.

143 Atkins L. Can you catch Parkinson's? The Guardian. 04 April 2002. www.theguardian.com/education/2002/apr/04/medicalscience.healthandwellbeing

144 Kumar A, Calne SM, Schulzer M, Mak E, Wszolek Z, van Netten C, Tsui JKC, Stoessl AJ and Calne DB. Clustering of Parkinson disease: shared cause or coincidence? Arch Neurol. 2004; 61(7): 1057-60.

145 Mertsalmi TH, Pekkonen E and Scheperjans F. Antibiotic exposure and risk of Parkinson's disease in Finland: A nationwide case-controlled study. Mov Disord. 2020; 35(3): 431-42.

146 Sleeman I, Aspray T, Lawson R, Coleman S, Duncan G, Khoo TK, Schoenmakers I, Rochester L, Burn D and Yarnall A. The role of vitamin D in disease progression in early Parkinson's disease. J Parkinson's Disease. 2017; 7(4): 669-75.

147 Dick FD. Parkinson's disease and pesticide exposures. Br Med Bull. 2006; 79-80(1): 219-31.

148 Massano J and Bhatia K. Clinical approach to Parkinson's disease: features, diagnosis and principles of management. Cold Spring Harb Perspect Med. 2012; 2: a008870.

149 Chan KH, Cheung RTF, Au-Yeung KM, Mak W, Cheng TS and Ho SL. Wilson's disease with depression and parkinsonism. J Clin Neurosci. 2005; 12(3): 303-5.

150 Mizuta E and Kuno S. Effect of D-penicillamine on pharmacokinetics of levodopa in Parkinson's disease. Clin Neuropharmacol. 1993; 16(5): 448-50.

151 Dickman MD and Leung KM. Mercury and organochlorine exposure from fish consumption in Hong Kong. Chemosphere. 1998; 37(5): 991-1015.

152 Jin L, Wang J, Zhao L, Jin H, Fei G, Zhang Y, Zeng M and Zhong C. Decreased serum ceruloplasmin levels characteristically aggravate nigral iron deposition in Parkinson's disease. Brain. 2011; 134(1): 50-8.

153 Fulgenzi A and Ferrero ME. EDTA chelation therapy for the treatment of neurotoxicity. Int J Mol Sci. 2019; 20(5): 1019.

154 Surathi P, Jhunjhunwala K, Yadav R and Pal PK. Research in Parkinson's disease in India: A review. Ann Indian Acad Neurol. 2016; 19(1): 9-20.

155 Liu B, Fang F, Pederson NL, Tillander A, Ludvigsson JF, Ekbom A, Svenningsson P, Chen H and Wirdefeldt K. Vagotomy and Parkinson disease: a Swedish register-based matched cohort study 1996-2002. Neurology. 2017; 88(21).

156 Svensson E, Horváth-Puhó E, Thomsen RW, Djurhuus JC, Pedersen L, Borghammer P and Sørensen HT. Vagotomy and subsequent risk of Parkinson's disease. Ann Neurol. 2015; 78(4): 522-9.

157 Gomm W, von Holt K, Thomé F, Broich K, Maier W, Fink A, Doblhammer G and Haenisch B. Association of proton pump inhibitors with risk of dementia: a pharmacoepidemiological claims data analysis. JAMA Neurol. 2016; 73(4): 410-6.

158 Breydo L, Win JW and Uversky VN. Alpha-synuclein misfolding and Parkinson's disease. Biochimica et Biophysica Acta. 2012; 1822(2): 261-85.

159 Brundin P, Ma J and Kordower JH. How strong is the evidence that Parkinson's disease is a prion disorder? Curr Opin Neurol. 2016; 29(4): 459-66.

160 Cersosimo MG. Gastrointestinal biopsies for the diagnosis of alpha-synuclein pathology in Parkinson's disease. Gastro Res Pract. 2015; 476041.

161 Sampson TR, Debelius JW, Thron T, Janssen S, Shastri GG, Ilhan ZE, Challis C, Schretter CE, Rocha S, Gradinaru V, Chesselet M-F, Keshavarzian A, Shannon KM, Krajmalnik-Brown R, Wittung-Shafshede P, Knight R and Mazmanian SK. Gut microbiota regulate motor deficits and neuroinflammation in a model of Parkinson's disease. Cell. 2016; 167(6): 1469-80.

162 Laforenza U, Patrini C, Poloni M, Mazzarello P, Ceroni M, Gajdusek DC and Garruto RM. Thiamin mono- and pyrophosphatase activities from brain homogenate of Guamanian amyotrophic lateral sclerosis and parkinsonism-dementia patients. J Neurol Sci. 1992; 109(2): 156-61.

163 Jinsmaa Y, Sullivan P, Gross D, Cooney A, Sharabi Y and Goldstein DS. Divalent metal ions enhance DOPAL-induced oligomerization of alpha-synuclein. Neurosci Lett. 2014; 569: 27-32.

164 Duce JA, Wong BX, Durham H, Devedjian J-C, Smith DP and Devos D. Posttranslational changes to alpha-synuclein control iron and dopamine trafficking, a concept for neuron vulnerability in Parkinson's disease. Mol Neurodegener. 2017; 12(1): 45.

165 Wolff V, Schlagowski A-I, Rouyer O, Charles A-L, Singh F, Auger C, Schini-Kerth V, Marescaux C, Raul J-S, Zoll J and Geny B. Tetrahydrocannabinol induces brain mitochondrial respiratory chain dysfunction and increases oxidative stress: a potential mechanism involved in cannabis-related stroke. Biomed Res Int. 2015: 323706.

166 Sunderman Jr FW. Nasal toxicity, carcinogenicity, and olfactory uptake of metals. Annals of Clinical and Laboratory Science. 2001; 31(1): 3-24.

167 Calderón-Garcidueñas L, González-Maciel A, Reynoso-Robies R, Kulesza RJ, Mukherjee PS, Torres-Jardón R, Rönkkö T and Doty RL. Alzheimer's disease and alpha-synuclein pathology in the olfactory bulb of infants, children, teens and adults <40 years in Metropolitan Mexico City. APOE4 carriers at higher risk of suicide accelerate their olfactory bulb pathology. Environmental Research. 2018; 166: 348-62.

168 Ping Pong L, Zhang Y, Wu T, Shen Z and Xu H. Acid-extractable heavy metals in PM2.5 over X'ian, China, seasonal distribution and meterological influence. Environmental Science and Pollution Research. 2019; 26: 34357-67.

169 Morton-Bermea O, Garza-Galindo R, Hernández-Álvarez E, Ordoñez-Godínez SL, Amador-Muñoz O, Beramendi-Orosco L, Miranda J and Rosas-Pérez I. Atmospheric PM2.5 mercury in the Metropolitan Area of Mexico City. Bull Environ Contam Toxicol. 2018; 100(4): 588-92.

170 Haehner A, Hummel T and Reichman H. Olfactory loss in Parkinson's disease. Parkinson Dis. 2011; 450939.

171 Tower J, Pomatto LCD and Davies KJA. Sex differences in the response to oxidative and proteolytic stress. Redox Biology. 2020; 31: 101488.

172 Wang H, Liu H and Liu RM. Gender difference in glutathione metabolism during aging in mice. Exp Gerontol. 2003; 38(5): 507-17.

173 Monti DA, Zabrecky G, Kremens D, Liang T-W, Wintering NA, Bazzan AJ, Zhong L, Bowens BK, Chervoneva I, Intenzo C and Newberg AB. N-acetyl cysteine is associated with dopaminergic improvement in Parkinson's disease. Clinical Pharmacology and Therapeutics. 2019; 106(4): 884-90.

174 Sharma S, Raj K and Singh S. Neuroprotective effect of quercetin in combination with piperine against rotenone- and iron supplement-induced Parkinson's disease in experimental rats. Neurotox Res. 2020; 37(1): 198-209.

175 Wagner C, Vargas AP, Roos DH, Morel AF, Farina M, Nogueira CW, Aschner M and Rocha JB. Comparative study of quercetin and its two glycoside derivatives quercitrin and rutin against methylmercury (MeHg)-induced ROS production in rat brain slices. Arch Toxicol. 2010; 84: 89-97.

176 Singh S, Jamwal S and Kumar P. Neuroprotective potential of quercetin in combination with piperine against 1-methyl-4-phenyl-1,2,3,6-tetrahydropyridine-induced neurotoxicity. Neural Regen Res. 2017; 12(7): 1137-44.

177 Yokel RA. Blood-brain barrier flux of aluminium, manganese, iron and other metals suspected to contribute to metal-induced neurodegeneration. J Alzheimers Dis. 2006; 10(2-3): 223-53.

178 Flora SJS and Pachauri V. Chelation in metal intoxication. Int J Environ Res Public Health. 2010; 7(7): 2745-88.

179 Bernhoft RA. Mercury toxicity and treatment: a review of the literature. J Environ Public Health. 2012; 460508.

180 Böse-O'Reilly S, Drasch G, Beinhoff C, Maydl S, Vosko MR, Roider G and Dzaja D. The Mt. Diwata study on the Philippines 2000 — treatment of mercury intoxicated inhabitants of a gold mining area with DMPS (2,3-dimercapto-1-propane-sulfonic acid, Dimaval®). Sci Total Environ. 2003; 307(1-3): 71-82.

181 Esdaile LJ and Chalker JM. The mercury problem in artisanal and small scale gold mining. Chemistry. 2018; 24(27): 6905-16.

182 Yorifugi T, Tsuda T and Harada M. Minamata disease: a challenge for democracy and justice; late lessons from early warnings: science, precautions, innovations. European Environmental Agency. 2013. www.eea.europa.eu/publications/late-lessons-2/late-lessons-chapters/late-lessons-ii-chapter-5

183 Farkas CS. Commentary: Potential for and implications of thiamine deficiency in Northern Canadian Indian populations affected by mercury contamination. Ecology of Food and Nutrition. 1979; 8(1): 11-20.

184 Bell L, Evers DC, Burton M, Regan K, Ingram I, Digangi J, Federico J, Šamánek J and Petrilikov L. Mercury threat to women and children across 3 oceans: elevated mercury in women in small island states and countries. IPEN / BRI Technical Report. 2018; doi:10.13140/RG.2.2.11554.99525

185 Sokol J. Something in the water: life after Minamata's mercury poisoning. The Wire. 6 October 2017. https://www.google.co.uk/amp/s/m.thewire.in/article/environment/minamata-bay-japan-life-after-mercury-poisoning/amp

186 Michael's story. www.michaeljfox.org/michaels-story

187 Seyd J. Ocean pollution tracked by scientists at West Vancouver lab. North Shore News. 20 February 2018. www.nsnews.com/local-news/ocean-pollution-tracked-by-scientists-at-west-vancouver-lab-3068110

188 Tang YZ, Koch F and Gobler CJ. Most harmful algal bloom species are vitamin B1 and B12 auxotrophs. PNAS. 2010; 107(48): 20756-61.

189 Krabbenhoft DP. Mercury studies in the Florida Everglades. US Department of the Interior – US Geological Survey. 1996. FS-166-96. https://pubs.usgs.gov/fs/0166-96/report.pdf

190 State warns of mercury in fish. Tampa Bay Times. 28 August 2005. www.tampabay.com/archive/2004/10/05/state-warns-of-mercury-in-fish

191 Mirlean N, Baisch P, Machado I and Shumilin E. Mercury contamination of soil as the result of long-term phosphate fertilizer production. Bull Environ Contam Toxicol. 2008; 81(3): 305-8.

192 Koizumi A, Aoki T, Tsukada M, Naruse M and Saitoh N. Mercury, not sulphur dioxide, poisoning as cause of smelter disease in industrial plants producing sulphuric acid. Lancet. 1994; 343(8910): 1411-2.

193 Rush T, Liu X and Lobner D. Synergistic toxicity of the environmental neurotoxins methylmercury and β-methylamino-L-alanine. Neuroreport. 2012; 23(4): 216-9.

194 Maxson P. Trading Mercury. UN Environment Programme. www.unenvironment.org/interactive/trading-mercury-health-effects/

195 Matheny K. Scientists puzzled by mercury's jump in Great Lakes fish. https://www.google.co.uk/amp/s/amp.usatoday.com/amp/99631216

196 Davies C. Fight the power: Why climate activists are suing Europe's biggest coal plant. The Guardian. 26 September 2019. https://www.theguardian.com/environment/2019/sep/26/fight-power-climate-activists-europe-biggest-coal-poland-bechatow

197 Jastrzab K. Database for content of mercury in Polish brown coal. Air protection in Theory and Practices. 2018; 28: 01017.

198 Appunn K. Germany's three lignite mining regions. Journalism for the energy transition. 7 August 2018. www.cleanenergywire.org/factsheets/germanys-three-lignite-mining-regions

199 Keinänen M. The M74 syndrome of Baltic Salmon becomes worse. Natural Resources Institute Finland. 6 April 2017. www.luke.fi/en/news/m74-syndrome-baltic-salmon-becomes-worse/

200 Hawley C. Tons of mercury found in the Baltic Sea. Europe's underwater chemical dump. Der Spiegel. 30 August 2006. www.spiegel.de/international/tons-of-mercury-found-in-the-baltic-sea-europe-s-underwater-chemical-dump-a-434329-amp.html

201 Mercury management in Sweden. Swedish experiences of mercury control and management. Swedish Chemicals Agency (KEMI). Swedish Environmental Protection Agency. Naturvardsverket. www.naturvardsverket.se/Documents/publikationer6400/978-91-620-8691-6.pdf

202 Nguetseng R, Fliedner A, Knopf B, Lebreton B, Quack M and Rüdel H. Retrospective monitoring of mercury in fish from selected European freshwater and estuary sites. Chemosphere. 2015; 134: 427-34.

203 Oakes JM, Fuchs RM, Gardner JD, Lazartigues E and Yue X. Nicotine and the renin-angiotensin system. Am J Physiol Regul Integr Comp Physiol. 2018; 315(5): R895-906.

204 Busse LW, Chow JH, McCurdy MT and Khanna AK. COVID-19 and the RAAS — a potential role for angiotensin II? Crit Care. 2020; 24: 136.

205 Cho S, Jacobs DR and Park K. Population correlates of circulating mercury levels in Korean adults: the Korea National Health and Nutrition Examination Survey IV. BMC Public Health. 2014; 14: 527.

206 Fox SE, Atmatbekov A, Harbert JL, Li G, Brown JQ and Vander Heide RS. Pulmonary and cardiac pathology in African American patients with COVID-19: an autopsy series from New Orleans. The Lancet Respiratory Medicine. 2020; 8(7): 681-8.

207 IMO restricts sewage discharge in Baltic Sea. The Maritime Executive. 29 February 2020 www.maritime-executive.com/article/imo-restricts-sewage-discharge-in-baltic-sea

208 Boseley M. 'A moral obligation': radical reform urged before cruise ships allowed to return to Australia. The Guardian. 30 May 2020. www.theguardian.com/business/2020/may/31/a-moral-obligation-radical-reform-urged-before-cruise-ships-allowed-to-return-to-australia/

209 Travaglio M, Yu Y, Popovic R, Selley L, Leal NS and Martins LM. Links between air pollution and COVID-19 in England. Environmental Pollution. 2020; 115859.

210 Cui Y, Zhang Z-F, Froines J, Zhao J, Wang H, Yu S-Z and Detels R. Air pollution and case fatality of SARS in the People's Republic of China: an ecologic study. Environ Health. 2003; 2: 15.

211 Dache ZAA, Otandault A, Tanos R, Pastor B, Meddeb R, Sanchez C, Arena G, Lasorsa L, Bennett A, Grange T, Messaoudi SE, Mazard T, Prevostel C and Thierry AR. Blood contains circulating cell-free respiratory competent mitochondria. FASEB J. 2020; 34(3): 3616-30.

212 Tyszka J, Kobos K and Tyszka A. Antibiotics against COVID-19 and mitochondria? Urgent thinking out of the box. Preprints. 2020; 2020040269.

213 Ryback R. COVID-19: mitochondria's pivotal role. Psychology Today. 16 June 2020. www.psychologytoday.com/gb/blog/the-truisms-wellness/202006/covid-19-mitochondria-s-pivotal-role-revision

214 Lippi A, Dominigues R, Setz C, Outeiro TF and Krisko A. SARS-CoV-2: At the crossroad between aging and neurodegeneration. Mov Disord. 2020; 35(5): 716-20.

215 Li G, Ma J, Cui S,He Y, Xiao Q, Liu J and Chen S. Parkinson's disease in China: a forty-year growing track of bedside work. Translational Neurodegeneration. 2019; 8: 22.

216 Bouchentouf S, Aïnad Tabet D and Ramdant M. Mercury pollution in beachrocks from the Arzew gulf (West of Algeria). Travaux de l'Institut Scientifique, Rabat, Série Zoologie. 2013; 49: 1-5.

217 Spiller HA, Hays HL, Burns G and Casavant MJ. Severe elemental mercury poisoning managed with selenium and N-acetylcysteine administration. Toxicology Communication. 2017; 1(1): 24-8.

218 Morris AA, Zhao L, Patel RS, Jones DP, Ahmed Y, Stoyanova N, Gibbons GH, Vaccarino V, Din-Dzietham R and Quyyumi AA. Differences in systemic oxidative stress based on race and the metabolic syndrome: The Morehouse and Emory Team up to Eliminate Health Disparities (META-Health) study. Metab Syndr Relat Disord. 2012; 10(4): 252-9.

219 Van Hecke O and Lee J. N-acetylcysteine: a rapid review of the evidence for effectiveness in treating COVID-19. The Centre for Evidence-Based Medicine. 14 April 2020. www.cebm.net/covid-19/n-acetylcysteine-a-rapid-review-of-the-evidence-for-effectiveness-in-treating-covid-19/

220 Barnhill LM, Khuansuwan S, Juarez D, Murata H, Araujo JA and Bronstein JM. Diesel exhaust extract exposure induces neuronal toxicity by disrupting autophagy. Toxicol Sci. 2020; 176(1): 193-202.

221 Sampson TR, Challis C, Jain N, Moiseyenko A, Ladinsky MS, Shastri GG, Thron T, Needham BD, Horvath I, Debelius JW, Janssen S, Knight R, Wittung-Stafshede P, Gradinaru V, Chapman M and Mazmanian SK. A gut bacterial amyloid promotes alpha-synuclein aggregation and motor impairment in mice. Elife. 2020; 9: e53111.

222 Nazemi K, Salari S and Eskandani MA. Assessment of the Escherichia coli pollution in drinking water and water sources in Sistan, Iran. J Water Reuse and Desalination. 2018; 8(3): 386-92.

223 Mercury in Europe's environment. A priority for European and global action. European Environment Agency. www.eea.europa.eu/publications/mercury-in-europe-s-environment/download

224 Won JH, Park JY and Lee TG. Mercury emissions from automobiles using gasoline, diesel and LPG. Atmospheric Environment. 2007; 41(35): 7547-52.

225 Bjørklund G. Parkinson's disease and mercury. J Orthomolecular Medicine. 1995; 10(3-4): 147-8.

226 Ngim CH and Devathasan G. Epidemiological study on the association between body burden mercury level and idiopathic Parkinson's disease. Neuroepidemiology. 1989; 8(3): 128-41.

227 Hsu Y-C, Chang C-W, Lee H-L, Chuang C-C, Chiu H-C, Li W-Y, Horng J-T and Fu E. Association between history of dental amalgam fillings and risk of Parkinson's disease: A population-based retrospective cohort study in Taiwan. PLoS One. 2016; 11(12): e0166552.

Acknowledgements

For their untiring support and guidance throughout the writing of this book, I thank my editor and publisher Danielle Wrate and her team, Abby and Alexa. I am very fortunate to be in their good hands. In addition, my gratitude and affection to Claire Urwin, Gill Nash and Raph Sergent, for their help and patience while reading through several drafts—their input was invaluable. Thank you also to my wonderful family for all the encouragement and IT support, with special thanks to Catherine for the endless hours spent at the research, writing and editing stages. This book would not have been possible without the work of many dedicated scientists and journalists, whose continued research provides a basis for new ideas. Finally, thank you to those willing to change to make a better future for all.

Biography

Jo Dixon is a retired hospital consultant. She is the author of *The Missing Link in Dementia: A Memoir.* This is her first novel. She lives in Norfolk with her husband, four children, four rescue hens and Maggie the dog.

For updates on Jo's work and research, you can sign up to her blog exploring misunderstood medical syndromes at drjodixon.wordpress.com/blog/